PRAISE FOR *The Way of Glory*

"One of the many impressive things about *The Way of Glory* is how lightly it wears its scrupulous research. This fine novel invites you to lose yourself to the compelling character and tumultuous life of a young woman trying to find God and love at the heart of a crusade rooted in greed and hate. This is a remarkable debut by a writer to watch." —Naeem Murr, author of *The Perfect Man*

"*The Way of Glory* convincingly portrays a place, a time, and a people vastly different from our own. Historical fiction is a fantastically difficult genre to get right, but Pat Boomsma manages it with aplomb." —Pinckney Benedict, author of *Dogs of God*

"*The Way of Glory* is a riveting read from first page to last, as it expertly traces the trajectories of several compelling characters caught up in the Crusades. As the protagonist, Cate will steal your heart; she's as complex a fourteen-year-old as you will ever meet, and the fate she struggles against is a complicated and often frightening vortex of forces, made ever richer by the intense evocation and very thoughtful depictions. This is a remarkable novel. —Fred Leebron, author of *Welcome to Christiania*

THE WAY
OF GLORY

Patricia J. Boomsma

Edeleboom Books

CHANDLER, ARIZONA

Patricia J Boomsma/Edeleboom Books
edeleboom.com

Publisher's Note: This is a work of historical fiction. Although some characters and events are based on historical sources, the work as a whole is a product of the author's imagination. The timeline roughly follows that in the relevant primary sources listed in the historical note at the end of this novel. I have given certain historical figures—including Robert, the First Earl of Gloucester, Afonso Henriques, Bishop Pitões, and Ramón Berenguer IV—speeches and actions that, while based on my understanding of the historical record, are fictional. With the exception of such historical public figures, any resemblance to persons living or dead is coincidental.

Book Layout © 2017 BookDesignTemplates.com
Cover Photo: Crusaders' Ships. Date: circa 1100, by Archivist.
        Adobe Stock #162290342, licensed 8/11/2018

The Way of Glory/Patricia J. Boomsma . -- 1st ed.
ISBN-13: 978-1-7326820-0-9 (Print)
ISBN-13: 978-117326820-1-6 (Ebook)

For Jen,
and in memory of my mom

"The boast of heraldry, the pomp of pow'r,
And all that beauty, all that wealth e'er gave,
Awaits alike th' inevitable hour.
The paths of glory lead but to the grave."

> — Thomas Gray "Elegy Written in a Country Churchyard"

If I speak in the tongues of men and of angels, but have not love, I am a noisy gong or a clanging cymbal. And if I have prophetic powers, and understand all mysteries and all knowledge, and if I have all faith, so as to remove mountains, but have not love, I am nothing.

> — 1 Corinthians 13:1-2, English Standard Version

PART ONE

BRYCGSTOW, ENGLAND
1147

ONE

The twig in Cate's hand made a pleasant clacking sound as she dragged it along Brycgstow's massive stone wall, but it provided little distraction from the choice her father demanded she make. Cate knew it was time for her to marry now that she was fourteen. Her sister Darryl had not been much older when she married. But the men her father had picked! She shuddered thinking of Wulf, an old farmer who leered at her whenever he came to town, and Sene, a carpenter from Gloucester she had never met, but who must be horrible if he could find no woman there.

Cate's coarse blouse and skirt chafed against her body as the cold wind gusted, and long loose strands of ash brown hair lashed her eyes. She dropped her bucket in dismay when she saw the long line of women filling the steps near St. John's Well and heard the chaos of merchants yelling to attract the attention of farmers crossing the Frome Bridge.

Just a few minutes, she thought, *a little time away from everyone's demands to bring the water, sweep the floor, tend the chickens, replace the bed straw. To choose how to live the rest of her life.*

St. Giles's church was nearby. How much better to wait there and dream, if only for a moment, of Ruth and other saintly women who sacrificed all for Christ. How glorious it would be to be like them, instead of grinding grain or mending tears in her father's shirt. Or being forced to marry an ugly old man.

As she neared St. Giles's, the sound of water rushing in the river on the other side of the wall called to Cate. She knew she needed to help her mother prepare the garden now that the ground was softening. She knew she would get in trouble if she went outside the gate to sit by the river. Her mother often warned her Christian girls were not allowed there alone, or almost anywhere it seemed, but right now Cate needed peace.

Silly stories, Cate thought about the tales her mother told about the dangers of the false king Stephen's prowling knights and the pirates who took young girls for slaves. Cate had watched the river many times, whenever she felt sad or lonely or confused, and she'd always felt safe. No bridge crossed the river here, and the few ships that sailed this far up the Frome congregated upstream near where the Jews lived outside the wall. And she'd heard her brother gloat many times that the false king's men didn't dare approach. The traitors had lost many men when they'd failed to rescue Stephen from Earl Robert's prison. Why would they come now?

Old Radulf kept watch in the huge archway that led to the marshes, his face obscured by his hood with only his white beard and a few straggles of long white hair stark against his dark, bent silhouette. She glanced quickly up the wall to see if her brother Sperleng or any of his soldier friends were on guard today. Two Norman archers paced the wall farther down, facing the river and forest that surrounded the town.

Cate hid her bucket behind a bush. She was sure Radulf saw her but, as always, pretended he didn't, looking to the right as she turned quickly to the left along the path that followed the curve of the outside wall before sloping downward. She headed toward the place she liked to sit, far from the boats and the soldiers and the noise.

She loved the whispering dark of the river and the fawn-colored grasses waving against the blue of the sky. Her clogs squished through the soft ground, and brambles clung to her long, stiff skirt as it brushed against blackberry bushes just beginning to flower. Lilacs, too, were opening, and she breathed in their glorious perfume. She lifted her face to shafts of light breaking through the clouds, letting the sun warm her. The wind was less biting here. She sank to her heels, calmed by the white tops of the waves shifting in the wind and the young leaves of the whitebeam trees across the river waving white and green.

A flock of crows circled overhead, their huge black wings glinting purple in the sunlight. They lifted on the wind currents, then dived toward the willows whose branches dragged along the bank of the river. Several landed near the water's edge, interested in something long and dark. She stayed still, fearing it might be a wounded animal, but when it didn't move curiosity overtook her. Grabbing her skirt in one hand, she skidded carefully down the hill. She took a few cautious steps forward. The birds flew to the tops of the trees, cawing raucously.

Cate saw a hand and froze. A child's body lay in a shallow trench, partially covered with marsh grasses and willow branches. She picked up a large branch and held it protectively in front of her. When she reached the body, she waved away the flies and brushed the grass and leaves with her stick. Bile rose to her throat when she saw the distinctive coppery hair and familiar shape of Oxa, the blacksmith's son, lying face down in the trench.

"Oxa! Is that you?" Cate dropped to her knees and shook him as she spoke. "Are you hurt? Say something."

Cate felt stuck in a nightmare, unable to move. *Get up! Get help!* she told herself, but she couldn't. A crow, lulled by her stillness, landed near Oxa's feet, tilted its head to one side, and hopped forward.

"No!" Cate shouted, waving her branch in the air as the crow flew away. She bolted toward the gate, screaming for Radulf.

"Come quick," Cate said, gasping for breath and holding her side. "Oxa's lying by the river!"

They ran back through the muddy marsh, Cate tripping on her skirt, landing face first in the tangled grasses. She pushed herself against a rock, pulled off her clogs, lifted her wet and muddy skirt, and hurried to where Radulf yelled and prodded Oxa. Now she saw the dried blood darkening Oxa's matted hair. Radulf turned the body, and Oxa's unseeing eyes stared at them.

"He be dead, girl," Radulf said quietly. "I'll get the sheriff. You be off to your father's house."

Cate stared at Radulf, eyes wide. She had seen Oxa just yesterday, laughing happily atop his father's shoulders.

Several large crows stood guard high in a tree screeching at them. *Am I screaming too?* she thought. *No, Radulf would be shaking me if I were screaming.*

I should do something.

I should go.

It cannot be true. Christ, let him be alive.

"Go, girl!" Radulf growled.

~

Fire sprang up in a burst of yellow and orange, casting long shadows in the morning gloom of the armory as Sperleng bent over the hearth to inspect the metal of the sword he'd promised Gilbert FitzJohn today. Sperleng jumped back and peered into a dark corner of the room shaded by racks of tools and a large bellows.

"Whoa, Yffi! A little more gently on the bag when I'm nearby," Sperleng shouted to the young boy pushing the top of the bellows with his arms and back. "I'd like to keep my beard!"

Yffi hung his head, his long, ash-covered hair hiding his eyes.

"Oh, don't look at me like that," Sperleng said, laughing, "I like your vigor. You need to learn when to pump hard and when gently, and gently's difficult when you're tired. Don't worry, you'll get it."

Sperleng wiped the sweat from his soot-blackened face. He pulled the sword from the fire and beat it with a huge iron hammer, the clangs echoing against the shields and scrap metal lining the armory. He lifted the blade with his massive, leather-wrapped hands to test its balance, inspecting it for bends and scratches, and repeating the process until satisfied everything was straight and smooth.

"Heat it high, now," Sperleng commanded, placing the blade in the center of the hearth, then watching closely until it glowed orange. When he felt the time was right, a time he struggled to explain to Yffi, he quickly lifted the weapon and plunged it into a barrel of cool water that sizzled then splashed as he pulled the sword out again.

"Rest awhile," Sperleng said. "We need to let the fire cool for the final stage. Then we'll heat the blade again, slowly, to prepare it for sharpening and polishing."

He took water from a tub near the entrance, drank some, and splashed his face.

"Be that sword for Jerusalem?" Yffi asked.

"Aye," Sperleng answered. "Gilbert's blades were much damaged in the last battle, and he wants a fine new sword to slay the Saracens."

"I pray Stephen's war will slow once all of you leave. It seems the best of you are leaving."

Sperleng grimaced. "Most are staying."

"But many leave with you, and we know who fills the front lines," Yffi said.

Sperling shrugged, but knew others shared Yffi's fears. The men of Brycgstow lived on Robert FitzRoy's fiefdom, and, when called to fight in the Normans' war over who should rule after King Henry's death, they picked up their axes and knives and farm implements and fought. Sperleng fought not for Henry's daughter, Empress Matilda—or his nephew Stephen, that treacherous weakling—but for Earl Robert and the people of Brycgstow and Gloucester. Earl Robert had chosen to follow his half-sister Matilda, and that decision belonged to him.

Nearly ten long years of war since Earl Robert rebelled against Stephen, and why? *Earl Robert should be king. He's Henry's eldest son. Who cares that his mother wasn't Henry's wife?* Sperleng shook his head at the thought. *Henry's father William was a bastard too, but he became king. Earl Robert is a strong and fearless leader of men. He deserves to be king.*

Sperleng also thought Gilbert, his unit leader, deserved to inherit his father's land and title. *Gilbert's cruel and lazy brothers don't deserve those honors.* Sperleng had fought beside Gilbert and seen his bravery at

Lincoln as well as on that horrible day at Stockbridge when Stephen's men captured Earl Robert. *But that's not the way the world works,* Sperleng thought. Gilbert was a third son, with little chance of land or wealth. Only military victories could increase his fame and prospects.

Gilbert had volunteered quickly when Abbot Bernard and the Holy Father called for soldiers to defend the Kingdom of Jerusalem from the heathen Turks. Sperleng felt honored when Gilbert asked him to join him. There seemed little to lose. Fighting in Jerusalem against the Saracens seemed a finer thing than killing men here, and the Holy Father promised forgiveness of all their sins and a place in heaven for joining God's soldiers in the fight. Sperleng didn't care much about the promise of heaven. He much preferred coming back home with plunder.

Gilbert arrived just as Sperleng was sharpening the blade. Sperleng could see Gilbert's satisfaction in the way he balanced the sword in his hands, swung it back and forth, and fingered the fine detail in the hilt. Sperleng had designed a cross in the center surrounded by intertwining snakes.

"A fine sword for killing Mohammedans," Gilbert said, pointing the blade toward the sun flooding through the open door. "Yffi, put this in my favorite scabbard and bring me my old steel." Yffi carefully carried the shining new sword to Gilbert's squire standing near a rack filled with weapons and returned with a dull gray sword whose tip was gone. "Sperleng, you will need your own weapon as we fight together in the Holy Land. Take this one, and fashion it for your use."

Sperleng bowed, flustered and gratified by Gilbert's generosity. A knight's cutter! "Thank you for this gift. I promise to defend you well with it."

"Kill many heathen—that will be thanks enough," Gilbert said, leaving as quickly as he came.

Sperleng had never owned such a fine piece, relying on the staves and axes and farm tools foot soldiers used to pierce the sides of horses or gut the enemy. He handled the blade easily, his muscled shoulders and arms flexing and releasing as he tested it. He was stronger and taller than Gilbert, so Sperleng decided to change its balance by thinning and lengthening the blade. Without a horse, he feared a long sword might prove impractical, but he loved it anyway. *Won't the enemy be surprised when this comes from behind the shield wall*, he thought, thrusting it with satisfaction. *Tomorrow I'll make a scabbard worthy of such a fine weapon. Now all I need is a decent mail shirt, and I'll be ready to leave.*

The afternoon sun blinded Sperleng as he left the smoky warmth of the armory. His stomach rumbled, eager for his mother's pottage. He hurried past the looming walls of the fortress guarding the moat bridge, greeting the soldier in the gatehouse before turning toward the shade of St. Peter's.

As Sperleng neared the carpenters' street, he felt a mixture of pride and sadness about leaving, a year in the planning and now just weeks away. He wondered if his brother Willard would be home, or if he'd be hanging around Father Simon, as usual. Sperleng had never understood Willard, a pious soul who wanted to be a priest, of all things. Sperleng would miss his mother most of all. He knew she was crushed by the thought of his leaving, but what could he do? A man must follow his lord to bring glory to his family.

His mother smiled as he opened the door, then laughed when he wrapped his arms around her and lifted her high before he settled next to Willard on the bench near the table. She piled the pottage high on Sperleng's plate, gave him the largest slab of bread, and patted his shoulder as he ate.

~

Cate stumbled uphill towards the gate, beginning to run when she reached the hard-packed streets of the town. She barely noticed the nods and calls of people she passed, or the clanging of metal on metal the blacksmith made, or its sudden silence. Her thoughts careened as she tried to force the image of Oxa's staring eyes from her mind. Maybe Aunt Mary or the sisters at the abbey could wake him? Her father would know what to do. What would she tell him? How could she tell anyone about this, explain how she came to be outside the gate? *Radulf found the body and made me come see who it was. No, he'd never do that. He'd find a soldier.*

"Well, I'm old enough," she complained to herself. She must have spoken aloud as Samuel smiled at the ground as she passed him. *What's he doing inside our walls, laughing at me?* she thought. *Probably demanding money from some poor soldier. Jews belong outside. Even rich ones. Oh, no time to worry about that.*

The smell of beef and mutton fat filled the air while soap makers lifted their heads as she rushed past. Several dogs joined her in the race, some barking happily as others bared their teeth and growled. Her eyes and nose dripping, her lungs burning, she wanted to stop but dared not slow.

Breathless, Cate pushed open the heavy wooden door. Her muddy clothes dripped onto the well-swept dirt floor. The sun streaming in through the open door lit a smoky path in the otherwise dim room. Her youngest sister, Linn, looked up from stirring the pot over the fire and tucked a long strand of chestnut-colored hair behind her ear. Cate heard Sperleng laugh with muffled surprise and turned to see him sitting with Willard by the trestle table near the hearth. Sperleng's massive arms and shoulders dwarfed Willard's thin frame and folded hands.

"Ho, Cate. Where have you been? Swimming?" Sperleng said, laughing.

"What has happened to you? Where did all this mud come from?" her mother complained from the shadows, frowning. "And where is our bucket?"

"Father!" Cate shouted.

"Here, girl. What is this noise about?" her father said as he entered the house, sawdust radiating off his broad body.

"Oxa! We found Oxa dead! Near the River Frome!"

Sperleng stood. "Who found him?" he demanded.

"I saw! And Radulf saw too! He went for the sheriff!"

"Piers, go and see," her mother said firmly.

Cate's father nodded and left quickly with Sperleng and Willard.

"Go Cate, find your aunt," her mother said. "Tell her she is needed to clean the body. We'll deal with this mess you've made, and you'll tell me why you were outside the wall, later."

Two

The highest spire in Brycgstow, taller than the High Cross that marked the town's center, taller even than the spires on the chapels sitting atop the gates, marked the abbey shared by the churches of Saints Peter and Mary. Cate bowed her head and slowed as she approached the small arched entrance, ignoring several of the nuns who squinted at her hostilely then turned away.

Sister Ann, the nun who ran the infirmary, was cooling the face of an elderly sleeping woman with a wet cloth. In the far corner lay a young girl covered in a coarse blanket, watched over by a woman in a thin and tattered tunic. Cate knew they were the last of the tenant farmers who had stumbled into Brycgstow during the winter, the rest having returned to the country once the weather began to warm. The girl's body lay flat and unmoving, barely alive, as her mother cried softly and held her hand.

Cate remembered when they had come, four families stumbling through Brycgstow's gates begging for food, telling the abbess that bandits had taken what little they'd had to last them through the snows. Cate and Aunt Mary had spooned broth into children's limp mouths and listened to their hollow-eyed mothers lamenting those who had died during the trek to Brycgstow. Some children never opened their eyes, and some, like this girl, could scarcely swallow, the bones of their arms and legs covered by thin, pale skin that contrasted oddly with their distended bellies. The older children and adults had flaking skin and blistering rashes, stunk from diarrhea, and had difficulty using their swollen feet and hands. Most died soon after arriving. Watching the children starve was the worst thing Cate had ever seen.

Sister Ann smiled at Cate. "Mary is in the kitchen. Is that what you need child?"

"Yes, sister. Thank you."

Cate heard the clanking of metal and wood as she came into the kitchen, and saw Mary bent over a large pot, her scrawny arms and red, rough hands moving briskly as she scrubbed. The sleeves of Mary's blouse were damp, and food stains dotted their threadbare gray cloth.

"Aunt, you are needed to clean a body," Cate said.

Mary looked to the chief cook, who nodded. "We can finish. Do what needs be done."

"Who?" Mary asked as she strode toward the washbasin.

"Oxa," was all Cate could say before choking on her tears.

"Galan's son?" Mary gasped, wiping her hands then embracing Cate. "How did it happen?"

"I found him," Cate said between sobs. "Next to the river."

"You found him?" Mary stopped and stared at Cate. "Were you outside the wall again?"

Cate nodded. "Radulf was there, too."

"Did Oxa drown?"

"I don't think so."

Cate twisted the coarse cloth of her skirt as Mary gathered soap, vinegar, oil, and lavender in a bucket. Mary apologized softly to Sister Ann, explaining where she needed to go. Cate and Mary didn't speak as they traveled the dusty paths toward St. Giles's. Cate grabbed her bucket from behind the thicket and followed Mary through the gate and down the hill toward the river. The sheriff was already there, talking with Oxa's mother and father. Someone had placed a flat length of board near Oxa's body, but otherwise he remained as Cate had last seen him, staring upwards. Mary walked to the river's edge and picked up two flat stones to cover his eyes. Willard wore a black tunic over his clothes. He hovered near Father Simon, holding a candle and bell while the priest chanted over Oxa's body. Oxa's mother, Acha, stood turned away from the body, silently staring at the river, her thin body rigid.

Galan paced a circle around the body, occasionally thrusting his bulk threateningly toward the sheriff.

"You know who is at fault," Galan shouted. "That Jew he works for!"

The sheriff stood his ground, neither flinching nor moving back despite Galan's greater girth. "I do not know that," the sheriff replied calmly.

Galan lunged toward the sheriff, hands clenched, but Sperleng grabbed him and pulled him aside. "Don't make this worse, Galan."

Galan shook off Sperleng's hands, then began to weep uncontrollably.

Mary approached Acha, "Let me wash him while you find a shroud." Acha nodded and trudged towards the gate. Galan stormed ahead of her, yelling something wild and incomprehensible.

The sheriff crouched near Oxa. "The body isn't completely stiff," he said more to himself than to anyone in particular. He stood up. "The boy didn't die here. There's little blood on his head or in the grass, and no dung. Does anyone know where he might have gone before dawn?"

They shook their heads, but Sperleng said: "It's well-known Oxa brought firewood and cleaned the stables for Samuel. Maybe he was there. Galan seems to think it was Samuel's fault."

The sheriff frowned. "Some think every bad thing is a Jew's fault."

Cate filled her bucket from the river, and Father Simon blessed the water before plodding uphill towards the gate with Willard.

Mary removed Oxa's clothing as Cate took a cloth and slowly washed his feet and legs. They worked in silence as Mary tenderly cleaned the numerous bruises that covered Oxa's arms and chest.

Cate felt the dust hardening on her face alongside the tracks of the tears that kept coming. Death was not strange to her. She had lost her baby brother two winters ago, and a sister had died shortly after she was born last advent. She knew several young women, some not much older than she, who had died in childbirth. And many men, young and old, had died in the battles against Stephen.

But this was different. Only evil explained this. Someone had killed a sweet young boy and abandoned him here.

~

As Mary wiped the dirt and blood from Oxa's face, her mind was a morass of sadness for Oxa, for his parents, for herself, and for Hafoc, her husband of one year, who was killed in an early battle of this wretched civil war. They had never returned his body, and she hoped that someone had done him the kindness of washing his body and burying him in sacred ground. She would never know. During the long years since, Mary worked for Norman priests and nuns who barely acknowledged her as she did the work they were too fine to do. She was eager to leave with the pilgrims from Brycgstow, to honor soldiers fighting for Christ instead of a Norman lord.

"Thank you for helping," Mary said, "I know this is hard."

"Someone needs to do it," Cate said quietly. "And after you leave, Sister Ann wants it to be me."

Mary grimaced. "Or you can come with us. Not many women have agreed to come to help the soldiers, and more are sorely needed to cook for them and care for the injured on our long journey."

"Leaving scares me," Cate said.

"It scares me too," Mary said. "Having you with me would help, though, and you know as much as I do about the plants and remedies."

Cate gave Mary a weak smile. "It will be many years before I know as much as you. And anybody can cook like me: throw whatever we have into a pot and let it boil. Even Sperleng can do that."

"Aye, but he thinks it beneath him," Mary said. "As they all do."

"Not sure I want to stay, either, though. Just today father told me I must marry. He's thinking Wulf would be a good match! If we were rich, I'd ask father to purchase my way into the convent."

"For that you went outside the wall?" Mary asked.

Cate looked toward the river. "I like sitting in the sun, watching the river. I like being alone sometimes."

"Cate. We all must accept the fate God has given us whether we marry or not."

Cate shrugged and looked away.

Once Oxa was clean, Mary and Cate warmed dried lavender and lanolin in their hands and smoothed it over his body. *How I love this girl!* Mary thought, taking furtive glances toward her niece. *And how sad that she was the one to find the body.*

Childless herself, Mary had helped raise her sister's children, especially Cate, a middle child lost in her mother's tumble of annual births, some deaths, and the needs of her other children. Mary remembered the day Cate was born. Mary had worried for her sister as the births were getting more difficult, not easier. When Cate finally came, Alma, exhausted from hours of labor, let Mary hold Cate first and wipe clean the blood from her tiny face and hands. At that moment, all Mary's love fell toward Cate. When Alma eventually demanded to hold the child, Mary felt pangs of jealousy and said she should sleep. The midwife glared at Mary, took Cate, and handed her to Alma to be fed.

But later, when Alma was too busy with cooking and cleaning and corralling her other young children, Mary would hold Cate. As Cate grew, Mary played games with her or showed her the best way to plant a seed and how to tell the difference between a good plant and one that needed to be pulled. Mary took Cate on market days and showed her the grains that made the best pottage and the differences between fine wool and poorly made. Mary showed her niece how to make thread on the abbey's spinning wheel, how to dye it with the plants they gathered, and how to weave it into a cloth.

And now this. Mary was glad she hadn't left yet for Jerusalem. Cate would need comfort.

They were finishing when Acha returned with a bolt of gray cloth.

"This is all I have to cover the body," Acha said so softly Mary could barely hear. Mary took Acha's hand and kissed it.

"Thank you. We are very sad for you."

Acha's body stiffened, and she did not look up. "Thank you," she mumbled. "I appreciate your help. I've cleared a place in the house for him and set out four candles. Galan has gone away."

Piers and Sperleng arrived, pulling a cart slowly through the mud and grass. They lifted the board with Oxa onto the cart, then trudged in silence to the blacksmith's house. The women followed. Willard and Father Simon were already at the house, lighting candles. Piers and Sperleng placed Oxa on a table shoved next to a window and propped open the shutters despite the cold.

Mary brought another bench next to the body and Acha dropped onto it, covering her face with her hands.

"I will watch with you," Father Simon said, sitting next to Acha.

~

A cloud of insects rose from the marshes, their annoying whine increasing as the dark gathered. Sperleng pulled up his hood. The sun sank quickly, and a blast of cold air convinced him to head toward the inn where he knew his friends would be. Not that he needed much encouragement. He enjoyed sitting among them, drinking ale, and recounting their exploits. He needed their energy to help dispel his gloom.

Oxa had been a baby when Sperleng began his apprenticeship with Galan seven years before, and he remembered Oxa's first faltering steps and surprised laughter when he fell. Sperleng had learned a lot from Galan, who had been a patient and thorough teacher when sober, giving Sperleng small jobs like making hooks to sell at market day so he could learn how the metal formed when hot, and how hard he could hit it before it broke. And Galan was generous, too, often giving his work to farmers too poor to pay or accepting a small sack of grain on the promise of a chicken that never arrived. But Sperleng had spent too many nights roaming the dusty streets with Oxa in his arms avoiding Galan's drunken rants. He'd been glad when his father had found him a new apprenticeship with the castle blacksmiths. He hoped Galan was not at the tavern, that he knew enough about women to comfort Acha rather than drinking in self-pity.

Sperleng entered the small, crowded inn, and stood in the doorway as his eyes adjusted to the hazy light. A serving maid brushed closely by and winked at him. He smiled and let his hands linger on her hips as she passed. The inn had several small rooms, each with a fireplace and tables and benches crowded almost on top of each other. "Sperleng, here!" he heard from a corner of the room and saw four of his fellow soldiers laughing and waving at him. As he sat down they all spoke at once, asking why was he late, was there a woman involved, how fast could he drink this ale?

"Why the glum look?" Egric asked. "No one was hurt in the war today, in't it?"

"Oxa was found dead along the River Frome," Sperleng said.

The table fell silent as Sperleng told them what he knew. As he finished, Galan stood and lurched toward their table, tankard in hand. Sperleng swore to himself; he had not seen Galan in the dark corner, sullen and alone.

"Samuel made Oxa clean out his horse's stables until he was so tired he could barely stand and stunk of horseshit and piss," Galan roared. "Then he refused to pay Oxa his due, cutting his wages for this and that, denying us the small pittance he earned. A rich man treating him like that, shaving coins and pretending they are full value. And Oxa too meek to ask for his due." Galan stumbled toward the door, his huge body crashing against the jambs. "Samuel will pay! I'll make him pay!"

"Galan!" Sperleng grabbed his arm. "Wait. Don't do anything you will regret. I'll walk you home. If Samuel killed Oxa he must pay, but now you should be with your wife. Leave punishment to God and the sheriff."

Galan turned swiftly, his arms flailing and ready for a fight. "Do you think the sheriff will do anything? The sheriff cares only for the Normans, and do you think the Normans want to lose their precious Jew? How will they pay for their wars against each other? As if any of us care whether Stephen or Matilda rules. No, the sheriff cares nothing for the son of a blacksmith."

Sperleng hurried Galan outside. "Don't talk like that in the alehouse, no matter how true it might be. Go home to Acha. Watch with her. You don't need the Normans taking away your livelihood or worse."

Galan pushed Sperleng away and stumbled in the direction of the wall. As Sperleng began to follow, Galan waved him back. Sperleng watched until he was sure Galan was headed toward his own house.

Everyone at the table sat silent and grim when Sperleng returned. Kendric slammed his tankard on the table. "Galan is right, you know. There will be no justice from the Normans."

Sperleng lowered his voice. "I wouldn't put it past Samuel. All he thinks about is making money, no matter who he hurts. I still owe him for the vest and mace I needed to join the Earl's foot soldiers."

"Me too," Kendric said.

Sperleng shook his head. "Samuel's happy to take the protection of the Earl's men, but then charges interest making it impossible to pay back! And Galan's right a Jew is more important to the Normans than we are. We mean nothing to them and must go into battle with whatever we can muster. I long for the old days when a generous lord honored his soldiers for service with suitable arms and land. Now the arms and the land go to the rich Normans instead of to the bravest of soldiers."

"Well, it is a lovely dream, that," Kendric said, poking Sperleng in the side. "I think those days may be gone."

"Maybe not," Egric said. "The Earl promises booty to all who return from Jerusalem, in't it?"

"Yes," Sperleng conceded, remembering Gilbert's gift. "And Gilbert is a generous lord, one of the few I'm sorry to say. He gave me one of his old knives this afternoon. And the Earl has gotten Samuel to stop the interest while we're gone."

"But he must pay for killing Oxa!" Kendric shouted. "He must know that killing a Christian boy has consequences!"

"Be quiet!" Sperleng hissed. "Norman spies come here too you know."

Egric, who had been sitting quietly and listening until now, suddenly said: "Maybe there is a different reason. Remember the Christian boy in Norwich a few years ago? The Jews killed young William as part of their Passover rituals. That seems a more likely reason than for Samuel to save a few coins."

"Yes, I remember, they need the blood of a blameless Christian boy for Passover! Murderers!" Kendric, maudlin from too much ale, began to weep. "Something needs to be done."

Sperleng imagined how frightened Samuel would be if a crowd surrounded his house, showed their force with a few fires. *It'd serve him right, that leech on Christian souls. Teaching him a lesson might be a good idea whether or not he killed Oxa. He is surely guilty of usury and blasphemy.*

"Maybe we should set fire to Samuel's stables after Oxa's burial to warn them against using Christians' blood for their rituals," Sperleng said. He leaned toward them and lowered his voice. "Spread the word quietly. The sheriff can't find out."

THREE

Stars still shone as the dawn began to lighten the edges of the clouds when Willard trudged toward Galan's house. The only sounds were of birds gathering in the trees and Willard's feet cracking the thin skin of ice over puddles in the street. He dreaded this part of a priest's job, sitting with families grieving over their dead. And this time it was Oxa, a young child, an only son!

As he neared the house, Willard put on his compassionate face. He was sympathetic, but angry too. Outraged. He knocked softly, and Father Simon greeted him with a sad smile then left.

Acha slouched near the smoldering fire, handing Galan a bowl of pottage. She silently offered Willard a trencher. He shook his head, then kissed then marked the sign of the cross on Oxa's forehead. He knew he shouldn't stare, but couldn't stop himself, seeing the blues and blacks and yellows along Oxa's cheek. He wanted to check Oxa's hands and feet but decided to ask Father Simon instead. This family had seen enough. Willard moved slowly toward the bench along the open window, pulling his hood up against the wind. It was going to be a long, sad day.

Galan left quickly, mumbling "work to do" in Willard's direction. Acha dropped onto the bench, shoulders hunched forward.

"Sleep, Acha," Willard said, taking her hand. "I can watch alone, and there will be neighbors coming soon."

Willard could see her stubbornness battling her exhaustion as she looked up at him. Then she nodded and lay down on a pallet as far away from the body as possible. Willard could tell she wasn't sleeping but was glad not to have to make conversation. *What is there to say?* he thought. *That Oxa looks peaceful? He does not. That he is in a better place? True, but she would hear that too much in the next few days. That this wrong will be avenged?* Willard feared it wouldn't, at least not in this life.

Willard's thoughts drifted as he sat in the stillness. He wondered how Cate was handling all this. What good were soldiers on the walls if they couldn't tell when someone dumped a body? Lazy, useless Normans. Cate was inconsolable last night in her muddy clothes, her eyes shining with tears. It was all he could do to maintain his priestly reserve and direct his sympathy toward Acha instead of holding his sister close in his arms. She seemed very young then, young and sad and confused.

Was it just yesterday morning Cearl was teasing Cate about getting married? Willard stifled a sigh. Families. He knew Cearl's mockery hurt Cate more than she let on. Why didn't Cearl see it and leave her alone? Willard had seen the tears forming in her eyes as her parents discussed her marriage prospects. Cate had told him more than once she'd rather live in a convent than marry. Was that fear or religious feeling? He guessed a little of both. He knew from watching Cate with Sperleng's friends that she was not immune to the attractions of men. But she also loved the stories of saints and fervently prayed on holy days. Not that their parents could afford to buy her a place. But how could he dismiss her desire for a religious life when he'd lived with similar dreams?

Willard knew Cate was more like him than the rest of their practical family. He often wondered when he watched his huge, strong brothers if he'd been a foundling, dropped off at their door one winter night. He knew they loved him, but sometimes it felt like the love of an adult for an infant or a stray kitten. The protectiveness of the strong for the weak.

He had tried to find humor in men's comments about the local midwife's voluptuousness and the sights she has seen but could not. He preferred Father Simon's stories about Jesus's travels with his disciples, the prophets, St. Augustine. But he never should have told Cate the stories of female saints or of holy women who refused marriage like Christina of Markyate. It had filled her head with impossible dreams.

And who could tell if a sister was beautiful, attractive to men who might want to marry her? He guessed she was pretty in her own way, taller than most girls, with light brown braids that blanched in the sun. He just loved her. Cate had the energy and joy of a child, but was responsible too, cleaning scraped knees and herding back a wandering child. He'd often seen her in the lanes surrounded by children grabbing her skirts and demanding kisses. Oxa had been especially attentive to her, running whenever he saw her, hugging her leg and handing her rocks to throw for a game or wanting to hear her tell a story. Willard guessed Oxa found Cate's quick smile and hugs a welcome change from the quiet stiffness of his mother. Willard shook his head and glanced toward Acha. Some women just didn't seem to know what children needed from them.

Willard got up and looked again at Oxa's face, checking to see if by some miracle he breathed again. Wouldn't that be glorious? But he saw nothing and walked to the window, barely noticing the smoke lifting from nearby houses. Oxa had been a fine boy, always interested in Willard's stories about the saints. He was likely in heaven already. Willard wondered what Oxa's life would have been like had he lived. Would he have been pious and silent like his mother? A generous drunkard like his father? So many expectations were put on an only child. Willard brushed a tear from his face.

A loud knock roused him from his reverie. "Acha," he said softly, "They've come."

Acha rose quickly, smoothed her skirts, and opened the door to the sympathy and noise and curiosity of the town.

~

Cate slept restlessly, Linn complaining several times during the night for her to be still. Cate arose as soon as she heard their mother moving in the common room, leaving the pallet so Linn could sleep a little longer. Gray showed through a crack in the shutter covering the window. She reached for her clothing at their usual place next to her bed, then remembered they were hanging to dry near the cooking fire. She scampered quickly toward the fire and pulled a long shift over her head. She fingered her muddy overblouse and skirt, remembering Oxa's face with sadness, anger, and fear. Was anyone safe? Maybe her parents were right, she shouldn't go alone outside the wall.

"Looks like it will be sunny today. A good day to wash," her mother said. "There should be other women at the river but be sure to find someone to keep you company."

"Linn can come with me, can't she?" Cate asked.

"Linn will be helping me," her mother said.

Cate shrugged. Usually she looked forward to doing laundry — it gave her an excuse to spend time with her best friend, Aedra. But today Cate wanted to be alone, to forget, to have her life be the same as it was before yesterday. She put on one of her mother's blouses and belted it with a thin rope, moved a stool near the warmth of the fire, and scooped pottage onto a small, smooth piece of wood. Smoke drifted upward toward the hole in the center of the roof. She ate silently, then gathered the family's few clothes into a straw basket.

"Your father made us a new washing bat and board from wood left over from the priory construction," her mother said. "That should make things easier."

"I'll see if Aedra has laundry today," Cate said, opening the door and leaving quickly.

Cate wound her way through the yards and workshops of her neighbors, most of whom were carpenters like her father. She loved the smell of cut pine and the sound of sawing that filled the air. As she neared the street where the woolmakers had their homes and shops, the floating sawdust changed to small bits of fleece and the strong smell of lye and wet wool. Aedra stood in front of her house, feeding chickens, when Cate arrived.

"Want to do laundry today?" Cate asked. "My mother says I need to be sure I don't go alone."

"Yes, I heard what happened yesterday," Aedra said. "It looks like today will be a good day to do it. Let me make sure my mother doesn't have other plans for me."

Cate leaned against the door frame of Aedra's house as she waited, noting the subtle differences from her own. The house was similar to Cate's with its wooden frame covered with straw and mud and its thatched roof. Her father had helped build or repair his neighbors' houses, so that was no wonder. But Cate's father had taken particular care when building his home, making sure everyone knew a master carpenter lived there. He'd carved a figure of St. Peter on his family's door frame, an elegance that led people to bow slightly before entering and made Cate proud. *Although Aedra has better cloaks and blankets*, Cate thought.

Aedra pushed open a shutter and waved Cate closer. "Mother agrees. I'll get things together and meet you in front of your house after I get my brothers' breakfast."

Cate wandered back home slowly, petting the black-and-white cat that strolled the neighborhood screeching for a handout whenever anyone passed. She picked weeds in the garden alongside her house and listened to the chopping, sawing, and pounding of her father and Cearl as they finished their work in their shed before heading off to the priory.

"Finally!" Cate said when Aedra arrived, and Aedra made a face at her as they headed toward the river.

"I don't really want to talk about Oxa. Do you?" Aedra asked.

Cate shook her head. She didn't want to talk at all. The soothing thing about Aedra was she usually did all the talking.

"Good. Did you hear?" Aedra said. "I'll be playing Martha at the Easter play this year. No more sitting on the ground with all the babies for me. Her sister, Mary, would be better, though. Don't you think I'd be a good Mary Magdalene, too? Many more lines! And so dramatic. Can't you just see it? Me, using my hair to wash Jesus's feet? I'd put a lot into the part if Trace played Jesus, I can tell you that. What about you?"

Cate grimaced. "Oh, Aedra, you know I can't say two words when I'm in front of people. I'll be laying branches down ahead of the donkey, as usual. And I can't think of a single boy whose feet I would wash with my hair! It's bad enough when I have to clean my father's boots."

Aedra laughed. "Come on, Cate. There must be one."

Cate looked away. "Well, Egric seems nice."

"Egric? Sperleng's friend, the archer from Gloucester?" Aedra shook her head. "Your father would never allow that."

Cate nodded, blushing. "Sperleng wouldn't like it either."

Aedra leaned toward Cate and whispered, "What's nice about him? His long black hair? His strong arms?"

"His eyes," Cate admitted. "His deep brown eyes. And he has the longest, darkest eyelashes of anyone I've ever seen," Cate paused. "And don't you ever say anything!"

They ambled through the Aldgate to the upstream part of the River Frome near where the Earl's men had built a rock dam for the laundresses of the castle. The river wasn't too deep or too swift here, and there was a large clearing near the castle wall they used as a drying field.

"Oh, look," Aedra said, disappointment creeping into her voice, "Your Aunt Hawys and her friends are using all the rocks here. We'll have to go farther." Aedra scanned the river for another suitable place.

"Don't worry. My father made me a new washing board, and I brought the old one too. We can stay here." Cate put down her laundry, waved with one hand, and cupped her other hand over her mouth to shout, "Hello Aunt Hawys, Willa, Edita!"

"Good morning, Cate and Aedra," Hawys shouted. "Come join us! And Cate, we all want to hear about yesterday!"

Cate frowned as she put her basket on the river's edge, took off her clogs, tied her shift with her belt, and waded into the cold, clear water. She dreaded all the questions but knew the women would not be deterred.

After only a few words, Edita interrupted: "You went outside the gate? Alone? Do you know how dangerous that is?"

Cate fought the desire to argue as she dunked and lifted her father's tunic.

Willa stood straight. "What did Oxa look like? Were his clothes torn? Was he bleeding? Did he have wounds on his sides or his hands?"

"Please stop," Aedra cried, "I can't bear to hear what he looked like."

Cate saw tears running down Aedra's face, and remembered that she, too, had watched over Oxa. "I'm sorry, Aedra."

For a while, the women were uncharacteristically silent, the only sounds the chittering of birds, the swoosh of the water as they dunked and lifted the clothing in the river, and the occasional crack of a board beating out mud or food from the cloth. As Cate finished each piece, she hung it on a branch to dry. Soon a swarm of arms and legs waved in the slight breeze, like the wraiths in her grandfather's stories.

Hawys broke the silence by telling the women her daughter's fever had finally broken, and Willa then bragged of her son's beginning an apprenticeship at the castle. Slowly Aedra began smiling again, telling the women of her role in the Easter play, but leaving out the part about Trace.

Hawys waited until Cate stood alone hanging wet clothes on the branches before talking to Cate quietly. Edita quickly scrambled up the rocky shoreline to listen, then whispered, "Easter is coming. It's just like St. William."

Cate returned to the water quickly and whacked clothing against her board in between violent rinses in the river. Cate wondered if it could be true. She remembered Samuel smiling yesterday when she passed him on the lane. Could someone murder a boy and then walk around smiling? Maybe, if sacrificing a young boy were part of a religious ceremony like in Norwich. Cate shuddered. No matter how hard she tried, she could not stop remembering Oxa's cold, lifeless body, his eyes wide open with fear.

As they finished hanging the last of the clothing, Cate decided to wash out the mud still clinging to her hair. Her aunt and friends were talking happily about their plans for Easter and breaking the Lenten fast.

"Aunt Hawys, I'm going upstream a little."

Hawys waved her understanding, and Aedra followed Cate a few feet to where several large rocks sat along the edge of the river. Cate dipped the bottom of her hair into the icy water rushing between the rocks, unbraiding it slowly. When she finished, Cate twisted the water out of her hair, and shook it. She found a rock in full sun, and sat there, loosening the knots in her hair with her fingers. She shivered each time the wind picked up. Cate looked at Aedra, who was uncharacteristically quiet.

"You're sad, Aedra," Cate said.

"Yes."

"Would talking about Trace cheer you?"

Aedra gave Cate a fragile smile. "Not now." Aedra hesitated, then blurted, "What have you decided?"

"I don't know," Cate said. "My father wants me to marry Wulf, and my aunt wants me to come with her to Jerusalem. I just want things to stay the same as they've always been."

"I think marriage is better than not. Sure your father can find someone better, or at least younger, than Wulf."

Cate grimaced. Images of Wulf grinning at her through his black teeth popped into her head.

"I don't care whether the man I marry is handsome," Aedra said, "although Trace is that! And Sperleng. He's handsome too, although no soldiers for me. Maybe once this stupid war is over. So long as he's kind. It may be a sin, but sometimes I think I know a way to be sure I marry the man I want," Aedra continued, smiling mischievously.

"Aedra! You don't mean that," Cate said. "Do you?"

"Cate!" Hawys shouted. "We're leaving. You come too!"

Cate and Aedra rose from their rocks and began scuffling through the water.

"So," Cate said, "you think Sperleng is handsome?"

Aedra gave Cate a little push. "Everyone knows that. Including him."

Cate and Aedra quickly pulled their clothing off the branches, stuffed them into their baskets, then ran to catch up.

FOUR

Piers' House
Lent 1147

C hickens crowded Cate as she threw bits of grain at her feet, then swept cobwebs and sawdust from the corners of the shutters as she waited. Her father and Cearl had left before dawn to make a delivery to the construction site at St. Augustine's abbey across the river, returning just in time to make the sad trek to St. Peter's.

The service was short, and few others attended, just Galan, Acha, Aedra's family, and the several old women who attended every funeral. Oxa's body was laid out in a white shroud tied at the ends, but during the Mass Willard helped Father Simon cover the body with a black drape. Willard moved capably around the church. To Cate, his confidence was the one bright spot in this awful day. Willard had hoped for a religious life for as long as she could remember, but as a carpenter's son he'd had little hope. He'd followed Father Simon and assisted him for years, and eventually Father Simon taught Willard how to speak, and even read a little, Latin. As more young Normans died in the civil war, fewer became parish priests, and Father Simon obtained the bishop's permission to formally train Willard. He would be ordained in less than two months, just in time to leave with Brycgstow's pilgrims.

Father Simon and Willard led the mourners through the misting fog to the burial ground as Cearl, Sperleng, Egric, and Kendric carried the black-draped bier, followed closely by a loudly weeping Galan and a silent, stiff-backed Acha. Aedra, Linn, and Cate rang small bells, their noise muffled by the increasing rain and the bodies that joined the procession. Between the rain and her tears, Cate found herself constantly wiping her eyes to avoid slipping in the muddy puddles ahead of her. At the cemetery, clusters of townspeople formed a circle around the newly dug grave filling with water, while others gathered under the eaves of the abbey. Father Simon gave prayers and a blessing in Latin and then began speaking to the crowd.

"Today is a sad day for us, but we may find comfort knowing that Oxa is in heaven with Our Savior. We must cope with our grief and turn our hearts to our loving God who transforms this flesh into spirit and who will raise the dead at the sound of the trumpet in the last days, when we will join Oxa in the bliss of paradise everlasting."

Cate and those near her nodded. A soft murmur ran through the small crowd, mothers hushing their children and quiet conversations among neighbors.

"For we know that death does not win this battle. It merely separates the body from the spirit until they are joined again on the Day of Judgment," Father Simon continued. "And on that day, this fine young boy, a loving support and help to his parents, a boy who prayed every day for forgiveness of his own sins and those of the world, will sit at Christ's right hand and bring judgment on the one who has murdered him."

The crowd grew quiet, tension clear on their faces.

"Be not despairing! *Ante Dei vultum nihil unquam restat inultum.* His murder will be avenged, if not in this life, then in the next. In this life, we grieve for young Oxa, for our sadness at his loss. But do we turn the other cheek and not seek justice? Is that what Christ meant? God forbid! For in this life we are the instruments of God's justice. We may ask, why does not God send his angels to avenge this senseless death? Because God has ordained that for our salvation we must carry the sword of his truth to bring his peace. We must make sure that the base and unfaithful person who cut off Oxa's short life pays for his crime and repents of this grave sin."

Cate felt blood rushing to her head and heard the stirrings of angry murmurs. "Yes!" several people exclaimed. She might have been one of them.

Father Simon's voice grew louder, angrier. "So, too, we must seek justice throughout the world, making sure Christians everywhere are safe from the violence of unbelievers. Several of those standing here today have taken up the cross and will soon leave on a pilgrimage to

Christ's holy war against the blasphemers who have defiled the holy places in the land of his birth. Our soldiers and young men, formerly fighting each other in this terrible civil war will instead join together against our true enemies: the enemies of the Cross."

As the crowd's angry murmurs increased, the priest's tone became resolute. Almost gleeful. "We know the hardships these pilgrims will face in the name of Christ, but we also know the glory they will achieve and the forgiveness of all their sins. Let those among you who are able join in this great cause, perhaps by journeying with them or by providing for their needs. Be the arm of God's justice on Earth, and in this way, avenge Oxa's murder, and St. William's, and the desecration of Christ's holy places. Let the devil flee at the sound of our swords and let our triumph be in the Cross. *Memento mori!* See in Oxa's body a reflection of all of us, for we will all die." Father Simon threw his hands into the air and looked to the sky. "May God have mercy!"

Cate could not move. Suddenly all became clear to her. She must do this—a holy pilgrimage of justice! She understood it now. She would go with Mary and Sperleng and Willard. This was her life's purpose. God was calling her.

In front of her, Galan wailed loudly, and he threw himself towards the grave. "I will go! For Oxa!"

As the priest chanted prayers, Acha placed a small leaden cross on Oxa's body and closed her eyes, swaying slightly. After the final prayer, the crowd trudged slowly towards the abbey, led by the weeping Galan and silent Acha.

Loaves of bread, slabs of cheese, and tubs of ale for the mourners filled tables in the shelter of the abbey's walls. *How could Galan afford that?* Cate wondered. Many huddled under the eaves, eating what was likely their only meal of the day, and many had already drunk too much of the ale. The conversations grew louder, and men gestured broadly, moving from group to group. Cate overheard *Oxa* and *avenge* and *Jew* several times. Cate broke off bits of bread and cheese, and she and Aedra leaned against the wall as they ate.

"Sister Ann told me that Samuel's men brought the food," Aedra said.

Cate's eyes widened. "What?"

She threw the bread toward the birds hovering nearby but put the cheese into her mouth. More birds arrived, bobbing their heads toward the bits of bread, the larger ones sometimes taking it from another bird's beak in an angry flurry of wings.

~

Galan took Sperleng by the arm and pulled him away from a group of men.

"I want to join you in this pilgrimage to Jerusalem," Galan said loudly.

Sperleng patted his arm. "Galan, this is no day to make such a decision. You are young and can have another child."

Galan glared at Sperling. "No, I'm sure. A good blacksmith will be useful."

Sperleng tried his best to hide the revulsion he felt as Galan staggered toward him, his ale-breath hot and close. *That is all we need*, Sperleng thought, *an undisciplined drunk in the camp*. Sperleng was glad of the priest's support but hoped it hadn't encouraged others like Galan who would disrupt the fighting force.

"There is a more immediate enemy," Sperleng said, "Think on that. We are ready to go to visit Samuel. Come with us there."

The surrounding men nodded, and several more townspeople joined them. Sperleng left Galan with them, all expressing their sadness, and ambled toward Aedra and Cate. "We're going now."

Cate and Aedra followed Sperleng to where several of his friends had gathered. Kendric and Egric each held a long pole, and rocks protruded from the bags tied to their belts. Once the food was gone most had left, but others were forming a circle, murmuring angrily.

"Friends," Sperleng said in a casual voice, "we know the cause of Oxa's death, this Lenten season while the Jews prepare their Passover rituals."

"We know!" several shouted.

"Father Simon has told us that we are the arm of God's justice, and so we must be!"

"We must!" many more joined in.

"Let's go then!" Sperleng cried. The crowd massed forward, pushing and shoving toward the path leading out of the cemetery. Small boys picked up rocks and sticks, and men felt for the knives they always carried as they surged past the church and into the lane that led past the guildhall. Young mothers looked at the crowd uncertainly, taking the hands of the youngest children and hurrying them in the other direction.

Sperleng's Aunt Hawys ran up to him, her excited voice loud and piercing. "I saw one of Sir Robert's men heading the other way. I fear he is going for the sheriff."

The crowd surged toward the Frome Gate, then spilled down the stairs toward where the town's Jews lived. Here the buildings were much more solid than where the tradesmen lived, masonry instead of the rough and drafty wood structures of most people. Stones paved the streets. *How nice that must be when it rains*, Sperleng thought resentfully.

Samuel's house was dark and quiet.

"Come out, you cowardly heathen," one man yelled, soon joined by a chorus of others.

When there was no response, someone threw a stone. All at once many rocks flew, and men began smashing pillars and statues and fences and walls. Another group ran to the back, setting fire to grasses and hay. Sperleng slipped toward the edge of the crowd as the flames grew.

The sheriff and several of Sir Robert's men rode up, swords drawn. The crowd opened for them as the sheriff jumped off his horse and brandished his sword.

"This must stop!" he roared, "This area is protected by Sir Robert! Leave now, or we'll end this with your lives and your freedom!"

At the sight of the horses and armed soldiers, Sperleng, Kendric, and Egric stole into the shadows of the narrow alleys. Many others ran away or milled about shouting angrily at the soldiers who began putting out the numerous small fires. Soldiers grabbed men wielding sticks, tied them on horses, and rode toward the castle. Young boys hurled stones at the soldiers until their parents dragged them away. Sperleng caught a glimpse of Samuel watching from inside.

"Who led this attack?" the sheriff demanded.

No one responded. More and more of the rioters melted away from the rear of the crowd, hiding behind the shelter of nearby buildings before running toward their homes.

The sheriff continued glaring at the crowd and the soldiers began forming a circle enclosing them. At last, a woman came forward, "We want justice for the boy who was murdered."

"He will have justice," the sheriff told her angrily. "But not this way."

~

Willard followed Cate into his parents' house to find Sperleng and two of his friends already there, their wet capes dripping on hooks along the back wall. Willard pushed his dark, damp hair back from his face and smiled and Cate leaned in to him, his soft body and arms surrounding her. When Cate started crying inconsolably, he patted her head and repeated her name for a while.

Willard took Cate's hand and said "Come, let's go in Father's workshop and talk." He led her to a bench in a quiet corner and waited as she wiped her dripping eyes and nose with her sleeve and kicked bursts of sawdust into the air.

"Oxa's dead," she finally said between gasps, "and I'll never see him again."

Willard held her hand and said softly: "But you will, Cate. You heard what Father Simon said today. Oxa is with Christ, and they are waiting for us."

Cate stared at him, her eyes both hostile and questioning. "How do you know?"

Willard sat back, trying to disguise his shock. "Because the Church tells us! We're here for just a little while, but death isn't the end. Christ has promised us the victory over death and sin. Don't you believe it?"

Looking down, Cate nodded. "Yes. Most of the time. But sometimes I'm afraid everybody will be in heaven but me."

"None of us deserve it," Willard said kindly.

"I'm going with you to Jerusalem!" Cate suddenly declared. "I want to go on this pilgrimage and help you and Sperleng seek justice and destroy the enemies of Christ."

Willard stared at Cate and said nothing.

"I am serious, Willard. When Father Simon was preaching I knew he was right. We must do what we can. And I can do this. I've worked with Mary. I know about medicines and dressing wounds. I can make pottage and ale. You know I'll be able to help you and Sperleng and his men."

"Women are coming, of course. Mary is going," Willard said slowly. "But there will be fighting and more blood than you've ever seen. Sperleng's warned me about it. *Dulce bellum inexpertis.* Mary is older, no children, unlikely to marry again, but you have your whole life ahead of you."

"Oh, Willard. I want to do something good and important. I want to deserve to join Oxa and Uncle Hafoc and grandfather in heaven."

"I understand your wanting to do something important, something beyond the everyday. I want to be a priest for the same reason. But Cate, you are very young!"

"Mother was married when she was my age, and Darryl is married, and she is only two years older! If I'm old enough to marry, I'm old enough to cook and clean and care for Christ's soldiers."

"Our little arguer," Willard said. "That may be true, but I want you to be safe. This pilgrimage will be long, and not at all safe."

"Everyone tells me how much harder life will be later, the sadness of losing a friend or a husband or a child. Staying here might be less dangerous, unless Stephen invades us of course. Don't forget there is war here, too. But going to Jerusalem is much more important!"

Their mother pushed open the door to the shop. "Come, join us. Eat something before Sperleng's friends finish everything off."

FIVE

*M*ary sat next to Sister Margaret, an elderly nun who was telling her, again, the history of the abbey, how they'd been here before the Normans built their great castle on the hill, how they'd saved the plundering Norsemen from their hideous gods. Mary smiled and pointed to a stack of dried plants on the table near the wall when Cate hurried in. Cate nodded and began grinding the brittle gray-green leaves with a rounded rock in a small stone bowl. When Sister Margaret fell asleep, Mary joined her.

"Half this yarrow is for the abbey, and the other half for the journey. Put the pilgrim's portion into this wooden box. No need to grind the mint; just put as much as you can in this leather pouch. And make sure we have enough ingredients for *dwale* - if we don't, let's collect more this afternoon. We'll need a lot of strong pain medicine, strong enough that we can cut someone to remove an arrow or sew a spear wound."

Cate nodded and looked at the stores of herbs. "Then we'll need more lettuce, poppy, and henbane."

"If you'd like, we can look for them and more yarrow in the meadows outside the gates after we're finished here." Mary shoved mint into the bags. "There's a lovely patch of yarrow near Aldgate."

"Should we make more vinegar?" Cate asked. "We've only saved two barrels."

"No, there's no time. And Sir Robert and William Viel are providing more."

"Will you join us at the market fair tomorrow?"

"If I can. The sisters are demanding much from me these last few weeks," Mary said.

"Sometimes my mother acts like I'm already gone," Cate said. "I guess she won't miss me."

"Cate, you know that isn't true. She's grieving in her own way."

Cate shrugged. "They were trying to get rid of me anyway."

"Self-pity does not become you," Mary said, frowning. "Stop it. Have you changed your mind again? There's still time."

"No; I don't know what's wrong with me," Cate said.

But I do, Mary thought, remembering the weeks before she married Hafoc. She wanted to marry him, knew it was right, but starting off on a new life was frightening. And Cate would be doing that far from her parents, far from all that was familiar. Mary decided to be as helpful and kind as she could, even if it meant listening to Cate grumbling.

"Will all our sins be forgiven too?" Cate asked suddenly. "Or just the soldiers."

"I would think so," Mary said. "We'll be pilgrims too, doing God's work."

"But we won't be fighting. We'll be helping the sick and the wounded far away from the battle."

"You'd better ask Willard, then."

"Father told me sometimes he wished he could join us. He could, couldn't he?"

"Your father has many responsibilities here, and he isn't as strong as he used to be. Better that Sperleng should go," Mary said, stripping the leaves from a fresh yarrow plant, then hanging them to dry along the wall. "It's to your father's honor to have raised such god-fearing children."

"I hope you come tomorrow," Cate said. "It might be the last time we're all together."

She's right, Mary thought; *I should go. I don't owe the sisters any more than I've already given.*

~

The fog was lightening to a dull gray when Willard joined his family for the trek to the market fair. Mist made the path slick and muffled the earl's hounds baying for breakfast. Willard, not used to physical labor, strained to help his father and Cearl pull the cart. Cate, Linn, and their mother followed behind to make sure none of the tables, benches, carvings, or household tools they'd brought dropped off.

Willard usually avoided the raucous fairs, preferring the solemnity of church services or the instruction of the miracle plays. But he was leaving soon and knew his parents wanted him to join them this one last time. Cate had begged him too, regaling him about the grandness of the harvest fair, one of the first since the battles of the civil war had lessened. He enjoyed her excited descriptions of the farmers who brought their harvest from the countryside, their wives exchanging thread and hides and sheep and vegetables for the blankets and coats they would need for the coming year. Willard's family went for the spectacle as much as for the chance to sell their goods. Craftsmen also had weekly market days in Brycgstow, but his father and Cearl seldom participated as they had plenty of carpentry work at the site of St. Augustine's and the new church Sir Robert was building for St. James.

Along the bank of the Frome, the family passed the smoldering remains of several bonfires. Willard's grandfather had told him old stories about Beltane, when the spirits came looking for mischief and countrymen led their cattle between the bonfires to protect them while young men and women covered themselves with yellow flowers and consummated their relationships near the heat of those fires. *Pagans*, Willard thought, glad of his family's conversion to the one true God. He watched his footing closely to avoid sleeping bodies. Willard couldn't help but wonder if anything had gone on here last night. He hoped those old traditions were gone forever.

When they arrived at the field just east of the castle, Willard could see the faint outlines of the stalls of those who had slept there. His family always set up as close to the market cross as they could, knowing that everyone would pass by. Aedra's family was setting up their wool stall across the lane, and the families smiled and nodded at each other.

Father took a bench and five poles from the side of the cart, and Willard began pounding them into the rocky ground. Cearl soon took the mallet from Willard's hand to drive the posts deeper. Cearl didn't say a word, but Willard felt chastised, weak. Together they covered the frame with a linen awning.

They set up tables and benches, and Cate unpacked several of her father's carvings—crosses with intricate designs of intersecting arcs and lines, haloed Madonnas, and many small foxes, dogs, and cats. Mother moved several of the more detailed carvings away from the front edge, and Cate replaced them with items she had made: baskets and straw dolls with small bits of fabric clothing them. In front of and alongside the tables the men put the large, heavy items the local farmers would need: wheeled carts, rakes, plows. In the back, they piled rough benches and stools.

"I wonder where Sperleng is. He promised to help us," his father grumbled.

"It's Beltane, Father. I can guess," Cearl replied, smirking at Willard.

As the mist thinned, only a few small patches of fog scurried in the wind along Market Lane. Soon it would be time for Sir Robert to open the market. These fairs were a major source of income for the earl, and his men kept a close watch while collecting stall fees. Willard's father had worked for hours on a waist-high carved statue that he proudly said he was sure Sir Robert would accept for his fee: St. James with a staff in one hand, a sword in the other, walking away from a fishing boat that formed the background. St James's cloak was painted a deep red and his sword gray with a red hilt. The rest of the carving was polished and oiled. Willard's father placed this statue in front of him.

Sperleng arrived just as a stone-faced Sir Robert, wearing a dark red woolen cape trimmed with fur, approached the market cross followed by his wife, Mabel. Mabel's face was hidden by a thin cloth. Her handmaidens lifted the hem of her long flowing gown of heavy red brocade with long, wide sleeves lined in blue. Her dress was tied at the waist with a woven gold belt secured with a gold clasp. Over this she wore a thin blue woolen mantle tied with a braided gold cord, its hood trimmed with blue and white striped squirrel fur. Willard pondered how much their splendor cost. *How much better to use that coin to spread Christ's truth and drive out heresy.*

"Where were you?" their father demanded.

"There's much to do in the armory to get ready for our journey, Father." Sperleng grinned at Cearl when his father turned to face Sir Robert.

Several knights in tunics covered with chain mail surrounded the earl and his wife, holding large, long shields. Some bore a standing gold lion on a blue background, others three clarions on a red background. Each knight had a long sword with ornate metalwork on the hilt in a scabbard hanging at his side. Sperleng pointed to the closest knight and said, "I made that sword, isn't it beautiful?" Cate nodded, as she rested into the crook of Willard's arm. Their mother held Linn's shoulders tightly, leaning her chin on the top of Linn's head.

The fog was now a haze that made everything seem slightly out of focus. Yesterday's towering clouds were gone, and the little bits of sky that peered through the low, gray ones had brightened to a dusky blue. Sir Robert climbed the few stairs to the stage next to the market cross and arranged his cape to display the shimmering blue surcoat with gold-embroidered lions underneath. His knights planted shields in front of them on the small platform and began staring suspiciously at the crowd. The Earl surveyed the gathering crowd imperiously, demanding quiet without saying a word. When he saw Pier's statue of St. James, he bent down and spoke to one of his knights, who then climbed back down.

"Your stall fee? The earl will accept this as payment."

Piers nodded, and bowed slightly, lifting the statue to the knight, who displayed it to Sir Robert and Mabel, then hoisted it to the platform for all to see.

Sir Robert kept his hand on the statue as he spoke, pausing often to let a local merchant, Robert

Fitzharding, translate the Norman French into the language of the countryside.

"My people, I welcome you to Brycgstow Fair. I know that times are hard as Stephen's men seek to punish those who side with Empress Maud. Many have died, and even I endured a long, bitter imprisonment."

Willard, having worked with the Norman priests, understood more of the earl's words than his family did, and he could hear the gravity and sadness in the earl's voice which Fitzharding matched while translating for the crowd. The earl seemed much older and frailer than Willard remembered.

Sir Robert continued with a lighter, happier tone. "But we at Brycgstow are fortunate, as God has provided us with the protection of his rivers and strong men and has saved us from the rule of greedy interlopers. Christ and his mother have blessed our harvests and provided our sheep with long, soft coats. Your industry has brought an abundance of goods to this fair, goods to share with each other and the world. Look to the ships in the harbor. Merchants have crossed the sea to purchase your fine goods. Your wool and blankets and coats are coveted, and there are no finer craftsmen in all of England." The crowd murmured their approval, and Willard saw his father stand a little straighter.

"Sadly, there are those who would try to take these riches from us, thieves and pirates for their profit, and others to support their false king. But I promise you the protection of our great army. The goodness of our Lord, the strength of our men, and the prayers of our priests will support us!" Sir Robert put both hands on the statue. "And James, the saint of soldiers and pilgrims, protects us!" Willard joined in the crowd's great shout.

"Let us thank Christ and his saints with our praise but also with our actions. For we have pilgrims here too. Pilgrims and soldiers of Christ, the faithful of St. Peter, who will be leaving soon on a great journey to save the Holy Land from the tyranny of the Mohammedans and their godless caliphs. I wish, but cannot go, for I feel the sickness of my age and the terrors of my imprisonment, and I must fight the false king Stephen and protect this land in honor of my sister and her son Henry, the true heir to his grandfather's throne. Instead, I will provide a tithe of supplies and armor for God's work." The crowd shouted again. "For those of you who have heard and answered Christ's call, I bless you for it. My son Philip will be joining you. We will pray every day for your safe return."

Mary put her arm through Cate's, and Willard pulled them both close. Sperleng hugged Linn and his crying mother.

"Many others have also contributed to this great enterprise. Robert Fitzharding and William Viel are providing ships and much cloth. Samuel is financing several of our young men, providing them with mail shirts, swords, and helmets, and forgiving them their debts." The crowd murmured at this, and Sir Robert stopped and glared until there was silence.

"I call on all to provide food supplies for this noble cause," the earl continued, "in whatever way you are able. Go beyond what is comfortable, for our pilgrims are sacrificing their comfort too for God's glory." The Earl lifted both his arms. "May God be with you!"

Sir Robert climbed down the stairs, joined his wife and their entourage, and began making his way along Market Lane, accepting fees and gifts from the stalls and heading toward the edge of the market where he and his wife would provide food and coins to the poor. Despite the clamor and clapping that surrounded him, Willard stood still, shocked. Samuel was financing a war in Jerusalem? Was this how he was buying off the town for murdering Oxa?

～

Mary and Alma wandered through the market stalls, inspecting the wool, trading spring herbs for honeycombs, laughing at the clowns and jugglers who jumped in front of them. The sisters had grown close since Hafoc's death, Alma always including Mary in family activities, and Mary helping with the care of Alma's children. Alma had begged Mary weekly not to join the pilgrims, and even in Alma's silence Mary felt her reproof. They had become dependent on each other to share their joys and worries, to help each other understand the little cruelties of children and clergy. Alma was her best friend.

But what Mary felt for Cate was entirely different, deeper, more primal. She was elated Cate had decided to join the pilgrimage. Cate said that God was leading her, and it certainly was an answer to Mary's prayers. But although Alma had begrudgingly accepted that two of her sons were leaving, as men had to do what was required of them, Mary feared Alma saw her and Cate's leaving as betrayal.

"I can see something is on your mind, sister," Alma said.

"I'm just thinking this will be my last May festival for a long time, and I'm trying to enjoy it instead of being sad."

"Maybe your last forever," Alma said curtly.

"Don't say that!" Mary said. "Sperleng says two, three years at most."

"Only if the Saracens don't kill you first."

"Some will die and will wait for us in heaven, but only Sperleng will be in battle."

"You know the Saracens will kill everyone if they get the chance—women, children, priests too," Alma said. "They may save a few nobles for ransom, but not my poor family." Alma turned to look at Mary. "I know why you want to go, and why you've talked Cate into going."

Mary opened her mouth to protest, but Alma stopped her. "Oh, I know she says God is calling her, whatever that means, but she's going because of you. But she's my daughter! I can't be the fun aunt who plays games with her and gives her plants and listens to all her complaints. Coddles her and makes unrealistic promises. If she dies, it's all on you."

Alma's words stung Mary. *So that is how my sister sees me.* But she saw the truth of them too. Being an aunt freed her from the mundane and the difficult. *But I love her too,* Mary thought stubbornly. *I don't want her to come to harm.*

Alma covered her face in her hands. "Oh, I'm sorry Mary. I shouldn't have said that. I know it's time for Cate to leave home and there's nothing for you here anymore. It's just hard. If she married Wulf at least Cate would be nearby, like Darryl."

"As I recall, our father didn't want you to marry Piers," Mary said.

"True enough," Alma nodded. "Thankfully he didn't make me marry that awful old butcher. Now I have beautiful children and a husband who still is alive."

"You are a lucky woman, Alma."

"Oh, I've hurt you again. I am full of that today. I am lucky I didn't marry a soldier, and that is the truth."

"I had a good marriage while it lasted. I can't complain."

"Of course, you can, you are my sister! And my children love you. I'm grateful for your kindness and attention to them."

"Look at Cate and Aedra by the players," Mary said. "They are so different, Aedra dancing and Cate smiling on."

"Sometimes I think Cate would do well to be more like Aedra," Alma said. "More outgoing, more spontaneous."

"Really? Aedra makes me tired sometimes with all her talking and moving about."

"True. But Cate can be too earnest sometimes. A lot like Willard."

"Willard has done well with his dedication, Alma. Almost a priest! I can barely understand him sometimes with all his Latin words."

Alma stood up straighter, her eyes shining. "Soon. In time for the pilgrimage."

"I wonder if Cate wants to go because Willard is going," Mary said.

"You might be right. They are close." Alma sighed. "And I know she prefers your company to mine."

"Alma, Cate loves you, you must know that. And like you said, I'm the fun aunt, not the person who tells her what she can and cannot do. I remember how I felt about our mother at that age! And now I miss her every single day."

Alma nodded. "Boys are so much easier."

The women walked silently among the booths, Alma fingering the wool and Mary touching the leaves of plants drying at a nearby table then leaning down to catch their scent. Small boys chased each other between them, then disappeared into the crowd.

"What does Willard say about Cate wanting to go?" Mary finally asked.

"He understands, but thinks it is no trip for a woman."

"Even me?" Mary asked, surprised.

"Yes, even you."

"As if any of them would want to do what the women will do," Mary scoffed.

"He knows why you are going, but Willard is protective of women's weakness, and fears they'll be a distraction to the soldiers."

"And to him?"

"No, he shows no interest," Alma admitted, "I think he'd prefer to be a monk."

As the women wandered back toward their stall, they joined Cate and Aedra in a circle around musicians playing a happy tune. One played a harp and sang, the other played a flute while dancing. To their side a young boy beat a small drum hung by what looked like the remnants of a ripped shirt. Trace came through the crowd and pulled Aedra into an open space where they started matching their steps and their claps. Soon others joined them in a line, Mary and the rest clapping in time. The musicians repeated the song for several rounds until the dancers began leaving the line in happy exhaustion.

As dusk approached, Mary helped pack the family cart with unsold items and the bags of flour, cheese, thread, and eggs the farmers had paid them. Often the men would sleep in the stall overnight, but today the clouds had thickened and darkened, and they feared a flooding rain. Cearl and Sperleng packed sullenly; the fair at night was very different from the fair during the day. Those who lived too far to return home were building cooking fires near the castle moat, passing jugs of ale and mead. Many were already drunk and laughing loudly.

"Father," Sperleng said. "Leave the canopy and a few benches. If it rains, the lane is sloped to take the water away from the Cross and this area, and my friends and I can sleep on the benches. We are soldiers; this is luxurious compared to battle conditions, and it will save you trouble in the morning. You can even bring more goods. Cearl, stay with us if you like."

Sperleng turned to Cate. "And you, Cate; you wish to be a soldier. Perhaps you would like to camp in the rain too?"

Cate shook her head, blushing, as two of Sperleng's friends laughed.

Mary frowned at Sperleng until he shrugged and walked away.

Six

*H*undreds of men rolled barrels of flour, wine, and vinegar, and hauled trunks of dried meat, wool, and linen to the six pilgrim ships moored along the banks of the Avon. Two high-sided Norman transport ships, provided by Earl Robert and William Viel, dwarfed the low-lying fishing boats and cargo skiffs moored west of the bridge. The large square sail of the Earl's vessel hung along the City wall, newly painted with a great blue cross. Merchants grumbled quietly that they would be glad when things returned to normal as their boats remained moored further inland while they waited the clearing of the harbor.

Gilbert and the other knights, all wearing new surcoats emblazoned with a large blue cross over their armor, had left the previous day, traveling overland to Dartmouth. The horses, and most of the knights, preferred the land to the sea. Before they'd left, Gilbert made Sperleng the leader of sixteen men, a quarter of his foot soldiers, and Sperleng still glowed with pride from the honor.

Sperleng greeted Cearl, who was framing a platform near the bow, and then lowered himself into the ship's bottom. He checked the slings for the horses to make sure they were securely tied to the broad crossbeams. Planks above provided some cover for the horses and tonnage. Sperleng helped the men load, placing the cargo when he could on the heavy, curved ribs supporting the ship's hull.

Egric and Kendric, their hair and bodies damp with sweat, rolled several barrels toward Sperleng.

"Your aunt and sister are near St. Nicholas with their supplies," Egric told Sperleng.

"You help them," Sperleng said.

"You're still angry at Cate?" Egric asked.

Sperleng kept working silently until Egric left. No need to speak about the fear and frustration he felt about his sister going on this pilgrimage. He needed to keep her safe and wasn't sure he could. He had men to lead, battles to fight. Cate would distract him. *At least Mary is coming*, Sperleng thought, *and she has sense.* Unease filled him. He couldn't ignore his family even when they were a burden. He walked quickly down the ramp to join Egric.

～

Cate saw Sperleng and Egric walking along the wharf and ran toward them as Mary waited with the medical provisions they had packed yesterday.

"Isn't it exciting?" Cate asked.

Sperleng wiped his forehead with his sleeve and looked away. "I don't know about exciting. It's a lot of work to load these ships, and we are going to war, after all."

Cate felt chastised. Sperleng was right. He had fought several times before, and she had overheard him raging when friends had died, thrusting away tears of fury and loss as he planned his revenge. "True," she said quietly.

"Everything needs to be in barrels or trunks," Sperleng said, looking at the loose bags of dried plants in their cart. "Is there room in your others?"

"Nay, we were told to find more here," Mary said.

Sperleng pointed Egric toward the gate where the harbormaster stood near hundreds of uncovered containers. "I think one will be enough."

Cate looked around, gaping. She'd lived here all her life but had never seen a vessel so huge and beautiful as the earl's new ship. The hull was painted a sky blue, its top edge lined with multi-colored shields emblazoned with lions and clarions, crosses, and birds and mythical animals. *Sperleng is in a mood, again,* she thought. She would ignore his attempts to dampen her exhilaration.

When Egric returned with a container, Mary and Cate carefully wrapped the bags in animal hides and laid them inside it.

"I'll bring this to the loading foreman," Egric said, rolling it toward the dock.

"He sure smiles more when you're nearby," Sperleng said to Cate. "Stay away from him."

Cate blushed. She thought Egric was kind and handsome, but she was not going to be distracted. She stared vacantly at the water, thinking about the grand pilgrimage ahead. Her mind raced between seeing herself standing at the site of the Crucifixion to tending to the wounded, the men's eyes filled with tears of gratitude.

"Look," Mary said, standing up and waving. "Alma is coming with Willard."

Sperleng put his arm around his mother and kissed the top of her head. "It was fine of you to come."

"Half my family is leaving in the morning. I needed to come."

"There is food and ale along the walls," Sperleng said, "Let's eat. I'll find Father and Cearl."

Men swarmed the tables of food. Cate was sure many of them were neither loading the boats nor going on pilgrimage. The men could brave that crowd. She followed her mother and Mary to a shady place along the wall. Her mother would not look at her or Mary.

"Alma," Mary said.

"I fear I will never see any of you again. Do you see why that's hard for me?"

"Yes," Mary said softly.

"Then stay!"

"I can't, and you know that," Mary said.

"A part of me would like to join you," Alma said. "Willard says you will be stopping in Hispania and may visit the grave of Saint James on your way to Jerusalem. How glorious that would be! But my doom apparently is simpler than both of yours."

They waited in silence as lines of men carried cargo towards the ships. Cate marveled at the speed of the loading but couldn't imagine they'd be ready to leave in the morning with all the stacks piled high along the river bank. A few fishing boats had come from upstream, the fishermen trying to find a space to lay out their nets and gut their catch. Cate saw Willard try to join a group of priests who mostly excluded him until the priest from St. Peter's opened a place. *Stinking Normans*, Cate thought, *Willard is worth a hundred of them.*

In the distance Cate saw Galan and Acha climbing the ramp to the earl's ship with several bundles. They stopped to talk with her father and Cearl along the quay.

"Acha is coming with us?" Cate asked, disbelief creeping into her voice.

"She has no children now," Mary said. "Only Galan."

The thought of seeing Acha every day filled Cate with dread. She chided herself for being uncharitable. Maybe Acha needed a cause to help her cope with her loss. But Acha was so morose, even before Oxa's death. Cate feared they'd constantly need to be careful of what they said and did, tiptoeing away from the subjects of children and death and blasphemers. When her father arrived, Cate looked up at him expectantly, hoping he'd be able to tell them what was happening.

"Well, it looks like you'll have another woman on this trip," he said. "Acha is joining the pilgrims, and I asked her to help Mary keep an eye on you."

"I'm glad," Mary said, "I feared for Acha being alone after Galan left, feared she would grieve too much the loss of Oxa. So much sadness for one woman!"

"Be kind to her, Cate," her mother said. "Accept her mothering and attention, even when you prefer to be left alone."

Cate nodded, although she didn't think she needed that much mothering.

When they returned home, Aedra was hovering near their garden, looking anxiously up the street. At the sight of them, she ran to Cate and threw her arms around her. "I thought you had left already, without saying goodbye!" Aedra said.

"I wouldn't do that." Cate felt tears stinging her eyes. "Help me in the garden. We can talk while we work."

Aedra nodded, and they began weeding as Cate's mother and aunt went into the house. Cate laughed as Aedra mimicked her scenes at the Easter play and whispered about her times alone with Trace. They talked about the storytellers at the fair, the new colors Aedra's parents hoped to dye this year's wool, everything except what was really on their minds, that this might be the last time they'd see each other. Listening to Aedra, it suddenly became real to Cate that she might not have these simple pleasures again for a very long time. No more watching Aedra dance with Trace. Or fishing with her father. Or harvesting the flax with her mother. She shook her head, trying not to think these things.

"Do you disagree?" Aedra asked.

"What? No," Cate said. "My mind was wandering."

"I thought so. Where to?"

Cate hesitated. She didn't want to ruin their last day. "Leaving you and my family is hard. I keep thinking about all the things we've done together, how you've been my friend for such a long time."

Aedra nodded. "It makes me sad too. Jerusalem! You'll be gone for ages! I'll have three babies by the time you come back. I want you here to play with them, not off in the land of the Amalekites. And you might never come back. I couldn't stand that. I'll be stuck here in boring Brycgstow while you are having an adventure."

Cate looked at Aedra with surprise. "Well, I think helping feed and bathe wounded soldiers won't be fun."

"Depends on the soldier," Aedra said slyly.

Cate laughed despite feeling a deep well of sadness. She would miss how Aedra made her smile.

"Pick strawberries and come sit with us while we wait for the men," Cate's mother said as she and Mary joined them in the garden. "And Aedra, stay and eat with us tonight."

The women hulled strawberries as they told stories about Cate and Sperleng and Willard as little children, about the time Cate wasted her strawberries by smashing them on her hands and coloring her face, then crying uncontrollably when she figured out there were none left to eat. They were laughing when the men joined them.

"We're a happy crew today," Sperleng said. "And Willard and I have good news. Willard is the priest for our ship."

"I'm proud of you, son," Piers said, clasping Willard's shoulder. "Both of you."

"Earl Robert gave me an alb and a chasuble to wear on holy days," Willard said.

Father reached into a large pocket in his shirt and showed Willard a carved wooden cross hanging from a leather lace. "I want you to have this."

"I have a gift for you too," Alma said, rushing inside and bringing out a length of cloth with a cross embroidered on one side and a pilgrim's staff on the other, "A stole to wear at services. Father Simon told me what it should look like."

"Thank you," Willard said, his voice unsteady.

"I carved crosses for Sperleng, Mary, and Cate, too, though not as fine as Willard's," Piers said, handing cords to each of them. "To keep you safe. Father Simon blessed them."

Aedra began to cry, and Cate felt her throat swell. *It is time to change the subject*, Cate thought.

"Who is in your regiment, Sperleng?" Cate asked.

"Soldiers I've been with before, mostly. Osbert, Kendric, and Galan, and a few Welsh from near Monmouth, including Egric." Sperleng tried to act humble and serious but couldn't. He looked cheerfully at Cate for the first time in weeks.

"Then that's what we will celebrate tonight," Alma said, getting up and moving toward the house. "I can't celebrate your leaving."

"We will be on your ship?" Mary asked.

"Of course, and Acha too."

"What did Galan say?" Piers asked. "He is no man to take orders, and you were his apprentice."

"He didn't say anything while Gilbert was there. He didn't look happy, that's the truth. Galan is no soldier, but he must learn to take orders, or he'll die. I think he'll learn that pretty fast."

PART TWO

FARE FORWARD PILGRIMS
1147—1148

SEVEN

The mid-day sun blinded Sperleng as the ship raced toward Dartmouth's shoreline. He could feel the lurching drag of oars trying to slow the ship while sailors quickly furled the massive sail. Two threw ropes away from the mast, two more held their lines firm as the remaining sailors fore and aft pulled and tied theirs, yelling to each other as the heavy linen sail folded into itself at the tree-sized yard near the top of the mast. As the weight of the sail shifted, the ship careened and swayed until it found its balance. Sperleng and his troops stayed far from the ship's center, standing alongside the small shelter near the rudder oar. He heard a distant shout, answered by the sailors on board with an incomprehensible stream of words and jolt of something heavy pulling the rear of the ship.

More than a hundred vessels crowded the port—huge cargo ships, slim sailing ships, galleys, hulks, nefs, cogs, small fishing boats—most with huge crosses painted on their sails. Sperleng's lumbering ship glided toward a long wooden pier jutting out from the embankment where, he suddenly realized, some sailors from the ship were already standing, pulling on the heavy ropes as the anchor set. *When did that happen?* Sperleng wondered.

When the ship finally settled, Sperleng swore to himself as Cate scrambled toward him, her gray-blue eyes shining with eagerness. He'd already warned his troops to stay away from her, but there were thousands of men here, and few women. "I cannot watch her all the time," he grumbled under his breath. He hoped she has some sense. Not that she showed any yet, with her delusions about the glory of saving Jerusalem and being a sister of mercy. She was just a woman, and a common woman at that.

Cate crowded Sperleng as he organized his troops for departure. He waved his hand at her dismissively and warned, "Don't go off alone, Cate. We'll find a room and return. Wait for us. And remember, if you disobey me it will be a simple matter to send you home or leave you here."

Galan pushed his way toward them. "Acha is coming with me."

Sperleng shrugged consent. *No point in antagonizing him over this.*

~

Hours passed, and more and more ships arrived while Mary and Cate waited, staring longingly toward the shore. The sun had begun to create long shadows of the many ships lining the harbor when Mary finally spotted Egric climbing the ramp. She and Cate hurried belowdecks to the ramp's entrance in the hold. The walkway was dark, and they were blinded as they left the shade. Mary put her hand above her eyes as Egric came to meet them.

"We've found a room for you at the Rose Inn," Egric said. "Sperleng is saving us a table at the tavern."

They followed him to a street filled with men spilling out of its many taverns. Shafts of sunlight broke up the shadows from the taller buildings. Each inn was a small wooden structure, most of them ragged from disrepair. Through their open windows and doors Mary heard laughter and singing. The stench of urine and scorched meat permeated the air between the buildings. Several men along the street raised their hands or tankards in greeting but looked away when Egric took both the women's hands.

They entered a massive wooden door. Part of the inn was lit from the setting sun coming through a west window. This tavern seemed larger and brighter than the ones they had passed, and Mary felt relieved that Sperleng's anger with Cate had not made him spiteful in his choice of rooms. Mary searched for Sperleng as Eric led them through the crowded room, finally spying him seated with several men toward the dim back of the room. There the servers had begun lighting candles in sconces along the wall. Egric asked one to bring three more bowls of stew and tankards of ale as they squeezed onto a bench.

Mary noticed only three other women sitting at the tables. These women, their breasts nearly falling from the tight bodices of their dresses, were sitting on the laps of men who were running scarred hands along their bodies. One woman seemed always to be laughing, her pock-marked face rigid with hilarity, and another kept whispering something in her man's ear. The third woman kept lifting a man's cap off his head, waving it in the air, and putting it back, displaying small dark circles along the palms of her hands.

"Pay no attention to those women," Egric said, leaning close to Mary and Cate. "They are not worthy of your notice."

"Where are Galan and Acha?" Cate asked.

"Galan said this place is too dear," Sperleng said. "They are sleeping on the ship with the sailors."

"Isn't it too dear for us too?" Cate asked.

"No," Sperleng said with a tone that brooked no further questions.

The room felt stifling from the heat of the sun and the many bodies lining the walls, sitting at the tables, and lurching through the small spaces between. The smell of boiling meat and sweating men was almost overwhelming. Despite her hunger, Mary longed for the open ship. The noise was so great, that she found it impossible to hear or talk, and so ate without speaking as the men around her laughed and cheered and sang.

Cate leaned over to Mary. "What are they speaking? I don't understand some of their words."

"I think there are many languages here," Mary shouted. "I don't think drunkenness explains all I'm hearing."

Cate leaned toward Egric. "Are there foreigners here?"

"Yes, many. Danes and Flemings and more. Karl here is Frisian. We helped him load his ship last summer when he bought some Brycgstow wool."

Hearing his name, Karl lifted his tankard toward Egric. Mary thought Karl was the biggest, and blondest, man she had ever seen. Even Sperleng seemed small sitting next to Karl, whose head rose above everyone else's and whose shoulders took the space of two men. His smiling eyes were the blue of an icy lake, his grin broad and gentle.

"Karl is easier to understand than the others," Egric said, lifting his tankard in response.

Mary steeled herself to the din that blurred together the languages, the singing, the scraping chairs, and the noise of dropped bowls. The windows darkened, the buildings across the street backlit in the dusk.

"Mary, I'd like to go to our room. This is too noisy and hot for me," Cate said.

"Yes," Mary agreed.

They went to where Sperleng was telling Karl and his friends about his battles. "Sperleng, Cate and I would like to go to our room."

Sperleng huffed, stood, and pushed Cate toward a small door along a side wall. Mary followed. Once through, Sperleng approached the innkeeper. "This is my sister and aunt. Take them to their room." He then stalked back to his table.

The innkeeper was a large, red-faced man who smelled of beer and other things Mary could not identify. "Anna!" he yelled, and an even larger woman rose from shadows by the stairs and lumbered to them. "Show these women the small room in the back."

Without a word, Anna took a candle from a table, and started up the narrow stairs, nearly filling the space between the walls as she climbed almost sideways. They walked to the end of a hallway where Anna undid a lock, handed a key to Mary, and motioned for them to go into a small, windowless room. Once they squeezed past her, Anna lit a candle on the wall, turned, and went back down the stairs.

In the gloom Mary saw a single pallet covered with straw, and a large pot in the corner. The noise from the tavern downstairs was nearly as loud as when they had been in the middle of it, except that the words were more indistinct and the music clearer. And it was hot. Mary thought about stripping naked and throwing herself on the pallet.

"Maybe this is not such a good idea," Cate said. "Should we go back downstairs?"

Mary sat down on the pallet. "I don't think so. At least here I can close my eyes."

"I think I will, though, for a while. Maybe I'll stand by a window to get some air. Do you mind?"

Mary debated whether to make Cate stay. It was hot and airless here and she understood Cate's dismay, but all Mary wanted to do was lie down.

"Be careful. Stay inside and go straight back to Sperleng's table. Stay near them always and make someone walk you back here. When you return, knock twice then once."

"I will," Cate promised.

~

Cate felt her way through the dark hallway, Anna's bulk ahead of her blocked much of the little light the sconces threw. As she neared the bottom of the stairs, the inn-keeper was directing a tall, broad-shouldered man upstairs. The man looked at her and smiled, showing a mouth of gray and missing teeth. As he neared, she saw bits of potato and gravy in his long curly beard and looked away. He said something in a language she didn't understand and pointed toward the tavern. She nodded politely and went through the door.

Sperleng and his men were raising their tank-ards and laughing. Although it was brighter and somewhat less oppressive than her room, Cate decided what she needed most was cool, smokeless air. Only Karl, towering above the others, looked at her with a wondering expression as she walked toward the door someone must have opened to cool the room and thin the smoke. As she breathed in the almost fresh air, even the stench of ale and piss didn't seem so unbearable.

Suddenly, someone grabbed her arm and pulled her outside. It was the tall man she had seen with the innkeeper.

Startled, she tried to pull away. "I need to stay inside!"

He said something unintelligible to her.

"I don't understand," she said. "Let me go."

He repeated himself, louder this time, and waved a coin at her.

She looked up at him, confused. He placed the coin in her hand, put both his arms around her, squeezed her, then kissed her wetly and thrust his hand under her blouse. Now she understood. Sperleng warned her about soldiers buying women, and Willard had told her about Saint Wilfrida, although he'd never quite explained the rape that lead to the birth of Saint Edith.

His spittle dripped down her chin as he pushed her face into his neck and rubbed his crotch against her. She gagged from his smell of decayed food, stale beer, musk, and fish, and from his slick sweat on her cheeks.

"No, no, I am here with my brothers. I am not for sale!" she shouted, ducking her head and trying to pull away.

He gripped her tightly, pulling her further away from the door toward a dark corner near the inn.

"No, no, please," she cried. Fear numbed her body as she tried to free herself from the man's strong arms. She had never felt so helpless, and her mother's litany of terrible things that can happen to young girls who went out alone played in her head. Why did she not believe it until now when it was too late?

God, save me, she began to pray, *I'll be good and careful from now on. I'll never wander off on my own. I'll pray every day and help the poor. Whatever you want from me I'll do, but please save me.*

Terrible imaginings of Saint Wilfrida ran through Cate's head. She'd ask Willard what really happened. No, she couldn't do that.

"No, no, no," Cate pled as the man yanked and pushed her. She wanted to screech, like the feral cats some nights outside her window, but her thoughts wandered instead to her grandfather's goats rutting in the pasture.

If this is my fate, God, please let me die, or, if I live, become a saint too. How strange, Cate thought as she began to collapse, *if I have avoided marrying Wulf only to have a child this way.* The road's uneven stones pressed hard against her head and the man towered over her fumbling with his clothes. *Maybe I could pretend to die. Christ have mercy! Let me die now.*

Suddenly Egric and Karl were there next to them, and Karl was roaring at the man in what Cate assumed was Flemish or Frisian or some other strange language. The tall man swung at Karl, but missed, and Karl lifted him by the throat and shook him violently.

"Get back in the Inn," Egric hissed, pulling her arm.

Cate turned on her side and retched, adding to the already strong stench of waste in the street. When she recovered a little, she held her blouse close, stood shakily, and shoved the coin in Egric's hand.

"Give him his coin," Cate said.

Egric's eyes shot between her and the coin, then he threw it toward the man. "What were you thinking, taking that coin?"

"I didn't take it! He forced it into my hand." Cate was weeping from indignation, frustration, and relief.

"Why are you here?" Egric asked, staring at her. "Do I need to explain to you the dangers of taking a journey where there are many men and few women?"

Cate shook her head, looking down at the ground, afraid Egric's anger and sympathy would make her cry harder. She had to be strong. Had to show them all she could take care of herself.

"You like to be on your own. I understand that. But it is not safe. We can't always watch out for you. Never look at men you don't know. Never travel without a companion. Better still, go home. Grow up. Help Christ's cause by being charitable and helping the sisters at the abbey. I am sure we can find someone to take you back to Brycgstow. I will take you if needs be."

Egric's words stung, partly because Cate knew he was right, partly because she could not go home, and partly because Egric now thought her a silly, headstrong girl. How humiliating it would be to be brought back to Brycgstow less than a week after she left! *This is my mission, my calling*, she thought stubbornly. *I won't ever make this mistake again.*

"Egric, I thank you and Karl for saving me," she said, fighting back her tears. "And I know you're right. I act without thinking. I wander off on my own. I think I understand things that I don't. But I want to go on this journey, and I want to learn. I will work hard not to be a burden to you and Sperleng. Please don't tell Sperleng or Mary about this or they will send me home. I promise to stay with a companion and not to roam alone. I can learn. I am learning. Please!"

Egric's troubled eyes softened. "Promise me and God."

"I promise." She looked up at him gratefully, then bowed her head in prayer.

"Against my better judgment, all right. I will not tell Sperleng, but you should tell Mary. Karl? What do you think?"

"We need women on this journey, and I have to think you've learned your lesson," Karl said in his thick brogue, "Have you?" Cate nodded. "Egric and I will watch out for you when we can, but you must be careful and watch out for yourself, too. We have a war to fight and can't be your nurse."

"I will walk you to your room. Stay there this time," Egric said.

Egric followed Cate upstairs and stood in the shadows as Cate knocked on the door.

"That was quick," Mary said, as Cate slipped into the dark room, hoping Mary wouldn't see the tear in her blouse.

"Yes," she said.

~

At dawn, Sperleng pounded on Cate and Mary's door: "Get up if you want to eat!"

They immediately opened the door, already awake and dressed.

"Good morning, nephew," Mary said, kissing Sperleng's cheek.

Sperleng smiled and hugged his aunt. Cate looked away. Sperleng turned and led them down the stairs and toward Egric, Willard, and Karl who sat at a long table near the front of the Inn.

The servers threw bowls of pottage on the table in front of them and left without speaking. Sperleng saw Cate looking about furtively and wondered when Karl smiled at her. *Oh, God, not Karl too*, Sperleng thought. Egric, who he'd thought would be smiling, stared steadfastly into his bowl. *Something is going on here. Something is not right.* He would confront Egric later, but now he must take charge.

"Willard and I meet with our leaders this morning to set up divisions and rules of order," Sperleng announced. "We leave Friday morning, so stay close and stay out of trouble!" He looked directly at Cate, and she nodded meekly.

"Kendric, Galan: you will stay with the women until I return," Sperleng ordered. "I know this is not how you wanted to spend your day, but it can't be helped."

Sperleng and Willard left quickly, hurrying toward the tall-sided ships with giant masts lining

Dartmouth's harbor. The day was warm and sunny, and soon they removed their woolen capes and carried them in their arms. Along the quay, hundreds streamed toward a village of tents in front of one of the largest ships. Gilbert and William Viel joined Sperleng and Willard when they entered the largest of the tents, a luxurious place with blankets and carpets on the ground and several chairs lining the front.

Viel pointed toward a large group of men gathered near the front. "Much as I despise Stephen's men, they are the leaders here, so we need join Hervey of Glanville, Lord Saher, and the other Normans."

"We are one in Christ's battle," Willard said.

Viel snorted. "We'll see."

Sperleng felt the unease and hostility of Stephen's men as they joined the group. Gilbert approached several knights and began a fervent conversation with them.

"That is Hervey's priest over there preening," Viel said. "No doubt he thinks he's in charge."

Willard nodded, and walked that way, leaving Sperleng alone with Viel. Sperleng stayed silent as Viel pointed out men he cautioned them to watch. *Viel is a suspicious man*, Sperleng thought. He knew of Viel's reputation as a pirate, a man who felt justified in pillaging ships belonging to those who backed King Stephen. Or the French. Although Viel called himself a merchant, Sperleng and most people believed Viel became richer from other people's trade than from his own. Viel was a great friend of Earl Robert, and

Sperleng knew he would do well to be friendly to, but never trust, the man. Sperleng nodded respectfully to Viel's pronouncements.

Gilbert soon returned, and the negotiations as to leaders and rules began. After much debate, four nobles loyal to King Stephen were elected to lead the men from England. Brycgstow's ships were ordered to report to Lord Saher. The four nobles then joined the leaders of the Rhinelanders and Flemings to discuss the rules that would govern all pilgrims, and the tent soon filled with debates in several languages mediated by the ships' priests who carried messages between groups and to the pilgrim leaders. Sperleng wondered how they would ever all agree, but by nightfall they reached a common order. Willard joined Sperleng, Gilbert, and the men of Bristol around Lord Saher.

"Fellow pilgrims," Saher said, "despite our differences, and our earthly quarrels with men from other lands, we are united in our desire that God's law govern how we—and the world—live. The differences between soldiers from diverse lands and who speak other tongues are erased by this unity of belief and purpose. We must cleanse ourselves to purify the world!

"We know we face great danger and death ahead as we struggle to bring Christ's law to the land of his birth. To unify us in this struggle, we Christians of many lands have agreed to be governed by strict rules of behavior and principle. We will be humble before each other by wearing simple garments suitable for war—we will not try to seem superior to each other through jewels or costly apparel. Do you agree?"

"Yes!" the men shouted. Sperleng glanced at the well-dressed knights, and saw that they, too, had shouted in agreement. *A good beginning*, he thought.

"We are all soldiers and realize the importance of discipline and honor," Saher continued. "I know you all will follow the commands of your leaders."

The crowd hummed with promises and shouts of "We will."

"But we are men, too, and sometimes fail to live up to the laws and our beliefs. If any commit a crime against a fellow pilgrim, the punishment must be equal to the crime: an eye for an eye and a tooth for a tooth."

A roar of agreement spread throughout the crowd.

"But we must not take this punishment into our own hands. No, for every thousand of our men we will elect two judges to consider the proof of the crime and the justice it will require. And to maintain our holy purpose we all will attend services at least weekly and make our confessions and communion every holy day."

Sperleng stood straight, proud of the integrity of these rules, and the discipline he saw shaping their journey. He'd heard rumors of pilgrimages torn apart and failing from lack of discipline and was glad that these men wanted no part of such anarchy. He wondered who of the leaders would be the twenty elected judges. He would be honored to be one but knew it would fall to someone born a noble. And a follower of Stephen.

As the noise of the men's conversations died down, Saher continued. "Men, I know many of you will be away from your wives and family for many months and maybe years. But I command you to esteem the women who have joined us on this journey. Do not let your need overcome your calling. To protect all our women, we will keep them separate from the men. They will have their own sleeping quarters and will not be allowed to go out in public unless accompanied by a priest or family member or a guardian. These are women of God who have joined us to make us better able to fight. Treat them that way! There will be plenty of other women to take care of your carnal needs."

Sperleng smiled thankfully. He had suggested a similar rule to Viel and was glad it had been included. Maybe Cate and Mary would be safer because of it. He could only hope.

EIGHT

By the fifth day at sea the ship was rank with waste and vomit from men not used to the rocking waves. After a couple of brisk sailing days, the fleet had found itself in quiet waters with no wind to carry away the stench. *How did Noah bear being on a ship for forty days?* Willard wondered. *And with all those stinking animals! At least we only have a few horses.* Still, he marveled at the beauty of the sun rising red and orange in the east, purpling the low-lying clouds and the sea.

A kind breeze started the sails lightly shimmering. Overhead the sky was still a solid and lightening blue, but to the west clouds had formed shifting mounds, the edges lined in indigo with gray centers. Willard knew rain was likely as the sailors were quickly tying down everything they could and standing ready with the sail ropes as though they feared a great storm. They maneuvered the sails to catch the wind but hung on to the ropes as the wind shifted. *God will protect us*, Willard thought. He looked forward to the fresh water and cleansing showers.

No one had come to share morning prayers with Willard, not even Cate or Mary, and so he sang his hymn and prayed alone. He tried to be forgiving of the strong men, given so much power and glory, who ignored their religious duties. *Beware of pride and a haughty spirit!* he couldn't help but think. *These men aren't monks used to the routine of the holy hours*, he chided himself. The soldiers had much to do, caring for the horses and helping the sailors tie and untie the sails, and he knew many of the knights disdained a priest of low birth.

As the sky brightened, Mary and Cate began giving bread to the men, who seized it from their hands. Cate tripped toward Willard as a sudden wave jolted the ship, and he grabbed her arm to steady her.

"I fear a storm is coming," Cate said, lines creasing her forehead as she squinted toward the distance. "I hope we find a port afore then."

"No need to fear, Cate. We're on Christ's journey and he'll protect us. God never gives us more than we can bear."

Cate said nothing and moved toward a group of Sperleng's men peering over the side of the ship. *Yes, the waves are larger than yesterday's stillness*, Willard thought, *but no more than the first few days. At least we're moving*. In the distance, he saw other ships bobbing gently. Their sails filled the horizon, masts seeming to pierce the gathering clouds.

The wind increased, and the fleet passed miles of shore dotted with villages and cliffs. By afternoon, Willard could see the tops of mountains along the horizon. The clouds twisted into towers, and sheets of rain created a broken gray curtain in the distance. The captain shouted to turn the ship toward the open ocean, away from the shoals and rocks nearer to shore. Sailors climbed the ropes, pulling up and tying down the sails, handing out bailing sacks, and bringing tubs of tar and animal skins, dried moss, and loose wool to the hold.

The nearby ships dispersed as the sky grayed, and soon a fog hid them all. When the rain started, the sailors dropped the yard along the mast, turned it so the pole ran lengthwise along the center of the ship, and tied it with ropes. Willard knew it was time to find cover but dreaded the crowd of bodies in the belly of the boat huddled beneath animal hides and the platforms his father and Cearl had built. Suddenly a sailor grabbed his arm and pushed him downward into a lower part of the hull, then the sailor dropped a length of timber over him.

The hold was dark and foul, and Willard crawled to find a place to sit above the water sloshing along the planking. The hooded horses in their slings snorted fearfully as squires covered the horses' eyes and stroked their withers while speaking softly into their twitching ears. Even knights had come from their covered shelters on deck to help. In the gloom, he heard weeping and many prayers. He found Mary comforting Acha. Cate sat stiffly nearby and folded into Willard's arms when he sat next to them.

"Let's pray to St. Nicholas, protector of all who sail at sea," Willard said softly.

The cries and prayers of men and women grew louder as the ship's rocking increased. Waves crashed against the ship, erratically pitching them forward, then back, then from side to side. Cold water pooled along Willard's legs and feet. At times, the ship pitched so far, he feared they would tip into the sea. Throughout it all, sailors ran above their heads yelling at each other and dropping things with a heavy crash.

Willard jumped at a sudden, loud crack immediately followed by a great boom of thunder. Willard thought he smelled burning. He hated how helpless he felt. *Pray*, he told himself.

"Willard?" Cate said. "I think this is more than I can bear."

"Keep praying to St. Nicholas, and remember God's promises," Willard said in as soothing a voice as he could muster, wondering himself how long they could stand this. He felt like Jonah, tossed on an angry sea, in a dark as black as the belly of a whale. *What is God telling us?* he thought. *Is someone running from God? How could that be when we are on Christ's sacred pilgrimage?*

"All men!" someone shouted. "Bailing needed! Come quickly!"

Willard felt his way toward the voice. In the dim light he saw soldiers filling buckets and sacs with water from the boat's bottom, handing them to sailors on the planks above or tossing the water out the bailing holes as quickly as possible. Someone thrust a pile of loose wool at Willard and told him to fill any leak he could find. Willard rushed toward a man warming a bowl of tar.

"Here!" a sailor shouted, and Willard tore off a wad of wool. The man jammed the wool into a leaking seam, then another sailor poured in hot pitch and tamped in the tar-soaked wool. A third nailed a shim of wood to hold it in.

"Here!" another man screamed, and the three of them moved on. Praise Christ, the leaks were few and small. The earl's ship was new and well-built.

Throughout the night, the storm worsened, and the men wailed their prayers. Wind howled. The ship groaned as waves pounded. Soldiers shouted out their sins and asked for forgiveness and mercy. They pleaded with Willard to intercede for them, and soon they demanded he pray as they worked. "Find us an answer!" one sailor begged.

When Sperleng joined him, Willard pulled him aside and whispered: "I fear God is punishing us all for someone's sin."

Sperleng scoffed. "Hush. And how could we find the guilty person among the thousands in the many ships?"

"They cast lots for Jonah," Willard said.

Despite their quiet, a sailor overheard, and soon all were demanding that the priest cast lots to see who should be thrown overboard.

"Enough!" Sperleng roared. "We will not be throwing anyone overboard! We will live or die together as soldiers!"

Hearing the noise, Gilbert, his face bleeding in places from lashes of hail, moved to Sperleng's side. "Well said, Sperleng. Who knows, but that Christ has not sent this storm to test our faith? He will save us, or there will be some greater purpose in our death. We aren't running away from God's mission! We are headed to save Christ's land from the Muhammedans," Gilbert shouted over the thunder. "The captain has told us the earl's ship is strong, and he fears more for the smaller and older ships in our fleet. Pray for the lightning to stop, or at least to stay away from our mast, and we will get through this."

The men returned to bailing, praying, sleeping if possible, and Willard hunched down, alone in the wet dark, wondering how to comfort and help these men. A huge hand grasped his shoulder.

"It's me, Father. I have caused this tempest. Have the men cast me overboard." Willard recognized the growl as Galan's.

"Galan, every man here thinks his sin is the worst. Pray for forgiveness, and do your part to steady the ship," Willard said.

"No, you must believe me! I can save the rest. God has spoken to me through the wailing storm. I've heard the devil laughing, and the voices of angels calling me."

"Have you been drinking?" Willard asked.

"No more than anyone, and no I'm not drunk. I heard the sailors talking about casting lots to find out whose sin has caused this storm, and God told me it was mine."

"Do you wish to confess something, Galan?"

There was a long silence. "God has put the lives of these men in my hands and told me my penance is to throw myself into the maw of the sea," Galan said. "If God wills it, I'll be taken up by a big fish, like Jonah, and given a second chance."

"Galan, be calm," Willard said. "Acha needs you. Don't leave her and us alone. We need your skills and strength to fight the Saracens."

As they spoke, Willard felt the presence of a crowd growing around them.

"What have you done, Galan, to cause this storm?" one angry voice shouted.

"Yes, tell us!" another demanded.

"Galan, be still and recover yourself," a woman's voice commanded.

A soldier lit a torch, making grotesque the faces and shadows surrounding Galan.

"We all are afraid, Galan," Mary said as she stepped forward. "Come, find a dry place and try to sleep."

"I know what I must do," Galan said, his eyes looking crazed in the light of the flame. He pulled himself to the platform where sailors cowered under deck shelters.

"Galan, don't be a fool. We all are in this together!" Sperleng shouted.

The crossbeams and planking were slick and the rain blinding, pricking like small needles against Willard's skin as he tried to reach for Galan.

"Fools!" one sailor yelled. "Are you crazy? There is nothing for you to do here!"

Willard clung to the ropes lashed to the towers, but Galan grabbed the ship's side, hoisted himself over, and disappeared.

NINE

ate's fear grew while the rain beat relentlessly. A sodden Willard lowered himself next to her. Frowning and grim, he looked toward Acha, and she burst into tears. It was the first emotion Cate had seen from Acha in a long time, maybe ever.

In a hushed voice, Willard told them what he'd seen. There was no body to wash or bury, no corpse to pray over. Cate was surprised at the tears that came to her eyes. She'd never liked Galan.

"I should join Galan in the sea," Acha kept repeating. Mary spoke calmly to her and held her hands tightly. Willard was stern, reprimanding her about the great sin of taking one's life, saying they must pray for Galan's soul, not add to the misery. Mary added a little valerian and yarrow to some ale to help Acha sleep, but her dreams were violent as she thrashed about mumbling incoherent things about Galan then Oxa.

Cate lay alert next to Acha as the brutal winds roared and the soldiers' prayers and confessions continued.

Toward evening the waves and rain lessened, and Cate heard men shouting words of praise and thankfulness as they continued to calm the horses and throw buckets of filthy water into the ocean. Cate brought food to the men, and Mary followed with ale and words of thanks to each.

Despite continuing rain, the next morning, the women and every man who could joined Willard on deck to celebrate the Feast of Ascension. Cate knew there were tears mixed with rain on the men's faces as Willard lifted his arms toward the clouds. As the waves gentled and the dark enveloped them again, sailors crawled into damp places and fell into exhausted sleep. Cate settled in next to Acha who had slept the entire day, reaching for Mary's hand across Acha's now quiet body.

Cate woke to the sound of timber against timber. She quickly climbed to the deck to see men raising a newly patched sail toward waves of clouds lined in pink and blue that reminded her of the scales of a great fish. Parts of the spar looked like new wood. Cate thrilled at the cross unfurling and billowing out as the sail caught the wind. She looked to the sliver of sun shining through low-lying clouds and prayed *thank you* for their salvation. She scanned the sea looking for the rest of the ships but saw only two in the distance.

"Where are the other ships?" Cate asked Sperleng who stood nearby talking to the pilot.

"I don't know," Sperleng answered, his forehead lined in worry. "We're to gather at the port on the north of Hispania. We'll take a count then."

Cate wanted to ask about Galan but feared Sperleng would become angry at her again. She stood by him silently for a while, formulating questions in her head.

"Has anyone seen Galan?" she asked softly.

"Nay." Sperleng shook his head. "But we've likely traveled far from where he sacrificed himself."

Cate heard a note of regret and sadness in Sperleng's voice. "Why did he do it?" she asked.

"Fear, I suppose. Fear that made him exaggerate all the big and little sins he could think of. Many of the men were becoming a little crazy from fear, and Galan was a man of strong emotions."

"Do you think he brought God's wrath on the fleet?"

"Willard would know better than I how God's justice works, but the storm didn't stop just then, did it? And I find it hard to believe God would send a tempest that kills many men and destroys ships for the sin of a single soldier," Sperleng said. "Especially one heading on a pilgrimage blessed by the Holy Father."

"He died for nothing?" The thought appalled Cate.

"Who can say?" Sperleng shrugged. "For all his strength and bluster Galan was a weak man who covered his weakness with drink and bullying. And his only son is dead. I think it was too much for him."

Sperleng brushed his hand against his eyes, then looked at Cate. "Now, shouldn't you be bringing me food?"

Cate nodded and hurried toward the ship's stores.

By midday, a coast was visible. Large rocks jutted out of the bay, forming an entrance to a port. Much of the shoreline was lined in rocky, green cliffs, but the ships headed toward a peninsula that curved to protect a large expanse of beach. As they neared, Cate saw several ships had already arrived, and a few more were following behind. Deckhands rolled up the sail and dropped the yard as oarsmen rowed in past jetties protecting the harbor. The peninsula narrowed here, and Cate saw another, unprotected, beach on the other side. The ship jolted as it ran aground, then tipped slightly as they dropped anchor.

Cate was eager to leave, her legs twitching from too long confinement, but she knew she would be one of the last. Mary and Acha joined her at the ship's side as the gangway lowered and horses and men began to depart. The sailors began dragging buckets of water from the bay along the hull, throwing water on the decks and mopping vigorously, trying to rid the wood of the stench. Cate raised her face, reveling in the warmth and freshness after so many days of rain and being trapped under wet wood and wool.

Once the sun touched the edge of the still choppy sea, Cate thought most of the ships had gathered in the large bay, until she overheard the captain telling Gilbert that many were still missing. Finally, it was their turn to leave, and Cate and Mary carried their packs and food down the gangplank, splashing through the rising tide with Sperleng's men. The water felt surprisingly warm, the beach rocky. To Cate it seemed both a familiar and alien world, one with mossy cliffs, oak and mulberry trees, but also plants unlike any she had ever seen— bent bushes with small pointed leaves and stems of small red blooms, trees bearing unrecognizable fruit.

They climbed to a low bluff near the beach, setting up their tents and mats and lighting cooking fires. As the edges of the long, thin clouds turned red and gray, Egric and Kendric accompanied the sailors to collect fresh water and fish in the river that emptied into the bay. It felt good to be off the rolling ship and to smell the sweetness of the meadows.

Over the campfire that night Willard's eyes flashed, his face a riot of emotion, as he preached about God's mercy and the sin of suicide. Men who previously would have walked away or talked over Willard's words listened raptly. Cate felt Acha's body stiffen as Willard's condemnation of those who took their own lives intensified. Cate reached for Acha's hand, discovering that Mary was already holding both.

Finally, Willard finished speaking. It was a warm night, and the men moved away from the fire looking for softer soil to sleep on. Gilbert invited Sperleng, Willard, and the women to sleep in his larger, sturdier tents. Several soldiers took the first watch, positioning themselves along the edges of camp.

Cate and Mary gathered the tankards, rinsed them in sea water, and left them to dry on the rocks encircling the fire. Mary tended the flames, and Cate threw dirt along the edges and spread seawater along the circle of rocks. They did not ask Acha to help, and Cate saw her sitting on a rock in the shadows away from the heat of the fire with her head in her hands, shaking. Cate touched Mary's arm and nodded her head toward Acha. Mary put down her rake and sat next to her. They sat for a while in silence, as Cate put out the last few sparks outside the fire's stone barrier, then joined them.

"Acha," Mary said, "I am so sorry."

Acha wiped her face with her sleeve. "I am a useless old woman, better off dead. I am no one's wife anymore, and no help to these pilgrims. The two of you can do what needs to be done. And my doom is cursed. I bring bad luck and death to everyone. Oxa dead, Galan dead, two babies dead afore they were born." Acha's voice grew increasingly louder and more shrill. "I asked Willard, why does not God take me too? I should join Galan in the sea. Oxa left for the birds and Galan for the fish to eat! I should have kept them safe. I am a useless old woman." Acha buried her head in her hands.

Cate was stunned. Acha was younger than her mother and Mary, not that much older than Sperleng. Not an old woman at all! "Acha, you're young!" Cate said. "You can have more children. And you are not useless! You are a much better cook than me."

Acha frowned, her eyes piercing Cate. "Tell her, Mary. Tell her about what happens to poor women who lose their husbands. Tell her about the pity and the poverty and the sadness. And even if I wanted to marry again, what man would take me when there are so many younger, prettier, happier girls like you, Cate? I'm sad and bitter and weak and I wouldn't blame them either. Galan went to the tavern every night and then came home still angry about a spoiled dinner or clothes not clean enough. And who would want a woman who loses her babies? Oh, don't pretend you don't know, Cate. Sperleng lived with us for a while. Everyone knows."

Cate had not known and hearing it filled her with sadness. "Oh, Acha," was all she could think to say.

Mary put her arms around Acha. "Stop blaming yourself. That was Galan's fault, not yours. We all knew he hit you. That's why you lost those babies. And Oxa! You can't protect a child from every danger, and certainly not from wicked Jews."

Acha caught her breath, then began sobbing. "If I had been a better wife Galan wouldn't have hurt me and wouldn't have been so angry all the time." She looked around, then whispered, "And I don't believe Samuel killed Oxa."

Confused, Cate asked, "Do you know who did?"

Acha tried to control her crying. "I was afraid. I didn't protect him."

"Protect him from Galan?" Mary asked quietly.

"Galan was furious when Oxa gave him the few coins Samuel had paid for his work. He accused Oxa of keeping back some of the money. Galan hit him across the face, then lashed him with a stick. Oxa pleaded that he hadn't, that Samuel had held back some because he thought Oxa tipped over some feed into dung and it had to be thrown out. Galan struck him for that. Oxa begged him to stop and said it wasn't true. Samuel's son had done it out of meanness. Galan stopped at that, shook Oxa, said he must go to Samuel and demand what was owed. When Oxa hesitated—he was in such pain!—Galan shoved him toward the door and Oxa struck his head against it. He fell to the ground and I couldn't wake him."

Acha tried to catch her breath as she choked on her tears. "Galan kept trying to wake him too, crying and swearing and saying it was Samuel's fault for cheating us. Then he lifted Oxa and took him out of the house and didn't come back. I was sure Oxa was still alive, though. I hoped someone was taking care of him until you found the body, Cate. I should have protected him! I should have said I would go with Oxa to Samuel. I should have done something, but I didn't. I didn't!"

Cate was dumbfounded. All these months she'd been blaming Samuel. Her mind raced, trying to sort what she knew and didn't know. They had all been quick to accuse Samuel, who might be a cheat and a Jew, but maybe no murderer.

"Did the sheriff know?" Mary asked.

"I think he guessed. I never said anything to anyone until now, and Galan kept saying it was Samuel's fault. Even to me, though he was silent when I asked him what happened after he left. But the sheriff's no fool. He came by one night a couple of weeks before we set sail. Said it was a good thing Galan was going on the pilgrimage as he needed forgiveness for all his sins. Said Galan might want never to come back. When Galan heard that, he demanded I join too. Said a woman must be with her husband."

"You could go home now, if that is what you want," Mary said. "Viel's merchant ships could take you."

"And do what? There is nothing for me there, either. It's better I should die. I will put on Galan's vest and use his ax to fight. It would be good for a Saracen to kill me. And until then I'll try to be of some use here."

"We're glad for your company, aren't we Cate?" Mary said in a soothing voice.

Cate's mind raced, not knowing what to think or feel. She felt sad again for Oxa, angry at Galan for lying and at Acha for her silence. Cate tried to make sense of Acha's story but could not. Why didn't Galan just say it was an accident? Some children died after they were disciplined, sad but not unknown. Had something happened after Galan left the house? It made no sense to Cate, and she knew she could never ask Acha.

Cate remembered her own outrage, her fear of the Jews' Passover rituals, her fervor during the priest's funeral sermon. Her sense of outrage deflated now, replaced by confusion. Her mind raced, and she no longer listened to Mary's consoling words.

When Acha said goodnight and stood to leave, Mary rose to join her.

"I'll finish banking the fire," Cate said. "You go ahead. I'll be fine."

"No, I'll stay, too," Mary said. "Goodnight Acha."

Cate gathered loose stones that had fallen and piled them around the fire as Mary raked the embers into a tight heap surrounded by a band of ash. The guards moved closer to what was left of the fire, and Cate brought them tankards of ale as they sat in a wide circle facing all directions. When they were sure the fire's sparks had died down, Cate and Mary headed silently for Gilbert's tent.

That night, Cate kept picturing the birds circling the Frome. In the morning when she saw Acha stirring the porridge she turned away. All day she tried to treat Acha as she always had but found herself talking too brightly when Acha was near or avoiding her altogether. She'd always found Acha a gloomy presence, but now found her unbearable.

When yet again Cate turned to leave as Acha neared, Mary pulled Cate toward her and hissed in her ear, "Get hold of yourself!"

Chagrined, she stayed and said an altogether too cheerful "hello." To her surprise, Acha grimaced and hugged her.

"Oh Cate, I shouldn't have burdened someone as young as you with my troubles. Please forgive me."

"No, I am sorry," Cate stuttered. "I don't know what to say, so I just leave."

"Don't say anything," Acha said. "But keep me company. Please."

Cate nodded, looking down. She didn't know if she could do that. She felt suddenly homesick for

Aedra's easy companionship and her mother's clear expectations. *Maybe we both should go back,* Cate thought. *Sperleng would like that. There is a long journey ahead, and we are closer to Brycgstow than to Jerusalem.*

TEN

After two days' recovery, Lord Saher ordered them to set sail. The pilgrims' ships spent the next week hugging the shoreline of Hispania, staying at least a day in each port to hunt and gather food and lessen the fear of the horses and men. Each day Cate scanned the horizon as one by one more ships joined the fleet. Her head was full of all she had seen, from strange plants and animals to massive buildings and ruins. She marveled at a bridge with many arches, much taller and wider than the bridges at home. A lighthouse soaring on a bluff at the edge of the world filled her with wonder, a tower the Captain told them had been built by Julius Caesar. Cate had no idea who that was but could see the awe on Willard's face as he listened, and even she could see how solid and ancient it was.

One afternoon, the fleet navigated up a large inlet toward the mouth of a river where they would remain for ten days. No one said, but everyone knew, any ships not arriving by then were lost forever.

As Cate rinsed and skinned several of the rabbits Egric brought back from his hunting, she watched Willard, deep in conversation with Gilbert and the Captain, nodding and gesturing toward the east while Sperleng crossed his arms and frowned. When they settled whatever it was they were discussing, Sperleng strode toward the soldiers and women eating near the fire in a rush of officiousness.

"We're less than a day's journey from the Shrine of St. James, and many wish to go there for Whitsunday, including Willard and Gilbert," Sperleng said. "But some of us must guard the ships and provisions. I will stay. Who wants to accompany them?"

"I do!" Cate and Mary shouted, nearly at the same time.

"I will stay with the ship," Acha said.

"I will do whatever you think best," Egric answered. "But I, too, would like to take the pilgrimage." The remaining soldiers under Sperleng's charge nodded and murmured their interest.

"Half of you must stay; the rest must guard the travelers," Gilbert said. "You six will come with me," he told the men closest to him, including Egric. "We'll leave at first light. Everyone should pack sufficient supplies for five days, as this is a little-traveled way, and we can't count on hospitality until we reach the hostels near the Cathedral of St. James. Even then we don't know what we'll find. The captain tells us the path follows the river much of the way, but the river near here is brackish, and close to the Compostela it is often befouled from the many travelers. We will fill our water skins as soon as the water sweetens. Be sure to bring enough!"

How many wonders! Cate thought, glad she had not given in to her doubt and despair by going home. She would visit the tomb of St. James! Cate and Mary returned to the ship, collecting empty water skins, and filling their sacks with cheese and bread from the stores on board.

"How long will we stay?" Cate asked. "How much food should we bring?"

"Don't worry," Mary said. "God will provide."

"I'm not worried," Cate answered, smiling.

At the shoreline Egric was with the many looking for unbroken scallop shells to carry with them, and he gave Mary and Cate several as they headed toward the camp.

"Here are some shells to bring. Gilbert tells us that is what pilgrims do, that they're symbols of Saint James." Egric said hesitantly.

Cate put most of the shells in the sack with the food but saved the largest for the personal bag she attached to her belt. Night enveloped the camp quickly when they returned, and Cate lay awake for a long time imagining the miracles she was about to see.

~

Willard woke to the first bird songs, just as the light began revealing the outlines of trees along the bluff. Cate and Mary were already up, and soon they joined about a hundred others on a narrow path along the river. He felt as if he were in a dream, wondering if it could be true that he was on his way toward the great Shrine of St. James. He barely heard the others talking excitedly about what they hoped to see and do. He needed the forgiveness he hoped the Saint would bring, forgiveness for not inspiring piety among his shipmates or not providing sufficient comfort and encouragement to Galan. The horror of watching Galan lift himself over the side of the ship into the angry ocean burned in his memory and each night in his dreams. Every night he prayed for Galan's soul and his own.

As the sun became hotter and the path dustier, the pilgrims' pace lagged. *Do they not wish to reach the shrine quickly?* Willard thought, irritated at the laughter and dawdling. *Maybe I should tell them the stories of Saint James, so they know how important this pilgrimage is.* Willard had talked many nights with Father Simon about James's miracles and assumed everyone else loved to hear stories of the saints.

"On Whitsunday, the Holy Spirit gave to James the gift of speaking the language of Hispania. We will be at his shrine tomorrow, and we will celebrate this great gift!" Willard began, unable to contain his happiness at the marvel of this providence. "Christians, are you interested in hearing the miracles of St. James as we walk toward his bones?"

Cate and Mary quickly came closer as several others nearby nodded. As Willard told the story, many more drew near so that they could hear too. Willard found himself in the middle of a hot, sweating crowd.

"James went to Hispania to preach the good news to all who would listen, but only a few changed their ways to follow the Christ," Willard continued. "When James returned to Jerusalem with seven of his followers, his miracles angered a Pharisee who sent his demons to destroy James. But the demons recognized James's godly power as a disciple of Christ, the true God, and instead sought his protection. They brought their master to James. After casting out the Pharisee's devils from him, James commanded him to do good and no longer harass the people of Christ. The Pharisee repented, and laid at James's feet his many books and charms of enchantment, begging James to burn them. But James, fearing the smoke of such a fire would attract more demons, told the Pharisee to throw them all in the sea."

The crowd near Willard murmured approvingly. He thought himself a better storyteller than preacher and was glad for this opportunity to impress his fellow travelers. He wondered whether he would ever have the power to cast out demons. He hoped so. The knights mostly kept their distance, but one of their women elbowed her way between Cate and Willard. Cate grabbed her arm, and the woman pointed to her ears and said, "I don't hear so good. Let me be close, girl." Willard nodded, and Cate let go of her arm.

"But other Pharisees, jealous of James's power, stirred a mob against him, put a rope around his neck, and led him to Herod. 'This man preaches treason. He preaches that we should follow only Jesus Christ,' the mob shouted. Hearing this, Herod ordered James's beheading."

Cate and several in the crowd shouted, "Death to the Pharisees!"

A righteous anger filled Willard as he talked, and his voice became louder and deeper. "James knew that he was in God's care and marched willingly to the place of beheading. On the way, a crippled man cried out to him: 'James, apostle of Christ, make me walk again!' And James blessed the man, who stood up to walk, praising God. On seeing this, Josias, the man who led James by the rope, fell to the ground, repented his sins, and asked to be baptized. James asked his executioner for water and baptized Josias, after which they both laid down their heads, singing of God's mercy, and became martyrs. The Pharisees left their bodies in the open for birds to eat."

Willard paused, filled with emotion. What sacrilege to leave a saint's body as carrion. He prayed that he would have the strength and faith of James and Josias in the tests he knew would face them in Jerusalem.

The crowd had grown, no longer just the soldiers and sailors and women from the ships. Now there were families, many wearing necklaces of sea shells. Children ran in front of and behind Willard, their parents and grandparents straining to keep them in view. A priest not much older than Willard, wearing a large wooden cross surrounded by small shells and carrying a walking staff, appeared to be leading several of these family groups. He raised his hand to Willard as he joined the fringes of the crowd.

Willard brushed his hand across his face and continued. "In the dark of night, James's disciples crept to the place of beheading and wrapped James's head and body in a white shroud and carried him to the edge of the Sea. They placed him in a boat that had neither a sail nor a rudder, pushed the boat as far from shore as they could, and two climbed in. God guided them to the shores of Galicia.

"As the boat neared the shore not far from where we are now, a bridegroom was riding his horse along the beach. Suddenly the horse ran into the sea. As the bridegroom sank beneath the waves to the screams and tears of his wedding party, James's disciples lifted their arms to the heavens, praying 'James, beloved of Christ, save this man from drowning so that he may live and bear many children to God's glory!'

"The sun, which had been hidden behind large clouds, suddenly burst forth and shone a shaft of light on where the bridegroom and his horse had disappeared. They rose from the sea, covered in scallop shells. The horse found footing on the sea floor and carried the bridegroom to the wedding party where they rejoiced and praised God."

"So that is why we bring scallop shells," Cate said, grinning.

Willard smiled at her as he nodded. "James's disciples continued farther along the shoreline, near to the place we landed our ships yesterday. They placed James's body on a stone, which miraculously took in the body and created for James a burial chamber. It took many months, but Christ provided a crypt for his Saint!"

"Praise God," Mary said, echoing the crowd.

James never doubted, and neither should we, Willard thought. He despised the story of Thomas, who doubted Jesus even when the resurrected Christ stood in front of him! Such weakness.

"In Galicia reigned a queen named Lupa, and James's disciples went to her and asked for a place to build a shrine. Lupa was a treacherous woman and sent them to the land of an evil giant. The giant easily captured the disciples and put them in prison. But God sent an angel who opened the prison doors. When the giant discovered this, he sent his soldiers on swift horses to recapture the disciples, but God stopped them by smashing a bridge as they crossed and they all drowned. When the giant heard this, he knew it was the work of the Lord, and offered a place to bury James's body.

"But Queen Lupa was not so easily persuaded, and did not want James's bones in her kingdom, knowing their great power and fearing James's miracles would turn the people away from the old religion. When the disciples returned to her, telling her of the land the giant offered and requesting oxen and a cart to carry James's body there, Queen Lupa pretended to agree. In her cunning, she sent them to gather oxen from hills where only enchanted bulls roamed, bulls that would run in circles and smash any carts attached to them against the rocks and kill anyone who tried to yoke them.

"James's disciples brought the Queen Lupa's cart to the hills, finding only wild bulls running and roaring. They prayed and held up a cross, and the bulls quieted and submitted willingly to the yoke of the cart. The disciples then took the bulls and cart to the shore and carried James's great stone to Queen Lupa's court. The queen, amazed, was converted to Christ. She offered up her castle as a church and shrine dedicated to Saint James."

The woman next to Cate clapped happily. Even Egric's eyes shone with appreciation as he edged a little closer.

The travelers found a shady spot near the river to stop for rest and water, and the young priest approached. He spoke a Latin just understandable to Willard, his church language mixed with the common and less recognizable Latin Willard heard surrounding them. When Willard told him they were headed to Jerusalem, the priest waved to his companions, who shared their fruit and drink with him. They talked for a long time, the young priest smiling and gesturing to the sky and to the fields surrounding them while Willard asked questions and nodded.

As they stood to resume walking, Willard introduced the young priest. "Father Josef has told me about how the Saint James's tomb was discovered. Would you like me to continue the story?" The group shouted their approval.

"The world does not stand still, and many went back to the old ways. The godly were persecuted and went into hiding, forgetting about James's bones for hundreds of years. Pagans roamed the land, killing Christians and crushing their holy places. The faithful wandered alone, hiding from curved swords.

"One evening, a holy hermit saw strange lights hovering over a field, lights he had never seen. He felt the lights beckon him. He told the bishop he had seen stars like angels. The bishop and this man of God waited until nightfall, when they followed a new star in the sky that led them to the field of lights, which in Latin is *campus stellae*. Here they found again the tomb of St. James, and the bishop built a new shrine to venerate the saint. Praise be to Christ!"

The crowd shouted and clapped. They walked more quickly now, eager to see the place of these miracles. Willard smiled, proud that his words inspired this energy.

~

Many in the crowd dropped to their knees and lifted their arms when the towers of the Basilica rose in the distance. Cate clung to Willard's and Mary's tunics so as not to lose them and kept her eye on Egric's tall body as he navigated through the sea of people. Their path had merged with others as they neared Compostela, and the river's bridge was crowded with sweating bodies and chanting pilgrims, many of whom had taken off their sandals or were crawling across.

Cate and her group finally passed through the city's pilgrim gate in the afternoon, the crowd dispersing as they entered a large plaza. They paused in prayer at the front of the massive church, its towering arches rising high into the sky, until the hordes behind them pushed them forward. Masons in the square cut stone into blocks while others chiseled faces and animals into pillars and arches for the unfinished parts of the Cathedral. Cate stopped to stare at a lovely image of a woman holding a small child. It reminded Cate of her father's carvings.

"Amazing," she said, "to create such beautiful images from a stone!"

"Father Josef tells me that the Moors destroyed the cathedral about a hundred years ago," Willard said. "That's why King Afonso is rebuilding it. Praise God, the bones of St. James were left undisturbed. Even heathens must fear him."

Soon they passed a hostel for poor pilgrims, filled beyond capacity. Many pilgrims congregated nearby where the monks had set up canopies and strewn rushes and grasses and handed out small bits of bread to the crowds. Egric found several soldiers he recognized from the ships and joined them. Cate and Mary shared their cheese and dried meat with the pilgrims surrounding them, and they received grapes, figs, raisins, and other strange fruits in return.

Exhausted from the walk, Cate lay down and quickly fell into a dreamless sleep, wakened only when Mary shook her as Willard stood to leave. Cate ran her fingers along her braid, removing a few sticks from her hair as they walked toward the shade of the north entrance. They passed a large stone fountain, its sides ridged gracefully. In the middle of the fountain's basin four stone lions' mouths spouted water. Many pilgrims stopped to drink or put their heads underneath one of the spouts.

"These waters have cured many people," Willard said. "Father Josef says this is called the Fountain of Miracles."

Cate and Mary dipped their hands into the fountain, drinking several handfuls and splashing some on their faces and arms. When they'd had their fill, they rejoined the stream of pilgrims heading toward the basilica's great doors. The crowd pushed them past a market where merchants had set up stalls selling shells, staffs, and figures of St. James, as well as a variety of breads and fruit. Cate fingered the shell in her pouch and smiled. She didn't have any money, but still she would have a remembrance, holy from its journey.

As they climbed the stairs to the entrance to the Cathedral, Cate gasped at the sight of the stone carvings along each of the columns and along the massive multi-layered arches. In the center, a huge figure of God the Father seated on his throne seemed to bless the pilgrims as they entered.

"Do you see the four figures holding up the throne?" Willard asked, his face shining with joy, the furrows almost always creasing his forehead invisible now. "Those are Matthew, Mark, Luke, and John. And over there? God is banishing Adam and Eve from Paradise for their disobedience. And here, above the door, do you see the angel telling Mary she has been blessed to be the Mother of God?"

Cate, struck dumb by their beauty and detail, felt her face frozen into a perpetual smile of curiosity and marvel. She approached a pillar that showed a man in a long tunic holding a broad sword in his right hand and caressing the head of a boy with his left hand. The man had a halo above his head and was looking up. A lamb rested by the boy's feet. Cate found it beautiful and troubling at the same time.

"Who is this?" she asked Willard.

"This is Abraham sacrificing his son Isaac."

"Tell me," she said. "I never knew he did that."

"Abraham loved Isaac more than anything in the world. God tested Abraham's faith by commanding him to sacrifice Isaac. Abraham took Isaac to the wilderness, bound his hands and feet, and raised his sword to cut off Isaac's head. Just before the downward swing, an angel of God appeared to Abraham, and said 'You have shown yourself faithful. Do not kill Isaac. Sacrifice this lamb instead.' Together they sacrificed the lamb God had provided and went home rejoicing."

Cate, troubled that God would seek the death of a young boy as a test of his father, whispered to Mary: "Didn't God know his heart?"

"Remember, Cate," Mary said gently, "God sacrificed his son for us. Sometimes faithfulness requires great sacrifice. It shows God's mercy, too."

Cate nodded. Another mystery.

Cate wished she could stare at the sculptures for hours, but the crush of people drove her forward into the cool of the church. As she crossed the threshold, she joined the mass of pilgrims laying their hands on the pillar just inside the doorway. She gaped at the height of the ceilings and at the light that seemed to shine directly on the main altar. Everywhere she looked she saw carvings and paintings of saints, their faces glowing with expressions of joy or kindness or devotion.

The scale of the church dwarfed the pilgrims, and Cate felt small in the face of the glory of God. Inside, everyone hushed, some bowing their heads while others lifted their hands to the light. Cate, made dizzy from looking up at the ever-opening arches, clutched Mary's arm. When she turned, she saw tracks of tears lining Mary's dusty face.

Light from high windows and the music of monks chanting filled the church. Willard bowed, then knelt in front of the altar of Saint Nicholas to thank him for a safe journey. Cate and Mary knelt on either side of him. As Cate closed her eyes, the music began to seep into her soul. She did not understand the words, but the chanting spoke to her of sadness and strength. She couldn't name what she was feeling, joy or grief or wonder filled with the images she had just passed and the fire of the candles.

Willard led them, stopping at each of the saints' chapels. He took Cate's hand and squeezed it as they approached the altar of Saint James, hemmed in by the throngs of pilgrims unwilling or unable to move. Cate, too, stood stunned with awe at the majesty of this place, the tomb of Saint James. The saint's bones were in a stone casket on a raised marble platform encircled with candles. Three large censers hung near the altar, perfumed smoke drifting out toward the high ceiling and making Cate feel unsteady. When a few pilgrims finished their prayers and pushed past, Willard pulled Cate and Mary closer to the altar. They knelt for the bishop's blessing.

They moved with the crowd as the pilgrims behind pushed ahead for a blessing. In the Chapel of the Savior at the head of the apse, Willard knelt and put his face on the stones, praying this way for a long time. When they finished praying at each of the side chapels, they headed back to the center and walked silently through the nave, overwhelmed. Sun brightened the upper spaces from curved clerestory windows at the highest points of the columns, lightening the nave and shadowing the arched aisles on the side. Here, too, carvings of angels and saints beckoned them. Some were brightly painted, but as Cate neared the main entrance, the carvings seemed newer and less decorated. The glare of the setting sun filled the area nearest the large open doors.

"We'll fast and keep vigil tonight," Willard said.

"Shouldn't we eat something and come back?" Cate asked.

Willard frowned at her. Mary squeezed her hand, looking away and barely hiding a smile. *That's probably what the monks are doing*, Cate thought.

ELEVEN

Santiago de Compostela
Eve of Pentecost 1147

Throngs of pilgrims planning to keep vigil filled the cathedral, and more kept crowding in. Cate found a small space of open floor near the main doors, and Willard knelt and began praying. Cate and Mary, not ready to spend more time kneeling, dropped their packs next to him, then wandered the aisles viewing the intricate carvings and paintings that filled the walls and stone columns. They followed a line of pilgrims to an upper gallery bright from the sun streaming through small arched windows.

The swarms of people in the plaza below looked tiny, and Cate, suddenly dizzy, steadied herself on a pillar. Only a short ledge separated her from the vast expanse of the nave. From here she could see the great height of the ceiling, and the details of many carvings that she hadn't noticed before, fish and rabbits and trees mixed with intricate swoops of circles and stars. Bits of sweet-smelling smoke rose from the censers toward them.

Cate peered from a balcony and saw Willard and Father Josef, their heads bowed in prayer, and Egric looking up and around the church. When he noticed Cate and Mary, he smiled, and Cate gave him a small wave. He lifted his hand and pushed his way through the crowd toward the stairs. Cate, too full of her own thoughts to speak when he joined them, smiled in greeting. Cate touched the many spiral columns, amazed at their smoothness, as the crowd circled the darkening church. They stayed until the dark made it difficult to see, and pilgrims began stretching themselves out along the floors and walls. Egric took Cate's hand as they made their way down the stairs, and she felt a surge of happiness, then a sense of loss when he released her hand at the bottom of the stairs.

The three rejoined Willard, the floor even more crowded than before. After Evening Prayers, the monks lit candles in the nave, and a priest replaced the bishop in blessing those who continued to flow past the altar. Cate bowed her head, but her mind was a jumble of thoughts rather than prayer, thoughts about St. James's wonderfully sad life and all his miracles, thoughts about Egric that she tried to banish. She might have slept as she was startled by the bells announcing Night Prayer. When all was hushed, several monks in gray tunics filed into the choir, their faces hidden by their hoods. They lined up in two rows, then lowered their hoods and began to chant. Cate was struck by the simplicity and anonymity of these brothers, a stark contrast to the vivid reds and golds of the altar cloths, and the riot of painted sculpture surrounding them.

Cate tried to keep vigil but could not after the droning of the readings and prayers of the Night Office. As the snores of her companions lulled her, she dreamed of many black birds circling, more and more gathering. She saw Oxa and Saint James, their heads on a rock as dark angels holding battle axes stood above them. She awoke suddenly, sure she had cried out, but Mary and Willard shifted only slightly. As she dreamed again, she saw Samuel sending his demons, their shapes shifting through the darkness until they came upon Cate and carried her to the burning stables behind Samuel's house. The sound of a blacksmith pounding metal against metal clanged as the fire spread. She then saw a boat gliding along the River Frome, a boat from which a light shone to the shore where Oxa lay covered in scallop shells. Oxa rose from the riverbank, shedding his shells as he walked.

Monks chanting at dawn startled Cate awake. Many people began stirring now, some drinking, some pacing.

"I'll be right back," Cate whispered to Mary as she got up.

"I'm coming with you," Egric said.

"Me too," Mary said.

Willard frowned at them. "We can eat after morning mass."

"It isn't eating I am worried about," Egric said, frowning back.

The trio passed men standing in front of large pots along the walls, then pushed through the crowd to the huge front doors. Empty scaffolding and half carved statues surrounded the entrance; stone dust layered the front steps, and Cate's skirt brushed a path behind her. They moved to the relative privacy of the gardens, then joined several other groups of pilgrims near the fountain to drink the blessed water.

When they returned to the church, the throngs had grown even denser, and Egric needed to shove their way back to their place. Some of the larger men refused to move, saying incomprehensible but clearly angry words. Egric simply moved to create a different path. When they returned, Willard wouldn't look at them.

Cate saw the bishop at the altar, praying, and the four joined a long line of pilgrims congregating to the left of the altar. The air stunk of unwashed bodies and piss pots, and Cate's hair and body itched. Her stomach was empty; her eyes threatened to close.

The bishop raised his hands in welcome and blessing and spoke in a loud clear voice. Several monks swung the largest censer, pulling it by ropes like a bell. Pungent smoke poured from the vessel, its perfume filling the space and the void in Cate's soul.

"Amen," the bishop and Willard said in unison. A monk in the choir, a boy, really, who Cate guessed was younger than she, stepped forward and sang a single high, piercing note. An older, larger monk stepped next to the boy and began to sing a low note in a deep, resonant voice. Soon the boy matched that tone at a higher pitch while the bishop swung incense above the altar. The monks on the south side of the choir then sang, and the monks on the north side replied. Suddenly Cate recognized their words:

Alleluia in Gloria

Cate breathed the strong, intoxicating scent of the incense, closed her eyes, and leaned against one of the broad, cool pillars. The boy and a single monk sang again, a chant that made Cate feel sad and happy at the same time. The choir soon joined the two voices in a plaintive harmony unlike Cate had ever heard, some high, some low, some matching, some wandering off on a new note that went higher and lower with the cantor's music, singing "Gloria" again and again. She found herself filled with the music, the voices of angels.

Rex inmense pater pie eleison

Again, one high voice wandered alone in the vast spaces, then another joined in, keeping a single low note. Then the entire choir responded:

Kyrie eleison

Somehow Cate became the wandering melody, alone and lonely, and she felt the strength of God in the deep constancy of the bottom notes. Time stopped. She felt neither discomfort nor hunger, only joy and longing.

"*Gloria in excelsis Deo,*" the priest announced.

"Et in terra pax hominibus bonae voluntatis," the choir responded. *"Laudamus te. Benedicimus te. Adoramus te. Glorificumus te."*

Cate felt the ecstasy of the choir, of the crowd, of herself in the music. She seemed outside of herself, outside of the dusty, hot city, outside of the world, somewhere she had never been before. As the service continued, she lost track of the differences between word and song and just felt the music. Felt as if angels held her.

Without warning, doves flew inside the Cathedral, and the choir sang to the rhythm of the birds' wings. Pilgrims dropped to the floor; others raised their arms toward the birds. Cate stood still, in awe as the white birds flew in front of the red banners hanging from the gallery.

A sudden silence brought Cate out of her reverie, and she felt Mary's hand holding hers. Tears streamed down Mary's face. Willard and Egric seemed lit from within.

The bishop lifted the Host, then the chalice. Cate saw that many pilgrims were crying, and most had expressions of awe and joy on their faces. The choir resumed their singing, interspersed with the bishop's prayers and chants, and Cate felt the world and its sadness creeping back into her. Her body itched again, and she was hungry. She cried at the loss of her sense of peace and holiness. Egric squeezed her hand, and she looked at him, fighting back the tears. She was glad again she had not returned home. *The storm was just a test of faith*, she thought, *and God has rewarded me with his spirit. I'll not doubt again. I'll be holy and obedient, worthy of my calling. Help me, Lord.*

After the final *Deo Gratis*, the crowds pushed the four of them somberly toward, then squeezed them through, the massive doors. Cate shaded her eyes as she peered into the sunlit plaza. The mood was festive here. Many headed toward the city gates, but most milled around the cathedral. A group of young pilgrims made a circle in the plaza, clapping and dancing and singing. Cate thought of Aedra, and how she would have loved this.

Pilgrims surrounded the several sisters and priests who handed out bread and fruit near the hostel as merchants hawked small carved doves and shells strung on leather bands. Cate touched Egric's arm tentatively and asked him if Sperleng had given him any money for them.

"Sperleng gave me offerings to place at St. James's altar, and some for food if we need to supplement what we have, but none for trinkets," Egric said.

"I know, but I'd just like something for one of the shells you gave me, and the bishop blessed, so that I can wear it always and not lose it," Cate said.

Egric's eyes softened. "Sure there be something in one of my packs."

Egric rooted in his pack and took out several linen threads that he twisted into a cord then knotted at one end. He slowly carved a small hole in her and Mary's shells and two of his own. Finally, he measured and cut

137

several cords and strung the shells, tying the open edges when he finished.

"I always have threads for my bowstring with me," Egric said as he handed them the necklaces. "You can wax the string if they start separating too much."

"Thank you, Egric," Mary said. "You are very kind."

"Yes, very kind," Cate repeated.

Cate and her companions recognized no one at the place where they had rested the day before, so they wandered toward the lion fountain where they joined a group of Viel's men filling their water sacks. The men recognized Egric and invited the four of them to a shady place up a small hill nearby where many of the ships' pilgrims had gathered. But first they headed toward a great mass of men where, they'd been told, monks were distributing ale. They filled their tankards and ale skins, climbed the hill, and joined the ship's pilgrims to share their bread and cheese and dried meat.

~

Willard and the ships' pilgrims stayed three days, returning repeatedly to the shrine. Each day the crowds thinned a little more. Many of the remaining pilgrims wore the sign of the cross, and Willard discovered that wearing this sign got them larger portions of food and the thanks of every churchman they passed.

As they began the journey back toward the ships, Willard felt a sense of conviction that they were part of something huge and blessed, a great mission of justice. He felt his soul had been filled with the Holy Spirit.

Every day since Whitsunday, he prayed that his feelings of joy and purpose would remain strong, would help him through the difficulties and disappointments of the battles ahead. He prayed to remember the peace he'd felt listening to the bishop's words and the choir, and how when the birds descended on the congregation he felt on fire. *The fire of the Spirit! This*, he thought, *must be how the disciples felt that first Pentecost. Holy, blessed, called to convert unbelievers.*

Willard wished he had been given the gift of a new language but thanked the Trinity for Father Simon's lessons in Latin. Even now, Willard's body felt energized, and he burned with the desire to turn away from the temptations of comfort. *Yes, a pilgrimage is better than locking myself away in a monastery*, he thought. *How easy it is to feel holy when nothing distracts, and how honorable it is to bring the Gospel to unbelievers, to create Christ's kingdom on earth.* Willard felt a great love for the soldiers, ready to die for Christ and ready to bring God's justice to the unfaithful. How he coveted Sperleng's strength!

Eager to return to the ships and be on their way, Willard picked up his pace. He could tell many of the soldiers did not experience this sense of purpose, and came on this pilgrimage out of duty or, worse, greed. *I will change that*, he vowed to himself and to God. *I will show them through my words and actions what it means to be a soldier of the cross. Starting with Sperleng!*

Willard had been surprised at first that Sperleng had given up this chance to spend Whitsunday in the

Cathedral of St. James, then realized that earthly honor and glory meant more to his brother. Sperleng had been glad of the Holy Father's promise of heaven to all who fought the Saracens in Christ's name, but Willard knew Sperleng looked for glory and land in this life as his reward. *How many others?* Willard wondered. *Well, I am their priest now, I will talk to them and help them find their way.* He quickly joined several of Sperleng's soldiers who were walking together.

"St. James didn't see the fruits of his work while he was alive," Willard began. "That must have been a great sadness for him. But look at what came of it in God's own time, the thousands who became Christ's followers because of him! Who can tell what glory will come from a simple act of faithfulness?"

The soldiers nodded but didn't encourage him.

We all are tired and filled with our own inspiration, Willard thought.

When they arrived back at camp, those who had stayed pressed toward them, wanting to know what it was like, had they seen any miracles? They listened in awe as Willard described the music, the carvings, and especially the doves.

"A miracle," one man whispered.

"A sign from God," another said.

"Yes, a sign that we are blessed!" Willard said, warming to his message. "So long as we act with Christ's mission in mind. Let's recommit ourselves to that with daily prayer. I will read from scripture and talk with you about the holy stories every day. Soon the trials of our journey will worsen, and we will face the enemies of Christ. We must be prepared, wearing not only earthly protections of vests and shields, but putting on the whole armor of God to be ready for all the evil that may come. We will stand firm, strengthened with the truth and wearing righteousness as our breastplate. Let us bind our feet with the Gospel, put on the helmet of salvation, make faith our shield, so we can pierce the enemy with the sword of God's Word. Christ did not ask his followers to be still, but to spread the Gospel to the entire world. He brings not peace, but a sword!"

Many men shouted their agreement, offering Willard ale and bread, several promising to pray with Willard every day of the journey.

One soldier muttered that he would prefer a hauberk as he wasn't sure righteousness would protect him from a Saracen's arrow.

Oh well, Willard thought, *it will be many weeks before we reach Jerusalem, plenty of time to encourage the doubters.*

"Eat, then rest," Sperleng shouted to the returning crowd. "Tomorrow we hunt for provisions and load the ships. We leave in three days."

TWELVE

Willard felt at peace, a serenity that not even the shouts of the sailors preparing to dock could mar. Cate smiled at him. He saw the calm in her face too, her eyes bright and focused first at him, then toward the large cluster of monks and clergy waiting on Oporto's sandy beach. Willard felt a burst of pride to see that the bishop's retinue came first, with elaborately dressed nobles behind them. At the edges of the welcoming party, curious locals crowded close. A mild wind caught strands of Cate's hair, and the sails of the many ships billowed white against the bright blue sky.

Gilbert commanded Willard to join him, and soon they headed down the ramp toward the waiting crowd. Willard nodded solemnly to the other priests and their nobles who joined them in a long line to greet the solemn, close-faced bishop who stood at the front, his large, purple-stoned ring glittering in the sun. The bishop held in front of him a tall, curved rod that reminded Willard of a shepherd's crook, except it was intricately carved and gilded. The bishop's loose-fitting white shirt was trimmed at the hem and sleeves with intricate lace that covered the longer, close-fitting purple tunic underneath. Despite the heat, the bishop also wore a heavy, hooded purple cape tied at his chest with an intricate gold pin that matched the design in the curve of his staff. Over it all the bishop wore a massive gold cross on a chain about his neck, and on his head wore a double-peaked purple cap.

Willard couldn't help but stare; he had never seen such fine vestments before. Upon reaching the bishop, he bowed his head and knelt, heard the bishop's blessing, stood, and moved aside to make room for the next fortunate priest. Once the bishop had greeted the ships' leaders and priests, he climbed on a pedestal and began to speak, his face opening into a welcoming smile.

"I am Pedro Pitões, Bishop of Oporto. The glory of your journey to Jerusalem has been told throughout the kingdoms of Hispania, and we have waited and wished for the honor to meet you. Our king, Afonso, is not here to greet you because he also is pursuing his Christian duty to rid this country of the blaspheming Moors. But he has written a letter asking me to invite you to join him in defeating the unbelievers and driving them from Lisbon. He has charged me to make whatever agreements and security you need to encourage you to join our holy war. Please, tell the men on your ships about Afonso's request and offer. Discuss this amongst yourselves, and tomorrow we will gather at the cathedral for Christ's blessings on your journeys."

As the bishop's procession marched toward the cathedral on the hill above the port, the beach buzzed with priests translating the bishop's words for each ship's leaders. Willard heard some voices raised in protest, and nearby he overheard William Viel commenting that he didn't trust Afonso. Several soldiers listening to Viel kicked rocks with their feet and cast angry looks toward the retreating bishop.

When they got back on the ship, Gilbert gathered his men. Cate eagerly asked Willard what was happening, and he described to her the glory of meeting Bishop Pedro and the decisions that needed to be made.

Cate clenched her hands when she heard of the bishop's proposal to stay and fight the Moors here.

"I don't like it. Lisbon is not the land where Christ was born and died," Cate grumbled. "It's not our fight."

~

In the morning, as the soldiers gathered on the hill near the cathedral to hear the bishop speak, the women and sailors remained on board. Cate scowled as she cleaned, throwing pails of water to try to rid the deck of the stench of spilled chamber pots and vomit. "I am doing this for the sake of Afonso?" she muttered under her breath. Mary grabbed Cate by the shoulders and turned to face her.

"Look at me, Cate," her aunt demanded.

"We were going to save the Holy Land, not stop here," Cate said.

"It is not decided yet," Mary said, "but we aren't the leaders of this pilgrimage. Learn your place and be content! You want to be treated like an adult, now act like one! Whatever decision is made will be God's plan for this journey." Mary turned away, her hands in a fist and shoulders stiff.

Cate spent the next few hours fretting and complaining to herself as she thrust tankards into net sacks and threw them underneath a waxed linen cloth. When she finally went ashore, the crowd on the hill was beginning to scatter into small cadres of men, some in tight groups and others wandering along the beach making wild gestures. A few drifted back to the ships lining the long shoreline. She ran to Willard.

"What happened?" Cate asked.

"We are going to Lisbon," Willard replied.

"And you are all right with that?" Cate was indignant. Mary came up and glowered at her.

"Bishop Pedro gave a convincing sermon about how this, too, is holy war," Willard said. "So, yes, I think it is God's will that we join Afonso to rid St. James's land of the unholy Moors."

"Help me understand," Cate said.

"You have to let go of your stubbornness and open your heart, sister. Can you do that?"

"I'll try."

"The bishop reminded us of the importance of sacrifice in Christ's name, and how sometimes God's plan for us is not the one we would have chosen for ourselves. Do you agree?"

"Yes," Cate nodded, looking down. Her plans never seemed to be God's.

"Sometimes we would rather stay in our beds and sleep than chase a lost lamb, and sometimes we would rather eat all the bread than share it with our brother," Willard continued.

"Sometimes we would prefer to sit with the men on the hill than clean the privies," Mary added.

"We made the decision to put God's cause ahead of our comfort when we joined this pilgrimage. But now we've been asked to make another decision to help rid Hispania of the Moors. Bishop Pedro told us about many Christians murdered and deprived of their lands by the vicious and greedy Moors. I'll spare you those stories, they are too gruesome for women's ears. But it made me realize how God protected us in England, governed by Christian rulers even if they couldn't decide amongst themselves which of them should rule."

Cate felt her resolve weakening. "But how do we know we should stay here instead of going to fight in Jerusalem? We made promises to God before we left!"

"The Holy Father himself has promised the same indulgences to those who fight the Mohammedans in Hispania as to those who fight in Jerusalem."

"He has?" Cate was astounded.

"Yes, and for good reason. Abbot Bernard told us how important it is to save the lands where Christ lived and died from the rule of the false prophet Mohammed.

Bishop Pedro reminded us that on our way to Jerusalem we should also do good works, ridding the land of St. James from the same stranglehold." Willard's voice grew louder and more excited as he continued, his eyes shining with resolve. "The war against the false prophet is a holy and just cause, no matter where it happens. It is not evil to slay the evil ones, and by stopping the spread of falsehood here we protect the lands to the north."

"But what if too many die here, and we can't save Jerusalem?"

"God will protect us, I am sure of it, and when we finish here, we will free Jerusalem and the holy places from the Saracen." Willard's eyes blazed as he looked past Cate and up the hill. Without warning, he grabbed Cate and held her close, and his tears dampened the top of her head. "What God wills will be!" Willard released her, then walked quickly toward the ship.

Stunned, Cate stared at his retreating black shape.

"Cate," Mary said, "we need to feed the troops. They are coming back, and they'll be hungry."

Cate's head buzzed with these new ideas. *Fighting evil here is as important as a pilgrimage to Jerusalem,* she tried to convince herself. But how she had dreamed of praying before Christ's empty tomb and gazing on the remaining pieces of his cross! She longed to feel again the holiness she felt in the Cathedral of St. James. *Willard is right, though. We should fight heathens wherever we find them,* she decided. *Spending Whitsunday at the*

Saint James's shrine was a blessing to show us the need to save Hispania.

Feeling chastised for her pride and single-mindedness, Cate bowed her head as she filled her arms with dried meat and tankards.

~

Cate had little time for worry once the choice was made to begin the battles here instead of months from now in Jerusalem. Bishop Pedro commanded the people of Oporto to supply the ships, and soon they brought oranges and pomegranates, figs and dates, almonds and chestnuts. They brought fresh bread and meat, bolts of fabric and blankets. They showed the pilgrims where to gather olives and the best places along the river to fish, and where in the forest to hunt boars and rabbits and deer. Egric's arrows brought down several of these, and soon the smell of drying meat pierced the air nearest the beach.

Cate overheard Sperleng tell his men as they camped on the shore that Lisbon was a strongly fortified city, and they could expect a long siege making large food stores necessary. *Large stores of medicine, too,* Cate thought as she and Mary followed the soldiers into the forest looking for betony and vervain, hemlock and henbane. But they found little that was familiar.

Baskets half-empty, Cate and Mary began laying out the plants to dry near the meat tents. They stopped when local women rushed toward them, shouting and waving their arms. The women led Mary and Cate to a large barn with drying tables where they sorted and laid out their pickings. These women nodded approvingly and made it clear they wanted to join the next time. Then next day, they showed Mary and Cate stands of poppy, rosemary, sage, mint, and fennel, some grown in gardens on the local commons, and some flourishing wild in the forest.

The gathering and hunting went on for ten days. The soldiers ate well, and the pilgrims celebrated Sunday and many evening meals at feasts with the churchmen and the people of Oporto. Most days, Cate saw William Viel wandering among the camps, talking with the men. Once she stood in the shadows to listen to what he was saying.

"You can't trust Afonso," Viel said. "Some of us have been through this with him before. Two years ago, my ships stopped here, and they asked us to join in the war against the Moors. Afonso promised us booty and ransom from captured knights, but when the time came to pay, he was nowhere to be found. Stay away from Afonso and his great plans. We will be better off supplying ourselves from smaller Moorish cities than Lisbon! Along the northern coast of Africa there are many Moors to kill, easier prey than in Lisbon. That is better for us and for Jerusalem as we won't lose as many men and arrive earlier. Think! Staying here may help Afonso, but how does it help us, or our pilgrimage?"

Many men nodded, asking questions about Lisbon's fortifications and how likely they would be to take the City. Cate slipped away, troubled again.

THIRTEEN

Tagus River
Vigil of St. Peter 1147

Lisbon's tall towers sat high on a hill not far from the inlet where the pilgrims' ships gathered. A menacing stone wall crawled down the hill toward the Tagus River, its top notched for the warriors and watchers Sperleng knew hid there, ready to dump vats of boiling water and burning oil on any enemy who dared approach. From the height of the bow, he gauged the defenses, saw a deep ditch circling the walls and large slits in the stone where archers could get more distance and soldiers could shoot fire at anyone attempting to run a siege engine close. Viel was right. This would not be an easy city to take.

The plain between the fortress and the inlet was filled with houses, some small huts but many large compounds with stables and barns. Sperleng saw armed Moors on horses dispersed throughout these settlements, standing guard as families frantically collected their children and anything they could carry towards the peaked gates of the city.

The ship swayed as the sailors dropped the ramp and a few knights led out their skittish horses. Like the horses, the soldiers itched to leave the ship, crowding at the beach-side edge of the deck, leaning over the railings as they watched the procession. One young soldier, already wearing his leather helmet and vest, raised his fist and yelled, "Death to the unbelievers!" Most men grabbed the lumps of bread and cheese Mary and Cate gave, not wanting to lose their place along the edge, but one looked at Cate and grinned, "Will you have me when I kill my first Moor?" Sperleng thrust himself between her and the soldier, who quickly hid in the mass of men. Cate looked down, and Mary, following behind, pushed her forward.

Once the knights and their horses reached the shore, foot soldiers rushed down the gangway. The surges of men leaving their ships reminded Sperleng of ants swarming toward a slab of honeyed bread left on the ground. Several men in ragged leather caps and others in torn chain mail began running toward the city, stopped by the shouts of their leaders and the knights on their horses who galloped to corral them, creating a barrier to keep the eager men on the beach. The men then spent their energy shouting and waving their weapons and shoving each other.

Sperleng led his men to join the chaos of men harbored too long and ready to fight. They found the houses closest to the beach mostly abandoned. Smelling smoke, Sperleng turned toward the walls to see spirals of smoke and flashes of fire rising from homes and stables. Men and women carrying sacks and holding children's hands ran through the streets as a flank of Moors on horseback, holding curved swords high as a warning, separated these families from the growing pilgrim army. Gilbert and several knights galloped along the beaches as foot soldiers swung their axes and bats at stragglers.

Moors in full battle armor, metal helmets and breastplates glinting in the sun, began streaming out from behind the walls. The foot soldiers in their caps and leather vests were no match for the long, curved blades of men high on their horses, and their screams as they fell alerted the Christian knights to the new threat. The knights turned toward and rushed the Moors, who attacked, then swung to protect other fleeing families, creating small skirmishes throughout the streets. When the streets emptied of women and children, the Moors hurtled away, the city gates quickly bolted behind them.

~

Cate feared the blazes in the streets that sprung up nearer and nearer the ships. Soon she saw soldiers carrying wounded men, and she and Mary hurried toward them, grabbing vinegar and cloths on their way. Other women grabbed mats, poultices, buckets, and bandages, as soldiers pitched canopies near the shoreline. Mary and Cate rushed toward Willard, who was praying over the several dead already lying in a row, and Mary knelt and began washing one.

"Tend to the living!" Willard said gruffly. "They need you more."

Mary glowered at Willard but turned toward the tents.

Sperleng and Egric each carried a wounded man. Sperleng dropped his on one of the mats the women had just laid and thrust his sword into a nearby fire. Cate soaked her cloth in vinegar and began washing the blood from a deep gash in the moaning soldier's arm. Sperleng pushed her aside and took his sword, now glowing red, and lay it flat against the wound.

Cate winced as the flesh sizzled. The soldier screamed, then was silent.

Mary rushed to Egric's soldier, who appeared dazed from the pain of a barbed arrow lodged beneath his shoulder.

"Pray there was no poison on that arrow," Mary said.

"Maybe we should pray there was," Sperleng responded grimly. "Is there hope for either of them? Or should I put them out of their misery?"

"With God there always is hope," Willard said firmly as he approached. "It is not our place to speed up God's time."

Sperleng snorted disdainfully. "How many battle deaths have you seen, Willard? How many times have you listened to men screaming in pain from infected wounds, begging for the kindness of a sword to their heart? You would treat Gilbert's horse with more mercy than a man." Sperleng stalked away, and Egric followed.

Cate tried to put Sperleng's words out of her mind as she looked at the soldier's cauterized arm. *Is he dead?* She lay her head on his chest. No, she could feel it move. *Of course, we must try everything to keep them alive.* She washed then laid a poultice of yarrow and lard on the wound.

"Move on to a new soldier," Mary commanded Cate. "You've done all you can for him now. Come back to check on him when things settle."

Cate looked up to see the wounded multiplied, six unattended men now lay beneath the canopy, a dozen more outside, most on bare ground. They wore no chain mail like Samuel had supplied to Sperleng and Egric. She saw no knights as she carried her cloths and an urn of vinegar to a young soldier bleeding from the several slashes on his stained leather vest. He was desperately crying "Help me, help me, help me."

"Mary, have we something for him?" Cate yelled over the din of screaming and moaning men.

"Give him some mead. If he's still in pain later, I'll give him some dwale I'll use when I remove this arrow."

As Cate gently pulled his filthy vest away from the bleeding skin, he grabbed her arm. "Please, please, please help me," he said, a wild look in his eyes as his back arched.

"I am trying," Cate whispered. She held a flask to his lips and poured a little as he gulped it down, then slowly pulled away more of his vest and shirt. Some of his skin came with the shirt, causing him to scream again.

"No, you are trying to kill me! You are a devil, I know it! Get away from me!" the soldier cried, swatting her hand.

Cate sat back on her heels, frozen, not knowing what to do. Should she keep trying to bare and clean the wound like Mary had taught her, or burn it like Sperleng had, or walk away? She just didn't know.

A woman from another ship shoved Cate aside. "You're no help if you are weak. Bring in supplies if that's all you can do. Get more cloths, more vinegar, more mead! Heat up the cautery!"

Her face burning, Cate fled to the ships' stores to bring more supplies. How useless she felt! She tripped up the ramp to the hold, barely able to see through the tears clouding her eyes. Her first skirmish, and she had showed herself a coward. She ran back, her arms filled with cloths and pots. Women and men grabbed them from her as she passed. As she shuttled between the ship and the shore she came into the rhythm of the chaos, running for supplies and giving cider and dwale to screaming men.

As dusk neared, the number of wounded slowed, and weary soldiers came to the tents to see their injured friends. Severed limbs littered the ground, and the air stank of blood and fire. Those who had died from their surgeries were carried out to the rows of bodies near the river. Those who had survived, and the less wounded, moaned and cried and pleaded, a cacophony of pain.

Mary and several other women walked from soldier to soldier, changing soaked bandages, applying mixtures of vervain or yarrow with butter on the wounds, and giving them burdock juice mixed with wine. Cate knew she should, wanted to, do this, but still felt humiliated by her earlier failure. She filled her bucket with river water and began washing the bodies of the dead. *At least these soldiers don't call me a devil.* When she finished one, she put pebbles on the soldier's eyelids and moved on to the next body. Sadness slowed her steps, and she was beginning to understand why Sperleng thought their deaths might be a mercy.

"Cate, we should eat something," Mary said, placing her hand on Cate's shoulder. "Are you able?"

Cate nodded, silent.

"It is hard, I know. You did well."

"No, I did not," Cate muttered. "I froze when I was most needed. All I could do was bring supplies from the ship. Anyone could do that."

"That is what was needed, and not everyone was able. Acha hid herself away and did not even bring food or crush herbs! Don't judge yourself harshly for a moment of fear. We all fear! You will learn to work through it."

Cate didn't believe Mary, but her words comforted.

"We'll sleep in the tent with the wounded tonight," Mary continued. "Soldiers will stand guard, and we can tend and comfort the wounded."

Soldiers were cooking fish over the several fires surrounding the makeshift infirmary. The light was almost gone, but there was a bright moon low on the horizon. Cate spotted Sperleng close to the river. As Cate and Mary approached, they saw Gilbert pacing and William Viel waving his fist at them.

"Only you fools fought the Moors before we had a plan. The Flemings didn't! The Rhinelanders didn't! Have you no discipline at all? How can we get good terms from Afonso if you start fighting for him before he promises us what we came for?" Viel shouted.

"That is no surprise, William," Sperleng shouted back. "The Flemings are cowards. See where they have their ships? As far from the action as possible."

"We need to get Afonso to swear his promises in front of us, so he can't back out again," Viel continued to rant. "Think! Take control of yourselves."

Gilbert stopped pacing. "This battle was nothing; small groups of men who had been cooped up in ships too long and inspired by the bishop's words. And we did force stragglers into the fortress, giving us a place to camp and set up our siege. Afonso must know that the Moors will come back if we leave, and now he's seen our skill and spirit. We can use that!"

Nothing? Cate thought, remembering the pain she had just seen.

"Well, be sure to be there tomorrow morning at Afonso's camp. The greedy Flemings have already pledged themselves, but there are Rhinelanders who remember Afonso's betrayal too." Viel stomped toward the next campfire's circle of men.

Cate felt frozen and confused, remembering her long talk with Willard about holy war. Were these men here instead of Jerusalem for plunder? She'd heard rumors in Brycgstow that Viel and his men were pirates, but Sperleng and Egric and Gilbert? Was that poor soldier with a barbed arrow in his chest in such pain so Viel could be rich? Cate closed her eyes in horror, wondering what to do and think.

Her turmoil must have shown on her face because Willard sat next to her and took her hand. She looked at him and asked softly, "Are we pilgrims or pirates, Willard?"

"It isn't so simple, Cate. Some men are both. And the Church has promised forgiveness of all sins, even the sin of greed, for helping conquer the Mohammedans. God calls the weakest of us to his Great Cause. This is all our chance for salvation—all of us, Cate, not just those with pure motives. People do good things for impure reasons all the time. Surely you know that already?"

Cate nodded. "But how can war for plunder and ransom be holy?"

"Because the followers of Mohammed have held this land for too long. The Church has asked its warriors to take up arms in Christ's name, even pirates. And you and I are here to help and support them."

Cate shrugged, disturbed and unsure.

When Mary and Cate returned to the hospital tent most of the wounded were quiet, the dwale calming them at least for now. The women checked each soldier for fever or for the coldness that indicated death. When Cate reached to the soldier who had called her a devil, she saw he was tossing and turning, delirious in his sleep. Cate checked his wound, then washed it with vinegar and bound it with a fresh cloth as he moaned and strained. Suddenly he opened his eyes and stared straight at her.

"Why?" he asked.

"Why what?" Cate asked, patting his hand in what she hoped was a soothing manner.

"Why?" he responded, baring his teeth and making a fist.

"I don't know," she mumbled. "I really don't know."

FOURTEEN

الصلاة أفضل من النوم

Prayer is better than sleep. —Pre-dawn Adhan

A faraway voice chanting, some notes clear and piercing and others seemingly lost in the air, woke Mary just as the sky began to lighten. She could not understand the words, but found the mournful sound strangely moving. She looked toward her sleeping niece and felt again that burst of protectiveness and joy. Mary rolled up her blanket and made her way through the rows of moaning men toward Willard, who stood between the bodies of the dreaming and the dead.

"Did you hear the voices?" Mary asked. "Or was I dreaming?"

"I heard them, too," Willard said. "The sailors told me it was the Moors, asking for Allah's help."

"I guess they've seen how many ships we have, then." Mary said.

"They've known for days," Willard said. "It's hard to hide 200 ships sailing along the coast. Most of the Moors are inside the city walls by now, with only soldiers guarding the gates."

Mary curled her nose as she pulled molding cheese and dried fish the sailors had given them from the ship's stores. She hoped they'd find a few hens running loose but knew they'd likely been taken into the gates. Cate and Acha were distributing bread from large netted bags, their eyes drooping.

"There may be more fighting today," Mary warned. "Feed them well this morning."

Cate nodded and struggled to tap a barrel of ale until Egric broke through the crowd to help her. Mary smiled as Cate gave him one of the larger pieces of cheese with his bread and filled his tankard a little higher than the rest.

~

Sperleng paced the beach, worrying about Viel's mutiny. Sperleng thought Sir Robert and Gilbert were honorable leaders he gladly served. But he mistrusted Viel, who laughed in the taverns and said if everyone simply acted in their own best interests the world might be a better place. Viel certainly looked out for his own interests and ignored everyone else's, plenty of proof of that. Sperleng considered plunder and ransom for a successful campaign their due, but he had no stomach for abandoning the massed army to go plundering the coasts of Africa. He hoped a deal would be struck.

Gilbert commanded Sperleng to join him, and together they climbed the hill toward Afonso's camp north of the fortress. All the other armies had come too and had formed divisions by geography and language. The Flemings turned their backs as Sperleng approached. Gilbert and Viel began talking animatedly with Lord Saher and Hervey from Glanville. Eventually Hervey motioned to the troops from Brycgstow to come near.

"I understand your fear that we will waste many days and many lives fighting here with little profit, only a depletion of our forces for Jerusalem. I share your concern but want to remind you that we made this decision in Oporto. We discussed this at length then, and what kind of men are we if we give our word and then go back on it?"

Viel stepped forward. "I need to hear Afonso promise us ransom and plunder in front of his troops and the bishop as well as to our men and priests."

The soldiers shouted their agreement, and Saher and Hervey joined the leaders of the other armies in the procession toward Afonso's tent, leaving Gilbert and Sperleng to calm the troops.

As the hours dragged on, the army's restlessness increased. Soldiers began wandering back toward the ships or toward the Portuguese camps looking for food. Others went to a nearby stream to spear a fish or cook at one of the small fires that began to line the shore. Several Flemish soldiers raised their fists and shouted what sounded like curses, then moved farther away. Karl emerged from the crowd and approached Sperleng.

"You've made no friends of the Rhinelanders and Flemings," Karl said, his face lined with a mixture of worry and amusement. "We're all sure we can make Afonso keep his word. We outnumber Afonso's troops."

"I think Viel is trying to humiliate Afonso a little," Sperleng said. "A lot of Viel's men felt Afonso betrayed them."

"I'm sure Afonso would like some of the Moors' wealth to help pay his troops. How do you think they'll react if he suddenly announces all the money from this campaign goes to us?" Karl said.

"I guess that is easier to say in Oporto than here, where all his troops are gathered," Sperleng said. He offered, and Karl accepted, a drink from his ale-skin.

"How's your sister doing?" Karl asked.

"Cate?" Sperleng stiffened. Was Karl interested in Cate?

"I got the impression she was in over her head."

"She definitely is that. I told her, my father told her a battlefield is no place for her. She does work hard and learns fast, and our Aunt Mary is keeping a close eye on her. But she is not ready for a man, either," Sperleng said, a warning in his voice

"Ho, not me Sperleng. I know better than to try to seduce a friend's sister. Worry instead about other men," Karl replied.

I do, Sperleng thought, thinking about the changes in Cate in just these few weeks. Her hair had lightened and skin browned from the sun, but more striking was the strength of her silences. There was a power to her he'd never noticed before. Begrudgingly, Sperleng had to admit Cate's conviction and passion gave her a kind of beauty. She seemed more assured, not so much a child as he had thought. *Christ, more things to worry about.*

Karl clasped Sperleng's shoulder with his large hand. "Well, friend, if I stay much longer the Flemings won't talk to me either. Let's hope for the best, whatever that is." Karl's tall form was soon swallowed up by the restless crowd.

The armies meandered about for what seemed hours. Abruptly a horn sounded, and everyone turned to look as Afonso stepped outside his tent surrounded by his generals and the pilgrims' leaders. Afonso climbed a large platform, high enough for all the roving troops to see him. He grimaced a little, his expression haughty as he looked over the tops of their heads. He wore fine clothing of a thin, soft material that moved easily in the breeze, a light-colored long-sleeved shirt that reached his ankles, covered by a green and white tunic which glinted in places with gold threads. A long sword hung by his side fastened to a girdle around his waist and half-hidden by a pine green mantle edged in red that was tied at his chest with an elaborate silver pin.

Sperleng longed to dress as nobly as Afonso, commanding by his mere presence, no matter how unlikely.

Sperleng edged close to Willard, wanting to hear but unable to get close to the translators who lined the front edge of the platform on both his sides. Afonso spoke in a dialect that many of the priests found difficult to translate, sometimes discussing the meaning amongst themselves before speaking to the crowd.

"My Christian friends," Afonso began, "On this Sunday honoring Saints Peter and Paul, as we start on this great conflict to recover the land blessed by Santiago, let's come to an agreement on how we will help each other for the glory of Christ and his Church."

Afonso's troops cheered as he paused waiting for the translators.

"I understand that some of you believe I am not a man to be trusted, a man who does not keep his promises. I deny this accusation."

Afonso's men shouted their support, and those on the platform pounded their feet and spears.

"But to calm the fears of the wary, to assure those who need to hear the words said before God, the Church, and all those present here today, I reaffirm my pledge to you. The Christians of the Kingdom of the Portuguese, and I as its leader, welcome your help as Christian brothers to reclaim our land from the Moors. This is our only concern. We do not seek the Moor's wealth, but only a return of our land."

Afonso's men shouted and pounded again, although with somewhat less vigor.

"For your aid in this holy and just endeavor, knowing the great sacrifices you have made traveling so far from home at great expense, we offer you the booty and plunder from Lisbon's Moors when they are defeated. You will have the right of ransom from those wealthy Moors who are captured. When we regain control of the city, you will have the wealth of the Moors to do with as you please. In the names of Christ and Santiago I promise you this!"

A loud shout, "God help us!" came from those who first understood, and a wave of singing and clapping ran through the camps. As the mayhem increased, Afonso climbed down the steps without looking at anyone and disappeared into his tent, followed by his generals. The pilgrims' leaders separated into their armies, which quickly moved toward the ships, each singing their own battle songs.

~

In the lengthening shadows, Sperleng headed toward the ship as Afonso led a squadron of his knights to the City's main gate and one by one ships unmoored and began leaving. Large battalions of soldiers streamed away from the beach toward the other side of the City. Cate ran to Sperleng as he approached.

"Where are those ships going? Are we leaving too?" Cate asked.

"No, we are staying," Sperleng said. "Afonso went with his leaders to propose a truce that would give the Moors the chance to give back the city to the Christians. I doubt they will agree. We are staying on this side while the rest will attack the east side of the fortress. The Rhinelanders say the possibility of tunnels and using siege engines is better on the other side. Karl told me they don't trust us and don't want our help. Combat on two sides is a good plan, and frankly I don't trust the Flemings either. Tomorrow we begin the fight."

Bands of men ran through the nearly abandoned nearby streets. Cursing, Sperleng looked to see if his men had disobeyed him. Egric ran to him.

"Viel's men," Egric told him, pausing to catch his breath, "are emptying the houses. Killing. Old or ill."

Sperleng strode toward where Gilbert was talking and waving his arms with Hervey and Saher. He stood close by and waited until Gilbert marched in his direction.

"At least it's not our men this time!" Gilbert shouted angrily, then stopped to calm himself. "But Saher thinks as long as the encounter has started, clearing out the western side is probably a good thing to preserve our advantage here and to keep laggards from terrorizing our camps. Gather your men but stay together. If we are lucky, just the sight of our men advancing will make the heathens move faster."

Sperleng nodded and went to put on his mail and helmet. When his men saw him dressed for battle, they gathered what weapons and protection they had and joined him in his march through the streets.

"Make a lot of noise," Sperleng ordered. "Get them to leave. Give the Moors more mouths to feed. The soldiers are already within the walls."

In one house, Sperleng and his men came upon an old, sick woman guarded by a young man brandishing a sword too heavy for him. Sperleng held back his men and motioned that the Moor should pick up the woman and leave. When he instead launched himself toward the soldiers, Sperleng quickly beheaded him.

Sperleng walked to the old woman's pallet, took her hand, then put his dagger to her chest. She mumbled something that Sperleng took to be assent. He crossed himself and her, then stabbed her in the heart. She died instantly.

"Throw their bodies into the river," he commanded two of his soldiers. The rest moved on to the next house.

Armed Moors on horses formed an arc in front of each of the city's gates, advancing only to gather stragglers inside. As the sun set, the Moors retreated and closed their gates.

Lord Saher organized his troops to seal the area west of the City from any Moor who tried to return. They threw bodies into the Tagus, some headless as Christian soldiers impaled turbaned faces on sharpened sticks and planted them as near to the walls as they could despite the danger from arrows the Moors sent toward anyone who came too close.

Saher ordered the leader of each ship to appropriate abandoned houses, preferably large compounds where troops could congregate. They found food in some and brought it to the common stores. They unloaded hay and supplies from the ships, putting them far away from any fiery arrows and where troops could guard them easily.

Sperleng and his men dismantled the enclosures on the ship's deck and brought them ashore as the beginnings of a siege engine. Knights claimed the best and largest barns near the water for their horses, so Sperleng assigned the women a smaller, less convenient one that Mary and Cate stocked with their dried plants and vinegar and bolts of cloth.

As the days passed, the bodiless heads facing the fortress withered and stank in the sun, their faces drooping into agonized frowns.

~

As the routine of siege began, women drifted in from the countryside hoping to trade their time, their bodies, their information for a little bread or dried meat. Lisbon's Moors congregated each morning at dawn along the breaks high on the fortress's stone walls, yelling incomprehensibly at the troops patrolling the perimeter just outside of arrow range. Sperleng wondered why the Moors gathered along the steepest incline of the west side. On night watch, just before first light one morning, he saw the shadow of a woman slowly moving along the wall, and decided to follow her, wondering why any woman would be so foolish as to leave the fortress. The woman crept furtively toward the base of a hill in a forested area north of their camp and disappeared.

Swearing to himself, Sperleng ran to the place he'd last seen her, thinking perhaps she was a messenger on her way to seek help from other Moorish cities. As he rounded a curve, he suddenly saw a break in the grasses covering the hill. The woman was carrying two sacks. When the woman saw him, she ran, her headscarf slipping away in the wind. She did not get far. Sperleng grabbed her arm, threatened her with his knife, and opened her bags filled with flour and jars. Then he dragged her to the opening in the hill where he saw the cave was lined with flour sacks and oil jars and shelves of dried fruit and cloth. When Sperleng saw the food, he released her, knowing she would tell the leaders their provisions had been found.

There was a great celebration that night, Lord Saher himself thanking Sperleng. Afonso rode up on his tall horse covered with glittering blankets and laughed when he saw the caves. He raised his spear in the air and shouted toward the castle, then pranced his horse in circles until the Moors congregated silently to watch as more and more of the Christian knights came to see the celebration. A great shout went up as each new faction arrived.

They opened bottles of stored wine, and their singing filled the valley, attracting even the Flemings from their camps. They cooked their newly caught fish and newly slaughtered boars over the fires they lit as the day darkened, taunting the Moors with the smell of fresh meat. The Portuguese chanted something loudly and repeatedly, something the Moors, but not Sperleng, understood. The Moors did not waste their arrows; they knew they would not reach the rioting Christians.

In the morning, the pilgrims set up guards in front of the caves, and in the first week Sperleng's men had killed twenty Moors, some soldiers, some women, some children, who tried to approach during the night. The Christian troops soon found three more small caves, also filled with jars of olive oil, bins of grain, dried meat and fish, enough to feed the armies for many months. The Moors had taken their books and gold with them inside the fortress but had left these great stores of food.

And so more women came from the countryside, some hungry and some sure already, as Sperleng was, who would be the victors.

FIFTEEN

*C*ate felt like a prisoner. Sperleng had moved his troops nearer the caves to a compound of houses even more isolated than before. Every day for weeks now she woke to the muezzin's mournful chant and another day of drying the fish the soldiers caught, cleaning the common privies and piss pots, and preparing meals for the soldiers when they returned from patrols. Another day of bewildering taunts shouted from the towers above them. Soldiers accompanied the women when they washed in the river, and the priests watched them always, alerting the leaders if any strayed too far from the camps. An armed guard was required simply to pick fruit at the orchards up the hill, and doing laundry was no longer a social occasion, but a silent chore done while soldiers tried to spear fish. She missed joking with Aedra. She missed her mother and father, Cearl and Linn.

Few people came to the makeshift infirmary: a woman who'd eaten meat that had turned, a soldier burned from hot oil dumped over the wall onto the battering ram, a knight with an infected cut, a priest bitten by something and becoming feverish, several men with painful urination, and the occasional fever, diarrhea, and vomiting. The knights required attendance in their lodgings by the doctors, and the foot soldiers often refused to leave their barracks where Sperleng absolutely forbid Cate to go. If a camp follower or one of her children became ill, she was banished to the countryside, so few ever complained of anything at all even when Cate could see they were in pain or their children's eyes shone with fever.

Cate longed to recover the sense of purpose she had when she was preparing to leave Brycgstow, or in St. James's church, or even when caring for the men wounded in the first battles. Those men had recovered or died, and the siege had become a war of battering the city walls, mining their foundations, and starving those inside.

Be glad for so few injuries, Cate chided herself.

This was nothing like her daydreams of glory and mercy, of bowing before the remains of the true cross. She tried to convince herself she was doing God's work but felt cheated.

Sometimes Cate envied the country women who came and went as they pleased, moving into abandoned houses near the camp. She often heard laughter and moaning coming from their open shutters. A part of her wanted to listen and look, another part to shut her ears and run. Her parents never made those kinds of noises! She doubted these men would still be here when the babies came and wondered what the women would do. Willard and the other priests warned the women against using their tansy or pennyroyal or wallflower to induce a woman's bleedings, telling them such a deliberate use was a sin against the God of Life that even this pilgrimage could not erase.

"Stop the men from visiting them and there will be no need," Mary grumbled quietly to Cate, and even Sperleng shook his head in disgust when he heard this pronouncement.

One of the country women brought a grandmother who had her own medicines, including pomegranate seeds and violas, but when Willard learned of her magic, he had her sent to Afonso's camp for punishment. Cate overheard a soldier saying that her hands been chopped off, and her body burned.

During the long, hot days, the camp followers helped Mary and Cate plant a garden and brought water from the wells and the river in exchange for sharing a piece of bread or leftover pottage. Sometimes these women would try to talk with them over the relentless booming of boulders striking Lisbon's walls. They pointed to things and slowly learned a few of each other's words. The local women wanted to learn words they could use to barter with the soldiers, words like *me* and *you*, *hair* and *hands*, *lips* and *kiss*, *river* and *fish*, *clean* and *sweep*, *bread* and *meat*. They laughed at their inability to understand each other and the odd ways each had of pronouncing their words. It helped Cate forget about her loneliness for a while.

One woman, called Milah, took a particular interest in Cate, watching her as she worked, and smiling when she caught Cate looking at Egric. "You, man?" she asked, clasping her hands together.

"Me and Egric? No!" Cate answered, not sure how to explain that Egric was just her brother's friend.

"Yes," Milah said. She fingered Cate's hair and smelled it, making a disapproving face and waving her hands in front of Cate's breasts and legs. "Anglica, fish."

Cate felt her face get hot as she realized Milah was telling her she smelled like fish. Cate turned quickly, but Milah grabbed her arm, took Cate's face in her hands, and looked at her kindly. "*Al-hama*."

Milah then began a long conversation with the other local women, pointing toward the hills up the estuary. Whatever they were discussing excited them, and they patted Cate's head often, saying "Yes" and "Clean."

Mary watched it all, bemused and as clueless as Cate. "I think they want to beautify you, although I don't understand how they intend to do that."

As the women huddled together, Mary and Cate continued hoeing, Cate newly aware of the sweat running along her nose and sogging her blouse. She looked up only when a squadron of Afonso's men came seeking supplies from the caves. The women ran to them and chattered excitedly. The soldiers kept shaking their heads in refusal until Milah whispered something in the leader's ear and stroked his beard. He looked at Cate, then at Milah, then shrugged his shoulders.

"Anglica," the leader said, "Milah says you want to go to *hammam*. Yes?"

Cate had no idea what *hammam* meant but was fairly sure it meant leaving the compound, at least for a little while, so she nodded her head. "Yes, but I cannot leave without soldiers. Or Mary."

The leader nodded and motioned to one of the soldiers sitting near the opening to the cave. "Come," he said.

Egric was also standing guard nearby and approached the leader. "I'll come. This is Sperleng's sister."

The leader nodded and returned to telling his men which supplies to load on the horses. Milah pointed to some thin, smooth cloth colored in oranges and browns. As a soldier handed it to Egric, Cate frowned and shook her head, sure that the limp, unabsorbent cloth was valuable even if useless.

"No," Cate said.

"Yes," Milah said. "For you."

Cate looked at Egric, who shrugged. "You cannot keep it, but we can see what it's for."

Soon the small group of soldiers and women began their trek to Afonso's camp. The grasses grew denser as they headed along a creek towards the forest. Cate's wooden clogs became heavy, so she took them off and followed the rocks of the stream. Small white birds seemed to follow them, gliding on the air for a while, then diving toward the water.

Egric stayed near Cate. "Where are we going?" he asked.

"I have no idea," Cate said happily, "But it's nice to feel the water and the breeze. It's stifling close to the hill."

At this, Milah turned and patted Cate's hair encouragingly while looking at Egric. "*Al-hama.*"

Once they reached Afonso's camp, the leader signaled his soldiers to unload their horses. Two soldiers then led the women downhill into a denser meadow. They followed a well-worn path through the brush until they reached to a few huts near a large stone structure. Several women ran ahead to one of the huts and came out with blankets and cloths and small clay jars.

Milah led Cate and Mary inside the structure but stopped Egric when he tried to enter its inner room. The Portuguese soldiers had already stopped to stand guard by the entrance, and Milah pushed Egric to join them. She hung a brown blanket in front of the doorway and pulled Cate toward a large, bubbling pool, one of several within the stone enclosure.

"It's a hot spring!" Mary said, clasping her hands and laughing. "Like the baths they say the Romans built in Baðon!"

Milah pointed to their clothes, and when Cate and Mary did nothing began tugging at them until slowly they removed their tunics and skirts. They stood naked in front of the largest pool. Milah and the other women had removed their clothing, too, and stood on a stone ledge built inside the pool.

Cate found it difficult not to stare at Milah's firm sun-browned body, her breasts drooping only slightly, or the mass of dark hair under her arms, along and between her legs. Cate was abruptly aware of her own body as she felt her nipples harden. Overcome with the need to hide herself, Cate jumped into the darkest part of the pool, creating a great splash and causing the women to laugh and scoop handfuls of water to throw at each other.

The pool's warmth gave Cate a jolt of pleasure, and she felt a tingling sensation along her body, first along her stomach and breasts, then her legs and arms. Cate had never taken a warm bath. In the summers at home she bathed in the Frome, which was always cold. In the winters, she warmed snow or icy water over the cooking fire, but her family did not have a large tub as she heard the Earl's wife used. The blocks of stone rather than silt beneath her feet surprised her.

When the laughter slowed, Cate saw that Mary, too, had entered the pool and was sitting along a ledge, her graying hair loose and dripping on the ends, and her skin whiter and more scarred than Milah's. Cate watched more women come in and take her and Mary's clothing, washing them in a small pool then carrying them outside to dry in the sun.

Cate closed her eyes and leaned her head on the pool's edge. Just when she felt she might fall asleep from the warmth and the water, Milah and another woman

179

began washing her with lotions from their jars. Milah pulled Cate's hair gently until she submersed it in the water and undid her braids. Cate's hair floated around her, shining gold and copper where the sun came through the openings that lined the top of the structure. When she sat up, Milah dripped another lotion on Cate's hair and massaged it into her scalp.

No one had ever touched Cate the way these women did, rubbing her shoulders and back with lemon-smelling soap, and it felt strangely comforting and arousing. *Is this how ladies live every day?* she wondered. Milah gave Cate a soft cloth to wash herself, then put a heavy cloth underneath her head in a shallow part of the pool so she could soak and enjoy the warmth. Cate felt loved. Not like her mother or Mary loved her, no, this is something different. Kindness, maybe, a stranger taking away some of her fear and solitude. Cate watched the women as they washed each other, lifting and jiggling each other's' breasts, combing each other's thick, dark hair, and she felt both alone and part of them. Mary lay with her eyes closed on the other side of the pool, smiling slightly. Cate felt a sudden rush of love for them all.

A yell from the guards outside roused the women, and Milah shouted something back as she motioned for Cate to come out of the water. A warm pool darkened the stones beneath them as the women dried her with thick towels and began rubbing her with a lotion that smelled of lavender and olives. Milah brushed Cate's hair with an oil that smelled of oranges, then tied it with a ribbon of fabric.

Other women brought in Cate's clothing, but when she began putting them on, Milah grabbed her skirt and overblouse and wound the thin cloth they brought from the caves around Cate's shift, creating a colorful new dress much lighter and cooler than what she had worn on the trip there. Milah handed Cate new sandals, made from leather rather than wood. Cate hugged her in gratitude.

"Pretty," Milah said, grinning this time as she waved her hands in front of Cate's body. "Clean."

Cate felt wonderful, contented and warm, and, she realized with surprise, no longer itchy. Mary looked contented and softer than Cate ever remembered. But she dreaded Egric's reaction, feared he would think she looked and smelled like the whores Willard and Sperleng kept warning her to avoid. As she came out of the structure Egric's eyes widened in surprise before he looked away. Egric nodded to Mary, and the soldiers and women started down the path.

Cate caught up with Egric, needing to know right now if he disapproved. "Egric, are you angry?"

"No," he said. "Although I worry what Sperleng will say."

"It was just a bath," Cate responded, stubbornness creeping into her voice.

Egric studied her. "You seem different somehow, and you were with those women a long time. Look, the sun is setting."

"Acha and the other women will have made the soldiers supper."

"You are wearing different clothing. You know Willard won't like it."

"And you, what do you think?"

"I think it will be hard for me to keep thinking of you as Sperleng's little sister," Egric said, slowing down to guard the rear of the procession.

Mary caught up with Cate and took her arm. "What did he mean by that?" Cate said.

"I think he stopped thinking of you as Sperleng's little sister some time ago," Mary answered. "But today you seem soft, happy, even glowing. It's hard not to notice. I like it."

"Me too. And this clothing is so much cooler and more comfortable. Egric is right, though. Willard won't like it."

The Portuguese women sang songs as they walked, Mary and Cate braiding each other's hair and humming as they caught the tune. Afonso's soldiers marched them to the edge of the camp as the dusk deepened, turning back when they were greeted by soldiers who stared at Cate and Mary in surprise. One by one the Portuguese women stopped to touch soldiers' faces, diverting their attention, until Mary and Cate stood with Egric at the edge of their compound.

"You should put on your ordinary clothing before coming to eat," Mary said.

Cate ducked into the door of the women's house. She slowly unwound the thin cloth and placed it where she knew she could find it again. She then pulled on her overblouse and skirt and met Mary at the cooking fire. Acha filled wooden bowls with stew and bread that they carried to the waiting soldiers. Egric sat next to Sperleng and Willard, and Cate and Mary brought bowls to them first.

Sperleng turned and seemed to be examining them. "Egric tells me the country women brought you to a hot spring today."

Mary answered quickly. "Yes, and it was lovely. Lisbon is a dusty, hot place, and we all needed a bath. The springs were a surprise though! I heard rumors the Romans built such places in Baðon along the Avon, but I never saw one."

"I've been there. The Earl's men enjoyed them," Sperleng said. "I'd like to see these baths."

"Maybe you could ask Afonso's men? Milah called it *al-hama*." Cate said.

"I will. Although that word does not sound Christian to me. What do you think Willard? Are our camp followers Christians?"

Willard stiffened but ignored Sperleng, continuing to tell nearby soldiers the story of the discovery of the spear that had pierced Christ's side. Cate was simply glad Sperleng's attention had moved away from her. She gathered the bowls, throwing some soggy remainders towards the feral cats slinking near the fire, but not too much—the cats needed to be hungry so they would keep rats away from the grain. She caught a glimpse of Egric in the shadows, watching her. She loosened her braid as she slid away, aware of the way her body moved, and her hair shone in the firelight.

~

On the Feast of St. James, the pilgrims joined the Portuguese for a celebration in a valley near Afonso's camp. Booths decorated with shells offered cakes brightly decorated with symbols of scallops, red dagger-shaped crosses, or walking sticks. Bishop Pedro invited the pilgrims' priests to participate in a miracle play about Santiago Matamoros, although only as slaughtered Moors, Willard told Cate sadly.

The play was staged on the hill above the plain. At the far edge stood a large, ripped tent whose too-short poles allowed the awnings to sag in the middle. Cate watched, mystified, as a few of Afonso's soldiers in their uniforms clashed with others dressed in brown and wearing turbans, including Willard. Most of Afonso's soldiers lay on the ground with the turbaned players standing over them and shouting, when three men carrying a sheet with a painted moon and stars processed in front of the audience. The remainder of Afonso's soldiers sped toward the dilapidated tent, and the turbaned men gathered on the other side of the hill.

Count Afonso raised his hands to the sky when Bishop Pedro appeared on a white horse dressed all in white with a large shell painted on his surcoat. Cate had no idea what the Bishop was saying, but the Portuguese soldiers in the audience were cheering raucously, shouting "Santiago."

The three sheet carriers walked back across the front of the audience now displaying a crudely drawn yellow circle that Cate surmised was the sun as the bishop galloped away. The turbaned soldiers reappeared, and Afonso's soldiers met them, shouting "Santiago!" The Bishop on his white horse then galloped back in. When he came near a clutch of turbaned soldiers, all of them dropped to the ground.

No more of Afonso's men fell, and all the turbaned soldiers were dropping as the crowd began yelling louder and louder "Santiago! Santiago!" The shouting continued long after the play ended as the audience drank more ale and wine and danced in circles with each other.

When an un-turbaned Willard rejoined Cate and Sperleng, his eyes were laughing. "That was fun!" he said.

Cate couldn't remember Willard ever saying that about anything. "I think I understood most of it," she said. "I take it St. James joined a battle against the Moors and Afonso won."

"Close," Willard replied, "This was a story about King Ramiro, not Afonso. Father Josef told me the story when we were at the Cathedral. Two hundred years ago, King Ramiro fought valiantly against the Moors, but suffered a terrible defeat. That same night, the king and his men retreated to the safety of a nearby ruined castle, where Ramiro was given a vision of St. James in a dream."

"The ragged tent must be that castle?" Cate suggested.

"Yes, and Bishop Peter was St. James."

"That much I figured out," Cate said, laughing. "From the big shell on his surcoat."

Willard nodded and tried not to smile. "'Do not fear the Moors,' St. James told the King. 'I'll fight them with you. You'll know me by my white clothing, white horse, and white banner. We'll defeat the Moors together, to the glory of Jesus Christ.' When he awoke, Ramiro told his troops about the vision. They charged against the Moors, crying 'Santiago!' In the middle of the skirmish the white knight suddenly appeared, killing many Moors and giving the victory to Ramiro. That is why St. James is known here as *Matamoros*, the Moor killer."

"No wonder King Afonso is making such a celebration today," Cate said.

"Afonso also wants the Moors to smell the cooking fires," Sperleng said. "Look how close to the walls he's put the spits of roasted pig and the bread ovens. Sure they are hungry, and soon they'll be starving."

Cate faltered at the thought of children starving as she feasted, remembering last winter's starving families. An image of children unable to swallow and women with oozing rashes sprang into her head and she shuddered.

"Won't we breach the walls before they starve?"

"God willing. We need to be on our way before too long or we'll need to winter here," Sperleng answered. "But Lisbon's walls are thick, and the Moors know that if Lisbon falls so will much of the countryside. The elders won't accept that without a fight."

"Then they should send their women and children away. They aren't fighters and that will leave more food for the soldiers," Cate said firmly.

"Clearly you don't understand war," Sperleng said. "We don't want to make it easy on the elders and soldiers. We want them to feel the pain of their children starving, or of the hunger they face if they keep feeding everyone. We've already offered to let everyone leave if they give the City to us, but they've refused. Afonso reminded them that first day that this country belonged to the Christians before the Moors stole it, and their only answer was to mock us saying they had been here for over three hundred years."

"But the children, they are innocents here," Cate persisted.

"Innocent?" Willard shouted, his voice making Cate jump. "No one is innocent without Christ. Are you really that ignorant, Cate? Even Christian children must be baptized. And these people are worse than the heathens because they know about Christ and call him a mere prophet inferior to theirs! You hear the taunts every morning, but do you know what they say? They mock Jesus' mother as a whore and call Jesus a bastard! They deny that Jesus is God! One morning they took a cross and spat on it, pissed on it, and threw it off the wall! Do you think their children would do anything different? You know they despise and mock Christ, just like their parents. They deserve to die along with the soldiers." Willard shook his head in disgust, turned, and stalked away.

Cate had never thought about it that way, never thought about it at all, really. She could understand why letting children starve would encourage their fathers to surrender, and she knew the Moors' children wouldn't have been baptized. But it bothered her. She hated the thought that the pilgrims were causing children to die such a horrible death. She decided she'd better keep those thoughts to herself.

"Come on, Cate. We need to get back to camp," Sperleng said. "Don't worry about any of this. Just let the leaders make the decisions and you take care of the sick. These people are our enemies and the enemies of God, and that is the end of it."

Sixteen

Near the Tagus River
July 1147

Willard frowned as he watched the whores' children playing naked in the mud. How many more would come? How could Lord Saher allow these wild heathens to eat his soldiers' food? Willard trudged to the small chapel he and several other priests had set up next to burial places of the martyred dead. He needed to pray, to think, to calm himself.

As he knelt before the makeshift altar covered with silken ivory cloth, Willard found himself unable to form a prayer to hold the disorder of his feelings. He stared at the large, carved cross hanging from the wall. *Help me,* was all he prayed.

Willard and the ships' priests took turns administering the Holy Sacrament at the altar, but most mornings only one or two soldiers and women joined the priests. The soldiers' confessions were always the same, and of things Willard knew they would do again:

sins of fornication and adultery, sins of pride and anger and envy. Most seemed to rely on grace abounding.

Willard moved to a bench along the side of the building and studied the other priests who came to kneel at the altar, looking for a sign. After a while, Father Peter, a priest from Devon who had become Willard's friend, joined him.

"You look troubled, brother. What is the matter?"

"I'm not sure," Willard said. "I find myself angry almost all the time lately: angry at how few soldiers come to pray, angry at my sister's flirtations with a soldier, angry at the women who come in from the country to tempt our soldiers, angry at their filthy children who eat our food. I think much of my anger is justified, but it eats at me and makes me sullen and unwilling to forgive. I have confessed this many times, but nothing seems to change."

"I know what you're feeling," Father Peter admitted, "because I feel some of the same things. I think we need to do more. We dwell on the bad things when we are not busy enough with Christ's work. I've been thinking we should start a school for the boys. We can teach them about being warriors for Christ and why they should be helping us instead of getting in our way."

Willard thought about this. "But we don't even know if these people are Christians. They could be Moors!"

"All the more reason to teach them," Peter said. "And it may be they'll bring their mothers to Christ. I was going to talk to our leaders about it. Would you help me?"

"Yes," Willard said, warming to the idea. "There is an empty house near my camp."

Lord Saher approved, saying it would be great to get those infernal kids out of the way for at least a couple hours of the day, and maybe it would teach them the fear of God too. Willard also talked with Milah who, when she finally understood that the priests were going to take charge of the boys for a few hours every day, looked grateful.

Somehow the Portuguese soldiers learned of their plan, and a young Portuguese priest, Father Martim, came to offer his help with translation until the boys learned the foreign priests' way of speaking. The priests spent two days talking about how they would start and decided their first lesson would be to tell the boys about the battle at Jericho. Father Martim sang them a song he'd learned as a young boy in a priory that included marching around a table seven times and then dropping to the floor. He remembered it as being great fun and hoped it might dissipate some of the boys' energy.

Mary suggested that providing food might be the best way to make sure the boys came as they seemed always to be hungry. Despite himself, Willard agreed, and Milah went to gather them with the promise of lunch. Almost immediately, eight ragged boys and their sisters, including two who had just learned to walk, ran in, followed by three young women whose children clung to their tattered tunics. Willard shooed away the women and girls, who then sat on their heels just outside the door.

Father Martim clapped his hands to attract their attention, shooing them away from the food. *Canticum post nos!* he said. He taught them the song about Jericho, all of them dropping to the ground with torrents of laughter when the invisible walls fell.

Cate and Mary brought in what was left of the midday meal for the boys, and they grabbed the pottage and fought over the little bits of bread. The first few days the boys seemed mostly interested in the food, but soon became captivated by the many stories the priests told. By the second week, the priests allowed the women and girls to listen to the stories, so long as they stayed in the back of the room and replenished the food and water when needed.

As the days passed, Willard noticed even more boys coming, many of whom he had never seen near the camps. When older boys from the countryside began to arrive, Willard suggested Martim alert Afonso. Some might be Christian boys, but the priests feared many were not. Within a day a summons arrived: the three priests must meet with Bishop Pedro at Afonso's camp.

The following day, five of Afonso's soldiers escorted the three priests to a large tent where the bishop and Afonso sat on elaborately carved chairs. The three bowed to Afonso and Bishop Pedro, knelt on rugs on the ground in front of them, looking up only when the Bishop began to speak.

"We hear you're doing good work with the boys from the countryside."

Relieved, as he had thought they were about to be disciplined, Willard smiled. Martim said, *"Gratias, episcopus."*

Afonso stood, towering over them. Willard couldn't help but notice the sword shining at his side. "We need young Christian men to fight. Do you think these boys will join?"

Willard, shocked at this suggestion, exerted all inner strength not to fall back on his heels. "We are not sure yet they are all Christians, King Afonso. And we have not been teaching them how to fight."

"I understand," Afonso said, pacing in front of the churchmen. "But soon you'll be able to tell who is with our cause, and who isn't. Particularly among the older boys. Bring your school to our camp. We'll feed the boys and train them to be soldiers. You can train them in the Truth, and my soldiers will train them to fight. The believers can stay. Those who come only for food will be sent away. But we're only interested in training boys who can be useful, no younger than seven. We aren't child minders here, and you shouldn't be either."

The next morning the three priests assembled the boys as usual, told them stories, sang songs with them. As the women brought in the meager midday meal of dry bread and cheese with a bluish mold forming on the edges, Father Martim gathered the children in a circle.

"Boys," he said, "you know why the soldiers and pilgrims wait outside the gates of Lisbon, don't you?"

They all nodded happily. "To bring down the walls and let Christian people rule there," one young boy said, clapping his hands and bouncing on his feet.

"Would you like to be a part of God's army?" Martim asked.

"Yes!" they shouted, beginning to sing their Jericho song, except for one quiet, older boy who looked puzzled. "But we have no swords or bows," he said. "We would all die."

Martim walked over to the puzzled boy, took his hand and pulled him to a standing position. "Davi is right. You must prepare to be Christ's soldiers. You can't just circle the wall and expect it to fall as it did for Joshua. You must learn to fight, and you must have the tools you need. But we can help you with that! King Afonso has asked us to recommend to him brave boys to be his squires!"

Martim's voice rose over the boys' exciting chattering. "King Afonso has promised these lucky boys food every day, and when they are ready, arms. But you must be able to leave your family and live in his camps. Who would like to do this?"

Milah rose from her place in the back of the room with the girls, clearly in a fury. "You cannot have our sons, priest." She grabbed the hand of her son, one of the youngest in the group. "Come, Iacob, let's go."

Mortified, Iacob pulled his hand away and ran behind Martim's long, grayish-white tunic.

"Milah," Martim said soothingly, "Iacob is too young to live in a soldier's camp. Afonso is looking for boys ready to be his squires whose families agree." He turned to the boy behind him. "Iacob, today is not your time. But if this is what you want when you are old enough, I'm sure King Afonso will always need brave young men." Martim took Iacob's hand and put it in Milah's.

Milah stormed away, a sobbing Iacob in tow. "Yes, Afonso will always need young boys to die for him. But not my boy."

As the younger boys left, picking up sticks and thrusting them towards each other as they left, the three priests spoke with the five oldest boys. "Talk to your families," Martim said. "And if you decide to join Afonso, meet us here after the muezzin's second call tomorrow morning."

Four boys joined the priests for the trek to Afonso's forest camp. Davi, the oldest and most solemn of the boys, had come, as had three others: Belem, Iohan, and Lopo. Willard gave each a bundle with bread and cheese in a cloth, and a waterskin.

Martim led them close to the stream that followed the base of the hill where the rocks were smoother on their bare feet. Iohan's energy seemed boundless as he threw rocks at small animals or into the stream and ran ahead, only to dig in the ground with a stick and fall behind.

As the castle towers disappeared behind the scrubby pines at the edge of a sparse forest, Willard started singing familiar songs from their mornings at the camp. The boys quickly joined in, marching to the beat. They passed large gnarled oaks and gathered chestnuts from the forest floor. At midday, they entered a meadow, sat in its low grass, and opened their sacks. Willard let them eat as much as they wished and felt the happiness and excitement exuding from their bodies and their smiling faces. Belem grinned at him as he grabbed for yet another clump of cheese.

"Are you happy?" Martim asked the group.

"Yes!" they shouted almost in unison.

"Then let's thank God for all his good gifts." They bowed their heads, each mumbling their own words as Martim chanted a prayer in Latin. When he stopped, the boys looked at him expectantly. "Today you're on your way to becoming Christ's soldiers. Christ called you, and you answered willingly. Praise be to God!"

"Praise to our Lord," the boys mumbled, their mouths full.

"But, remember, Christ's soldiers are different from all others. The Saracen kill Christians because of their hatred of Christ and their greed for land and profit."

"Heathens!" Iohan hissed.

"But you," Father Martim continued, "you will only kill to bring Christ's honor to the land, and for the conversion of unbelievers. The enemies of the cross mock the true Gospel and will try to weaken your resolve. Don't be fooled! You know the truth, and your cause is just. Learn what these Christian soldiers have to teach you. Be obedient to them and to Christ, knowing that your sins will be forgiven when you conquer in Christ's name. Now, let's see your new camp!"

The boys clambered to their feet smiling and singing bits of whatever songs they could remember. Soon they came to several large tents near a small, stone house. Willard hugged each of the boys tightly, overcome with a sudden sense of love and responsibility for them. Afonso's men led the boys inside one of the tents and showed them where they would sleep. Bishop Pedro soon arrived with several priests, and led Willard, Peter, and Martim to another tent nearby.

"We hope you'll stay with us a few days," the bishop said. "The boys will find it easier, and we'll enjoy your company. And, if Afonso's troops are called away, we'll remain here and need you and your soldiers' help to train these and the other boys Afonso has recruited. A few Hospitallers have come here seeking Afonso's support. They'll do most of the training at first. When Lisbon is conquered, Afonso has promised them land."

Willard had heard of the orders of warrior monks and lay brothers, men who had dedicated their lives to protecting pilgrims and defending holy places but had never met one. He yearned for their life, the life of a monk and a soldier. Willard had no interest in being a scholar or manuscript copier. He wanted to fight to protect Christ's people and holy land. He'd felt useless at the battles where his only role seemed to be to pray over the dead. He envied Sperleng's fearlessness and strength, his knowledge that he was advancing Christ's kingdom on earth.

But Willard knew he was lucky to be a priest to a band of pilgrims as his family couldn't buy him a place in a monastery and had no land to donate to the orders. He could, though, help train these boys, and he would. Maybe he would win the right to join them.

Two Hospitallers collected the new boys and marched them to an open area. The leader looked regal in his long black cassock with a white branched cross embroidered across his breast and a long, plain sword attached to his belt. The shorter, younger monk shuffled behind the first and was without a cloak, wearing similar black vestments. His cassock was too large, its blousy sleeves dropping over his hands, and the brother had tucked its hem into a simple rope belt.

About twenty boys of varying ages were silently eating their midday meal near a small fire. Willard saw no women. An older boy stood cooking a fish on a stick while two younger boys handed the newcomers small chunks of bread. Belem snuck a glance back at Willard, who smiled encouragement. The silence continued until everyone had eaten and the few leftovers gathered and stored.

The Hospitaller leader then stood, commanding attention, and all eyes and bodies turned his way.

"My young brothers, we welcome our new recruits to Christ's army." Despite his aggressive bearing, the knight's voice was gentle, and Willard saw by their rapt attention that each boy felt the knight was talking directly to him. "Choosing to leave the comforts of home and your family is never easy, and we celebrate the strength and commitment that led you here."

The group murmured their assent. A few said "welcome" and "we praise you."

"You must have questions about me and about what you will face in this journey," the knight continued, "and over the weeks and months you're here you'll receive the answers you need. For now, I'll just tell you a little about myself and brother Tomas, and what you can expect for the next few days.

"I am Brother Rodrigo, and I was raised in a noble family in Galicia. I was trained as a knight but heard God's call to the Brotherhood of St. John when I went on a pilgrimage to Jerusalem with my father and older brothers. We sought Christ's blessing on the war with the Moors here in Hispania, and my father gladly granted me leave to join the brothers in their work comforting the sick and protecting Christ's pilgrims."

Rodrigo began pacing, stopping in front of one boy and taking his hand, then moving to another and grasping his shoulder. "When Prior Raymond heard from pilgrims of the holy wars in Hispania and the successes of King Afonso, he sent Brother Tomas and I to provide whatever small help we could, for we knew your language as well as the perfidious ways of the Mohammedans. And, so, here we are, ready to teach and encourage you in the ways of reverence and the skills of war. Some of you might think these are separate things, but they are not!"

The monk's hooded black cloak moved smoothly as he bent toward one of the younger boys, displaying a small white cross sewn on the left shoulder. "As brothers, we commit to the peace of Christ and to living humbly, chastely, and obediently. This is not easy, and our prayers throughout the day help us maintain our resolve. You need not become monks like us or join our order, but discipline and routine will help you overcome your fears and the difficulties you may soon face. You will join us in these prayers and in our discussions to help you focus your heart on the will of the Lord and the task before us.

"We are also brothers in arms, dedicated to fighting against evil. The evil that we face here, in this time and in this place, are the Moors who have overrun Hispania and filled it with unholy practices. When this devil is sent running, there will always be more evil to take on. Christ forgives you for violence done in His name against evil and promises you the blessing of heaven.

"But Christ wishes you victory in this life as well as in the next, and so you must learn how to skillfully use a sword and a bow, and you must have the strength to kill many Moors and to survive your wounds and such deprivations as little food. Brother Tomas and I, as well as Afonso's knights, will teach you these things as well."

Belem jumped to his feet in excitement, and blurted: "Brother Rodrigo, will we learn to ride a horse?"

Willard worried Belem would be chastised for his interruption, but Rodrigo laughed softly, "Not today, young man. But someday, if Christ wills it."

Belem sat again.

"Now is a time for individual reflection and prayer," Rodrigo said. "Meet here again at the ninth hour."

Willard returned to his tent, fully intending to pray and reflect, but instead quickly fell asleep. At mid-afternoon, the noise of people gathering woke him. He hurriedly smoothed his tunic as he joined the others.

Father Martim waved for Willard to join them alongside a small clearing. Several of Afonso's men stood in a straight line behind Brother Rodrigo, and the boys made another line facing him. Brother Rodrigo gave each boy a straight, arm's length branch stripped of its leaves and twigs, one end wrapped in cloth. Each of Afonso's men held similar sticks, and first they showed the boys how to hold them. Then the soldiers had the boys run with them toward bushes.

When the boys started rushing at each other, clacking their rods against each other's, Rodrigo pulled them gently aside. "Not yet," he said. The soldiers then showed the boys how to use poles to protect themselves. When the boys' energy waned, Afonso's soldiers had each boy hold one of their shields. Invariably, each child dropped the shield, amazed at its weight and embarrassed at their weakness.

"You see now," Rodrigo said, "why you must build up your strength before using real weapons. Don't worry. We'll work on that too."

As the boys prepared the evening meal, the priests joined the bishop and the Hospitallers where they sat on benches in front of their tents. Willard burned with questions and soon engaged Rodrigo in a discussion about the Hospitallers. Rodrigo's humility and simplicity impressed him. The knights he'd met barely spoke to commoner priests like Willard. Rodrigo was a noble, and yet he treated Willard as an equal, gently mocking his accent as they talked, and listening intently to Willard's ideas about training the boys.

"You have more experience than I in forming the minds of young, undisciplined men," Rodrigo told Willard. "I need your knowledge and welcome your suggestions. My life was one of privilege and now is one of order and discipline. I fear I don't understand the needs and concerns of young men like these, born to poverty and allowed to run wild."

Willard was speechless at this flattery, but quickly recovered. "You have a fine manner with them from what I can see. I think they need praise and encouragement as well as discipline. Many of the boys attracted to our camps have never known a father's love or discipline and need both desperately. And food. They need food. They've spent their lives so far mostly hungry."

Rodrigo nodded reflectively. "And you, Brother Willard. What do you need? What brings you to Lisbon?"

Willard's mind raced as he decided what to say. Could he tell Rodrigo he had been made a priest just a few months before only because so many young noblemen had died in the civil war, and then only because he agreed to be the ship's priest? Tongue-tied, Willard looked up fearfully at Rodrigo.

"Willard, I know you're not a Norman. I can tell by the way you speak," Rodrigo said gently. "And yet you're a priest, honored to lead a group of pilgrims. That tells me you're brave as well as committed. You could be in England with a lovely wife and sons of your own, but you're here. Why?"

"I want to serve God," Willard exclaimed. "And all I've seen since joining this pilgrimage makes me want to do that even more. I want to fight evil, like you do, not just with words and praying over the dead, but truly fighting evil, wiping it off the earth and making the world Christ's kingdom. St. Paul tells us women and families make men weak, detract them from God. If I'd been noble born, I may have joined a monastery, maybe even the Hospitallers," Willard looked at Rodrigo hopefully. "But I wasn't. God led me to this pilgrimage instead."

Rodrigo nodded, then stood. "Who knows where Christ will lead next? If you'd like, I'll write you a letter introducing you to the prior when you reach Jerusalem. There's always a place for brave priests in the Order of St. John, noble or not. We have many lay brothers too. For now, though, we're called to train these boys."

Elated, Willard rose and followed Rodrigo toward tables underneath an awning. They ate in silence, served by sleepy boys who could barely keep their eyes open. Afterwards they marched to the stone house now being used as a chapel for the evening service.

Brother Tomas had a clear, strong voice and taught the boys psalms in Latin. Willard smiled as he heard their voices grow surer and stronger, and when the older boys' voices suddenly changed pitch. Many of the boys did not know what the words meant, but he could hear their awe in the tone of their voices, no longer sleepy as they struggled to learn. Willard found himself singing softly with them, trying to learn the rhythms and melodies of the familiar words. A universal language of God! His heart overflowed with joy, and he hugged Davi and Belem, Iohan and Lopo when they filed past him leaving the chapel.

Again everyone gathered near the fire, waiting expectantly as Rodrigo began to speak.

"My young brothers, scripture tells us to pray without ceasing, and wouldn't it be wonderful to spend our lives singing psalms and feeling God's presence as we pray before the altar? Tell me, Alvaro, do you pray without ceasing?"

Alvaro bowed his head in shame. "No, Brother Rodrigo."

Rodrigo walked over to Alvaro and lifted his chin. "Don't be ashamed. We all must eat. And sleep. Is there anyone here who doesn't eat or sleep?" The boys laughed quietly. "So, what can it mean to pray without ceasing?" Rodrigo paused again. "It means we must live our lives as a prayer. Sometimes that means talking with God in his church or in quiet contemplation in the still of our hearts. Sometimes it means singing psalms of praise to His glory, or, yes, eating in thankfulness for all his gifts. But, do you know the most important form prayer takes?"

Rodrigo stood silently for a moment as the boys waited for the answer to this mystery. "It is to do good actions, acts that will bring about the kingdom of God here on earth! Yes, we must pray often, and at first you will not like getting up in the middle of the night or awakening early for prayer, but soon it will become the cadence of thankfulness and purposefulness, a time of rest and reflection. Much of our time must be spent doing what Christ commands, rooting out the evil that we see everywhere. Every good work is a prayer, and we must pray without ceasing.

"God commands us to put on his armor, my young brothers, and over these next few weeks we will guide you on putting on this armor, teach you how to use the sword in the fight against the forces of darkness that surround us, and build up your strength as you wrestle each other as Jacob wrestled with the angel. When you're ready, you'll learn to hunt while riding a horse and to ride your horses together in formation.

"Christ's army needs brave boys like you to take up arms in his name. And this is a battle where you cannot lose, for God rewards both victory and death!

You're promised forgiveness of sin, and the glory of heaven awaits you. I think some of you may have family, uncles and cousins perhaps, maybe even fathers and brothers, who have not yet seen Christ's light. Maybe some of them now live in fear behind Lisbon's fortified walls. It will be difficult to go against them. But consider this: we are now your family. We will fight with you and share our food with you. We will comfort you and praise God with you. You'll never be alone or hungry as long as you stay faithful. For Christ promised that those who have given up their families for his sake will be rewarded a hundredfold, in this life and in heaven. Tonight, as you go to your rest, think about this, seek God's revelation in your evening prayers. Even sleep is prayer as it readies you, makes you able to do good works throughout the day. Good night, rest well, and pray without ceasing!"

~

The next two days fell into a pattern of prayer, preaching, discussion, and training. They arose twice during the night for prayers and psalms, and then at daybreak for prayers before the first meal of the day. They ate in silence, so they could contemplate the day and give thanks to God, Brother Rodrigo explained in his talk following their first breakfast. The meals were meager, and the boys took turns cooking, serving, and cleaning up afterwards. At first, the new boys resented this as they considered it work for women. Rodrigo chastised them, saying they must be prepared, and women were weak and a distraction. Soldiers must be self-sufficient, he told them.

The afternoons were spent in military training, the boys' favorite part of the day. The younger boys concentrated on stick play, learning to thrust their cudgels and staves against bales of hay and to throw them upward towards shields held by Afonso's men on horses. The older boys alternated this with learning to shoot arrows high and far. Each afternoon there was a competition, with the winner receiving the honor of being Rodrigo's or Tomas's squire the next day. Willard often saw boys practicing during the siesta that followed the midday meal.

Each morning Rodrigo filled the boys with fiery words and zeal, and each evening he gave them encouragement and words of reflection. They loved him, followed him, sought his approval in everything they did.

On Willard's last night, at the gathering following Vespers, Willard and Fathers Martim and Peter joined Rodrigo at the front of the assembled boys. Willard spoke first. "Boys, I admire your courage and dedication, and wish I could stay with you, but Father Peter and I have duties to the pilgrims and we must return. Four of you came with Father Peter and I, and any of you may leave with us if you've decided this is not the life for you. There is no shame in this. It just means God has not called you to this service." The camp stayed silent except for the guttering of the fire as Willard's pause stretched on. "Davi," Willard said gently. "Will you return with me or stay?"

Davi jumped to his feet. "I am Christ's soldier."

Belem, Iohan, and Lopo stood quickly. "Me too," Belem said, and Iohan and Lopo repeated.

Rodrigo then stepped forward. "The heavens rejoice hearing you speak! I can hear the angels singing in heaven. Let's join them!"

Brother Tomas began singing *Conditor alme siderum* in his rich tenor, and soon they all were standing and singing, hands opened and arms lifted to the sky.

At the final line, *Cum Spiritu Paraclito, in sempiterna saecula,* Rodrigo shouted, "Creator of the stars, Jesus save us all! Let us be with You and the Father and the Holy Spirit forever!"

Looking at the four boys near Willard, Rodrigo said, "Are you ready to commit yourself to this in front of God and all of us?" They nodded, their eyes glistening in firelight. "Then repeat these words: *I freely give my life to God.*"

Rodrigo waited as the four boys repeated his words, creating an antiphonal chant with the succeeding phrases.

I promise to God, in the presence of these brothers and the heavenly host, to live a life of obedience to Christ.

I promise to obey Christ's Church and his appointed leaders, including Brothers Rodrigo and Tomas, Bishop Pedro, and our Blessed Father Eugeni-

us. I will go where they command me and do all that they command.

I promise to pray without ceasing, in communal prayer with my brothers and in working to bring Christ's kingdom to the whole earth.

I promise to battle evil in all its forms, in all ways, in all times, in all places.

In the name of the Father and of the Son and of the Holy Spirit, now and forever.

Rodrigo, Willard, Peter, and Martim embraced each of the boys. As the group went toward their tents, Willard and Peter told them each goodbye as they would be leaving with a few of Afonso's soldiers at first light. The boys then raced to join the others as Willard and Peter went solemnly to their own cots.

"I wish I could stay," Father Peter said.

"I do too. How happy they must be!" Willard replied. As he lay on his pallet, reflecting and praying, Willard repeated the vow in his head. He had made similar vows, most recently at his ordination, but this one seemed bigger, more important somehow.

As Willard drifted to sleep, visions of battles between the devil and the heavenly hosts filled him.

SEVENTEEN

Anglo-Norman Camp
Lammas 1147

"Tell me about Afonso's camp," Sperleng said as he joined Willard around the fire. Cate hovered nearby, serving those closest to her brothers slowly, hoping to hear the details that so far Willard had refused to share with her.

"The boys who went are lucky! They're getting a lot more training than I ever did before I joined the Earl's army, and it was never from the knights," Sperleng continued. "Just the village sword and bow competitions. And hunting, of course."

"It was remarkable," Willard said "After Bishop Pedro left, the leader was a Hospitaller knight named Brother Rodrigo. What a great man! A strong bearing and a kind heart. Eloquent, firm but gentle, and could beat Afonso's men in shooting and sword fights. The boys loved him too. They didn't complain about the midnight prayers after the first time and had such fun learning to use a stave and bow. He fought in the Holy

Land and told us of the atrocities occurring every day. When we come to Jerusalem, I hope to join the Hospitallers, to have a life filled with God's work!"

Cate sat next to Willard hoping to hear more. Willard turned and looked at her fiercely. "Don't you have work to do?"

"Don't you?" Cate shot back. Willard rose quickly, but as he began to leave Cate held his arm. "Willard, I'm sorry. I just wanted to hear about the camp and the Hospitaller."

"It is no concern of yours," Willard said.

"But I think it's fascinating that you want to be a Hospitaller. You've never said that before during the many times we've talked."

"You are a woman, Cate, and some topics are not suitable for your ears."

"I'm your sister!" Cate said.

"My family is the Brotherhood of Christ." Willard stalked off.

"What was that about?" Cate asked, trying not to cry.

Sperleng put his arm around her shoulders. "He'll get over it. He is over-impressed right now with this new monk he met. Monks are worse than priests when it comes to women, thinking they are the cause of everything evil. As if Adam wouldn't have sinned except for the temptation of Eve."

Cate wiped her eyes, looking at Sperleng gratefully. "Do you need anything?" He shook his head as Cate stood and walked away.

Cate found it harder and harder to be with Willard. She hated and envied his self-satisfied assurance. The mothers missed their boys and feared they might never see them again alive. "It is a gain to die as a soldier of Christ," was all Willard ever said about it. Cate hoped he never said that in front of Milah, who eyed Willard with a mixture of distrust and fear.

Willard entirely ignored Milah's steely looks. Eventually he demanded that women and girls stay away from his and Father Peter's lessons with the new and younger boys, instructing Mary and Cate to leave food at the doors. Willard invited any willing soldier to join them, and many did as a diversion from the monotony of standing guard or the danger of filling the trench along the city wall.

In the afternoons, the girls sulked as their brothers played war games. To distract them, Mary and Cate invited the girls to help them plant and grind herbs, showed them how to make vinegar and poultices, weave cloth, knead bread, dry fish. The camp followers joined in when they weren't otherwise occupied with the soldiers and told the girls stories and sang songs with them. Cate began to understand some of these songs and was quite sure Willard would disapprove.

A tall, thin girl named Urra, whose face bore the scars of sunburn and thorn scratches, seemed instinctively to know how to mix the medicinal plants. She followed Mary everywhere, asking questions and learning their words for plants while telling Mary and Cate her words. Cate felt a little jealous watching Mary with Urra, seeing her younger self in the way Mary took Urra's hand to show her the right way to grind and blend herbs. Cate felt glad when Urra disappeared one day, and disturbed when she reappeared a few days later, arms loaded with plants and with fresh cuts and a smile on her face. When Mary asked where these came from and what they were, *"mulher bosque,"* was all Urra could say.

The local women seemed to know what these plants were and became most excited about a plant Urra called *cardoo,* a plant that looked to Cate like a thistle that sprouted thin purple petals radiating from the top. Despite herself, Cate was intrigued by their interest and watched carefully as they separated the spiny stem from the globed bud, and seeds from the flower. They crushed the seeds and some of the buds, then put them in small sacks hung around their necks. They put the stalks in a pot with water and wine, threw in a couple of the buds, and placed the pot over the cooking fire.

"Give you man," Milah told Cate, and all the women laughed. Cate shook her head and blushed.

~

Sperleng spent his days patrolling and working on a massive breaching tower to scale the city's walls. When the Norman tower builders learned that Sperleng's father was a carpenter, they quickly conscripted Sperleng for joinery work. Soldiers gathered wood from the houses, tearing them down for timber, and soon a huge scaffold rose in their camp, with enclosed platforms at intervals of men's height. The first floor had room for a hundred standing men.

The successive tiers narrowed, with ladders leading upward. Each floor had coverings made of animal hides on three sides. The ceiling of the topmost tier was secured with metal hinges, tied with thick ropes, then covered with fresh hides. The Rhinelanders and Flemings often sent their builders to watch, and they bragged their towers would breach the walls first, unless of course their tunnels and fires did.

The Moors occasionally shot fiery arrows towards them, but the towers were out of range. Most of the time the Moors saved their ammunition and heckled them. Sperleng learned their taunts were about how weak and cowardly the ghost-faces were and what their women were doing in their absence. When Sperleng tried to sleep at night, no matter how hard he tried to forget, his ears still rang from these mockeries set to the rhythmic pounding of metal on stone.

The pilgrims' leaders schemed for the eventual assault, and one clear morning, when the muezzins were chanting the first call to prayer, men underneath the cover of movable fortified shelters smoothed the ground in front of the wheels of all three towers while hundreds of soldiers began slowly moving the towers toward the city walls. Archers shot arrows at any Moors they spied on the walls, and armed men underneath the canopies of two battering rams swung iron-tipped trees against the city gates.

The English pushed and pulled their tower forward, but they had misjudged its weight and the sand's resistance.

"Stop!" Sperleng yelled when he saw the wheels begin to sink, but his words were lost in the clanging of the battering rams against the metal clad gates and the shouts and horns from both inside and outside the wall. Soon the tower was immovably stuck, the top-heavy structure teetering precariously each time they tried to push. Sperleng commanded his men to wedge loose lumber under the wheels, but the damp sand had already swallowed them, and each time they dug, more sand rushed in.

Smoke rose from the Rhinelanders' side of the wall as the Moors shot flaming arrows at the roofs of the Flemish towers and battering ram. Sperleng saw flames shooting above the wall line and despaired, knowing the other pilgrims were having no more success than they were. A trumpet sound of retreat carried across the plain, and the Moors chanted their taunts over and over.

The Moors continued their attack, using mangonels to thrust heavy rocks and burning logs toward the stranded tower, and their archers kept up a barrage at any nearby soldier. The field was littered with bodies, screaming and silent, as men rushed to drag them out of arrow range. When the melee quieted, and the smoke began to clear, soldiers began the sad work of carting men with burns and barbed arrows back to their camps.

Sperleng trudged toward Gilbert's compound, his hands raw from pulling rocks from the sand. Gilbert waved him inside, and they sat staring at their fish and ale for what seemed a very long time.

"There's no saving the tower," Sperleng said. "We need to let it go."

"Aye, but Saher wants us to try again tomorrow," Gilbert said. "We've spent a month building it, and if it takes a month to build another, we'll be here for the winter."

"It's stuck fast!" Sperleng's voice began rising. "We'll not save the tower, but we'll lose many men."

"There must be something we can save." Gilbert looked away as he talked. "Maybe the top tiers?"

"The top tiers are the most secure of all, as they must be to hold all those men." Sperleng pounded his fist on the table. "Perhaps the knights are stronger than my men and they can try."

Gilbert stood up, his brocaded surcoat falling to the floor. "You know how war works, Sperleng, the foot soldiers are the first line of defense. Go, tell your men to begin again as the sun rises."

Sperleng held back what he wanted to say and went toward the hospital tents to check on the wounded.

The second day went badly. Arrows, many lit with burning tar, flew over the wet hides the soldiers used to protect their heads as the men tried to separate the tiers and save as many nails and brackets and animal hides as they could. Occasionally an arrow set a corner ablaze, and the men rushed to douse the flames. By afternoon, they spent more time putting out fires than dragging off lumber as the Moors figured out the most vulnerable sections. Many men fell trying to save the tower, and more men were needed to drag away the bodies, living and dead.

Sperleng was glad when night finally came. He and Kendric swam in the river to rid themselves of the smells of sweat and ash and blood that clung to them. When they arrived at the caves, Gilbert and his squire stood waiting for them.

"Saher says it's no use. Leave the tower to burn," Gilbert said, his expression betraying sadness.

Sperleng nodded, refusing to speak.

"Sperleng, I know you are angry about all the men who were hurt or died today. I, too, must follow orders," Gilbert said.

"None of us wished to winter here," Sperleng said. "But it seems we will."

On the third day the fires took hold, and the dry wood burned quickly now that the men had stopped dousing flames. Rivulets of fire traveled along the posts setting each tier ablaze, and soon the tower was a scaffold of flame. The men stepped back as it burned to the ground.

What a disaster, Sperleng thought as he trudged to check on his men. The hospital tents were a riot of movement and screams and the smell of death, women running from mat to mat bandaging and cleaning or closing men's eyelids. *It's good Cate and Mary are here,*

Sperleng thought, seeing their skill and how they comforted the men. *Some will live to fight another day because of them.*

~

Cate recognized the stink of death wafting from within Lisbon's walls toward their camp. Large flocks of black birds circled over the city constantly and scouted the river's banks. Cate could only imagine what life was like inside those walls. Every night Sperleng's men killed one or two Moors who tried to harvest fruit or hunt in the dark. Every day, the troops noticed more bodies drifting from the water gates where Lisbon's walls met the Tagus, caught by the sides of the ships guarding those gates. Sometimes the living attempted to float with the dead to escape or merely to retrieve the garbage sailors threw into the Tagus.

One moonless night Gilbert's men captured messengers swimming in the Tagus who carried desperate letters to the leaders of nearby settlements. The translated letters made it clear the stores of food inside the walls were diminishing quickly and mostly reserved for soldiers while the poor ate rats. Many of the animals, even some horses, had already been slaughtered. The soldiers celebrated, and their leaders decided there was no need yet to risk a frontal attack. Cate tried to celebrate, too, but found herself dreaming of listless children with hollow eyes.

But still the Moors would not surrender. Shortly after the Feast of the Assumption, King Afonso abruptly left with most of his troops to deal with trouble elsewhere, leaving the siege to the ships' leaders. Willard left for the boys' training camps, with pilgrim knights now providing the military training. Sperleng's men grumbled at the evening meal that they would have liked a turn at the camps; better the boys learned from foot soldiers as those boys would hardly be given horses or armor.

"The knights will soon tire of the games," Cate heard Sperleng telling them, "and you will have your chance. Until then, we must work on a new siege tower, hunt, fish, and prepare the ships for winter."

One scorching afternoon, as the shadows of the ships began providing some shade for the men tying down the sails and sealing the ships' wood, Cate heard shouts, and looked up to see a Norman longboat skimming across the river towards them. Several more small boats followed closely behind and quickly beached as a crowd gathered to hear the news.

"We crossed the Tagus to fish and had nearly finished when a swarm of Moors on horses came out of the forest," Egric told them. "Most of us were able to reach the boats and push off, but the Moors killed the soldiers standing guard and those who didn't reach the boats in time. They took five of our brothers captive. I doubt they are still alive."

In a fury, Gilbert leapt on his horse, and dashed toward the compounds of Hervey and Saher. Hervey sent messengers calling a meeting of the Council of the pilgrims' leaders, and that night they made plans to punish the raiding Moors. All the next day men readied the swiftest boats to carry the soldiers and horses across the river, sharpened and oiled their swords, cut new arrows, and mended torn mail shirts. The following morning, they waited on the beach for the Flemish and Rhinelander troops to arrive, but by the third hour it was clear they were not coming.

"That's the Flemings," Viel said, "almost as unreliable as Afonso. You would think they would have come just on the promise of plundering Al-Mada. I guess they figure a few more dead Normans won't hurt anybody. No matter. All my men are willing to avenge their brothers. And I am sure there are enough of us to rout a few country Moors. Am I right?"

A shout went up from the troops who heard, and within an hour enough additional soldiers were ready to sail.

Cate spent most of the day watching anxiously for their return. As dusk turned the river gray, she feared the worst. Suddenly someone shouted, and Cate saw boats emerging from the hazy shade filled with singing men holding spears with bleeding heads impaled on them. Boat after boat skimmed onto the beach. Soon the larger ships with the knights and horses came aground along the beach, and the knights led out from the holds wave after wave of brightly dressed Moors covered in blood. None of the Moors wore armor, or even leather vests, only long tunics covering loose trousers.

The sailors and women lit torches, which they handed to the conquering soldiers as they marched toward the closest City gate. The Flemish, Rhinelander, and Frisian troops, hearing the noise, soon joined the parade that lined the impaled heads along the wall on the western side of the city. Cate, carried along with the surge of soldiers, glimpsed the horrified faces of Moors lining the breaks high on the city's walls as the knights forced the captured Moors to hold the spears while laughing men dug holes and others lit torches to display the dripping, lifeless faces. As darkness took hold, and the crowd quieted, Cate heard the gates opening and Moors wailing and pleading. As the assembled troops watched, one by one Moors claimed the heads, covered them with cloths, and brought them into the city. When only a few remained, the crowd dispersed, and the knights walked their captives away from the walls. Cate saw a few turbaned old men gather the remaining heads, blood seeping through the thin white cloths that covered the lifeless faces.

"It's time to go," Mary said pulling at Cate's arm as Sperleng, his clothing covered in dirt and blood, waited impatiently nearby. "There are injured to tend to."

"That was awful," Cate said, still staring at the hunched old men carrying their bloody loads. "And sad."

"That is war," Sperleng said, pushing her roughly away from the crowd toward their compound. "It is ugly and brutal, but now the Moors will be even more afraid, and even more willing to surrender. If we'd left the bodies on the field, they could put it out of their minds or pretend no one had died. Now they see that their cousins and uncles and maybe even fathers or brothers have been killed. They have to ask themselves, is it worth it?"

"Who of us died?" Cate asked anxiously. "How many?"

"Only one of Hervey's men. There are many wounded, though, who you should be caring about. Go!"

Cate followed Mary to the barns where the injured now lay. She filled a large bowl with vinegar and water and began washing the blood off a young soldier's face. As she gave him a draft from a wineskin, he smiled

"It's not much I don't think, just a cut on my leg."

"God was with you then," Cate said. "How did this blood come to your face?"

"That is from a Moor I stuck." he said.

Cate took a knife to the area on his breeches that seemed the darkest. A long, shallow cut ran from his knee to his calf. It reminded her of a cut she had seen on a farmer in Brycgstow who had fallen on his hoe.

"Does it hurt anywhere else?" she asked as she cleaned the edges of the wound. It didn't seem deep, so she placed a loose cloth on top.

"Nay, but I wouldn't mind some of that dwale to help me sleep," he said, "and a kiss good night."

"Needs we save the dwale for our surgeries, but I will find you some wine."

Cate undressed him carefully but found no other wound, then covered him with a blanket and kissed him on the forehead before moving on to the next soldier. He, too, was covered in blood, but although his arm was crooked Cate found no cut. She felt the length of his arm and found a bone that seemed out of place.

"What happened?" she asked.

"We ran toward the farmers in their field, and I tripped over a rock," he said, looking at his arm, then staring Cate in the eye. "But I got back up and killed my share. I carried two heads to the boats; the blood is theirs."

Cate's face froze as she congratulated him. "We are all safer now. I'll get Mary to set your arm."

Cate waved at Mary to join her, then moved on to the next soldier.

~

Lisbon's poor snuck out nightly, prostrating themselves before the first guard they saw, begging for mercy and food, claiming conversion to Christ. They told tales of corpses left to rot and hunting rats for meat. The Normans allowed the elderly, the women, girls, infants, and toddlers to leave, demanding ransom for the youths and men left behind guarded in empty caves. At first, they gave their captives a little food and water, but when no one returned within a few days to pay their ransom, soldiers killed them and threw their bodies into the river. Cate listened to these stories as she stirred the pottage, grimacing as Viel laughingly told anyone who would listen that the Flemings put out food as bait then slaughtered anyone who came to take it.

One morning, as Cate walked along the edge of the deserted streets toward a grove of pomegranate trees, her guard nuzzling Milah, she saw a small boy moving furtively from tall grass to the trunks of trees. The boy was thin with a hollow face, but his billowing clothes appeared clean and mended. Cate stood still and watched silently, remembering winters when her family needed to share what little they had left from the summer stores, as the boy tore open a fruit he'd found at the base of the tree and consumed it quickly. He then began gathering loose fruit and putting it into a net. He turned and froze, apparently seeing Cate but hoping she had not seen him.

Cate headed in the other direction, raising her voice to her escort who was still hidden by the trees. The boy dashed with his few fruits to the safety of high grass.

The next morning, Cate slipped out of her house early, past the sleeping guard, carrying part of a loaf of stale bread that she left near the tall grass where she'd seen the boy. She dared not check later to see whether it remained.

EIGHTEEN

As the days cooled and shortened, the pilgrims became increasingly restless wanting the warmth and safety of the walled city before winter came. Fights and gambling grew among the bored soldiers, and Sperleng encouraged competitions among the men to keep their unease at bay.

At the council's weekly meeting in early October, the Flemings bragged that their tunnels had reached underneath the eastern wall, and they were ready for a final assault. The Norman leaders offered to send troops to help, but the Flemings and Rhinelanders told them to stay on the east side, distract the dark devils instead. Sperleng conceded that making the Moors fight on several sides of the wall was a good strategy but was sure the Flemings wanted first chance at booty and hostages. The Portuguese would supply men for the towers and knights to guard all gates and launch boulders along the northern walls. The priests and young men from Afonso's training camps would join the battle. The Normans announced their siege engine was almost completed, too, which set the Flemings hooting and laughing, taunting them about building houses on sand. Norman foot soldiers responded that at least they didn't run like cockroaches from the sight of fire. Shouting and fistfights ensued, and the council sent everyone but the leaders away.

At dawn Sperleng saw black smoke rising from the eastern side of the city. Gilbert sent Sperleng and a few men to see what was needed while the rest of his men hurled a flurry of boulders against and over the west wall. When Sperleng reached the Rhinelanders' side, he saw smoke pouring from three holes on the side of a hill as Lisbon's wall above began collapsing. Large rocks and chunks of wall slid down the hill as hordes of foot soldiers climbed up the steep side, some slipping, and others brought down by falling stones. As Sperleng and his men rushed forward, a group of Flemish soldiers stopped them, waving their swords angrily and making it clear they wanted no help.

Sperleng stood a while watching from the shore as soldiers, shields on their heads, inched up the steep hill underneath a canopy of arrows flying in both directions. The Moors quickly brought large planks to barricade the breach and crumbled portions of the wall blocked the pilgrims' entrance. In the open spaces, armed Moors cut down many of those who made it to the top of the hill, and then began advancing downward.

The jumble of swords and soldiers and shadows obscured Sperleng's view, but he could see the numerous bodies near the top of the hill. The Moors didn't venture far from the wall, and when the pilgrims retreated, the Moors remained to guard the breach.

Sperleng reported to Gilbert the final assault had begun. English and Norman soldiers covered the roof and three sides of their tower with anything they could find to slow down the fire they knew the Moors would try to start. They filled buckets with water and sand and soaked tightly woven mats and hides from oxen and boars in muddy water before hammering them loosely to the tower. They made canopies to protect the lower levels.

Sperleng concentrated on making sure the floors were sturdy enough to hold a hundred men and that the movable top could swing easily as a bridge when needed. He knew the collapsed wall gave them a crucial diversion that could mean victory. Under the cover of a battering ram shelter, they tested the firmness of the ground as close to the wall as they could. While soldiers slammed the trees against the wall, others anchored pulley ropes into the sloping rocks nearest the wall.

When the breaching tower was finally ready, one of the Norman priests blessed it and everyone began filling sacks with water and wet moss and river plants, then hanging them from nails on each side and at each level. Mary and Cate poured vinegar into bags of weeds and chaff and sand, then handed them to men who climbed the ladders and tied them to the topmost tier.

Fifty men began pushing the tower toward the main western gate as four oxen protected by a shield wall dragged it forward. Sperleng made sure the wheels were always rolled onto something hard, whether on hard ground, rocks, or planks. Men crouched on each tier to balance the weight. The catapult and two large swinging beams on the highest tier made the tower top-heavy, requiring twenty men with sturdy ropes to keep it in balance as they inched toward the wall. Behind the tower, thirty more men hauled carts filled with barrels of river water, vinegar, and mud, and pushed forward a small covered structure covered with plaited willow branches. The October morning had felt cool, but soon the sun burned into their skin and heated up the heavy clothes and armor they wore. By nightfall they had moved the tower halfway to the wall.

The next morning, as the sky began to change from navy to gray, soldiers relieved the night guard and began again. When the tower came within range, the Moors began shooting fiery arrows. The blankets and hides that covered the oxen and machines soon had the look of hedgehogs. Archers raced up the ladders to send return volleys, the falling men soon replaced by others running upward. The Moors, weakened from months of little food, were driven from the top of the gate as the sun sank and the clouds along the horizon turned blood red.

Sperleng joined the swarm of knights and Portuguese who filled the Norman tower for the evening watch. As the dark deepened, he looked worriedly toward the river. High tide was coming. Although they were located above the tidal flats, the tide would surround them, cutting them off from the rest of the camp. He ordered men to wedge large rocks and pieces of wood underneath the wheels and bring whatever barrels and buckets they could find.

As the water rose, troops rushed to wet down the sides as the Moors relentlessly threw balls and arrows of fire. Seven young foot soldiers pushed a small covered structure between the tower and from here beat out and doused fires. Other soldiers strung canopies over them, fresh hides soaked in water and vinegar. Several men fainted and fell from breathing smoke and burning oil. Soldiers inside the tower released sacks of sand and chaff to douse fires, giving the sacks to others for refilling. They dumped sheets of water from the top, creating waterfalls that scurried along and between the covering hides and mats.

As the tide reached its height, the Moors opened the city gate and rushed toward the marooned tower, met by the armed knights who surrounded it. The screams of dying men filled the air as the waiting soldiers watched in helpless horror through the flashes of fire that illuminated the stranded troops. When the tide finally began to recede, armies of knights rushed to join the melee until the Moors retreated behind the walls leaving many of their dead piled with the bodies of dead Christians.

All the next day the battle raged. In the afternoon, the sea stranded them again, but this time hundreds more troops remained on the scaffold and within the tidal island near the gate. When the tide receded, the soldiers moved the tower next to the city wall. They cut the ropes holding the bridge, and it crashed on the stones of the wall.

Seeing the pilgrims ready to cross, the weary Moors put down their swords and bows, pleading for mercy and a truce. Most of the pilgrim soldiers were not interested in a truce; they wanted blood and kept pushing forward and climbing the ladders. Gilbert, Sperleng, and the other leaders had to block the bridge from the surging mass of grumbling and shouting men as messengers were sent to Afonso and the Council. As they waited, more Rhinelander and Frisian troops arrived, and the worn-out men who had fought for two days climbed slowly down the ladders and looked for fallen friends who might still be alive among the bloody mess of bodies.

~

The women and priests rushed from patient to patient as the wounded arrived. Soon the barn was full, and whoever was able quickly set up canopies nearby. Cate laid down mats, heated water, brought bandages and wine and vinegar, mixed dwale, called for a priest when it was clear a man was dying or already dead. The camp followers joined them, wiping foreheads with cool cloths and giving wine and ale to those who could drink.

Every time new wounded arrived, most on the backs of weary soldiers, Cate looked up, fearing to see Egric or Sperleng or anyone she knew. One of

Gloucester's knights carried in Kendric, and Cate rushed to him. He had an arrow in his arm and was unconscious from loss of blood. The knight shoved his sword into the fire while Cate broke off the top of the arrow and tightly tied a length of cloth above the wound and then pushed the barbed arrow through. When she finished, the knight cauterized both sides of the wound. Cate washed it with wine and vinegar before taking off Kendric's leather helmet and vest and wiping the grime off his body. She didn't see Egric arrive until he dropped wearily on the ground by her side and took Kendric's hand.

"Will he live?" Egric asked Cate.

"I don't know. He was unconscious when he came and didn't flinch when I pushed through the arrow." Cate wiped her eyes with her sleeve. "Those are not good signs. And if he does live, we may need to cut off his arm."

"Cate!" Mary yelled sharply from across the room. "Move on!"

Cate shrugged, irritated that Mary seemed to think she was wasting time. "Will you watch him and let me know if he wakes up?" Egric nodded as she rushed toward the arriving wounded.

Some soldiers now brought the dead as well, and Willard directed them to an open area where numerous bodies lay in rows. He stopped at the mats of moaning men, giving them wine, praying with them, checking for fever, telling them their sins were forgiven for their sacrifices in this glorious cause. Cate felt the old Willard had returned, the kind, thoughtful, generous one, and smiled at him gratefully.

Sperleng arrived hours later. Several loud groups of men passed by, shouting and cheering, as they headed toward their beds. Sperleng carried one of his dead men draped over his shoulder and wearily laid him on the ground with the bodies. He said nothing to anyone, just looked grim-faced, first at the dead and then at the rows and rows of wounded. Egric approached him, pointed toward Kendric, and together they sat silently next to him. After a few minutes Sperleng said they all needed sleep, and he and Egric trudged back toward their barracks.

The night seemed eerily quiet after the screaming and clash of swords the previous nights. Cate and Mary sat by the fire quickly eating the bread and fish Acha brought them, listening to the moans of the men and the occasional bit of faraway song. Cate, too, had been awake for two days, but felt more disoriented than sleepy, jumping at the crack of the fire or the cry of a man in his sleep.

"You need to rest, Cate," Mary said, patting her hand.

"You do, too! Besides, I don't think I can sleep, anyway."

"At least lie down for a while. I'll come in a few hours and we can switch."

Cate nodded and scanned the area for some place nearby to rest. She took one of the fresh blankets Milah brought earlier in the day and flung it on top of a small pile of straw just inside the open barn door, first poking it with a stick to drive out any rats or other vermin. She stared at the stars in the black sky, sure she wouldn't sleep, when suddenly Mary was shaking her. Cate got up and quietly brushed down her skirt and hair with her hands as Mary settled into her place. She passed Acha sitting by a heavily bandaged youth thrashing in his sleep. Several women roamed the aisles of bodies, touching heads and checking wounds. Men lay sleeping at the sides of their friends. Sperleng sat next to Kendric. After telling Acha to get some rest, Cate joined him.

"His arm is hot and swollen, and his wound is oozing. And he still hasn't woken up," Sperleng said.

Cate loosened the bindings and handed Sperleng a wet cloth to clean the pus weeping from the wound. She smoothed a salve of herbs and grease over the area, then covered it loosely with a strip of linen soaked in vinegar.

"He is alive, and Mary tells me the heat and swelling is a good sign. When did he fall?"

"Egric says he saw him shot while climbing the ladder in the morning. He was bleeding in the dirt for at least a half day before anyone could carry him here."

"He probably hurt his head, too, although I didn't see anything when I took off his cap." Cate felt Kendric's head but found nothing that worried her. "Are more of your men wounded?"

"Two are out there with the bodies," Sperleng said sadly. "I wish Kendric had taken a helmet and a chain shirt when Samuel offered them. But he was too stubborn to accept anything from the Jew. Blood money I think you called it? Well, it saved me from some arrows today."

Cate's face burned, thinking again about Galan. "I was wrong."

"Yes, you were too young to understand and too young to come on this pilgrimage. But you've proven yourself little sister. I wish you were home, safe. But I was wrong too; you are a help to us all," Sperleng said, his voice gruff from sorrow, then got up and walked toward the rows of bodies. He stooped over a few and closed their eyes.

~

The next morning Viel strode into Gilbert's camp in a fury, his ship's priest trying to keep up beside him.

"Wake up!" Viel shouted. "And learn of last night's treachery!"

Most of Gilbert's men were awake and ran to listen. Sperleng could tell by Viel's angry face that something had not gone well.

"Men of Brycgstow," Viel began, "I warned you of the treachery of King Afonso, a man who has gone back on his promises before and is planning to break faith again, this time with the help of that faithless follower of the false King Stephen, Hervey of Glanville. How many of our friends have been wounded or died these past two days to secure our victory? Yes, our victory! We were ready to cross our bridge over the wall, and only the pleas for truce stopped us from the final slaughter."

The soldiers shouted their agreement. "We should have crossed! Let's finish the job now."

"But we had Christian mercy," Viel said, "bolstered by the promise of five princes as hostages while the terms of truce were negotiated. Last night, those princes were given to Hervey who brought them to King Afonso's camp—the same Afonso who promised *us* the hostages and all ransom and booty from the City! Now the ransom will go to him. Do you trust he will deliver that ransom to us? I do not."

Even Sperleng felt outrage. This was not what they had agreed. How could Hervey do such a thing? He had the hostages in hand and turned them over to King Afonso? Afonso had barely participated in the siege, his troops coming and going, sometimes only a few troops in their camp to help with patrols. Yes, they had come back in force for this final assault, but most of the men who died the last few days were pilgrims. How dare Afonso claim these hostages? As Sperleng's anger roiled inside of him, other men shouted, demanding an explanation from Hervey and threatening to climb the breaching tower and cross into the city to kill anyone they saw.

Viel's priest, a small man with a long scar along his right cheek, climbed on a bench and raised his arms in a benediction to the crowd.

"Brothers in Christ," the priest began, "We came here on a holy mission to save the land of St. James from the blasphemers, and we have saved Lisbon. We should first praise God that he has given us the victory."

"Praise God!" the men shouted.

"But Christian men must keep faith with each other, and we should not sit silently by when they do not. Right now, our leaders are meeting to decide what is best for us. They sit in their Council with King Afonso to negotiate what has already been decided. The hostages, the ransom, the spoils belong to us! That was decided long ago, before we agreed to stay. What more is there to talk about? Think about this: when we arrived here, did the leaders and their council secure the areas outside the walls for us, or did we?"

"We did!" the soldiers shouted.

"And who destroyed Al-Mada after their soldiers took our men hostage?"

"We did!"

"And who would now hold Lisbon if the leaders had not stopped us?"

"We would!"

"Do we have need of leaders like these, men who break off amid victory? Who compromise our agreements by giving up the hostages promised to us? Whose faulty plans led to the destruction of three siege engines? Are these the leaders we want?"

"No!" the crowd roared.

"Then let's go to the council's meeting and demand our due!" The priest raised his hands, jumped off the bench, and followed Viel towards Hervey's camp. As they marched, more and more soldiers joined them, the mob's outrage growing as the bruised and tattered men added their complaints in the retelling. When they learned Hervey was in King Afonso's camp the crowd seethed in that direction, with shouts of *"Treachery"* and *"Judas"* repeated loudly and often.

Sperleng joined the hundreds who rushed to Afonso's camp, while others hurried to seek support from the Rhinelanders' camp. The Portuguese, having heard of the trouble in the pilgrims' camps, had set up a perimeter of armed knights. Foot soldiers shouted at the knights and the King for hours. When night fell, they left, exhausted and hoarse, vowing to gather in the morning and enter the city.

At daybreak, Sperleng joined almost 400 soldiers in battle gear, many wearing armor taken from fallen Moors, seething at the edge of their camp. Saher's general, his ruddy face lined and weary, blocked their way with scores of Norman knights and asked for patience.

"Men," he began, "Lord Saher and the council have heard your concerns. I assure you, the council is holding Afonso to his promises. The hostages were brought to the King's camp because the Portuguese are much better able to understand their language and know best what is important to the Moors. Your revolt has already emboldened the hostage princes to demand more concessions than they are due. Be unified in Christ! Give the council another day to resolve the truce. We have been here four months, at great loss. Can't you wait another day and save yourselves and your countrymen from further pain?"

After much loud discussion, Sperleng and the rest of his men finally agreed that waiting one more day was better than fighting. Sperleng overheard one soldier grumbling that he was ready to fight now, but he could see relief on the faces of others. In the evening, Saher's general returned to their camp with the news: a truce had been reached, and tomorrow morning one hundred armed men chosen from each camp would enter the City to occupy the inner keep. The people of Lisbon would bring their valuables to the castle, and these would be divided amongst the pilgrims. Any Moor or Jew found to have had held back money or possessions would lose both these and their heads. The Moors would be allowed to leave Lisbon, and the Portuguese would occupy it.

Sperleng was, and knew most of his soldiers were, content enough with the agreement, glad to have an end of the fighting and happy not to face death again tomorrow.

~

In the morning, Mary joined every pilgrim who was able gathering at Lisbon's main gate. She stood at the edge of the crowd as the archbishop gave blessings and thanks. The gate slowly opened. One hundred Norman knights joined one hundred Rhinelander and Flemish knights in a solemn march. In rebuff for the Brycgstow's troops mutiny, neither Gilbert nor any man from Brycgstow had been given the honor of joining this procession.

The archbishop and bishop led the procession, both in long ceremonial vestments of purple covered by white and each wearing a large gold cross that glinted in the sun. King Afonso on a tall white horse followed, accompanied by a knight on each side carrying banners displaying large blue crosses. King Afonso wore full armor and a circlet of crosses on his head. His sword with a gold hilt hung in a silver scabbard tied to his right side, and in his left hand he carried a shield with a dark blue cross on a white background. His white cape with a large embroidered blue cross furled behind him as he rode. Mary both admired and resented his finery.

The pilgrim leaders followed on horseback, each with a colored cross on his tunic and mantle and carrying a shield with his family's coat-of-arms. All the leaders looked resolutely forward, their proud faces etched into the deep blue of the cold sky. The chosen knights marched behind, also wearing over their polished armor tunics newly painted with the sign of the cross.

As the knights passed through the gate, Mary spied several foot soldiers from the eastern camps slipping in too, and pointed them out to Sperleng, who then pointed to other men climbing over the breach in the eastern wall. Mary's fists clenched in disgust. Those Flemings were always looking for an edge, first as mercenaries for Stephen and now trying to get the first spoils of God's War. One of them had surely killed her husband Hafoc. Mary doubted very much that their sins would be forgiven; they showed no remorse whatsoever.

Once the procession passed, Lisbon's gates slowly closed behind them. Mary grieved at the many unwashed bodies still sprawled in piles along the outer edges of the wall. Hordes of flies and birds circled and landed. Many of the bodies had lain there two days already, and the sulfurous sweet smell of decaying flesh burned her eyes and nose as she wandered through them.

Sperleng joined Mary, rolling corpses off one another with his ax and taking what useable weapons he found. Willard prayed over one of Gilbert's men, young Davi at his side looking ill but trying to seem brave. Mary noticed how much larger Willard seemed, stronger and broader.

Soon men arrived with carts, piling bodies five high and rolling them toward the river where they laid them out in a row. If they weren't claimed by the evening, the tide would take them during the night. Mary had to accept that not all the dead would receive the burial they deserved. There were just too many dead, and too many wounded to care for.

Mary knew numerous Moors had fallen outside the wall, but she saw none today. She wondered whether the Moors had taken them inside the wall, or if the soldiers had already tossed them into the river. When she could stand the smell and sight of death no longer, she walked upstream into the river hoping to rid herself of its stench.

After the evening meal, Sperleng came again to see Kendric and sat by his inert body.

Mary touched her nephew's shoulder. "There's been no change. We'll cut his arm tomorrow and pray that saves him."

"What good is a soldier without his arm?" Sperleng said, mostly to himself.

Mary moved to the next pallet where Cate tended a young man whose moaning kept growing louder, who screamed when she touched his forehead and demanded to know where Celia went. He calmed only when Cate told him Celia would be back soon.

"Who is Celia?" Mary asked.

"I don't know," Cate shrugged, "but telling him she'll be here soon is the only way I've found to calm him. He's been screaming and asking for Celia for two nights now. At first, he would wake up and be coherent occasionally, but then he was in pain he couldn't bear. He sweats and shakes and complains of the cold. Maybe the delirium is better. Who knows?"

"Will he live?"

"Only God knows, but I doubt it. See his wound?" Cate slowly pulled up a strip of linen covering a deep wound in his abdomen. The area surrounding the gash was inflamed and turning black in places and with abscesses filled with pus. "I've lanced the pus several times already, but it keeps coming back." She reached for a small knife, and as she touched the area near blackened skin, the patient screamed in pain.

"Can't you give him something for the pain?" Sperleng demanded.

"Don't you think I have? He's already had more dwale than is good for him."

"Good for him? Is this pain good for him? You're right, though. I've seen wounds like this before. He will die. He'll live in pain for maybe a couple more days and then he'll die, his body stinking from decay even before his last breath. I know what Willard says, only God can decide when a man dies, but I say no one should have to live like this." When he saw Cate was crying he softened. "Just find something for him. I'll give it to him."

Mary understood but was troubled by Sperleng's words. She mixed a small bowl of ground herbs with ale and handed it to Sperleng.

"He really shouldn't drink more than half of that," Mary said.

"Or what?" Sperleng asked.

As Cate lifted the soldier's head, he looked about wildly, asking for Celia.

"She is right here," Sperleng said. "She is holding your head; cannot you feel that?"

The young man nodded and smiled.

"Celia wants you to drink this," Sperleng continued. "It will help the pain."

"Thank you, Celia," the young man whispered, drinking a little of the mixture each time Sperleng brought the bowl to his mouth until it was finished. "Stay with me."

Soon his breathing slowed and finally stopped.

NINETEEN

Inside Lisbon's Walls
Advent 1147

Sperleng claimed a banished Moor's blacksmith shop and house in Lisbon for his troops once the entire army took over the walled city. Cate, Mary, and Acha spent many days and evenings near the forge as they twisted flax into strong bowstrings while Egric shaved and sanded the pungent cypress he'd gathered from the forest into bows nearly the height of a man. Sperleng spent most days over the hot blue and orange fire whose sparks sprayed into the smoke each time he pumped the bellows or pulled out a glowing sword. The fire's warmth let them spend most of their time outdoors or under the porticos that lined the walls of the enclosed yard. There was much to be done, and knights daily came bringing crushed and broken armor and demanding new swords and axes. The Normans had confiscated many curved swords from the Moors, but the Norman knights preferred straight ones and gave them to Sperleng to refashion. Kendric, his left arm gone, would sometimes join them, taking Acha's hand in his remaining one.

Milah and the other camp followers had moved with them, after being baptized at a huge ceremony in the hastily dedicated cathedral, a grand mosque Bishop Pedro rededicated to Christ soon after Afonso took Lisbon. Although it didn't have the glorious painted statues of saints and angels of the Cathedral of Santiago de Compostela, Cate found it strangely beautiful in its own way. She often found herself getting lost in the swirling patterns carved into the many arches, white over a shadow of blue, as she listened to the chanting of a service. Since the beginning of Advent, the new Norman bishop, Gilbert of Hastings, had ordered the hanging of pine branches and berries in the church, and although the piney smell and needles of the boughs weren't the same as at home it helped make this strange place more familiar.

Cate missed home and wondered what her family and Aedra were doing. Cate found it amazing that it was Advent season and still they had seen no snow. The gardens at their new home still produced bright, crooked vegetables and sharp, minty-smelling herbs that Milah had to teach Cate how to use in cooking or as medicine. Was it snowing in Brycgstow? Was Aedra going to marry Trace? Cate listened each night as the soldiers discussed what was happening outside their camp, hoping to hear word of home.

One night, not long after they settled inside the walls, Gilbert and Viel sat around their cooking fire talking with Sperleng and his soldiers. Cate brought them pork and ale and hovered nearby as close as she dared. Viel's booming voice was easy to hear, but Gilbert was softer spoken.

"My ships bring news that Earl Robert has died," Viel said, "of a fever on the eve of All-Saints' Day. They buried him at St. James's Priory. William is Earl now."

Cate nearly dropped the plate she carried, and a little ale slopped onto the ground near her feet. She hoped no one saw.

"William is a fine man, and a strong leader like his father," Gilbert said.

"And like his mother and aunt," Viel laughed loudly at his own joke.

"Sir Robert was good to me, took me into the armory when I needed a place and praised me in battle," Sperleng said, "but I saw little of Sir William, and I doubt he'd know me. Sure he won't keep my place in the armory as Sir Robert promised."

"Brycgstow is a strong fortress, but I fear Stephen will see William's youth as a chance to take over the Earl's holdings," Gilbert said. "Empress Matilda cannot be happy about that."

"Even more anarchy," Viel said. "Not a good time to go home."

Cate felt her chest hollow. Her father and Cearl often praised Earl Robert for his generosity in building the Priory and St. Augustine's Abbey, providing them work for as long as she remembered. She said a quick prayer his son would continue.

"Well, we're not going home. We're going to Jerusalem." Gilbert said.

"If we ever get there," Viel said, leaving.

Cate wondered if there were a way to go to Jerusalem without Viel. She was tired of all his complaining. After Viel left, Gilbert and Sperleng huddled closer together, making it even more difficult for Cate to listen. She brought an ale skin to them, and they nodded their thanks.

"Does Viel know something about Saher's plans?" Sperleng asked.

"Nay," Gilbert said. "He's just saving face after being wrong about Afonso."

Sperleng nodded. "He's right it's not a good time to return home. I wonder if it ever will be a good time. I'd hoped Stephen would be banished and Mathilda the Queen by the time we returned home. Seems unlikely now."

"It does, although William FitzRobert might be up to the task. I hope he is. But it won't change my doom. I will always be a third son, with little chance to inherit. And if Stephen succeeds, my family will likely lose all for their loyalty to the Empress. Perhaps I should meet Willard's Hospitaller, Rodrigo I think you said his name was? Although the Templars wear finer clothes and seem to own more land."

"Aye, Rodrigo," Sperleng said, his voice lightening. "Although I never saw you as a monk. Not sure your wife would like that."

"There are many kinds of churchmen, my friend," Gilbert said, laughing quietly. "Many kinds."

It seemed Sperleng suddenly noticed Cate. "We have enough for now," he said, "you can go."

Cate moved reluctantly away, offering ale to another group as Gilbert and Sperleng talked. She wondered if there would be a feast at the castle this Advent, or if all would be shrouded in black. So many changes, even at home.

~

As Christmas neared, families of the Portuguese soldiers began moving inside Lisbon's walls, the nobles and generals moving their families to the inner castle area while infantry officers took their pick of empty estates. Many quarrels arose when a Portuguese commander preferred a compound already occupied by the pilgrims, and Sperleng agreed to share their quarters with a friendly soldier who wanted to be sure to claim it for his family when Sperleng and his men left in the Spring.

The soldier's wife showed Cate how to bake with dates and figs, how best to grind and press olives, and how to reduce itchiness with a mixture of olive oil and lemon. Other Portuguese families helped replenish the pilgrims' stores of vinegar, wine, and cloth, knowing that the sooner the pilgrims were ready, the sooner they would leave. Cate enjoyed the camaraderie of the cooking and spinning and loved the greater freedom she had to wash laundry in the river and gather medicinal plants in the forest. Once a week, the women went to the baths in the city, small rooms heated by hot springs and stone fireplaces, where they removed the week's grime and talked as best they could of the future: Cate and Mary of Jerusalem, and the Portuguese women of the children they hoped would grow up in safety.

Most of the wounded from the final battles had died, some quickly from loss of blood, others of wounds that never healed but became gangrenous, and many from fevers and pains that no amount of blood-letting or poultices would cure. Some survived with a severed leg or arm, and many limped from broken bones improperly set.

Kendric's speech was slower, his gait awkward, and he often flew into rages over trivial things such as the size of his bowl or the heat of the fire. Only Acha seemed able to calm Kendric's rages. She had nursed Kendric through the amputation, changed his bandages daily, and helped him get used to eating with one arm. Cate was relieved that Acha bore the brunt of these rages. Acha never complained.

Occasionally Egric would tell a story and announce, "The women will like this one," at which the soldiers would groan because they knew the next story would be about love and children rather than the more exciting stories of battle. Cate always blushed when he said this, and the men would laugh and make lewd comments until Sperleng would remind them that she was his sister.

~

Willard preferred to stay with the Hospitallers at Afonso's training camps. He enjoyed the routine and brotherhood of the common prayers and meals, and found he was a decent enough swordsman. He practiced daily with Rodrigo and the boys, and Willard's body showed it. No longer was he the thin, mild-mannered priest's apprentice he had been in Brycgstow. He stood straighter, and the strength in his arms and chest were obvious even underneath his long, loose alb.

Rodrigo taught Willard to ride a horse, first by letting him groom and lead the horse, then set the saddle, and finally sit on the horse while Rodrigo held the horse's head. Willard felt foolish learning skills the others had known as young boys, especially when he first got on the horse and immediately fell off the other side. But he knew this was a skill he had to learn to have a chance at becoming a Hospitaller knight. The afternoon he and Rodrigo rode up to the training field together on horses he saw the admiration in the boys' eyes, recognizing their envy and desire. *Even Sperleng doesn't ride a horse*, he thought, dreaming of the day when he and Rodrigo would ride up to the city walls and show his brother his new skills.

That day came Christmas week when they all went to celebrate at St. Mary's Cathedral. Brothers Rodrigo and Tomas led the procession. Willard, astride his new horse and alongside Father Martim on his, carried a black banner emblazoned with the Hospitallers' cross. A group of about twenty young boys marched behind them, each in a simple brown woolen tunic on which they'd painted a cross. As they entered the gate, Willard thrilled to see the pilgrims and Portuguese lining the main street to the Cathedral to greet them. He searched for Sperleng in the crowd and felt a moment of pride when he saw Sperleng's eyes wide with admiration and mouth gaping in surprise. Cate stood next to Sperleng, waving and smiling, and Willard nodded his head as he passed.

When they arrived at the cathedral, the boys waited silently in formation as the brothers, priests, and knights tied their horses and led them into the church as the bells rang for Sext. They moved solemnly through the dim interior, then knelt at the altar. Bishop Gilbert raised his arms and blessed them, and Brother Tomas led them in singing psalms. Willard felt the admiration of the crowd and threw his shoulders back as he sang.

Afterward, he saw Sperleng and Cate waiting for him at the base of the stairs.

"Life in the country has done you good!" Sperleng said, grasping Willard's bicep.

Willard recoiled a little, finding Sperleng's touch too familiar, not respectful enough. "Aye, we work hard every day, practicing our swords and throwing hay."

"Well done," Sperleng said. "Perhaps we can fight together behind the shield wall next battle."

Willard thought that unlikely. He intended to fight on horseback with the Hospitallers. "Perhaps."

"And what a strong horse you were riding," Sperleng said.

"Yes." Willard could not hide his pride, despite attempting humility. "He was a gift from Afonso to the Hospitallers."

Sperleng's body stiffened, signs of jealousy mixed with his admiration.

"That's wonderful, Willard," Cate said, smiling.

Willard warmed at her praise but bowed only slightly.

"Come join us for dinner, Willard," Sperleng said. "We haven't seen you for a while and need to hear all about your adventures."

"Yes, please come," Cate echoed.

"Maybe another day. Afonso has invited us to stay at the inner castle and we should go there first," Willard said. Davi and Belem rushed toward him, pulling at his sleeve to leave. "Have a blessed Christmas."

Willard saw Sperleng and Cate again at the rear of the church late on Christmas Eve as he and other priests filed toward the front. After lighting candles, he joined a group of singing priests dressed all in white who carried torches through the lines of people, then surrounded a group dressed as shepherds near the front. Still singing, Willard and the priests led the shepherds to a woman in a blue shift and a white headscarf who held a baby. Standing next to the woman was a man in a simple wool tunic holding what Willard recognized as carpenters' tools. Davi, Belem, and several other boys came out of the crowd and knelt before the woman and baby, joining the song. All then processed out the side door, still singing.

What a glorious service! Willard thought. *Celebrating Christ's birth after saving this City from the heathen! And next year, Jerusalem.*

Willard attended all three Christmas services in a place of honor near the front. After the morning service, Rodrigo and Tomas joined the King in the great hall, and Willard, Father Peter, and the boys were given plates of bread and meat to eat in the open area outside. A maid dropped a couple of pomegranates and waved to Willard that he could have them as she rushed inside. He had never been this near a king's feast and was amazed at the number of dishes the servants carried into the hall. *How can anyone eat that much food, or drink that much wine and ale?* he thought.

Many of the boys wandered off to nap or practice with their wooden swords, promising to return for the afternoon service. Willard found a place in the sun near a massive tile oven, and lay there thinking how he, a poor carpenter's son, took up Christ's cross and helped deliver this land from the Moors. *What a turn my life has taken!*

When Willard dozed, he dreamt of Jerusalem and seeing Christ standing outside the empty tomb and of the angels at Bethlehem leading his group of boys to a stable filled with tall war horses they rode to save Christ's tomb from the Mohammedans. He awoke to the sound of trumpets gathering them for the third service. He shook the dust from his clothes and sandals and joined the boys as they passed. On the way down the hill they heard laughter and singing from open gates and windows. Many others joined them. The plaza in front of the cathedral was filled with people, some lining to enter the church while others stayed in the square to drink, eat, and watch jugglers and minstrels. At the far corners of the square masked actors were dressed as angels and shepherds. Inside the church near the altar, Willard could still hear the din.

~

Cate thought about Aedra as players dressed as kings carrying small chests passed her in the square in front of the cathedral. One player was dark and turbaned, wearing flowing trousers of red and yellow. Cate wondered if he was one of the converted Moors, not knowing whether to be happy about the conversions or to question their truth. Willard thought all the Jews and Moors should be banished, but Afonso decided to let converts and Jews remain. *It's his city,* Cate thought, *and we'll be gone before any false converts dare to fight.*

Afonso had declared the Feast of the Epiphany, the twelfth day after Christmas, to be a day of feasting and celebration, and promised on this day he would distribute his gifts to the pilgrims. The square was a riot of activity and anticipation. The entire right side of the square was an elaborate platform with many banners fluttering in the breeze, the largest in the center displaying Afonso's blue cross. The three kings climbed the stage from one side while a portly man in a Roman tunic and a circlet of leaves on his head climbed the other. Cate couldn't understand what the players were saying but recognized the story from the plays back home. When the kings presented their gifts to the Christ child, trumpets began blaring and Afonso's procession entered the square, followed by the six pilgrim leaders.

Afonso's armor gleamed under his blue velvet cloak edged in white fur. His elaborate gold crown displayed alternating red and blue gemstones topped with carved fleurs-de-lis and crosses.

Does the king never smile? Cate thought. *Always that blank stare like some statue.*

As Afonso stood at the edge of the platform, the crowd hushed and strained to hear. Those who couldn't understand him crowded near their priests for translation.

"Soldiers and pilgrims, for half a year we have worked together to reclaim this land for Christ and St. James. It has been a long and difficult time, and all of us have lost friends and brothers. Many still bear the wounds of war. They always will. The Portuguese people thank all of you, the Normans, Rhinelanders, Flemings, Frisians, and Franks, for your bravery and generosity in this holy war."

A murmur of assent went through the crowd. Kendric leaned against Acha, who braced him with her arm.

"You have earned much gold and precious stones from the stores and ransom of the Moors. I know you will use this wealth to continue Christ's war against the

Mohammedans. I pray you will be as successful in Jerusalem as you have been here. On this day of gifts, we happily give you whatever food and supplies you need. Our builders will help refit your ships, and our blacksmiths will help you rearm. Messengers from the South have told us that the Emperor and Count Berenguer of Barcelona, with the help of the Genoese, have delivered Almería from the bondage of the Moors, and we have asked them to welcome you and provide you with your needs when you arrive there as all of Christian Hispania wants to thank you for your help in defeating the scourge of the Moors."

Saher, standing at Afonso's right, nodded his head and seemed to be staring directly at Viel. Viel crossed his arms across his chest and smirked.

"But some of you are weary, or too injured to continue on. Some of you may have met women here whom you wish to marry. And some of you may have come to love this land almost as much as we Portuguese. To you I offer another great gift, the gift of land to live on and cultivate."

As the pilgrims began to understand, shouts of happiness and many conversations filled the air making it difficult for Cate to hear. She saw Gilbert and Sperleng stare at Afonso in surprise. As the din increased, a trumpet blew. Afonso was not finished.

"My kingdom needs leaders who have shown themselves in battle, as you have. We have conquered not only Lisbon, but much of the countryside. We have given farms to our knights and leaders, and we welcome any pilgrim knights who wish to join us. I will talk with your six leaders, my friends and brothers, to reward the worthiest of you as best suits your skills and honor."

Sperleng's shoulders sagged.

"What does this mean?" Cate whispered to Sperleng.

"Nothing for me," Sperleng said quietly. "I'm not a knight, and it's unlikely our leaders will reward anyone from Brycgstow. But we may lose many from other camps."

The next day Saher commanded all his troop leaders and priests to come to his estate. Saher seemed angry and couldn't stop pacing as he talked.

"Afonso is big on pomp and extravagant gestures, but he has no idea how much trouble his offer has caused. First, he appoints a priest from Hastings as Bishop, and now he offers land to our knights. But we have all made the promise to go to Jerusalem! We can't go back on that promise; you do understand that, don't you?"

The men around Sperleng nodded and mumbled that they did.

"Good. So here is what the pilgrims' leaders have decided. Any wounded knights unable to journey to Jerusalem may take Afonso's offer, but we will hold all other knights and foot soldiers to their promise of the cross. I will expect the priests to back this up! If any wish to return to Lisbon after Jerusalem, they can see if Afonso is still willing. Explain this to your men."

Sperleng had a question but didn't dare ask Saher. Instead, he approached Gilbert as he was beginning to leave.

"Gilbert, I too have wounded men unable to travel to Jerusalem. What shall I tell them?"

"It's pretty clear only knights will be given land," Gilbert answered, "Perhaps your men can offer their services to a knight who stays. There will be many who accept Afonso's offer, promise of the cross or not. They'll be looking for men they can trust, and if I were staying I wouldn't trust a Portuguese man who thinks this should be their land."

"Are you thinking of staying?" Sperleng asked.

"No, Saher made it clear to me last night that none of Gloucester's knights will receive land. I'm not sure if that's because of Viel, or because Gloucester sided with Empress Matilda. Probably both. Do you wish to stay?"

"Where you go, I'll go."

"Thank you, Sperleng. I've always appreciated your loyalty and will reward it one day."

The next day Kendric approached Sperleng in the courtyard near the forge. Cate and Mary carded wool nearby.

"Sperleng, my friend," Kendric said, "you know I am not much use as a soldier with one arm. I've heard Robert of Devon has invited any freeman from Brycgstow to share his land in return for services and rent. I'd like to do this."

Sperleng nodded. "I expected as much. You have my blessing."

Kendric hesitated. "And Acha wishes to stay with me. She agrees to marry me. She is kind and strong and hopes for more children."

Sperleng made his hands into tight fists, but his expression didn't change. "A woman should be with her husband. I hope you are happy. Go, quickly, before Robert of Devon takes no more men."

"Doesn't it seem a little quick to get married?" Cate asked after Kendric and Acha left. "Galan's dead only a few months."

"Be happy for her Cate," Mary said. "Remember how she wanted to die?"

"Aye."

"I think it makes perfect sense. They are both older, and not everyone will marry either a woman who's already been married or a man with one arm. And they know each other's families. They have the same beliefs. They both work hard. And Acha says Kendric makes her feel needed. Marriage isn't about physical attraction, I hope you know," Mary said as Cate blushed. "Yes, I've seen how you look at Egric, and he is a handsome man. But marriage is about loyalty and commitment and helping each other, not that."

Cate wasn't sure that was completely true, although she couldn't say that to Mary. She liked the warmth and disorientation she felt when she was near Egric She wanted more than the promise of stability. *I'm not from a noble family, and don't have to marry to make alliances,* she thought, *and Acha doesn't either.* She sensed Egric was afraid to approach her because she was Sperleng's sister, and she wondered how she could let him know it didn't matter without seeming bold or crass. She'd ask Mary after Jerusalem.

~

Cate loved Lisbon. Flowers and color were everywhere, from the huge bushes with blooms of white and magenta to the bright yellow buds of the mimosa tree to the riot of small blue and yellow flowers both in the meadows and in Lisbon's small gardens. And she was never hungry. Fish and fresh fruit seemed always available, and last week there had been a huge pig slaughter, celebrated with feasts of roast pork, cracklings, and blood pudding.

The rain misted often these last few weeks, but even the occasional downpour couldn't dampen Cate's joy in the warm house she lived in and the paved streets she wandered. King Afonso invited the pilgrims to visit the castle gardens, and whenever she could Cate sat on a bench in the warmth of the sunny, protected garden filled with vines of purple flowers spilling over the walls and rows of almond and orange trees, breathing in the strong sweet scent of their blossoms. Sometimes she was joined by a sad-eyed woman wearing a lovely light blue and gold headscarf who always made a point of crossing herself then looking down when she saw Cate.

Jerusalem will be even better, though, Cate assured herself. She closed her eyes and lifted her face to the sun, dreaming of Jerusalem, the City of God, the center of the world. She imagined herself braving the assaults of Saracen pirates who would suddenly fall face down at the sight of her guardian angels. In her mind, she saw herself crossing a plain to see the walls of the Holy City bathed in ethereal light and dropping to her knees in awe. She pictured herself at Christ's tomb lighting a candle whose wisps would reach to heaven, touching the hands of Christ. She wanted to hear the trumpets announcing Christ's return.

And yet, every ethereal image in her mind faded as she remembered the screaming men and their gangrenous wounds. Her reveries weren't clean anymore as memories of starving children and withering bloody faces on spears intruded. It grieved her that this was the path to the Kingdom of God, and she prayed for strength. She consoled herself with the knowledge that someday soon all this pain would end, and the world would be made right.

Cate could seldom get away to contemplate these mysteries as most days she and Mary gathered and ground the plants and herbs they'd need for Jerusalem. They soaked dried oats and barley, malting them once they sprouted in stone hearths they found in their new home. Once a week they set aside their other tasks to brew ale from the malted grains. Its sour smell filled the courtyards and kept the soldiers nearby where they practiced chess, a game the Portuguese had taught them. Acha joined Cate and Mary most afternoons, weaving undyed thread into cloths and blankets as quickly as they could. The three women fell into a rhythm of work, made less monotonous by singing songs from home.

~

Rain drifted onto the carts and slicked the bricked streets as Sperleng and Egric hauled their cart filled with barrels of water, sacks of grain, and bags of dried fruit toward the ships. The days since Epiphany had been cool and gloomy, but no ice had formed in the river and the Council decided it was time to set sail, so they could be in the Holy Land by Easter. Lent was approaching, and the council and the priests would vigorously enforce the fast. *Especially Willard with his new-found zeal,* Sperleng thought crossly. Better to be as close to Jerusalem as possible before they stopped eating meat and starved themselves all day.

Knights stood guard along the harbor as the sailors and soldiers loaded, some upon new mounts taken from the Moors. The holds were almost full and there were fewer soldiers now, but Sperleng knew these supplies wouldn't last. They'd need to restock all too soon. Sperleng had heard men who'd returned from Jerusalem tell about the weeks of siege, the lack of bread, the Saracens hiding near wells and springs to slaughter any who came to drink, and the hot, barren deserts. He thought it unlikely the Saracens there would store food outside their walls.

~

On Candlemas, the pilgrims were ready to leave. Bishops Pedro and Gilbert of Hastings joined them in the cathedral to bless their journey, and the pilgrims reaffirmed their promise of the Cross. Willard helped light the hundreds of candles that filled the church, thanking Christ the light of the world each time. He felt sad to be leaving Rodrigo and the boys in the camp but was filled with anticipation about meeting the monks of the Order of St. John at the Hospital in Jerusalem.

In a bag he wore underneath his clothing, Willard carried a letter Rodrigo had written to Master Raymond, leader of the Order. Willard tried to fight off the pride he felt thinking about this, knowing humility was the virtue the monks most prized. *I am weak, Lord,* he prayed, yet he couldn't fight the smile that kept coming to his face as they passed through the narrow streets and the hastily repaired city gates up the ramp into the ship. *Jerusalem!* Willard was on fire with anticipation to see Calvary and Mount Zion and venerate the True Cross. He and Rodrigo had talked about the meaning of Jerusalem many times, the place where heaven and earth touch, where Christ will return in glory to judge the living and the dead, the gateway to paradise. Rodrigo told Willard about the promise of paradise once Jerusalem was secured for Christ, that the land would become filled with milk and honey, watered by the sacred spring, a place where Jews and Saracens would see the Truth and worship Christ. Willard thrilled that such a paradise could be gained under the shadow of his sword. He would do all he was able to see that happen.

Streams of men boarded the ships. At the last, the knights walked their horses into the holds, talking gently to their covered heads. Many steeds tried to stop or pull away, but eventually all were loaded. The sailors dragged in the ramp, closed the doors to the hold, and pulled up the anchors. Oarsmen slowly rowed the ship to the middle of the river as Willard watched the castle's diminishing towers. Once they reached midstream, the sailors lifted the sail, and the ship jerked forward as it caught the wind and skimmed the calm water.

PART THREE

*A NEW LIFE
1148—1153*

TWENTY

W ary of cities in this hostile land, the ships kept the coastline barely in sight. They sailed past Moorish strongholds but anchored when they saw the mouth of a river or a small settlement that seemed easy prey for the fleet to replenish their water and supplies. Cate stayed on board most nights, preferring the safety of the ship to the noise of soldiers drinking a farmer's wine and looting his ranch.

The journey was slow. Some days the air was still, leaving the oarsman to make what progress they could. During calm days, Willard would bring out a chess set Rodrigo had given him as a gift, the dark wood pieces carved with turbans and curved swords and the light pieces having crosses painted on their chests. Willard refused to teach Cate or any of the women but used the game to teach soldiers of the martyrs in Jerusalem and the glory of their cause.

Cate sat nearby when Sperleng played Egric, trying to figure out what Willard refused to explain.

"How are you so good at this game?" Sperleng said after losing to Egric for the third time.

"It's like a game the traders played in the taverns at home," Egric said. "I've played it many times."

Sperleng held one of the serf pieces in his hand before placing it on the board. "This is us, lining up in front of the castle and king."

"The first to go," Egric agreed.

After Sperleng lost for the fourth time, he decided to watch the sea instead.

"Would you like to play?" Egric asked Cate.

"Yes!" Cate said. "But you will need to show me."

Egric was a patient teacher, first explaining how the serfs could only move one square at a time, but that the knights could sneak past, moving crookedly through them. The game was over, he said, when the other side took the king or eliminated all the king's protection. Once they started playing, Egric often touched her hand when she was about to make an unwise move, explaining why she might not want to choose it.

"This is hard," Cate said.

"You need to plan, to think many moves ahead," Egric said.

"But I don't know how you're going to move; how can I plan?"

"Try to figure out what would be my best move, then block it. Unless that opens up your king or queen to attack."

After a couple of games, it started to make at least some sense to Cate. Sperleng came back and watched their third game, clenching his fist every time Egric touched her. When the game was finished, Cate could see Sperleng was angry by the thin line of his lips and the creases in his forehead.

"Find us some ale," Sperleng said. "I'm ready to play again."

After the evening meal that night Sperleng and Willard approached Cate as she was bagging the tankards.

"It's not seemly for you to play games with the men," Willard said.

One more thing I'm not allowed to do, Cate thought to herself as she looked down and away.

Eventually the land curved toward the morning sun, and Cate sighted the towers of a large city that the sailors called Hairon. The council had decided this was a Moorish city worth sacking, and one by one the ships beached as men, women, and children fled their houses and streamed toward Hairon's gates.

The sailors lowered the ramps into the shallows, and the knights and their horses splashed their way to dry ground. One hundred fifty shiploads of knights, archers, and foot soldiers armed with swords and axes swarmed the land surrounding the city walls, cutting down anyone who had not yet sheltered behind the gates. The pilgrims unloaded several mangonels and battering rams, and directed them at the walls, whose stones soon loosened in several places. The assault went on for two days, until Hairon's elders stood on their tower gate, arms raised, demanding to know what the pilgrims desired.

The council agreed to discuss a truce, and soon the elders arrived at the council's tents with forty armed men, with hundreds more lining the open gates. The council demanded sacks of grain, dried fish and fruit, and a great sum of money. The Moors promised the food, but said they were a poor city, unable to give such a large sum. The Council sent the elders to find what they could, keeping the forty as hostages until their ransom was paid.

Throughout the next day men dragged carts filled with food and wine and oil outside the wall, and the leaders of each ship took their share. By nightfall each ship's stores were full, but the Moors had brought no treasure. The elders proclaimed they had given all they were able and asked to meet again at sunrise. In the morning, as the ships moved toward deep water, Cate's hands tightly gripped the sides of the ship while she watched the sun create shadows of the forty men hanged from trees near the city's walls.

By the first day of Lent they had depleted their supplies of dried meat and cheese, and the sparse meals became a monotony of pottage and the occasional fish. The journey to Almería took much longer than anyone hoped, and there were few places safe to land after leaving Hairon. As they sailed through the narrows between Hispania and Africa, tall, muscular black men on magnificent war horses lined the shores, and others in ships followed the pilgrims waving their large curved swords, sometimes clashing with the last ships. Two ships and their many men were lost. The sailors strained to keep the ships out of arrow range from the shore, often pulling up the sail so the oarsmen could better maneuver.

As they neared Almería, the outlines of its castle slowly emerged from the gray rock face of the hills, first two tall towers then a long expanse of merlons and crenels gray against the pale blue of the sky. Some ships already anchored in port had large triangular sails while a few galleys had a smaller sail in front of the large mid-ship sail. That they were Christian ships was obvious from the large red crosses painted on each sail, some with four smaller crosses embraced in the arms of the larger one. As these ships came into view, the pilgrims gathered on deck and shouted. Willard lifted his arms as he shouted a prayer of thanksgiving, and Cate, too, found herself weeping gratefully, safe again among Christians.

As always, the horses disembarked first, and Cate envied their excited splashing and neighing as she leaned over the shields lining the deck. Once again Sperleng ordered her to wait on the ship until they'd found a place to stay, so she decided to enjoy the spectacle rather than joining the crowd pressing toward the ramp. Soon a large group of men gathered along the beach, led by a tall man wearing a brown cap, its pointed top falling softly to one side. He wore a loose red tunic cinched at the waist with a woven leather belt from which hung a short sword. His flax-colored cloak was tied with a silver brooch over his right shoulder, and it lifted in the wind like a flag, showing a large red cross over his left shoulder. Next to him, armed men dressed in plain brown tunics and short boots stood straight, some wearing leggings but most not, with round brimmed hats to keep the sun out of their eyes. Saher clasped the hand of the man in the red tunic, and after a while the two men led their knights toward the city's main gate. Cate and Mary brought ale to Willard and the other men who stayed on board and sat with them as the afternoon dragged on.

Sperleng returned the next morning. He led Cate and Mary and his men through the gate past a large open area with a well and many cisterns. Cate looked up to see houses that grew larger and more colorful the closer they were to the citadel. Sperleng stopped in front of a large stone house. Inside, the floors of the house were of chipped brick, with many cobwebs drooping near the ceilings and in the corners. Most of the rooms were empty or contained splintered sleeping pallets. The house formed a square around an open yard that was sunny and inviting, and Cate saw several foot soldiers from their ship had already braced a large iron pot over the top of a fire.

Cate set a sack of grain she had carried in a bucket from the ship along an inner wall, then carried her bucket toward a nearby cistern. Egric joined her, taking Mary's bucket and offering to fill it for her.

At eventide, as Cate and Mary handed out pottage and ale to the soldiers sitting around the fire, Sperleng and Gilbert returned from a gathering of the pilgrims' leaders.

"Men," Gilbert said, "our Genoese brothers have asked us to stay in Hispania a while longer. The Saracens still hold much land here, and Ramón Berenguer, Count of Barcelona and Prince of Aragon, has asked all Christian soldiers to continue the battle in Tortosa."

Not again! Cate thought, and she saw Willard stiffen and frown.

"Almería was claimed for Christ through the bravery of the Genoese and the Christians of Hispania, and now Count Berenguer seeks to surround the Saracens and cut off their harbors and supplies. Many Genoese are already in Barcelona getting ready for battle. Barcelona and Tortosa are cities of great wealth, and Berenguer has promised land and reward to all who help in this just cause."

The camp quieted, the tension thick as the men frowned and fidgeted and whispered to their neighbors.

"Men," Gilbert said, "I know this is a lot to consider, and each man's choice is his own. I have decided to join the Genoese, and I will share my reward with any who join me."

"I will join you," Sperleng said. "Where you go, I go. And where you stay, I will stay."

Stunned, the group was silent. Then men began shouting questions.

"Who is this Berenguer," some asked. "Can we trust him?"

"Will there be land for us all, or only a few nobles?" others shouted.

Willard stood quickly, his body stiff and hands clenched.

"My own brother, violating his promise of the Cross," Willard shouted. "I never would have believed it."

"The Bishop of Rome sanctioned this fight. You agreed in Lisbon that this was God's will!" Sperleng shouted back.

"We cannot wait another year to help Jerusalem!"

"The King of Frankia and a mighty army are on their way to the holy land. We can fight the Saracen here and join them after."

Is this the same as in Lisbon? Cate wondered. Like Willard, she longed to go to Jerusalem. Would they delay forever, each time the Christians in Hispania asked? *There are heathen all over the world; isn't it our mission to save Jerusalem?* She heard them arguing long into the night and fell asleep to angry voices.

Egric was already awake when Cate gathered her bucket to find water, and he walked quietly with her as they checked a few depleted cisterns then went to the main well. After they filled their containers, Egric asked her to sit with him. He stumbled over his words, then took her hand.

"Cate, I know you are young and that we are in the middle of war, but when this is over might you consider marrying me? I think Willard will not join Sperleng and Gilbert in Tortosa. He wants to be a Hospitaller knight in Jerusalem, not a simple priest in Hispania. But my loyalty is to Sperleng, and so I am hoping you will come with us and not go with Willard to Jerusalem."

"I don't know what to say, Egric."

"But will you think about it?"

Cate squeezed his hand. "I will."

Cate spent the rest of the day in a daze. She wanted both Egric and Jerusalem. How could she choose? The divisions among the pilgrims became increasingly angry. Two other nobles, Gerald and Osbert, joined Gilbert in deciding to fight again in Hispania. William Viel came by, announcing that he had no interest in staying any longer, and inviting any of Brycgstow's soldiers to join him in following the African coast toward Jerusalem.

Lord Saher came in the evening. "I have heard the men of Brycgstow plan to break their promises again. Is it true?" he shouted as he shook his fist at Gilbert and Sperleng, then turned to the gathered troops. "Well, I and the rest of Christ's faithful will go to Jerusalem. I will find places on my ships for any loyal men not lured by Berenguer's bribes."

Willard stood quickly. "I will keep the promise of the Cross."

"Of course," Saher said angrily. "Only the priest among the men of Brycgstow is ready to keep his promise. I should have expected nothing less of you pile of mutinous dung. Come with me. The men of God always need another priest."

As Willard hurriedly gathered his things, a few other men stood, too, and asked to join Saher. Most avoided looking at Sperleng as they scurried off.

Cate's need to choose suddenly became real. She loved Willard and had always felt much closer to him than to Sperleng, despite how this pilgrimage had changed him. She had already lost so much—her mother and father, Linn and Cearl and Aedra, and all that was familiar. After so much death, the thought of children and a family called to her, a physical need. She was torn between her longing to complete her pilgrimage and her desire for Egric. These thoughts consumed her, and she found herself hiding from everyone, looking for every chance to be alone and worry.

In the quiet, Cate tried to imagine life with Egric, having children, spending her life spinning and cooking and caring for everyone like her mother did. Then she tried to call up her daydreams about the Holy City, imagining a different life without Egric, but that thought made her weep. Increasingly she thought about how she felt when she was with him, the warmth and dizziness she'd never experienced before. She knew Mary would scoff at that as a reason to stay with someone for the rest of her life, or even as a reason for choosing to stay in Hispania.

Cate wished for the first time that her father would make this decision for her. She did not know how. When she was with the group cooking or cleaning or fetching water, she did so in a daze, hearing but not comprehending what others were saying. After reminding Cate three times that she needed to stir the pot, Mary put her hands on Cate's shoulders.

"Cate, what is wrong with you?" Mary said in exasperation. "Why are you so distracted?"

Cate finally focused her attention on Mary. "I just don't know what to do!"

"Do? We stay with Sperleng and the men from Brycgstow, of course! We have no choice to make. We are here under Sperleng's protection, and that is the end of it."

"But Willard—"

"Willard is a man, a priest, who can make his own choices," Mary interrupted her. "He can't, and frankly doesn't want to, have his sister following him. Surely you know that from the way he's been acting the last few months."

Cate had to admit Willard was different. Maybe she was remembering a brother who didn't exist anymore. "But we promised to go to Jerusalem," she persisted.

"We are not soldiers, Cate. We promised to help the armies in their fight against the Muhammedans. And we've done that already, and we must help them whether they fight in Hispania or in the Holy Land. I hope that when we finish here, we will complete our pilgrimage at the Church of the Holy Sepulchre, but that is a vow Sperleng and his men have taken too."

"Women should encourage men to keep their vows," Cate said stubbornly.

"That may be, but our duty is to help, not lead."

Cate hesitated, then said quietly, "Egric says he wants to marry me."

Mary smiled. "Everyone knows Egric wants to marry you. Is that what you want? And you can say no but still follow Sperleng."

"I don't know what I want. How did you decide to marry Hafoc?"

"I didn't decide, not really. Hafoc and my father worked it out. I could have refused I suppose, but I didn't want to. Hafoc was a blacksmith; did you know that?" Cate shook her head. "He was from Gloucester and came with Sir Robert when he fought with Stephen. We were to move to Gloucester when we had children." Mary looked away as if seeing the life that never was.

"What should I do?" Cate asked.

"You should stay with Brycgstow's army; of that I am sure. Marriage is up to you if you have Sperleng's blessing. Talk to him. Egric is a good man, you know that."

Cate resolved to talk with Sperleng, but he came to her instead. He had spent most of the last few days with Gilbert at the estates of the Genoese, returning in the evening to talk with each of his men until late in the night. He returned this night as Cate was handing out bowls to the men, rubbing his hands together distractedly and telling her gruffly that he had something to say to her. Cate ladled a few more bowls, then followed him inside to a small room lit by a single candle on a table that sent their shadows flickering across the walls.

"You haven't given Egric an answer yet. What does that mean?" Sperleng asked.

"I thought we were going to Jerusalem and nothing would change until after that," Cate said. "Now you are going to Tortosa and Willard has left us and Egric says he wants to marry me and Mary is no help. I am afraid to marry Egric and afraid not to. I want to go to Jerusalem, but not without you or Mary. What should I do? Tell me!"

At this Sperleng laughed. Loudly. "Ah, my headstrong sister who always acts as if she knows what to do is asking for my advice?"

"Please don't make fun of me, Sperleng. I don't know what to do. Would I have your blessing if I married Egric?"

"Cate, Egric talked to me before he talked to you. He is under my command; he can't approach my sister without my permission. I told him he should wait until our pilgrimage was finished before making any decisions or promises, and that was our agreement until we came here and Gilbert decided to join the Genoese. Egric wants to stay with us but remembers his vow and is trying to decide whether to join Gilbert or go to Jerusalem with Saher's ships. He will stay with us if you will have him, but if you will not he wants to be wherever you are not. I've told him he must be settled before I will give you permission to marry. This marriage is far in the future even if you agree. Which I think you should."

"How long?"

"Egric has no money, no land, and his skill is as an archer. That's fine for a soldier, but not for a husband. He knows that too. I don't know when that will change because only God knows when we will have victory. If Gilbert is given land in Hispania, he has promised me a tenancy. If the acreage is large, perhaps there will be some for Egric. But as long as there is a war to fight, Egric will be a soldier. Who knows how long that will be?"

"And what about Jerusalem?"

"We will take our pilgrimage to Jerusalem as soon as we can."

Cate found it strangely comforting that she could accept Egric without marrying right away. After Tortosa they'd go to Jerusalem to finish their pilgrimage. Cate threw her arms around Sperleng, thanking him. Then she went to look for Egric. She found him sitting alone in front of the fire, glancing towards the archway where she emerged. She sat down next to him, smiling. She put her arm through his.

"Yes," was all she said.

TWENTY-ONE

Sperleng marveled at the bustle of men working in Barcelona's dockyards. In the harbor, Genoese galleys with their triangular sails were sleeker and taller than the ships the Normans preferred, but Sperleng felt proud of their ability to navigate rivers and moor closer to shore. Barcelona's harbor was not as protected as Brycgstow's or Lisbon's, and all the sails were lashed securely to their masts, their ropes creating a web of muscles for the skeletons of the ships. In the shipyards, Sperleng looked closely at huge round ships under construction, wondering how they would fare under battle. Gilbert had told him they were used for carrying goods and troops and pilgrims, but Sperleng couldn't help but worry that a ship like that would fall to the first swift pirate ship that rammed a hole in its side. Well, the smaller ships would need to make sure none got that close.

The Normans used the shipyards to start constructing new siege towers. Each day men dragged trees from the countryside and slowly transformed them into planks and poles. The Normans' tower designer had gone with Saher to Jerusalem, but the Genoese had several to oversee construction. Sperleng wished they all spoke the same type of Latin, but sometimes even the Barcelonans and Genoese didn't understand each other, and local priests began spending their days at the yards to help with communication.

Sperleng spat when he thought about Willard abandoning them. *There are Templars and Hospitallers here in Barcelona for Christ's sake. Why couldn't he wait to go to Jerusalem? Brycgstow's men need a priest.* Sperleng shook his head in disgust. Willard had vowed to rejoin Sperleng in Jerusalem, but Sperleng had no patience for disloyalty, and decided to think of Willard as one of his men who had died. He knew Cate was still grieving, but now she had the distraction of Egric's attention.

Sperleng smirked when he remembered Willard's reaction to the news of Cate's betrothal to Egric. Willard had rushed back to the house in Almería offering, then demanding, that he perform the sacrament immediately. Egric had readily agreed, but Sperleng took his father's role and said the time was not right as they were in the middle of planning a war and Egric had nothing for the bride price.

"People will think her a whore!" Willard shouted.

"I will cut down anyone who says that!" Sperleng shouted back.

"And I will take an arrow to their heart," Egric promised, "I will not allow anyone to dishonor her."

Willard then summoned Cate but stormed off after they met. *But Lord*, Sperleng thought, *let there be no bastards. This is no time for a marriage.*

Sperleng walked back through Barcelona's massive walls, thick enough for two knights on horseback to stand between the high arched entry and the city's streets. Soldiers patrolled from the top of these walls, pacing between the crenelated towers that interspersed the flat expanses every few hundred feet. Berenguer conducted his business and housed his family and the families of his favored generals in the citadel. Berenguer had given generously to the church, and Sperleng passed construction work on a cathedral, an abbey, several smaller churches, and a large building housing the Templar knights along the main streets in the walled city. Sperleng and his men set up camp near a blacksmith outside the wall near the market and the small convent and hospital where Cate and Mary spent their days tending the sick and preparing medicines.

Now that Lent was over, Sperleng spent evenings with his men in the market's taverns slowly forgetting the pain of Lisbon's battles and lost friends. Barcelona's women were welcoming, and Sperleng laughed and sang as he hadn't since leaving Brycgstow more than a year ago now. The crowded taverns were clean, with tables outside looking onto a large open square. At twilight, the innkeepers lit large lanterns that swung gently over the tables and along the square. Count Berenguer had decreed that the pilgrims were to be treated as guests, with food and wine given for free, but Sperleng found that the food came more quickly, and the portions were larger and of better quality, when he shared coins from his Lisbon booty. Sperleng and his men soon found a favorite place where they stayed long into the night telling stories and singing.

When Cate and Mary joined them, the tavern owner brought out his best bread and drove away the local women. Life felt almost normal again, and Sperleng dreaded the trip he knew was coming. *But that's what life is, days of plenty with friends and food and song interspersed with days of hunger and trouble and pain and loss. Only God knows which tomorrow will be.*

Some days Sperleng walked to the Hospitallers' complex north of the walls, where a few of the warrior monks lived in a small complex on the building site Count Berenguer had given them for a new church and monastery. Sperleng asked for news of the Holy Land. He had found one priest who understood him there, and they spoke of Willard's plans to join the Hospitallers in Jerusalem. The priest said he would ask the knights who came from Jerusalem if they had any news of the shiploads of pilgrims from Brycgstow. So far, they had heard nothing.

~

At the infirmary, Cate dressed the wound of a young farmer who had cut himself while plowing his field. The air was filled with the pungent smells of vinegar and blood and the sounds of his wife's crying. When the children weren't running around the room picking up jars and asking Cate questions she could barely understand, she tried to have them name things for her. Without Willard to help translate, Cate felt isolated. In Lisbon, they had lived surrounded by English soldiers, and first Willard and then Sperleng or Egric told her what was happening. The little language she'd learned from Milah and the other camp followers seemed useless here, leaving her to communicate by pointing and by telling the children "No!" a hundred times a day. They seemed to understand that.

But Cate wanted a teacher, someone who could help her learn the language of what she was sure would be her new home. If Sperleng and Egric received land, they would never return to Brycgstow. Unless she could convince Egric they should go home. But what would he do there? Egric told her his family were farmers, and his eyes shone when he talked about the possibility of having land to tend and children to teach the ways he'd learned. No, she knew in her heart this was where she would die.

Early the next morning, as the sun brightened the edges of the hills, Cate and Mary joined the lay sisters on their weekly trip to the market. They walked among the brightly colored stalls filled with oranges, almonds, figs, dates, and many other fruits and vegetables she did not recognize. They passed multicolored cloth that moved as they passed, silver crosses on strands of leather, carpets with intricate designs. She never knew there were so many kinds of fresh fish and dried meat, cheeses, and breads. Cate was always awed at the variety, although just once, she thought, an apple might be nice.

When she saw a round of cheese that looked good, Cate hoped for a taste before buying and tried to explain that to the merchant by pointing to it. He immediately handed her the whole wheel and put out his hand for payment. Cate shook her head, and the man began talking loudly and angrily. Her guards stepped toward him as Cate used the phrases she used most often since she arrived: "I'm sorry. I don't understand."

One of the sisters spoke to the merchant quietly, and he calmed down. He sliced a small amount of cheese and gave it to Cate. Cate smiled; it tasted wonderful. Mary then marked off a portion of the wheel and looked questioningly at Cate. Cate moved her hand to a larger portion and nodded her head. The sister then had an animated conversation with the merchant, starting to leave several times, until, finally, they agreed on a price. Mary paid from Sperleng's allowance, and Cate wondered whether they'd paid too much. She had to trust the sisters. What choice did she have until she understood?

Cate and Mary brought their purchases to Sperleng's camp early enough to help prepare the evening meal. When she saw Sperleng, Cate placed a plate of pork in front of him, garnished with olives and almonds. Sperleng grunted a greeting and tore a piece of flesh from the bone.

"Sperleng?" she said.

He looked up at her.

"I would like someone to teach me the language of this place."

"Why? You know the names for many things, and you never go anywhere except the convent and where we are."

"The merchants don't understand me. When we go to the markets, I fear we may be swindled because I don't understand what they are saying. I could bargain better if I spoke their language."

Sperleng considered this. "That's true. I often wonder what Berenguer's soldiers are saying." He sat back and thought for a while. "But I think we will learn soon enough."

"But the more quickly I learn, the more I can overhear what people are saying. Perhaps that would be helpful too."

Sperleng thought about this. "Where would you find a teacher?"

"Maybe Sir Gilbert would know."

"Why don't you ask Gilbert's priest? He is staying at the abbey too," Sperleng said.

The next morning, after the priests and nuns ate their morning meal and the leavings had been cleaned, Cate waited outside the chapel. She approached the Norman priest as he left mid-morning prayers and quietly asked if she could speak with him.

"What is it, young one?" he asked kindly. "Do you have a confession to make?"

"No, it isn't that," she said quickly, then hesitated, remembering some of her thoughts about Egric. "At least not right now. I was wondering if you could teach me the language of this place? I am finding it hard to understand the patients at the hospital, or even to buy fruit at the market. I feel I could be so much more useful if I could talk with people."

The priest nodded. "It would be helpful to better understand what they're saying, but I'm afraid I struggle too. The Barcelonans speak a kind of Latin, and I can usually make out what people mean if they speak slowly enough, but I'm no teacher. I'll ask the prioress if she knows of anyone willing to provide instruction."

Every day Cate waited for news from the priest, but after a week passed, she lost hope and kept asking the nuns to name things for her as often as she dared. When they began turning at the sight of her, Cate played naming games with the children who came in with their ill parents. One afternoon, as Mary mixed yet another remedy to help a pregnant woman keep down her food, Cate tried playing the naming game with her young son. The boy seemed to know only a few words: Petrus, his name, and *pila*, which seemed to be the ball he was holding in his hand. Suddenly the doorway darkened, and the imposing figure of Abbess Maria entered, her long black habit sweeping the dust from the stone floor.

"*Anglica*," she said, beckoning to Cate. "*Veni*."

Cate jumped to her feet and looked at Mary, who nodded her head. The abbess turned around and strode through the arched cloister to the courtyard where the Norman priest stood with a woman wearing the simple dark brown tunic and white headdress of a novice. She appeared to be a few years older than Cate. The priest took advantage of pauses in the abbess's speech to tell Cate that this young novice, Sister Ermessa, knew some of their language and would help Cate learn the language of Hispania. Cate smiled at Sister Ermessa and dropped to her knees, kissing the hem of the abbess's dress.

"*Gratias, gratias,*" Cate kept saying.

The abbess took Cate's hand and lifted her, a little brusquely Cate thought. "Si, si," the abbess said, letting go of her hand and then hustling away.

"Let's sit on these benches for a while," the priest said. "I would be glad to learn a little more, too, although the abbess made it clear that after today I must stay away from you and the sisters."

Sister Ermessa, Cate finally understood, was the second daughter of a wealthy merchant who had married a woman from Wessex, a woman of great beauty and uncertain, at least to Cate's understanding of the halting conversation, origins. Her father had bought her a place in the convent. She was eager to learn about her mother's home. The three of them struggled through the rest of the afternoon until the priest and sister left for Vespers, and Cate went to help Mary prepare the evening meal.

"What did the Abbess want with you?" Mary asked.

"She found someone to teach me their Latin," Cate said happily as she chopped olives and onions and other odd vegetables they used in Barcelona.

Mary stared at her, speechless for a few moments. "You asked the abbess to find you a teacher?"

"Well, no," Cate admitted, "I asked the Norman priest, and he asked the abbess. There's a novice here whose mother spoke our language, and she agreed to teach me when she and I have time. You should join us when you can."

"I might. And you can teach me what you learn," Mary said.

Two days passed before Cate met with Sister Ermessa again. They agreed to meet in the courtyard after Sext when they could, as this time between the midday and mid-afternoon services was when many took naps. The stone benches were cool, but the sun in the cloudless sky warmed them.

"I am grateful for your help," Cate said, looking at the intricate tiles that paved the walkways and pillars. She loved the way the designs turned and twisted, sometimes into flowers or suns or knots. The tiles along the edges were glazed with color, bright blues and greens and yellow with hints of red and orange.

Sister Ermessa nodded and smiled. "Let's go to the kitchen and see what you already know," she said in her heavily accented speech.

Cate pointed to pieces of bread and fruit on the table, *"pan, figues, limon, aranhas*. Should we walk around, and I'll name things?"

"Yes," Ermessa said.

Cate named what she knew, and Ermessa named the things she did not. They then walked to the hospital, where Petrus sat near his mother waiting for Mary, the ball in his lap. The boy jumped up and laughed when Cate entered and said "*Pila*" as he threw the ball at her. He followed her as she named things. Thinking this was a game, Petrus started naming things before she could. Ermessa frowned, and said something to his mother, who carried him toward the stream that ran alongside the convent.

"*Riu*," she heard Petrus say. "*Pedra*."

"You know many words," Ermessa said. "We will have conversation."

"That is what I cannot do," Cate admitted sadly.

"I will say; you will learn."

After two hours, Cate was exhausted and returned to her room to take a nap as Ermessa joined the sisters at None. Cate slept fitfully, dreaming of skeletal children reaching for figs, bread, and oranges as Ermessa named them and Willard snatched them away. Then Cate and Aedra were laughing beside the Frome, turning to see crows circling, but when she turned back, she stood alone next to the Tagus, no ships in sight. She began running in the river, looking for anyone she knew, but she could get nowhere as the sand and rocks stopped her progress. She tried to scream, but the sound would not come, and the bright sun glared malevolently. She awoke suddenly, sure she had heard the crash of stones, but when she opened her eyes, all was quiet and hot, her body covered with a thin layer of sweat. She lay back staring at the rough and cracked wood of the ceiling, waiting for the pounding of her heart to stop.

~

On the Feast of Saints Peter and Paul, Mary joined the pilgrims gathered with the people of Barcelona on a hill near the harbor to receive the bishop's blessing. For days the pilgrims, sailors, and the young men of Barcelona had been removing ballast stones from the ships and filling them with barrels of grain and wine, swords, arrows, axes, lumber, and the frames for siege towers. Today the ships sat low in the water, bobbing in the wind and the waves, their ramps leading to the shore or the shallows, their sails seemingly reaching toward the large white clouds scattered through the sky.

Mary stood with Cate at the edge of the crowd with the women of the abbey, unable to hear the bishop's words but able to see him as he raised the cross, then raised his arms in a sign of blessing. It was a blistering hot morning, and Mary dreaded the crowded ships filled with men and horses. She closed her eyes and prayed fervently for kinder, more generous thoughts. They were going to save Tortosa from the tyranny of the Saracens as they had the people of Lisbon.

When the bishop's blessing concluded, men surged down the hill towards the tables of food lining the harbor, seeming to fear they might not eat ever again. Several sailors stuffed oranges and cheese in their bags as Mary and the other women ran to refill the rapidly depleting bushels.

Sperleng stood nearby with Egric, directing his soldiers to their ship at the far southern edge of the shore. The men seemed eager to leave. Knights led their horses into the ships. When all others had boarded, Mary and Cate followed a Norman priest up the ramp, and Sperleng helped the sailors lift and secure it in the hold.

The Templar ships rowed out first, then raised their whitened sails to display a large red cross that billowed open in a sudden gust. Then went Count Berenguer's and the Genoese ships, a few double-masted, most with square or almost square sails, some with uneven four-sided or triangular sails. Each had a visible cross on the broad end of the large sail, Berenguer's ships obvious from the red stripes on their yellowed sails.

The Norman ships left last. They rowed toward open water, then raised their square sails. The winds were fair, and their ships soon ran even with the Templar ships as they lifted and dropped on the choppy sea.

Mary breathed in the clean smell of the water, and turned her face toward the wind, trying to forget the simple logic of battle: win or die.

TWENTY-TWO

Ebro River
July 1148

After a two days' sail, the fleet entered the mouth of a large river and beached their boats along an empty stretch of land. Sperleng splashed through the cool water to join the leaders on shore. Count Berenguer sent a third of his and the Genoese knights to scout the strength of the Tortosans and find a place to camp. They returned at midday, directing the ships upriver. Soon it was too shallow for the larger ones. The Templar and Norman ships could go farther, nearer the great fortress and the mountains.

As they passed the citadel, the stream turned, and Sperleng heard a distant rush of water. The Templars had taken over a mill along the Ebro river's stony shores, and Sperleng and his men helped them divert water towards cisterns on a nearby abandoned farm. Squires led the restive horses towards the troughs and corrals as bowmen set up a perimeter guard. The bottoms of the clouds briefly reddened then grayed as the sun dropped.

The night was hot with little breeze. No clouds blocked the moon, and Sperleng caught occasional glimpses of wild boar snuffling along the forest line, and tall deer-like animals with large curved horns standing alert and then darting up the sides of nearby hills. In the silence, he could hear the calls of the night birds. This hot, spare land amazed Sperleng, an alien land with cliffs higher than any he had seen and animals he would have thought a fantasy if he hadn't seen them with his own eyes. As the sky lightened he saw spirals of smoke downriver and knew it had begun. He resolved to fight as if this were already his home.

At midday, a rush of dust and hooves and striped banners announced the coming of soldiers. Count Berenguer tore off his helmet and threw it toward his page, calling for all the ships' leaders to listen. Just behind him the Genoese leader drew his sword and raised it high, an action that led the Templars to drop to one knee.

"Discipline, we need discipline!" Berenguer shouted. "Already some of the Genoese have stormed the citadel, unprepared, and they are lost. Fools! I thank the monks and soldiers here for waiting for orders instead of running off like children at some game. You've been in battle before and know we can't just run and kick the walls down or scare the enemy into surrender by waving our swords!"

Sperleng and Gilbert looked at each other, remembering the over-zealous soldiers at Lisbon and how angry the pilgrims' leaders had been.

"We must finish our siege towers, gather huge rocks for our trebuchet, fill in the ditches around the walls, cut off their water and food supplies! Do this first, and victory is ours!" The men shouted approval.

Gilbert and Sir Jaume, the chief Templar knight, walked the count around the camp. Berenguer nodded approvingly at the barley stores and flour at the mill and pointed toward the olive groves in the distance surrounding them. As the Barcelonans galloped toward their camps, Gilbert called his men together.

"Count Berenguer has a good plan. He wants us to patrol the closest sections of the wall to make sure no one enters or escapes and gather what we can from the farms around us, then burn them to dust."

Several men gasped, including Sperleng who had hoped for one of these farms for himself someday.

"We need to be able to see when anyone comes near," Gilbert said, "and can't let them hide in tall brush. We are surrounded by Saracens here despite the vast spaces and rugged terrain. And the fires will frighten others into leaving. But save those olive groves in the distance and bring any animals you can to the corrals. There are plenty of fish, but we don't want to live on just that for the next months."

Few crops were ready for harvest. Cate and Mary joined Sperleng's group of soldiers foraging closest to the mill to gather grapes, small figs and what barley was left in the fields. Egric watched bee swarms to find several hives, and he promised to return at dusk to smoke the bees and gather the honey. When they returned to camp, Mary spread out the grapes and figs to dry, and Cate began a pottage of water and barley mixed with what vegetables they'd found. Sperleng speared a large carp that he gutted then added to the pot. Soon more men returned, some with food, some carting large rocks, and others with yew branches that the archers quickly began whittling.

"One more day of foraging and we'll start the fires," Sperleng said to the grim nods of his company.

~

"It seems wasteful to me. The wheat will be ready for harvest in a month or so," Cate grumbled to Mary and Egric as they sat around the fire that night. "Can't the soldiers just guard it?"

"Those were our orders," Egric said calmly. "Count Berenguer knows this land and these people better than any of us do. And it takes a lot more men to patrol a field of wheat than to look out over a barren field."

"But I'd hoped," Cate said hesitatingly, "That we'd live in one of these houses."

Egric smiled. "We will build something new on whatever land we are given. It needn't be as grand as any of these, in't it? There's plenty of wood and stone near here, and fine hills near the river that will give us protection from floods and a view of what is coming. Just a small stone house at first, with barns for animals.

Mary will live with us, and we'll live near Sperleng, and his wife will be your friend." Egric looked into the distance, imagining. "Can't you see it?"

When Egric talked, she could. Cate's mind raced with the pictures his words created. She thought of the gardens she and Mary would plant, and how their neighbors would come to her for advice on how to stitch a wound or calm a fever. She thought of children, her children, throwing stones into the river and laughing as Egric chased them with a wooden sword. Such different visions from just a few months ago! She smiled happily at him.

"The fields look pretty dry anyway," Mary said. "There may not be much of a harvest."

Cate had to agree. In the week since they had set sail from Barcelona they'd seen nothing but blank blue sky, and during the day it was hotter than Cate had ever felt. Standing in the sun felt like standing near the cooking fire, and the few trees along the river bank filtered but didn't block the sun.

Already Egric's fair skin had turned bright red and hot to the touch. Cate knew it would peel tomorrow despite the oil mixed with lavender she and Mary handed out all evening to the fair-haired soldiers. The Templars from Hispania and Genoa laughed and said they smelled like women. Cate thought the Templars should try to smell a little better themselves, as even the time they spent in the river didn't rid them of the strong, gamy smell they gave off. *But, then, Milah thought I smelled like fish,* she remembered.

Cate got up the next morning before the muezzin's chant drifted from the castle walls, handing out bread to the men who needed to work while it was still cool. The foraging resumed just as birds began calling to each other and light outlined the spaces between the nearby hills. Sperleng ordered his troops to bring stones from the mountains for leveling the trenches near the walls.

Several knights left to patrol around the castle and see who was left in nearby settlements. Some soon returned herding a stray sheep or with directions to abandoned homes with remaining food stores. Gilbert and Jaume established the camp perimeter, and several men set small fires close by to create a dead zone to protect the camp.

Cate helped set up diversion channels so that the cisterns remained full and the river water was ready to quench any blaze that came too close. Sperleng stayed nearby, spending much of the afternoon working on the siege tower. At camp that night, Gilbert reported that the Genoese had already smashed through one of the wall's towers and removed many barrels of flour and wine.

In the still of the next morning, clusters of men surrounded a nearby field, carrying torches and carts filled with barrels of water. They created firebreaks along the olive groves and began by setting fire to the greenest of the wheat. It smoldered slowly and crept away from the clearings until the archers shot fiery arrows toward the dry grass farthest from the river.

Orange flames quickly outshone the pale yellow of the rising sun. Thick white smoke turned a dark tan as it rose. Burning paths ran through the fields, leaving behind branching black tributaries. Sparks floated upwards then dropped to start new fires.

As the conflagration grew, it created its own current that sped toward the standing grain. Men rushed to put out spot fires the sparks created outside the fire lines or that looked ready to jump toward the trees. Smoke drifted first toward the city then back towards the camps until everyone wore a film of ash on their bodies, and many were coughing despite the cloths covering their faces. By midafternoon the fields were barren and smoking, with only a few patches of orange flame visible when dark came. Soldiers raked ash over glowing spots, and the night watch kept a close eye to make sure no unattended fire took hold.

"As long as we have cool, calm mornings we'll move from field to field," Gilbert announced. "When that's done we'll start across the river."

When Count Berenguer decided the fields had been sufficiently cleared, the boom of boulders against the walls became louder and more frequent. Nearly every day another tower crumbled, and men ran under cover of shields and ox hides to retrieve anything they could through a shower of arrows.

Cate's stomach soured as the tents filled with yet another wave of wounded men, some carried in carts or in soldiers' arms. *How much more will there be this time?* she thought as she hurried to check their wounds. *When will it be finished?* She'd hoped she would be toughened against all this pain, but it took every bit of her strength just to begin. Sperleng rushed in to make sure his men were being cared for, his bloody sword slung loosely at his waist, then rushed out again for more.

How does he do it? Am I the only one who feels sick? Oh, grow up, Cate told herself. *Your stomach hurts; so what? Look at these men with arrows in their shoulders or half of their back covered with burnt flesh.* She tried to remind herself of the purpose of these battles—the glory of Christ, the battle against Satan, bringing the Kingdom of God to this place—but she couldn't get past the blood and the stink.

And how does Egric keep going? He never talked to Cate about it, and after a battle he would sit around the cooking fire telling stories of Arthur and other famous warriors and the glory they earned. Only once had she thought she'd seen tears in his eyes, standing over the bloody body of Gilbert's page, a boy no more than nine who had loved to listen to Egric's stories and often sat next to him as close as he could during the telling.

And after this Jerusalem.

She closed her eyes for a few seconds. It was too much.

"Cate!" Mary shouted. "Bring more cloths and vinegar. Now!"

At least I don't have to see what happens during the raids along the river, Cate thought.

Every day the knights would scout the country-side to make sure no Muslim armies were coming and to drive ranchers from the best land. Egric told Cate if the villagers refused to surrender, the knights would cut off their heads and line them up on poles in view of the wall. Cate hated those displays most of all. She knew it was a war strategy, but she could not look at them, still remembering the soulless eyes staring from a blood-blackened face the one time she did. She tried to talk with Egric about it, but all he would say is that they would do it to us if given the chance.

As the towers fell, the Christian army seemed to be winning. Why wouldn't the Tortosans surrender?

"It's an honor to die for their lords and families," Egric told her. "The Moors believe in a false prophet, and the rich elders are concerned about their loss of land and status, but they are brave in their way. No one wants war or to see their children die, but, like us, they see no other path. They know we will drive them from this land, as we must! The Moors took this land from the Christians and have harassed and killed and made slaves of Christians here for hundreds of years, forcing them to deny that Jesus is God, allowing the Jews to use Christian children in their sacrifices. Think, Cate! If they aren't stopped, the Moors will cross the mountains into France, Normandy, home. No Christian is safe if we turn away. The savagery, the blasphemy, the slaughter of Christians must end here. I'm willing to die for that, and the Tortosans are willing to die to stop us."

The inevitability of it filled Cate with grief. "How much more will it take?" she asked quietly.

"For this battle? Not much longer. The elders have already sent messengers to Count Berenguer asking for a truce. That would give us time to find reinforcements, and to finish filling in the moat near the citadel so we can roll up our siege engines. Berenguer seems confident they will eventually surrender, and we'll keep up the attacks until they do. But the battle against the Moors? I'm not sure it ever will be finished. When will God and the Devil stop fighting? Not until Christ comes again and there is a new heaven and a new earth. Until then, all we can do is to tell the devil: No more. This stops here."

Cate had never heard Egric so passionate about anything. She knew he was a loyal soldier, and the stories he told were tales of glory where the armies of good vanquished the armies of evil. She loved his certainty and his ability to make her more certain too. She leaned her head against his shoulder and he put his arm around her, his fingers brushing her hair from her face. As she looked up at him, Mary called, asking for help.

Cate smiled at Egric as she rose, and she saw the love and desire she felt reflected in his eyes.

TWENTY-THREE

During the weeks before Christmas Sperleng often spied dark shapes in the distance hurrying along trails leading into the mountains and knew the end was coming. Sometimes his men would surround a group, killing the men and children but bringing the women back to camp, tied in ropes.

When the siege ended the week after Christmas, Sperleng settled with Gilbert's troops north of the fortress along the cultivated borders of the city in the houses of the hostage nobles and other Moors who had fled the city. Count Berenguer gave the Suda, the Moor's fortress, to the Templar knights, and the Genoese received the best villas within the now crumbled city walls. The count slowly divided the surrounding ranches among the knights who chose to settle here, and men went out daily to the countryside to choose their land.

The Norman ships would be sailing soon, and the pilgrims had decisions to make. They argued amongst themselves about Jerusalem, the priests reminding them of their duty to complete their vow. But word had come of defeat in the Holy Land, and most knights preferred to go home to their wives and land than to join a defeated army. Hospitallers told Sperleng they'd received word that Willard arrived with the Order at Damascus, but no one knew what happened to him after. Sperleng hoped he was on one of Viel's ships headed here or returning home.

Sperleng had no interest in returning home. He wandered around Tortosa's hilly streets, admiring the grand houses given to the Genoese. Gilbert told him the Genoese, too, were arguing about whether to stay, and many of the Genoese second sons were glad of this chance for land and slaves. Count Berenguer had paid the Genoese with the lives of captured Moors. Those thought to be worth ransom had sent letters to the South, and daily the well-dressed and haughty redeemed by their families were loaded onto ships.

Sperleng often watched auctions of the Moorish poor who had no hope of being ransomed, dreaming of having servants of his own. Some men at auction had piercing, angry eyes, as they stood tied in chains and straight as spears awaiting their turns. Sperleng doubted any of them would make suitable servants. *Only trouble*, he thought. The women mostly huddled together crying for themselves and their lost children. He'd heard some women had taken poison or killed themselves with kitchen knives to avoid what they knew was their fate.

As part of the truce, Count Berenguer allowed some converted Moors to stay, but those who did were driven from their homes to a walled neighborhood of crumbling houses called Aljama that Christian soldiers guarded. Genoese and Norman knights forced rich Jews out of their fine homes, considering these the spoils of victory, while old men, women past childbearing age, the crippled and crazed were offered to Christians as slaves or sent to Aljama to make their way as best they could.

Count Berenguer divided the Moors' gold, silver, and horses between the treasury of Aragon and the nobles who had helped him. In turn, Gilbert shared a portion of his plunder with his men. Cate clapped her hands when Sperleng came home with bolts of expensive cloth for fine new dresses for her and Mary. And their evening meals now usually included meat.

"Gilbert offered to find us servants," Sperleng said.

Cate laughed out loud. "Then what would Mary and I do? We don't need strangers living with us. They surround us already."

As the heat of summer closed in around them, Sperleng prepared to join Berenguer and the Templar Knights in their raids on the Northern city of Lérida.

Sperleng rubbed his hands together with excitement as he told his gathered men what a prize Lérida would be. "We'll be safer, with less worry about a threat from the North or the West, and we can concentrate on protecting and advancing our borders," he said as he chose the men who would accompany him.

"Sir Jaume says you may stay in the Suda's women quarters with the knights' women," Sperleng told Cate and Mary. "It will be safer there."

~

Cate found the Suda fascinating and beautiful. The women had an entire wing of the castle, every window covered by intricate lattice work. As the weeks passed, the women fell into a rhythm of cooking and gardening. Even the noblewomen eventually joined them, putting aside their fine clothes for the softer, loose-fitting breeches the Moors had left behind.

At night the women slept in a common room, and the cries of children often woke Cate. It was comforting to hear the lullabies their mothers or nurses sang to quiet them. Cate felt safe and almost happy, except for her worry about Egric and Sperleng.

One morning, a few weeks after the men left, tower bells began clanging, and Cate looked up from retrieving water from the well to see the Templar brothers running across the courtyard as others dressed in armor arrived. She stopped the Norman priest as he rushed by.

"What's happened?" Cate asked.

"Moors from the south are gathering across the river. They must have heard the count and his men left," he said, then ran toward the armory.

All afternoon, boulders crashed against the river wall. Cate had never heard the boom from inside the walls, and the sound terrorized her. Messengers ran in and out of the gates, sometimes followed by armed soldiers. At the evening meal, the mood was somber.

Sir Jaume stood at the front of the great hall speaking in somber tones while the women served haggard and frowning men. The remaining leaders of Count Berenguer's, the Norman, and Genoese forces nodded their heads.

As she handed one of Gilbert's men a tankard, Cate leaned down. "Have men died?"

The soldier shook his head. "There have been no pitched battles, only the beginning of a siege. We've sent messengers to Barcelona, but no one will arrive in time. Sir Jaume says we don't have sufficient forces to survive and they are debating a truce."

Cate noticed several local women were listening intently. One strode to the front and spoke loudly and passionately, waving a wooden spoon.

"Now what?" Cate asked. She wished she'd had more time to learn from Sister Ermessa.

"That is the wife of one of Count Berenguer's leaders. She says not to give up so easily. She says all the women and children should dress in men's armor and make the Moors think we have more soldiers than we do."

Cate laughed. "Well, why not? It's better than being taken ransom or sold as a slave."

Word passed through the hall quickly, and messengers left to gather everyone in the walled city. Sir Jaume and several brothers brought helmets and axes and swords to distribute to any woman who wanted them. Cate and Mary rushed forward and took a dagger and a hatchet, two leather hoods, a chain mail vest, and a wooden shield.

"We will need to help the wounded too," Mary told Cate. "But until then, we'll go where we're needed."

The night was quiet as men and women lined the city walls. Mary and Cate slept, then took turns with nearby soldiers peering through the long thin breaks in the wall as the light crept up the sides of the mountain. At first, Cate saw nothing but ships lining the river bank. Then a black shadow raced between circles of darkness. She pulled at the sleeve of a nearby archer and pointed. When the shade galloped forward again, several arrows whizzed from the castle wall and the dark figure fell. The battle had begun.

Cate heard a shout and joined dozens of armored women who began rushing up stairs to the top of the wall. Cate saw many figures crouching behind pillars, moving for a few seconds to show themselves, then dodging behind the merlons again. When they reached the top, she and Mary did the same. Cate couldn't tell men from the women and marveled at the audacity of this plan. It just might work.

Skirmishes broke out over the next several days. Cate heard small parties of men crept out in the night, setting fire to whatever enemy weapons or camps they could. During the day, the Christians would shoot barrages of arrows at anything moving within range, and, if the enemy came close enough, sent fire bolts or torches, dropped boiling water or oil. Mary attended to the few wounded; most died instantly as an arrow pierced their body and they dropped from the wall's great height.

One morning Cate woke to cheering and stood to see the mill on fire and the last of the ships rowing out of the shallows. The woman next to her cried as she clung to Cate.

They'll come back, Cate thought.

~

Every day for the next months Cate looked for Egric and Sperleng, hoping to see a cloud of dust in the west that would announce their return, and every day her disappointed hope became fear. What if they never returned? Did the Moors win?

The Hospitallers encouraged Cate and Mary to work in their clinic, having seen their skill with plants and easing the pain of the wounded. As much as Cate hated the fear of not knowing, she was glad she didn't need to follow the soldiers into battle anymore. Now they treated injured soldiers who returned from raids on the countryside, but more often they delivered babies or treated men with painful urination or set children's broken bones and calmed their fevers.

One of the remaining soldiers grumbled about providing solace to the enemy when he learned Moors and Jews came to the clinics too. Mary reminded him this was a different place with different customs. "Count Berenguer has given the Moors *Aljama* and the Jews the old dockyards along the Ebro to build new homes. Who are we," Mary asked, "to question his decision to let them stay?"

The nights became colder, and the farmers planted the winter wheat. One morning, several days after the Feast of All Saints, Cate heard distant horns proclaiming triumph. *This is it,* she thought, *either they have returned, or we are doomed.* As the horses approached, Cate heard cries of joy and soon saw Gilbert's colors on the approaching flags. Sperleng rode near Gilbert at the head, followed by twenty more men. Cate searched anxiously for Egric, finally seeing him toward the rear. *Thank you, God,* she prayed.

"Only ten of Gilbert's men died, two of mine," Sperleng announced after awkwardly dismounting. "Today we'll return to the house outside the wall. Tonight we'll celebrate, and Egric will tell the story!"

Cate threw herself at Egric, to the laughter of the other men.

"Control yourself," Sperleng scolded, "You aren't married yet, and we have much to do." Cate kissed her brother on the cheek. The returning soldiers ran into the river, splashing and dunking each other, then standing in the warming November sun.

Cate couldn't stop smiling as she and Mary packed their few belongings into a cart. *Egric is home and unharmed, and the land is now safer for Christians!*

Once settled, Cate and Mary began preparing the evening feast. Men slaughtered three lambs and built cooking fires with spits for roasting the meat. Cate floured her hands and began creating loaves of braided bread, some with raisins and dates. She didn't look up again until streaks of orange lined the blue-gray undersides of the clouds above the mountains. She quickly changed into her favorite dress, re-twisted her braid, then ran toward the fires where women were carving the meat and giving generous portions first to the men who had returned. Egric waved for her to join him, but when the men around him made loud mocking noises, he picked up his trencher and tankard and motioned for her to follow him to a quieter place. Sperleng and Mary joined them.

"I want to hear about everything," Cate said breathlessly, "Even if it takes months to tell."

"You will," Egric said. "Sperleng's volunteered me to tell the whole crowd tonight, remember?"

"That will be the short version. I want the long one."

"You want to know everything?" Egric teased. "You want to know about how I got ill from eating rancid pork one night? Or how I couldn't sleep at night thinking of you, and what I did about it?"

"Well, maybe not everything," she said, feeling her face warm.

Sperleng laughed, "Egric is prepared to tell the high points. I think that will be enough for anyone, even you, Cate."

Everyone began gathering when Egric moved a bench close to the fire. Sperleng, Mary, and Cate settled near the front. Cate noticed the local laborers who had helped prepare the feast stood near the back of the circle, then slowly slipped away in the darkness.

Egric leaned forward. His deep voice carried without the need to shout:

> The days were long when we left the city's safety.
> Heat harried our horse's hooves as we headed
> toward the tops of mountains and the setting
>   sun.
> We roamed the river, urged our steeds
>   upstream.
> Close were the cliffs and far were the forests.
> Silently we strode until brave Sperleng spoke:
> "Constant companions, bold in battle,
> fate has found us hostage in this harsh land.
> Christ will crush the ones who deny the divine."

The men quieted, some nodding their approval. Cate settled comfortably on Mary's shoulder, lulled by the rhythm of Egric's tale.

> The sun set three times before we saw
> the site where the waters crossed.
> A fortress rose above the rivers.
> Bleak walls blocked the sun, that garrison of
>   gloom.
> Gilbert stood high on his horse
> Demanding the devils surrender their swords.

"Abandon your blasphemy and return the stolen
  lands.

Accept Christ the conqueror and let us live in
  peace."

Only echoes of silence answered him.

Aragon's armies soon came, filling the fields.

Legions of soldiers built a blockade.

The count conquered the castle for the glory of
  God,

then divided his troops, some guarding this
  garrison

when warrior monks joined Berenguer's
  battalions.

He led them to Lérida, strong Saracen city,

and sent us to conquer the fortress at Fraga.

Fearful Fraga!

Alfonso of Aragon wept at its walls.

Ramón sought revenge where many men died,

So sent strong Normans to capture this prize,

And left for Lérida.

Our soldiers went weekly to hear the count's
  commands,

Past pastures of pagans who warily watched us.

One morning we went, Sperleng, Osbert and I.

A cluster of youths stood silently staring,

Waving their weapons as our dust passed them
  by.

When the count heard this treason, he sent
  troops to join us.

The youths would not yield and ran into the
road,
With sticks and scythes, daring to danger.
Ramón's men raised their swords, when rushed
a crowd
Begging for mercy for their impetuous sons.
Osbert then bellowed: "Fall on your knees.
Kiss the blessed cross, our Redeemer's rood.
Abhor the devil's infamy and save your souls."
Children and their mothers, old men with their
crones
Bowed to Christ's cross, faces flat on the field.
But one young man stood, a scythe in his fist,
Stared at us all his eyes ablaze.
"There is no God but Allah, and Mohammed is
his prophet."
Osbert severed his head. Black blood ran
aground,
Sure sign that this body was the devil's abode.
In the silence they whispered as one woman
arose.
"My son spoke the truth and for this he has
fallen.
There is no God but Allah and Mohammed his
prophet."
Rage filled Ramón's men as their swords they
unsheathed.
We joined in the slaughter of Saracens
screaming.
With horses we chased those who would flee.

> Death crows came quickly to circle the field filled
>   with corpses.
> We left the bodies to rot and raised a cross on
>   the spot
> That all Moors might know of God's victory here.

Cate sat up. All around her men cheered and raised their tankards for Egric, Sperleng, and Osbert. "Death to the Saracens!" a man behind her shouted.

Cate found the story troubling. Slaughtering a whole village for the pride of a young boy and his mother? War seemed glorious in the telling, but in her mind she saw the headless bodies left to rot. She understood why the men killed the boy threatening them, maybe even the woman who blasphemed, but the old men, the other women, the children who bowed to the cross and asked for mercy? Or was this just a story told as a boasting? She moved into a shadow so that Egric couldn't see the confusion on her face. She knew Egric and Sperleng believed no Christian was safe until all Saracens were dead. *Maybe they're right*, she thought, wishing it weren't so.

Egric's voice softened as he continued:

> The nights grew long as we waited for word of
>   the fall of Lérida.
> Fog filled the valleys each morning, hiding the
>   hills,
> Cover for Saracen snakes to slither.
> We kept close vigil and slaughtered those satans.
> Closer came harvest, the Feast of St. Michael.

Archangels hovered, protection from harm.
We heard trumpets of triumph as winter drew
near,
And the moaning of Moors for the loss of Lérida.
We shouted the fame of the armies of Aragon.
Great joy as we joined the count in the conquest,
Received our reward and the promise of glory
As the Moors rendered tribute, laid down their
curved swords.
Great feasting followed, and wine flowed freely.
The count praised our valor and promised pro-
tection
Orchards of olives, bounty, and treasure.
With thanks we went back to our families and
farms.

At this, the men began singing and drinking and clapping, filling their cups with ale and wine, and congratulating the returning heroes. Mary took Cate's arm and led her away from the revelry.

"Let the men have their party. We need to leave," Mary said.

"Do you think Sperleng or Egric killed any children?" Cate whispered.

"I think they did what they had to do," Mary answered. "And because they did, we can be safe, and soon you and Egric will have a place of your own. Doesn't that make you happy?"

"Of course," Cate said, glad it was too dark for Mary to see her face.

TWENTY-FOUR

*A*s Advent neared, Cate marveled that this would be her third winter away from Brycgstow. She still dreamt of snow, of icicles falling from edges of roofs and the hovering silence after a storm. *I never feel cold anymore,* she thought, then sobered as she suddenly realized that she couldn't quite picture the faces of her parents or Aedra, only their shapes and the dull gray clothes they always wore. Gray, she remembered it all as gray: the sky, the city walls, the clothes they wore, the weather-worn cottages, the pottage over the fire, even the meadows and rivers dulled by the cloud-obscured sun. *Soon I'll be married, never to live in Brycgstow again. Now I live where the sun shines and crops grow all year. My life is just as I want it to be.*

~

Sperleng was not invited with the Norman nobles to spend Christmas in Barcelona, but he was sure his longing for land would soon be decided. For Epiphany, Berenguer returned to Tortosa and gathered the Templars and Hospitallers, Genoese and Normans for a feast and gift-giving. Sperleng hoped Gilbert's lands would be large enough that he would grant Sperleng a tenancy.

The day of the feast seemed longer than any Sperleng had spent as he waited for word. He went to the cathedral, hoping to see from the noble's faces who had received the greatest rewards, but couldn't see Gilbert among the many men. *I hate feeling so powerless,* Sperleng thought. *I wish I knew or could do something!*

"Will you please stop pacing?" Cate chided. "You can help with the meal if you've nothing better to do."

Sperleng looked at her with disdain. Vassals didn't help women cook!

Cate laughed when she saw the look on his face. "Gilbert will come soon. Stop worrying," she said more kindly.

Two long and anxious days later Gilbert finally came. The feast had included homage ceremonies where Norman and Genoese nobles became Berenguer's men, giving up their vows to their lords back home and accepting lands in Hispania. The Normans had been granted tenancy to lands along the Ebro north of Tortosa. They would visit these lands the next day.

Gilbert told Sperleng he preferred to stay in Tortosa until the frontiers were more settled. He was bringing his wife and children from England, and he knew his wife would prefer to live near the cathedral and the castle, in the more protected areas of Tortosa.

"Would you be willing to govern one of my estates?" Gilbert asked.

Sperleng knelt before Gilbert. "I would be honored."

~

Cate had never seen an homage ceremony before. During the months of preparation, Gilbert commissioned new armor, tunics and surcoats for Sperleng, and sent bolts of new cloth for Cate and Mary, finer than any they had ever touched, and seamstresses to turn the cloth into fashionable dresses.

Although the walk to Gilbert's estate was short, the trailing ends of Cate's sleeves kept dropping toward the street until she wound them around her wrists and clasped her arms at her waist. The seamstresses held the hems of her and Mary's dresses as they walked, unwilling to see all their hard work ruined by dragging over dung in the road. Cate had never had such a beautiful and uncomfortable dress, its brocade scratching her where the dress was laced tight around her chest and waist. *I don't know how long I'll last before I will have to scratch it,* she thought, knowing she must not.

Gilbert's manor was an imposing structure with arched doorways that rose to a point surrounded by carved swirls and circles that sometimes formed leaves and fruit. Cate tried not to stare, to act as if she were used to such finery but couldn't help herself when they entered the brightly tiled foyer, blue star-shaped tiles mixed amongst geometric patterns in yellows and whites and reds.

Cate walked past a glut of swords at the entrance to Gilbert's great hall. Sperleng's men stayed with Cate and Mary at the rear of the hall, as Sperleng walked alone to its center. Gilbert's wife and sons stood with him at the far end of the hall dressed in red velvet trimmed in white fur. The Norman priest stood in his black robe next to Gilbert, a small gold box in his hand. Gilbert touched his sword with one hand and beckoned Sperleng forward with the other. When Sperleng was a sword's length away, he fell to his knees and put his hands together in a posture of prayer.

"Sperleng, my soldier and my friend," Gilbert said, "are you willing to serve me and become my man, to honor and defend me and my family from now on and protect my lands, and to give aid and support to my lord, Count Berenguer, when asked?"

"I am willing and honored to be your man, and promise always to be faithful, to protect your family and lands, and to give aid and support to your lord," Sperleng said, bowing his head.

Gilbert clasped Sperleng's hands, then kissed both his cheeks. When the priest joined them, Gilbert continued: "In this reliquary are pieces of the True Cross, brought from Jerusalem by the Templars. Will you swear your fealty on this holy relic?"

Sperleng put his hand on the gold box. "I promise on my faith that I swear fealty to Lord Gilbert and will be faithful and observe my homage to him completely against all persons in good faith and without deceit."

Gilbert took an olive branch from his wife and a new sword from his eldest son. "Here are symbols of the gifts I give to you, tenancy of land along the Ebro near the village of Aldover, and my promise of protection in return for your fealty, aid, counsel, and a share in the abundance of the land. Do you accept these, and the obligations they entail?"

"I do, my lord, in humbleness and gratitude."

The priest began mumbling a prayer that Cate could not understand and barely heard, her head full of awe at the turn their lives had taken. Her brother, a carpenter's son and now a vassal! Vassal to a lord! She wished their parents and Willard and Cearl and everyone in Brycgstow could be here. Egric smiled at her, and she could see delight in Sperleng's men's eyes. They understood that their fortunes had changed. No longer were they villeins and farmers. They would be knights.

Sperleng kept his head bowed long after the prayer finished. The room stayed silent and Gilbert smiled over him until Sperleng looked up.

"Stand up, man," Gilbert said, "and let's celebrate!"

At this, Gilbert's servants entered with large amounts of food and placed them on tables around the room. Others moved tables and benches into a large rectangle. Many knights and nobles, Norman and Catalan, had been invited to the feast, and the hall was soon crowded with men and a few women. Musicians played reeds and lutes quietly as the feast began, then became livelier and louder as the guests drank more wine and laughed more loudly. As small cakes were brought in, Gilbert announced that the Count had sent one of his minstrels to the celebration, to tell the grand story of El Cid to the nobles who may not have heard it.

Cate couldn't understand every word but understood enough to know this was about an unjustly banished warrior named Rodrigo who became a great Christian leader by defeating the Moors in glorious fashion and uniting Christian Hispania against the heathen. She thought the minstrel said El Cid had defeated the Count Berenguer's grandfather, but his daughter married the count's father although she wasn't the Count Berenguer's mother. Confusing. *Well, that is the life of a noble, I guess,* Cate thought. *Like Sperleng's may be.*

Cate looked over at Egric, who seemed fascinated, although she didn't think he understood the words any better than she did. At the end of the poem many of the Spanish knights shouted *"Campeador!"* while others seemed disapproving. Cate's head buzzed with wine and happiness.

~

Sperleng wanted to move quickly to his new land, before Pentecost and the heat of summer. Cate and Mary joined Sperleng and Gilbert one warm day a few days after Easter to see the homestead. As they approached, Cate noticed a small, thin woman dressed in flowing robes walking along the river, holding the hand of a small boy. Her face and hair were covered against the dusty wind; only her eyes were visible. The little boy stopped and picked up rocks every few feet, and the woman waited patiently as the boy decided whether to put them down, throw them in the river, or hold them in his fist. The woman did not look up at the sound of the horses and carts, but Cate watched her stiffen and stand more erect the closer they came. After they passed the woman and boy in a flurry of dust and noise, Cate saw the woman's shoulders relax.

They went through a tall wooden gate in a clay-covered wall and arrived at a large clay building uphill from the river. The roof extended past the exterior walls of the building, held up by massive pillars that created a shaded porch around the structure. A wall of the same material blocked Cate's view of the entire building, but beyond the wall she saw several sheep and goats in a grassy area along the river. Large trees surrounded the area from the river to the house.

"This is yours?" Cate asked Sperleng.

"It's Gilbert's, but mine to manage." Sperleng stood tall as he spoke. "Gilbert has another ranch down-river, closer to Tortosa," he added. "A beautiful spot."

"Is there a village or a market nearby?" Mary asked. "Where will we go to church?"

"Many of the villages have been abandoned," Gilbert answered. "Moors lived on most of the ranches and in most of the nearby villages. The Jews and a few Moors still live in the villages, but the markets probably won't come back until we re-establish them." Gilbert pointed toward some mountains in the distance. "Count Berenguer told me that there are also villages in the mountains still in the hands of the Moors. Don't go there."

"Who was the woman we passed along the river?" Cate asked.

"I don't know," Gilbert said. "She's dressed like a Moor, but who she is or why she is on our land, I can't say."

Cate looked southward and saw three horses and their riders coming toward them in a cloud of dust. Soon, several soldiers arrived. They dismounted and spoke to Gilbert.

"Count Berenguer's men want to know if they can be of assistance," Gilbert said to Sperleng.

"Ask him about the woman," Sperleng said.

Gilbert talked awhile with the soldier. "The woman was the wife of the Moor who owned this ranch," Gilbert said. "He was killed, and his parents and brothers fled, but they left her and her son here. She's living in a small house on the land with her new husband, Razin ibn Faris, one of the farm laborers. They are yours to do with as you wish."

"These people are tied to the estate?" Sperleng asked.

"Yes. We need workers to tend the animals and work the crops and these people have promised loyalty in exchange for protection and food," Gilbert replied.

"Like the villeins at home?" Cate burst out.

Sperleng frowned at Cate. "Perhaps this woman could be our house servant?" Sperleng asked.

A servant, Cate thought, *we will have a servant?*

Berenguer's soldier approached the Moorish woman. Cate saw the woman never looked at the soldier but seemed to nod in assent.

"Her name is Tamu. She agrees to cook and clean for you," Gilbert said after talking with the soldier. "She asks only that she be allowed to live with her husband and son, and that you keep her husband to tend the orchards, as he did for her dead husband's family. And she begs that you and your soldiers respect her marriage vows."

"Have they been married in the church? Are they married in God's eyes?" Sperleng asked. "I've no obligation to protect a whore."

"She agrees to convert," Gilbert said. "Other than that, we'll need to find out."

"Let's talk with her husband," Sperleng grumbled. "I'm not sure about having a lot of Moors on the property, converted or not."

"You may not have a lot of choice, Sperleng," Gilbert said. "Someone needs to tend and harvest the crops. Not many Christians have moved into the area yet, and who knows if anyone but those promised land will."

Sperleng scowled but nodded.

They entered the house through a heavy wooden door carved in geometric shapes, and Cate suddenly missed her father, remembering the images he'd carved. The windows to the outside were tall and thin, thinner than a boy, decorated with iron disguised as branches and leaves. Once inside the high-ceilinged main room,

Cate could see through large, arched windows to the rear that the building was a series of rooms surrounding on three sides an open courtyard. The floor in the main room was tiled in a diagonal pattern of muted reds, browns, yellows, and beige. Cate closed her eyes, overwhelmed that she would live in this beautiful place.

They walked through the rooms silently.

"This will be my room," Sperleng finally said as they stood in a large room whose long, narrow windows to the outside faced the river. "The breezes off the river will be welcome in the summer."

Gilbert nodded and directed a soldier to bring Sperleng's arms and clothing. In the room were several platforms with mats; it appeared that several people had slept in this room previously. Sperleng stood in front of the largest one, a carved bed with a netted canopy.

"This bed should stay, but move the others," he commanded another soldier. "It will need a new mat," Sperleng directed Cate.

Cate nodded her head.

"Move two of the beds to the room on the other side of the kitchen," Sperleng told the soldier, pointing across the courtyard. "That will be where Cate and Mary sleep. The guards will sleep in the room next to me in the front of the house, facing the road. Cate, you may decide the use of the remaining rooms."

Guards? Cate wondered, then realized how dangerous it was to be living out in the open on land taken from the Moors.

TWENTY-FIVE

Cate sat and stared at the river, sometimes for hours alone, and thought ruefully about how many times her mother had forbidden just this. Now she wasn't sure being alone most of the time was better than the constant demands of her life back home. Mary lived at the Hospitallers' abbey several days a week, working much as she had in Brycgstow, and who could blame her? She said she felt needed there. She came to stay at Sperleng's estate only one or two days a week now, and Cate feared that soon even these visits would end.

Perhaps I should join Mary, Cate thought. *I liked working in the clinic and anything's better than this direction-less waiting.* She tended the small garden she and Mary had planted with medicinal herbs, harvesting those that hadn't wilted or burned, turning them into poultices and elixirs as best she could. Much of the garden wilted last summer under the hot, dry sun no matter how much water Cate dragged from the river. The mint had not survived the first year's planting, and the yarrow and vervain that grew wild around Brycgstow had to be coddled to survive.

Cate and Mary had tried planting their seeds in sun, in shade, near the river, far from the river, and slowly were learning what worked best. Most of their plants shriveled and died last summer, but this year they'd planted earlier and watched to see which needed daily watering or shade. Almost everything Cate learned about plants in Brycgstow seemed useless here. Still, every morning she weeded and watered, and every evening at dusk she walked the rows to see what had survived.

When Sperleng wasn't around to scold her that it was servant's work, Cate swept floors and made pottage the way she liked it, a skill Tamu never seemed to learn as she always added more spices. Cate's understanding of the local language had much improved while working with Tamu for a year, and for the gaps she and Tamu communicated mostly by pointing.

"Can I help?" Cate asked Tamu as they sat outside to catch the river breeze, Tamu kneading a kind of flat bread. Her son, Musa, clung to Tamu's skirts, tugging at them as if wanting to be protected.

"No, no, no." A look of panic crossed Tamu's face.

"Please?" Cate pleaded.

Tamu seemed to understand her boredom. She pointed to Musa, and Cate understood that playing with him would be a help.

She put her arms out. "Musa. Come?"

Musa wailed and gripped his mother's legs. Cate remembered a game she played with Linn and Oxa when they were young. She walked around the yard, picking up sticks and stones. Musa watched her closely. Cate went toward the shade of a tree where she used a stick to draw three lines and a circle in a row toward the tree. She pretended not to look at him but saw that Musa had loosened his hold on his mother. Cate then stood at the farthest line from the circle and threw the stone toward it, but intentionally missed.

"Awww," she said loudly and threw again. This time, the stone landed within the circle. She clapped happily and jumped up and down. She offered a small stone to Musa, who shook his head and buried his head into his mother's skirt. Cate turned back to the game, jumped to the second line, threw, and missed the circle.

"Awww." Cate said, making a sad face to Musa who was peeking from behind the cloth. He hid his face again, but he was smiling. Tamu smiled too. Cate threw another stone, this time within the circle. She turned to Musa, clapping happily.

This time when Cate offered a stone, Musa ran to her, took the stone, ran to the circle, threw the stone at the tree, clapped, and ran back to his mother. Cate clapped happily, jumping up and down. That wasn't the game, but at least he was playing. Soon Musa decided clapping and jumping and tossing stones was more fun than hanging on to his mother's skirt. Musa added running in circles and touching the tree.

Tamu smiled at Cate.

~

After the years of watching soldiers die and fields burned to nothing, Mary found taking care of the abbey's herb garden calming and birthing babies glorious. There still were many bodies to wash, but these deaths were gentler than the gaping sword wounds or gashed heads that had filled her days during the sieges. Sperleng asked her once if she wanted him to buy her passage home, if not now, once Cate married Egric, but she told him no. "There is only Alma for me in Brycgstow while here are you and Cate and Egric, and soon maybe Cate's children. And if I never see snow again, it is fine by me."

The Hospitallers called her Sister Maria, assuming—because of her fine dresses and knowing she was Sperleng's aunt—she was of noble birth. They gave her the largest room in the small house where the cooks and laundresses lived near the clinic that served the Tortosan poor, far enough away from their castle in Amposta and the brothers' local residence to avoid temptation. They apologized that there were no other sisters to keep her company but often told her more would come soon. The noble families in Barcelona were still too afraid to send their unmarried daughters to the frontier, but that would change.

"Perhaps you can be their prioress," Brother Diego said.

Mary tried to hide her surprise. *A prioress?* "I would need to take Hospitaller vows and learn to read and write your language before that happens," she told him, not wanting him to know she couldn't read or write at all.

"Easily done," he said.

And so began Mary's lessons, first with chalk on stone or drawing letters in the mud and then on scraps of linen. She knew Brother Diego soon figured out how little she knew, but he was kind and kept it to himself. *I should have asked Willard when I could have,* Mary wished, *but who would have thought I'd ever need to?*

On the days Cate visited, she joined them and quickly learned. Brother Diego showed them how to turn sheep hides to parchment, but he said such fine material should be used only for manuscripts and important letters. Mary asked Sperleng to buy some ink for her, and she made a small tenter frame over which she and Cate stretched strips of cloth to make practicing writing easier. When Egric saw them writing one day when Mary was visiting the farm, he scowled and asked them if there wasn't something useful they could do like spinning or weaving. Chastened, Cate began sewing with Mary on the days Egric was home, limiting her writing practice to her days in Tortosa or when Egric joined Sperleng on his expeditions.

Mary refused to be intimidated. She might be a prioress one day.

~

Early one morning, Cate woke to shouting. Her stomach grumbled from the Lenten fast as she tried to go back to sleep to dream of Sunday's Easter feast. As the shouting came nearer, she wrapped herself in a blanket and peeked through a window. She saw Tamu with an elderly man who was gesturing first at her and then at Musa, who looked at both in confusion. Cate quickly put on her skirt and blouse, grabbed a large stick, and ran toward the shouting. When they saw her, Tamu and the old man became quiet.

"What's the matter?" Cate asked

"This is my father, Harun ibn Walid." Tamu responded, then looked at her father and said, "This is Cate, sister of my lord."

Tamu's father bowed slightly, so Cate did the same. As the uncomfortable silence lengthened, Cate realized they would not argue in front of her. Convinced Tamu was not in danger, and not knowing what else to do, Cate went back into the house and stood in the shadows so they would not see her watching through the window.

Tamu's father soon began gesturing wildly again, as Tamu shook her head in disagreement. When Musa began crying, Tamu picked him up and walked toward the house, tears streaming down her face. Ibn Walid stood looking at her until she disappeared inside, then walked toward the bridge that crossed the river.

Cate put some bread and several oranges on the table.

"*Aranhas? Pa?*" she asked.

Tamu smiled and took some bread and an orange, peeled the orange, and handed both to Musa. He ate both quickly, too young to fast.

Cate wanted to know what had just happened but didn't know how to ask.

"Tamu, your father. Why was he angry? Why were you sad?"

Tamu hesitated. "In two weeks is a holy day. He wanted me to come home. And bring a sheep."

"A sheep? You don't have a sheep, do you?"

"He wanted one of yours. He said they belong to me, not to you. I said they no longer belong to me, and I will not steal or ask for one."

"Will you go home for the feast? You can, you know. I don't mind, and Sperleng will be on patrol. I can set out meals for the workers. Mary can help."

"My father is poor and has no animals. He will eat at his neighbor's table. I will stay here."

Cate felt the sadness radiating from Tamu. Although she and all the laborers had been baptized, Cate was sure she missed her old traditions and the days her husband owned the land. She wondered if this would be the first time Tamu spent the feast day with Christians. It might be like spending Christmas or Easter with a Moor or a Jew. Cate shuddered at the thought.

"Maybe you can make the meal and have your father come here? Easter will be past, and we have five new lambs. We can feed the workers too, and we'll dry some meat for the patrols."

Hope and gratefulness flowed in Tamu's eyes. "No, we're fine. Father needs to accept that things are different now."

"We all need to eat. We can eat a sheep prepared the way your father likes it. And I think the laborers would appreciate it, wouldn't they? I'm pretty sure it's a holy day for some of them if it's one for you."

Tamu nodded. "Your priests might disapprove."

"We won't be praying, Tamu, just eating the food you make. I think it will be fun."

"You are a strange Christian, Cate. Thank you."

Tamu told Cate the feast must be held at sunset two Thursdays next. Cate knew Sperleng kept close track of the animals, so the week before, as he prepared to leave with Egric on yet another patrol of the countryside, she told him as casually as possible that she would be killing a sheep to feed the soldiers and workers while he was gone.

"Why?" he asked. "We just had an Easter feast."

"Yes, and you'll be taking the meat stores with you on your raids. Tamu can dry much of the meat, and we need to feed the workers and soldiers," Cate said.

"An old ram, then. Not a young lamb," Sperleng said.

When the day came, preparations began early. Cate baked bread before dawn. A shepherd brought a newly butchered ram, more than half cut into small strips for salting and drying. Tamu covered the rest in a marinade of water, orange juice, and a dark brown paste that had been wrapped in fig leaves.

"What is that?" Cate asked, pointing to the paste.

"*Murri.* It's a barley paste that has been fermenting for many days."

Tamu poured the marinade over the mutton, covered it with a cloth, and put it in the coolest part of the house. Cate and Tamu then went outside to pick fig leaves, which they placed in a tub and covered with water. Musa started throwing stones and sticks at the tree, then at them.

"I think he's bored. Or needs attention," Cate said. "Shall I walk with him?"

"Yes, thank you." Tamu looked at Cate gratefully.

Cate took Musa's hand as he bounced along the river. Musa picked oranges from the ground while Cate searched the meadow for wild asparagus and berries. When Cate saw Musa's eyes drooping, they walked back to the house. Tamu placed her son in a nest of cloth in the shade of a fig tree.

Tamu had hollowed out an area on the high ground that had remained relatively dry despite the recent rains. She and Cate lined the hole with rocks they took from the river and covered them with wet fig leaves. Tamu then retrieved the mutton, watered a tree with the marinade, placed the meat on top of the leaves, and spread olive oil and garlic over the top. She then covered all with more wet leaves and rocks. Finally, she shoveled embers from the cooking fire and placed them with dried wood atop the rocks.

Tamu and Cate pitted and pressed olives, chopped eggplant and onions, and crushed almonds. Tamu took dried lentils she had soaked overnight, placed them in a cooking pot, added fresh water, lemon juice, and salt, and hung the pot over the fire. They then rolled into balls ground dates, almonds, and bread-crumbs, and Tamu cooked these quickly in butter, covered them, and set them aside.

When the shade shifted to put Musa in the sun, Tamu woke him up, put him on her lap, and gave him a bowl of bread soaked in goat's milk. Off in the distance, Cate saw a solitary man walking toward them. As he came nearer, Cate saw he carried a netted sack filled with fruit and vegetables on his back.

"Is that your father?" she asked.

"Yes." Tamu smiled.

By the time he arrived, Musa was ready to play. Ibn Walid hugged his daughter and kissed her cheeks. He bowed slightly to Cate, then turned to Musa, picked him up over his head, kissed him, and lowered him to the ground. Musa squealed in delight.

Ibn Walid said something to Tamu, she nodded, and he and Musa wandered off to throw stones in the river.

"My father's friend, al-Basir, grew these vegetables and provides them as his gift," Tamu said.

Cate was amazed at their size and color. She wished she could grow some like this. "Gratias," she said.

The hour before sunset was a rush of activity. Ibn Walid checked the meat regularly as Tamu prepared saffron rice, an eggplant dish with onions and almonds, and *manjar blanco*, a fish dish made with milk, sugar, raisins, and thickened with ground rice. They filled the tables with pomegranates, grapes, figs, and bread.

At dusk, the men wandered in, unsure how to approach. Cate understood that she was the host in their eyes. The soldiers should begin first, she told them, and ibn Walid began handing out plates of food. Tamu scooped the lentil soup into trenchers of bread and offered it to the workers as Cate poured glasses of wine or water sweetened with mint and sugar cane. Some of the laborers took their shares to gaunt women and children standing in the distance.

The eating and drinking went on for hours as the night blackened, until a sliver of moon and many stars shone. Ibn Walid built another small fire away from the cooking fire, so people could sit by its warmth. Most of the soldiers fell asleep along the courtyard walls, snoring softly. The laborers and their families returned to their houses. Musa slept quietly on Tamu's lap. Eventually only Tamu, her father, Cate, and the house guards were awake. Several guards mounted horses to prowl the perimeters.

"Why do you have a feast on this day?" Cate asked.

"Father, tell the story of Ismail."

Ibn Walid smiled at Tamu, then Cate. "No, my child. You must tell. She can understand you better than me."

Tamu nodded and began speaking in a soft and rhythmic voice:

"Ibrahim was a good man, loved by God. But he was a sad man too, for he was old and had no child. God had promised him many descendants, but his wife

Sarah had borne him no sons. So Sarah gave her servant Hajar to Ibrahim to marry."

Cate thought about the carvings of Abraham she had seen at the cathedral of St. James. Was this the same man?

"Ibrahim married Hajar, who soon became with child. Sarah was jealous and found fault with Hajar whenever she could. The conflict between the women became too much for Ibrahim to bear, and Ibrahim prayed to God for an answer. Ibrahim packed Hajar and Ismail's clothing and took them on a long journey. They rode many days and nights until they came to a valley in a desert in the land of Arabia where Mecca now lies. There was no water here, no people, only rocks. Ibrahim helped Hajar get off the camel, put her belongings and enough food and water for three days on the ground, and began to leave."

Cate sat up. Ibrahim left his wife and child in the desert to die? What a terrible story!

"Hajar cried to Ibrahim, 'Why are you leaving us in this empty place?' Ibrahim did not respond. Hajar cried again, 'Ibrahim, why are you leaving us here?' Again, Ibrahim did not answer. Crying more loudly, and with much grief, Hajar shouted, 'Ibrahim, did God command you to leave us here?'

"At this Ibrahim turned around. 'Yes.' Hajar bowed her head, saying, 'Then all will be well.'

"Ibrahim began walking again, praying that God protect Hajar and his son.

"After three days, they had drunk all the water and Hajar could no longer feed Ismail. She watched her son cry in the hot sun and desperately searched for water. She ran up the mountain on one side of the valley but saw no water or any sign of life. She then ran down the mountain and up another on the opposite side of the valley, but still she found no water, and no one to help her. She repeated this seven times in her worry and fear, praying to God the entire time. Finally, she collapsed, and waited to die."

I do not like this story, Cate thought.

"In the silence," Tamu continued, "Hajar heard a voice, and lifted her head to see an angel speaking to her. 'Hajar, God has heard your prayers. Look, here, beneath the sand is a spring of fresh water that God has given you.' The angel scratched through the sand, and Hajar saw fresh water bubbling up."

Much better, Cate thought, her head nodding sleepily.

"God told Ibrahim in a dream that Ismail and Hajar survived. Ibrahim praised and thanked God and went to visit them many times. But Ismail began to be what Ibrahim loved most: more than Sarah; more than Hajar; perhaps more than God. The year Ismail was thirteen, Ibrahim began having dreams every night that he must sacrifice Ismail. Ibrahim ignored these dreams until he could no longer deny that they were visions from God. He then made the long journey to Arabia. When he arrived, he went to Ismail and said: 'Ismail, my son, God has commanded me to sacrifice you. Are you

343

willing to give up your life as it is God's will?' Without hesitation, Ismail said, 'I am, father. Whatever God wills must be.'"

Cate feared she was misunderstanding again. Didn't God command Abraham to sacrifice Isaac? She was sure that was what Willard had told her.

"Ibrahim and Ismail climbed the mountain, and when they arrived at the top, Ismail laid his head on a flat rock, praising God. Ibrahim took his sword and lifted it up, but just before he began the downward swing God spoke: 'Ibrahim. You have shown your faithfulness and that you love God above all earthly things. I do not seek Ismail's death; sacrifice this sheep instead.' At this, a sheep appeared, which Ibrahim and Ismail sacrificed to God. They went down the mountain, praising God."

Cate was filled with a sense of peace, and too tired to fight this blasphemy. Other than getting the name of the son wrong, this was the story she knew. *A lovely story, at the end anyway,* she thought as she drifted off to sleep.

When Cate awoke at dawn, she found herself covered in a sheepskin. She rose, stretched, and went in the house.

TWENTY-SIX

*O*n the Feast of St. Barnabas, the sun rose hot and the tiles of the courtyard radiated heat from the day before. Cate gathered her bucket and rake and headed toward her kitchen garden. Thankfully a slight breeze blew off the river. As the cloudless sky brightened, she heard the animals complaining for their breakfast, and the scrapes and shouts of the laborers as they began the day. The yarrow had stopped flowering months ago, but she still saw hints of green under the browning tops. She bent down and sighed, pulling unwanted plants that had sprung up around the yarrow and vervain. When she heard knocking at the gate, she rose, brushed the dirt off her skirt, and let in Musa and Tamu, who had come to prepare her breakfast.

"You seem sad," Tamu said. "Has something happened?"

Cate gave her a weak smile. "My plants are dying, and I don't know what to do. The sun is hotter, and the air is dryer here than back home, but there must be some way to get them to grow."

Tamu held a purple flower from a wood betony, then bent down and looked at the brown-topped yarrow. "Many plants dry here in the summers. Most come back."

Cate nodded. "I hope so, but I'm afraid I won't have any seeds left by the time I figure out how to take care of them. Mary asked the monks at the abbey, and they made suggestions, but most won't take the time to guide her. Do you have a garden?"

"Trees!" Musa said. "We have trees!"

Tamu smiled at him. "These are medicinal plants, aren't they? I have a few the healer from my village gave me, but they don't look like these."

"Could you show them to me and tell me what you use them for?" Cate asked.

"Sure. But you should see the healer's garden. People come from far away to seek his advice and tonics."

Musa tugged at Tamu's sleeves. "Trees!"

Cate looked towards the hills where she knew Tamu came from. "Do you think he would help a Christian?"

"I don't know," Tamu said. "My father is grateful to you for your kindness to us. I will ask."

"We would need to bring guards. Sperleng and Egric would never let me go alone. They may not allow me to go at all."

"But no army!" Tamu said. "Too many horses and they'll run to the hills with their crossbows."

"And what are these trees Musa loves?" Cate said, taking his hand as they walked toward the house.

"His father and I planted three pomegranate trees when Musa was born. Musa and I water these trees once a week to remember him."

Mary arrived later that week and looked sadly at the remains of their garden. "You're right. We need to do something different."

"Tamu said the healer from her father's village is willing to show us his garden and help us understand what and how to grow here." Cate said. "Do you want to come?"

Mary broke into a wide smile. "Of course! The monks tell me the Saracens know many different ways than the healers at home, that they've found books from the ancients. Who knows if that is true, but I'd like to learn what they know." Mary paused. "But we must be careful that they don't teach us something that may poison our soldiers."

"The clinic treats everyone, not just soldiers. Surely he wouldn't teach us about potions that would kill his own people?"

Mary shrugged. "I guess I'm not as trusting as you."

Cate pondered this as she silently returned to her weaving. She knew everyone thought her an innocent, but she believed Tamu when she said the healer was a kind and generous man who loved to share his knowledge. Tamu's father told her the healer eagerly awaited the Christian woman who had been so kind about the feast. Cate hoped he wouldn't bring that up around Mary or Egric.

"When will you come next?" Cate asked.

"Five days," Mary said.

"Too soon, I think. Perhaps St. Martha's feast day? Nobody celebrates that much," Cate said, and Mary nodded.

"I'll talk with Egric," Cate said.

"Absolutely not," Egric said when Cate proposed a trip to the village. "The countryside is still dangerous. Why do you think we go on patrols?"

"Tamu says only women and old men have stayed there. Most of the men died in battle or moved south. She says the valley belonged to a warrior lord who came to the village only to collect his rent and share of the crops, but since the fall of Tortosa no one has ever come."

"I've heard of such cowardly behavior in many villages," Egric admitted. "No Christian would leave widows and orphans and old people to fend for themselves. We'll send scouts, but not you," Egric decided.

"Mary and I need to see their healer's garden. Can you send the scouts and allow us to follow far behind? And go only if it's safe?"

"Why is this so important to you?" Egric asked.

"You've seen my garden," Cate said. "We may end up with no medicines at all."

Cate watched the worried lines build on Egric's forehead as he thought. Egric grimaced, looked at Cate, and eventually nodded.

"On my terms," he said.

When the day came, Tamu rode with Mary as she directed the small group toward the mountains, following a barely recognizable trail next to a dry stream bed that wound through rocky land and low bushes. Musa cried when told he must ride with Cate on the small gray mare Sperleng had given her, but Egric refused to let Tamu and Musa ride together. Cate sang to him, and he eventually calmed.

Egric and three other soldiers rode their tall war horses, followed closely by their squires. When a bend in the trail appeared or Egric decided the brush was too heavy, the scouts would lead, and on open trail the soldiers would take turns riding ahead and alongside the three women. As the party neared the village, two scouts went ahead while the rest waited. When the scouts returned unharmed, they started again.

By midday, they arrived in a small valley where the stream bed split into two branches coming from the steep hills nearby. No wall protected the village that lay between the two streams, only a tall tower on the highest point of a ridge that looked over the countryside. Inside the tower Cate saw a large bell and a man pointing a crossbow, watching them. Cate pointed toward him and Egric nodded, making sure they stayed more than a cross-bow's distance away.

Cate saw few crops, but many sheep grazing in the sparse grasses. The houses were small, most lining the stream beds. They were made of the same stone Cate had seen on the trail, some with rush-covered roofs and others with tiles. Behind each house was a small garden shaded by stunted olive and fig trees. One house stood out, larger than the rest and with a garden shaded by grape vines growing over a tall structure made of branches. A well stood close to this house, the women near it hiding their faces then scurrying away.

As the group approached, Tamu's father came toward them with an elderly man whose beard and loose white robes moved erratically in the day's strong wind. The two men helped Tamu and Cate dismount, and Tamu's father took the sleeping Musa from Cate's arms.

"Welcome," Tamu's father said to the soldiers as they dismounted. Cate looked curiously at the older man, who noticeably refused to look at her and Mary. "I am called Harun ibn Walid, and this is ibn Yusuf al-Basir, our healer. Al-Basir, these women are healers too, and have come to learn from you."

Al-Basir nodded and smiled but kept looking at the ground. "Al-Basir is traditional and cannot look at you outside his house. It will be all right when we enter," Tamu said when Cate looked at her quizzically.

When they entered, an elderly woman in a loose white shift that covered all but her face motioned them to sit on large floor pillows. She offered them steaming tea, stew in a bowl of bread, and small, square, honey-drenched cakes. Everyone sat except Egric, the only soldier who came inside. He moved watchfully from the arched doorway to the lattice-covered windows. Al-Basir urged them to rest awhile, but Egric refused.

"We must return home today," Egric said. "Cate, get on with your task."

Al-Basir led them outside to a lovely garden filled with flowers and many green and thriving plants, so different from Cate's own. Her fatigue from the journey subsided into eagerness. How had Al-Basir had made such an oasis in this dry, rocky place?

Cate and Mary listened closely as Al-Basir, with Tamu's help in translating his heavily accented speech, talked about creating separate places in the garden for plants that needed more water or more sun than others. Closest to the patio grew plants shaded by grape vines growing over an arch constructed of branches, a few bunches of small, hard grapes drooping just above their heads.

Al-Basir's garden surrounded a small pool. Most months, he told them, it was fed by a deep spring his father had dug, but in the dry season he often had to fill it with water from the stream or well. The pool was lined in blue and yellow tiles, and he showed them hand-sized water gates that, when opened, allowed water to run through stone lined furrows between the plants he said needed the most water.

Furthest from the house, plants grew in the sun. Al-Basir told them the shadow of a nearby mountain would eventually shelter them from the setting sun. A tall lattice, bush-lined fence surrounded the garden, making it much less windy here than what they'd felt on their journey. A large fig tree shaded a far corner of the garden leading to a small olive, orange, and pomegranate grove.

"Al-Basir, I only recognize a few of these plants. Will you tell us what they are used for and how to care for them?" Mary said as they stood under the fig tree.

The old man slowly knelt near the base of the tree and plucked a few small, yellow-green flowers from a shrub that surrounded it and handed some to Cate and Mary. The blue-green leaves gave off an acrid odor.

"This is rue," he said, "which we grow near a fig tree so that its healing powers are strengthened. Do you have fig trees in your garden?" Cate nodded, dumb with interest.

"We rub it on our bodies to keep away fleas or to ease pain in our joints," Al-Basir continued. "You can chew a leaf for a headache, crush it and mix the virtue with water to help with coughs and stomach pain, or dry it to make a tea to keep your eyes healthy. One seed in a glass of wine will help fight poisonings. But don't ever use too much! It's poison to swallow fresh leaves or to drink too much of the tea. I can give you some dried rue for tea and some seeds, but they must be planted in the spring, not now in the heat of summer. Don't worry about adding to your soil — it can grow well in poor soil — but be sure to plant it in the shade of a fig tree."

Al-Basir's voice rose with excitement as he pointed out his favorite plants, schooling them in the best ways to grow and use them. In the sunny, irrigated part of the garden they walked through viney patches of orange and yellow flowers, some having closed into small balls that he called melons. He gave Cate and Mary crushed seeds to be used for intestinal worms and promised to send melons at harvest that they could eat and then use the seeds to plant their own. The fruit, he said, was good for blood diseases and constipation.

Nearest the stream were patches of low-growing plants.

"Here's rosemary," Al-Basir said as he broke off a few long thin leaves from a bush covered in clumps of small blue flowers. "Older people, like me and my wife, use it to help us remember. We also burn it in the rooms of the sick to purify the air. And here is dill. You can cook with this to add flavor or use it as a medicine for stomach ills. And capers, my favorite," he said smiling at his wife. "These love the sun and don't need much water so are wonderful for this land. It lessens stomach gas and helps men and women desire each other."

Al-Basir's wife laughed softly, and Cate forced herself not to look toward Egric.

As they walked through the garden Cate recognized several plants that were dying in her garden but thriving here. "Al-Basir, we, too, grow fennel and vervain," she said, touching each, "but yours are so much healthier. Can you tell us your secret?"

"Mistress, there is no secret," Al-Basir said. "You see how this plant you call vervain is on the border of shade and sun? It is too hot for it to be in full sun but will die if shaded too much. And don't over-water it. Do you water all your plants the same?" Cate nodded as he continued. "Make sure it's uphill from the river so it doesn't get flooded in the spring and place it near this plant, dill. Now, your fennel should be in a sunnier place, and cut off about half of the flower stems when they appear so the rest grow stronger."

"Cate and Mary, it is time to leave," Egric said gruffly as the sun approached the western mountains. "We need to be off the mountain by dusk." Cate looked at him anxiously as he and his squire stood sullenly in the shade near the pool. They had only begun learning what Al-Basir could show them, but she knew better than to contradict Egric. She saw in his face that there was no room for argument, so she joined him in walking toward the horses.

Al-Basir quickly gathered pouches of seed and dried herbs, and his wife filled their pouches with water and bread after Egric refused another meal.

"Al-Basir," Mary said, bowing slightly, "thank you for sharing your knowledge with us. This land is so different from Brycgstow where it is wet and cool most of the time. Please give me the rue and Cate the rest so we can keep it separate from the less dangerous seeds. I fear we will forget which is which when we arrive home."

"I will tie a sprig of each plant to its bag to help you remember," Al-Basir bowed.

"Yes, thank you," Cate echoed. "Maybe you can come in the spring with ibn Walid and guide us in the planting? I will ask my brother to give you a young lamb in return."

"If Allah wills it," Al-Basir replied.

Egric led his horse toward the trail. "Cate, don't make promises you cannot keep," he said quietly as he helped her mount.

~

"Tamu," Cate said as she worked on creating a pool in the garden, "when I marry Egric will you come live with us?"

"That's for my husband to decide," Tamu said as she dug.

"What would it take to convince him? Or are you just saying that because you want to stay here?"

"Cate, you must know I'd prefer to be with you and your new family than to stay here with all these restless soldiers. Sperleng will marry someday, and I cannot know what his wife will be like. I doubt he'll marry someone who will play with Musa or help bake bread. But my husband must have enough work, and neither of us wants to move too far from our families."

"It's hard being away from parents," Cate said, suddenly sad. "I wish I knew whether mine were still alive, or if I'll ever see them again. Although I doubt I will."

"I forget sometimes that Sperleng and Mary are all you have left of your family," Tamu said. "I can't imagine having traveled like you did. I moved less than a day's journey from my village when I married, and I cried for weeks. How could you do it?"

"I cried sometimes, but I came on a pilgrimage for Christ! The Saracens were killing Christians and destroying Christ's Holy City. It was my duty. I'm still sad that we never got to Jerusalem. The Holy Father tells us our victories here are equally blessed, but I would have liked to walk where Christ walked and seen where he died."

Tamu remained silent for a long while, and Cate feared she'd offended her. *But I've only told the truth,* Cate thought.

"Tamu, why do Saracens murder Christians?"

Tamu looked at Cate as if confused. "Why did Christians kill my husband?"

Cate felt stricken. "What I meant is, this was Christian land, settled by the followers of St. James, until the Moors came and made martyrs of Christians. And Jerusalem is our holy city!"

Tamu grimaced. "It is holy to us too. Our leaders want land and riches and power and never to bow to unbelievers. Isn't that what Count Berenguer and your brother want? It's what all men want. When my people were the leaders of this land, I bowed to no one," Tamu said, turning her eyes fiercely toward Cate. "Now I bow to you and all the Christian lords."

They worked in silence for a while. Cate's stomach churned as she thought about Tamu's words. "Tamu, would you kill us if you had the chance? Would your husband or the laborers? Your father or Al-Basir?"

Tamu looked at Cate sadly. "I've had many chances, and, yes, some have encouraged me to kill your brother and whoever I could in the night. I would be a martyr for Allah, they promise."

Cate sat on her heels, surprised.

"But I've searched my soul," Tamu continued, "and I'm not a murderer. I can't kill someone simply because you are misled about Christ and the Prophet."

Misled? Cate thought. *I'm not misled! And a martyr for Allah! Did her family really think that? Her family is damned and will go to hell. How sad to know Tamu and Musa and ibn Walid will burn for eternity, ever alone! At least I'll see my parents again in heaven.*

"And I can't kill the people who gave Musa and me food and a place to live when we were hungry. No, Cate, you don't need to be frightened of me, and my father is an old man who would never kill anyone. I can't speak for my husband's brothers, though. They traveled south but may return if they get the chance. Sperleng is right to keep guards at the house. I fear his brothers would kill me too if they could."

Maybe I need to be more careful if that is what the Moors think. Cate felt frightened now. *Maybe Egric is right, we should only have Christians near us. Here we are in this strange land, surrounded by people who hate and want to kill us.*

"I've frightened you, haven't I? I'm sorry," Tamu said.

"Sperleng and Egric have warned me many times. But it is hard to hear it from you." *Tamu could never kill us even though she feels threatened herself,* Cate told herself. *We are friends. And Musa, funny, gentle Musa who now runs to me and hugs me.*

"I think women and farmers just want to live with their families and work the land. It's the princes who want more land, and the priests and imams who talk of holy war. Let's talk about something more pleasant, like how the nights are getting longer and the days cooler."

"In Brycgstow that would be a bad thing, because it meant winter and the time of hunger were coming. Your winters here are short and summers long. Cate looked up to see two loose-edged clouds drifting above her. Despite the piercing sun, Cate felt cold.

TWENTY-SEVEN

Aldover
July 1151

"What were you thinking?" Sperleng roared when Egric told him of the trip to Tamu's village. "Has my sister made you lose all sense?"

"We took many precautions," Egric mumbled, looking at the ground.

"Never again. Promise!" Sperleng said, his voice icy now. "Idiot."

"And you!" Sperleng shouted at Cate as she rushed to defend Egric. "What are you playing at? Taking such a risk, for the sake of a garden? I could have paid a Christian farmer to come here."

"The village is filled with old men and women," Cate said. "Tamu's father told us the young Moors had left. And Mary said the Moors know things the Christians don't."

"And you believed Tamu? Her father and this healer are not welcome here either. That is all I'd need.

Moors wandering in and out of the compound, figuring out where our weaknesses are."

"Ibn Walid came here many times when Tamu's husband owned this ranch."

Sperleng slapped her. "You will obey me!"

But learning of this fine isolated and unprotected village in the mountains started Sperleng thinking about how easy it would be to take. Later that night, once Sperleng was calmer, Egric told him how he had spent much of his time there looking over the land, the mountain stream bed, and the grazing sheep.

"I would like land such as this," Egric said. "I miss the hills of Wales, and Cate loves the garden. And it's cooler there, surrounded by two streams that join on their way toward the Ebro. It's a small village, and I saw no soldiers and few horses. If we surprise them, it will fall in a day."

Sperleng nodded, thinking how the villagers had scattered before Egric and his few soldiers.

"The healer's house is the largest, not as large as yours, but fine enough for me," Egric continued. "And there are many other houses, enough to provide for a base of soldiers. Who knows what riches the Moors left behind? I saw gold and enameled vessels in the healer's house."

Let Cate be Egric's worry, and the sooner the better, Sperleng thought.

"I'll talk with Gilbert," he said.

~

Cate woke suddenly. Sperleng's and Egric's voices came from the central courtyard through the wide doors and windows left open to catch any breeze. She relaxed as she listened to the murmurs of the two men she loved most and almost fell back to sleep when she heard Egric say *Al-Basir*.

They were talking about her. Cate walked quietly to the window that faced the courtyard and tried to catch what they were saying but was only able to hear a word or two.

She peeked out the window and saw them staring at a drawing Egric was making with a stick in the sandy ground that surrounded the tiled patio, but they were too far away for her to see what it was.

"No walls," she heard next, then "one tall tower."

Cate froze. They must be talking about Tamu's village. But why?

Maybe Egric was assuring Sperleng that their trip wasn't dangerous, and they should be allowed to go again. *That seems unlikely*, Cate admitted to herself, but it was the best she could hope for.

Cate pulled back from the window as they headed toward the wall closest to the river.

"A morning's ride . . . stream bed . . . two branches join stream . . . few young men . . ." she heard Egric say. Yes, they were discussing the village.

Suddenly she remembered Egric asking her if she would like Al-Basir's garden. Of course, she had said. Who wouldn't?

Did he plan to get it for her? A wave of nausea almost overwhelmed Cate.

She would have to make it clear tomorrow that she wanted her own garden, not Al-Basir's. *That should take care of it,* she thought as she lay back on her pallet and fingered the down-filled cloth that softened the straw it covered. *I'll tell Egric we should move to one of the villages they've already taken, maybe the one near Xerta. Or we could live in Tortosa near the Hospitaller's clinic where we'd be near Mary.*

Except Sperleng had said there were no estates for them in Tortosa as the Genoese and the Barcelonans had taken the best of them.

Cate could not fall back asleep worrying about Tamu's village. *Why should I care about Moors? Tamu said that many had encouraged her to kill Sperleng. Still, they were kind to me, gave me seeds and advice when they could just have easily set a trap and slaughtered us. No, I'll just tell Egric I want to be close to Mary and Sperleng and that will be the end of it.*

As Cate tossed and turned and worried, the sky began to lighten, almost imperceptibly at first, and the birds began their morning song. *I may as well get up and start the bread. I'll make it with raisins and figs, just like Egric likes.*

The loaves were cooling by the time Egric and Sperleng finished their morning swim.

"Tamu was up early this morning," Sperleng commented as he took a loaf for himself.

"It was me," Cate said. "The birds woke me early, so I decided to bake. Tamu's taking care of the chickens. I hate that job."

"Chickens are nasty," Sperleng agreed. "And this bread is great. Cate will make a great wife; don't you think Egric?"

"I've always thought so," Egric smiled at Cate. "I hope our home is large enough for an oven. We brought our dough to the bakers' ovens in Wales. Only the great lords had their own."

"It was that way in Brycgstow, too," Cate said. "I guess Sperleng is a great lord! I didn't mind going to the baker's, though. It was always fun to talk with the other women when my mother would take me there."

"Do you miss it?" Egric asked. "I sometimes tire of all this heat and sun and brown. Even snow. Sometimes I miss snow."

"Really?" Cate asked. "I don't miss snow, although this heat is exhausting. I admit it. I take a nap every afternoon during the worst of the heat."

"Everyone does, the Barcelonans tell me," Sperleng said. "But have you ever been hungry since the end of the siege? It is nice to have such short winters."

"I wonder if all the villagers have enough. Maybe we're not hungry because you are a lord," Cate said.

"Whatever the reason, I am glad to be here, and wouldn't go back. Ever. Do you two want to go back, or are you just shining your memories?"

"No," Egric said, "I don't want to go back. I get homesick sometimes, but not enough to go back to the cold and the civil war. Everything I want and everyone I love is here. And at least here we are fighting unbelievers, not other Christians."

"I miss Mother and Father and Cearl and Linn and Aedra," Cate admitted. "But not Brycgstow. I wish they could come here. Could they? Maybe you could marry Aedra, Sperleng. She thinks you are handsome. She told me."

"Cate, Aedra will be married by now, and Mother and Father would never leave Brycgstow, you know that. Gilbert brought his family, and they are not happy. This place takes getting used to."

"I wonder what Willard is doing?" Cate said. "Have you heard whether he made it back to Brycgstow, or if he still is in Jerusalem?"

"I don't know," Sperleng said. "We'll probably never know. I think of him on a horse in Jerusalem or blessing the sick there. I don't like to think about the alternatives."

A wave of sadness passed over Cate. Sperleng was right, and they'd probably never know.

"Do you want to see the changes I've made to our garden?" Cate said suddenly. "I think next year it will be better than Al-Basir's."

Both Sperleng and Egric scowled at hearing that name. "No," Sperleng said. "I need to check on the horses."

"I'll come," Egric said. "I haven't seen you alone much."

"Practically never," Cate agreed as they went hand in hand out the patio gate toward the walled garden near the river. "We couldn't find a spring, so we put the pool near the river. See how the men have bricked up the side to raise the water to irrigate these plants? We'll be able to use water gates like Al-Basir had. We'll use the walls as shade for the plants that need less sun, and Tamu's husband will build an arch and plant vines here along the south wall. We'll seed what needs the most sun here, near the north wall, and move a couple of fig trees in the center."

"It would be easier if the garden were already made, in't it?" Egric said. "And you know we'll be gone soon. So much work that you won't get benefit from."

"We won't be moving far away, will we? And Mary will still be here every week. I don't think I'm wasting my effort."

"No, but I want you to have a fine garden at our home, too."

"Let's build a home on Sperleng's land, or nearby! I like it here."

Egric stiffened. "Sperleng promised me my own tenancy. I can't live off him forever."

"No, I know," Cate said, stroking his rough hand. "But there are some abandoned ranches near here, aren't there? Upriver near Xerta?"

"Yes, but I was thinking closer to the mountains where it is cooler, maybe by a mountain stream?"

This is it. Cate stiffened; dare she ask? "You mean Al-Basir's village?"

"Or someplace like it."

"Please leave them alone, Egric. Even Count Berenguer allowed Saracens and Jews to stay in Tortosa."

Egric shook his head. "You don't understand war, Cate, and it is not the same. If we leave a foothold, it gives them a place to build up a force against us. In Tortosa there are a few merchants and old men, and they are watched constantly."

Cate sat silently, her mind racing. She thought about how sad Tamu would be if her father were killed. *Should I say no, I'll never live there?*

"You may think Tamu's your friend and a Christian now, but she is a Moor," Egric continued. "We'll never be safe until all the Moors are gone."

"Al-Basir and ibn Walid were kind to us when they could have killed us," Cate said.

"They knew what would happen to their village if anything happened to us."

"And so it will happen anyway? Let's stay near here. I'd like to live in Tortosa where I could work with the clinic like Mary and we'd be near the Cathedral and the markets. Al-Basir's village is too remote! I'd feel so alone." Cate was pleading now.

"You will have me and our children to keep you company and busy. It should be enough. Sperleng warned me that you were headstrong and stubborn. Don't prove him right. And, besides," he said in a softer tone, "nothing is settled. Gilbert has the ultimate decision."

Egric kissed her gently. "Let's not argue about things that may never happen."

~

Every night Cate had trouble sleeping. How could something she wanted so much cause her this much distress? She knew Egric preferred the mountains to the lowlands beside the Ebro, and her heart warmed when she thought of them and their children working together in the garden and shearing sheep and planting wheat and baking bread.

But then she'd feel cold and hard when she thought of Tamu's father and Al-Basir dying at the hands of her brother and his soldiers. *Yes, they are heathens, but what was it Tamu had said? Should we kill people who were kind to us just because they were misled about the true God?*

And I would be responsible. I led Egric to ibn Walid's village. I exposed the villagers to my brother's soldiers. Their deaths will be on my head.

Night after night Cate tried to figure out what to do. *Maybe Gilbert or Count Berenguer won't allow another raid,* she hoped. *Maybe they'll think it is time for peace.*

Oh, don't be so naïve, she told herself. *The village's only hope is to go south, like Tamu's husband's family and the nobles of Tortosa did. Why didn't they? Surely they knew they couldn't stand up to a raid without the support of the Moorish lord who seemed to have lost interest in them.*

After a week of sleepless nights Cate had to drag herself out to the garden so she wouldn't lose the few plants that survived. Sperleng and Egric had gone to meet with Gilbert, and the thought of what they were discussing weighed heavily on her mind. She had no energy for Musa's games or to face Tamu, so she simply avoided them as best she could. But today there was no escape. Tamu carried water right to where Cate was weeding.

"Cate," Tamu said, "something's wrong. Tell me what it is."

"I'm not sleeping well; it's too hot. I'm just tired."

Tamu poured the water. It quickly rolled over and between the rocks they'd placed in furrows between the plants.

"Will you and Egric marry soon? Are you worried about that?"

"I am tired, Tamu. It's better if I am alone when I feel like this."

"Then I'll leave you alone, but I wanted you to know I'd like to visit my father when you go to Tortosa for the Feast of St. James. Is that all right?"

"Of course." Cate hesitated. She didn't want Tamu there when the raid came but knew she shouldn't warn her. "Tamu, why haven't your father and Al-Basir gone south like Musa's other grandparents did? It's dangerous for them here, in't it?"

"It's dangerous for everyone, everywhere. It's dangerous for you too! My husband was killed in the first battles, and his parents decided to leave. I stayed here because when they left Musa was very ill. They promised to send for us, but never did. Maybe they died. I don't know.

"We stayed with my father, and Al-Basir healed Musa, and after much time passed with no word, my father said I should marry again and claim my husband's land. Father agreed with Razin ibn Faris to marry me and live on this land, but soon Lord Gilbert arrived with his soldiers and we knew it was best to work for him, and now Sperleng. The most important thing to me is to live with my son and husband. This is as good a place as anywhere I think."

Cate sat back on her heels and closed her eyes, then slowly rose. "Tamu, let's walk along the river."

Cate led Tamu toward the shade of a large tree where the distance and noise of the water would hide their conversation. Tamu watched Cate curiously. "Tamu," she began, "I want you to encourage your father and Al-Basir to leave their village. Their generosity in helping me has put them in danger. I don't know what will happen, but I overheard Sperleng talking and I think they may be in danger. Please don't tell them what I've said, just encourage them to find a safer place to live."

"Cate, I've said that to my father many times, and he refuses to leave. If I tell him there's a specific threat, maybe he'll listen."

Cate nodded. "If they leave quietly, Sperleng won't know that I warned your father. Make sure he knows that if they come, it will be with a large army and no good can come from trying to fight. Remember, no one from the south came to help the great city of Tortosa during the siege and sent only a few soldiers after to try to take it back. And have your father tell Al-Basir. But no one else! If the village is empty, he'll feel betrayed. Please, Tamu."

Tamu's eyes seared Cate. "You want to protect the two men you've met, but no one else? Do you think my father will agree to have his friends slaughtered?"

"If they surrender, they'll be allowed to leave. That's what happened in Lisbon and Tortosa!"

"But hundreds were killed first. The Christians wiped out many villages, showing no mercy. Remember Egric's story? A village slaughtered because one boy stood up for Allah? I'll leave today. I'll tell ibn Faris that I received word my father was ill, and we must see to him. You must know we can't return. Sperleng is a cunning man and will know who warned the village." Tears had formed in the corner of Tamu's eyes. "I hope for your sake he doesn't figure out who told me. I should have known we couldn't be friends."

As Cate rushed past the whitewashed walls of the enclosure toward the villa's cool interior, her mind careened from relief that Musa would be safe, to fear if Sperleng found out, to sadness that Tamu would be leaving, to anger that these battles never seemed to end. Cate lay on her pallet and stared at the spider building its web in the corner, trying not to imagine what Egric might think about what she'd just done.

~

Sperleng returned with many soldiers. All his men had returned from patrols, and Gilbert sent twenty more to join them. Mary and Cate prepared bread and stew and ordered the steward to care for the horses and bring in more straw to sleep on.

"Where is Tamu," Sperleng asked, "Why isn't she cooking?"

"Tamu left four days ago. She said her father is ill and went to care for him," Cate said.

Sperleng looked at Cate, then shrugged his shoulders. "It's just as well. We should find a Christian maid, anyway."

Cate wished she felt the same, but for her the days were filled with anxiety and loneliness. She couldn't tell Mary, and certainly not Sperleng or Egric, what she had done, so she worried alone whether ibn Walid had time to escape and what would happen when Sperleng raided the village. She wished she'd never asked Tamu for help or visited the village.

But at least they had the chance to leave, Cate consoled herself. And if Sperleng and Egric didn't take the village, some Christians would eventually. She'd seen the excitement in Egric's eyes as he described the journey and the village to the soldiers. This was his chance to lead and receive the reward that would allow them to marry.

It was a beautiful place; they could be happy there. Cate hoped the soldiers didn't burn or trample Al-Basir's garden. *What a shame that would be.* She imagined her children playing in the stream and learning about the flowers and herbs. Egric would teach the boys to fish and hunt, and she would show the girls how to spin and weave and make medicines. Mary could live with them or nearby and maybe set up a clinic.

Maybe they would find Willard, and he would come be their priest. *If he's alive. I hope he is alive,* she thought. *If everyone has left the village, that will make it easier for Sperleng. No danger to anyone. They could walk right in and take it over. There hasn't been time for the villagers to gather reinforcements. Sperleng is weeks ahead in preparation. No, I've just averted a slaughter on both sides.*

Cate heard the soldiers leave in the night, knowing they hoped to reach the village near dawn. She wondered how long they'd be gone. Not long, she hoped.

The soldiers left behind as guards settled around the walls, their dark shapes moving slowly in the faint moonlight. *I may as well start baking,* Cate thought. *Anything to keep my mind off this.*

Mary soon joined her in the courtyard. They worked in the light from the torches nearby and the fire in the oven. Cate boiled grain and mixed in fish and dried lamb in the pot over the fire. Soon the smell of bread and pottage drew the soldiers into the courtyard. They talked excitedly as the sun rose, wondering what was happening, yet sure of Sperleng's success.

Only a dim twilight remained in the day when Cate heard, then saw, four horses running toward them. She saw Sperleng on one of them, but, disappointingly, not Egric. Men rushed to tend the horses, a stable boy grabbing the reins of two horses as Sperleng jumped to the ground.

"The village is ours," he said to the cheers of everyone. "Cate, bring us our food as I tell them what happened."

Sperleng hadn't commanded her like that for a long time, and his sharp tone worried her. She ran to bring ale and bread, cheese and pottage. Then she stood on the edge of the crowd to listen.

"I can't tell a story like Egric can, but it was an easy victory and not much to tell. We arrived at the village tower as the sun was coming up over the mountains, and were surprised to see nothing but smoldering fields, burned cottages, and toppled stones. The people were gone, the sheep and horses were gone. Egric took soldiers into the mountains to see if it was an ambush and saw that many people had recently crossed over a path south through the mountains."

Sperleng stood straight and still. "Someone betrayed us."

Cate's body stiffened with fear. Did he know? Why did he see this as a betrayal instead of a blessing?

"Praise God there was water running in the stream, because someone had filled the well with huge rocks. It will take days, maybe weeks, to remove them. It will be easier to build a new one. Their chapel still stood, but inside there was nothing: no gold or silver, no books, no rugs. Many of the houses had been built with stone, but those with thatched roofs stood open to the sky, while the tiled roofs had been smashed. There was nothing of value in any of the houses, just a few broken chairs and a table cleaved in half. We found no food stores, and the cisterns were filled with stones. Only one place remained. Egric said it was the house and garden of Al-Basir."

Sperleng paused for what seemed a long time. "Cate," he said, looking at her for the first time. "You've talked with the man. Why would the healer leave his garden?"

Mary stared at Cate, recognition dawning. "Cate, what have you done?" she whispered.

"I do not know the mind of the Moor," Cate said as casually as she could. "Perhaps he couldn't bear to see it destroyed? It was a lovely place."

"Perhaps that is the reason," Sperleng said, seeming to agree but Cate heard the menace in his voice. "Men, tomorrow I will return with supplies and four men. Decide who will come with me and be ready at dawn."

As the men dispersed, Sperleng joined Cate and Mary in the shadows by the main house. "It is time we talked about the future," he said, gripping Cate's arm and pulling her into the room he used for strategy sessions. "You," he said, grasping Cate's shoulders, "are a traitor and a liar. And I was a fool for not seeing your loyalty shifted from me to Tamu. And don't try to deny it like you pretended out there. There is no other way the village could have known. Egric admitted that he told you; he said you already seemed to know, and he reminded you to tell no one. Do you wish to live with the Saracens? Because you cannot live here with me." Sperleng released his grip and began pacing, smashing his fist into the palm of his hand. "Mary, what did you know about this?"

"Nothing, Sperleng. Nothing. I would never have guessed."

"Mary can't be blamed," Cate said. "I just told Tamu that her father should move south as her husband's family had. He was a nice old man, and kind to me! And I thought it would make it easier for you, too."

"Oh, you did it for me, did you?" Sperleng's laugh was hollow. "How generous to save us from having to drive old men away from an unguarded village. What you did was give them time to burn the fields and plug the well and destroy houses that could have held Christians. You've betrayed me and Egric, and Gilbert will wonder about my trustworthiness. I am not the only one who's guessed what happened. Egric, for one, is sure. I've relieved him of his marriage pledge to you."

Cate brushed the tears from her cheeks. *Egric shunned me? Just because I didn't want to feel responsible for the deaths of ibn Walid and Al-Basir? What will happen to me?*

"Crying helps nothing," Sperleng said, "and I don't believe your tears are anything but pity for yourself because now we know who you truly are. A traitor and a liar. How did we come from the same parents? Didn't we hear the same lessons? Watch the same slaughter of Christians at Lisbon and Tortosa? Why would you betray us to the Moors? I will never understand, and I never want to see you again either."

~

Mary had been quietly thinking as Sperleng raged. She understood how terrible Cate's actions had been, but, unlike Sperleng, thought it was a naïve but good-hearted mistake. She feared what would happen to Cate if Sperleng simply cast her out. *Would she kill herself, or, worse, sell herself? How would she survive? There must be another way.* Mary had promised Alma to watch over Cate, but would the monks let her live in the abbey if they learned what had happened? *No*, she thought, *they would not.*

"Sperleng, I know you are angry and I agree you have a right to be. Cate's warning Tamu was wrong and disloyal," Mary said. "But she is young and made a terrible mistake. Don't banish her."

"Young?" Sperleng scoffed. "Yes, she's acted like a child, selfish and thoughtless and stupid. But it is no excuse! My mother was younger than Cate when she had me, and I fought with Earl Robert when I was younger! We all have responsibilities, and must live up to them, especially when it is difficult."

Sperleng turned and shook his fist at Cate. "Do you think it was easy to besiege Lincoln when men I knew, Christian men! were dying there? Did I send a messenger in and say, 'We are on our way; get somewhere safe'? No, I did not, and would have been executed if I had. This is why women can't be soldiers, and why you never should have come. You are weak, soft, unreliable, and a temptation to my men. And soon I'll be laughed at by my men and cut off from Gilbert's favor."

"Who's guessed this, besides you and Egric?" Mary asked. "What are your men saying?"

"The men assumed the Saracen laborers saw us preparing for battle, and that because ibn Faris knew Egric had been at the village recently that was our target."

"Which could be true, right?" Mary said. "The laborers could be spies. They probably are! No one need know Cate warned them."

"But I know!" Sperleng shouted. "She's admitted it, and frankly it is more important to me to have Egric near me than Cate. And Gilbert's no fool. He'll guess something is up when Egric no longer wants the farm he practically begged for."

"I am a Christian," Cate interrupted, pleading. "I'm not a blasphemer! Send me home or put me in a convent. I'll pray for forgiveness every day, and help the poor, and be chaste, and pray that the Christians drive out the Moors from St. James's country."

Sperleng scoffed. "I don't have the money to buy your way into a convent. And why would I, even if I did?"

"You could suggest that Gilbert offer the land to the Hospitallers in Willard's name," Mary offered, "that your sister and aunt want to dedicate themselves to God and the mission of the Hospitallers and taking this village is your contribution to the Order. Say that Cate heard Christ's call, and no longer wished to marry Egric."

"I won't embarrass Egric that way."

"Or say Egric rejected her, realized he was a soldier and not ready to settle down, and that Cate saw no alternative but to live a life of contemplation and service to God."

Sperleng pushed them out of the room. "I can't look at you anymore."

TWENTY-EIGHT

Cate wandered along the shallows of the river, searching for flat rocks for the garden. Small waves kept drenching the hem of her skirt, so she tied it at her waist with the rope she used to carry her sack and waterskin. Plumes of swirling sand streaked dust along her face as she brushed the sweat from her eyes. When she reached the mill, she followed the water as it diverted to small streams downhill toward the grain fields and orchards. She bowed to Brother Jimeno who stood near the gate of the convent's walled garden, his sword mostly hidden by the folds of his dark tunic.

The oppressive, still heat inside the walls always caught Cate by surprise after the open river air, hot as it was, and she moved slowly toward the ditch she'd been building along the west wall. She laid her rocks along the bottom and sides, flattest side out, so the water would flow quickly rather than saturating the first plants it came to. She finished as the west wall began shading her, and she stood to stretch.

Silence washed over Cate like a balm, so different from the shouting and commotion all the time back at Sperleng's farm. Several women were harvesting those peppers, artichokes, squash, and eggplant that appeared ripe, but Cate was more interested in the herbal garden where Mary stood pinching leaves in a raised bed. Cate joined her, inspecting the rue near the base of the fig tree that shaded most of the herb garden, then moved on toward thriving beds of rosemary, fennel, and vervain. She found a large melon hiding among its creeping vines, tapped it, then lifted it to show Mary.

Cate braced herself for noise and busyness as she approached the house they lived in with five other women near the infirmary. Even after two years she still found it strange living with no men in the house, and the only men she met were their silent, and sometimes leering, guards and the priests and monks who led the services and criticized their work. She sighed. *Well, I wanted to join a convent. So why am I so sad?*

But she knew. Every day Cate thought about Egric, and every night she prayed for him, sometimes sadly remembering his soft touch on her cheek and other times angrily remembering that his loyalty to Sperleng exceeded his love for her. Now she thought of his voice booming happily as he told a story, and she missed him. Missed the fire in his eyes when he looked at her, missed his gentle reproofs when she acted unladylike—so much kinder than Sperleng's brutal comments that she acted like a whore.

Cate missed Willard, the kinder version of Willard untouched by war, and his stories too. *Stop feeling sorry for yourself,* she told herself. *Think how much worse it would have been if Sperleng had simply banished me instead of smoothing my way with the Hospitallers.* She knew Mary, and guessed Egric, had helped with that.

Sister Estafania clapped and shouted to the others when Cate set the melon on the table, and soon their cheeks were dripping with juice and laughter. They carefully placed their seeds in a shell bowl for later planting. *It is nice to be with women who believe like I do,* Cate thought, *who I don't need to fear will hurt me or run away like Tamu. But what would they think if they knew what I did? Would they still welcome me?*

"Save some for Mary!" Cate said, covering the end with a cloth. "She saw me with it, so she'll know if we don't."

"It's your turn in the infirmary, Cate," Sister Estafania said, pushing her toward the door. "I've been there all day, and we all prefer my cooking to yours."

Cate smiled. It was all too true. *Everyone has their gifts,* she thought, *and cooking is not mine.* She knew she was too impatient, preferring to throw everything in a pot or quickly cook fish over a fire to taking hours with slowly simmering sauces. But Sister Estafania was almost useless in the garden, the herbs seeming to wilt as she walked by. Go with your strengths, they all told each other, but take turns with the awful tasks, like emptying the chamber pots and cleaning the privy. They took turns in the infirmary, their favorite task, and yet everyone needed time away from the strains of treating dying children and comforting their anxious parents, trying to stanch the bleeding from a severed finger, and watching pregnant women die in childbirth.

Inside the small courtyard of the infirmary, a man paced holding his cheek, and a woman sat with a small boy sleeping fitfully on her lap. Mary was feeding biscuits and a tonic that smelled of vinegar and meat to a man who repeatedly clutched at his stomach.

"The boy has a fever," Mary said. "See him first."

Cate took the young mother's hand and lifted the boy onto a small bench. Cate took wet cloths and wiped the boy's body. He began whimpering, barely able to open his eyes.

"How long?" Cate asked his mother.

"Two days he's been hot and weak. Today is the worst."

Cate nodded and filled a small shell with the juice of several spring herbs, hoping the heat hadn't weakened them too much. She asked the mother to cradle his head as Cate held the tonic under his nose. She then put a few drops in each nostril. When he finished sneezing, she took ground wort and put it in a small amount of wine. As his mother helped the boy drink, Cate gathered a few burdock leaves and tied them to the boy's arms with a strip of cloth.

"Don't let him take off these leaves," Cate said. "And if he still is this hot tomorrow, come back."

"Thank you," the mother whispered, her eyes wet from worry and gratitude.

The pacing man then stormed into the room. "I need something for my toothache! Please. Now!" he shouted, circling.

As calmly as she could, Cate ground turnip roots with water and onion juice, and told the man to put the paste on the area that hurt. She mixed the rest with strong wine that had turned to vinegar and told him to swish it around his mouth, then swallow. She heated a thumb-sized amount of beeswax and directed him to cover his teeth with the mixture, leave it on until he got home, pray for relief, then peel it off and throw it in the river.

"When you are finished with that, leave some wine in your mouth for a little while to loosen any wax then spit it out. If tomorrow you aren't better, find a butcher to pull your tooth," Cate advised.

"It feels better already," the man said as he walked out.

Cate walked over to Mary and the groaning man. "Is there anything I can do to help?"

"Look at his eyes, how red they are! Prepare a salve for him."

Cate took a few leaves of dried rue from the shelf, ground it, and mixed it with honey. She put the mixture in his eyes, but he screamed and knocked her hand away. She then wet a cloth with spring water a priest had blessed and washed his eyes.

"Would you like me to take over for a while?" Cate asked.

"No," Mary said, "I know what I've tried already, and soon we'll finish for the night. Just keep me company."

"I saved you some melon."

"You'd better have! Now we'll see if it still is there when we get home."

"Have you tried mint already?"

"Yes, but maybe more will help. He needs to drink something too."

Cate mixed mint into mead, and the man drank it hungrily. It seemed to calm him. She then gave him some of the blessed water.

"There's nothing else I can do today," Mary said. "Don't eat anything until you feel better. Just drink ale or wine."

"I need to sleep," he said. "I may never eat again."

Cate and Mary ambled back toward the house, enjoying the evening cool. "Let's walk awhile," Mary said.

The houses they passed smelled of frying garlic and onions and smoke. Men stood in the streets and nodded respectfully as they passed. Many had been to the infirmary and recognized them, and others bowed to the large crosses they wore. It made Cate feel proud, made the sting of what she'd lost seem less important.

"One of Sperleng's men came to see me today," Mary said. "Sperleng is getting married this Spring to Gilbert's third daughter."

Cate clenched hearing the news, another reminder of the children she'd never have and the cousins playing she'd never see. "Will I be invited?" she wondered aloud. "Or will Sperleng decide I have too many obligations to attend to as he did these last Christmases?"

"We'll both be expected to be there, at least for the ceremony on the cathedral steps. It is close to here, and it would be hard for Sperleng to explain your absence. I am sure Gilbert never knew what you'd done and thought Tamu had overheard the men preparing. But try not to be too sad if you are not welcomed at the feast. Egric will be there, and we have no suitable dresses anymore, anyway. Religious women are often felt to dampen the spirit of a wedding with their barren wombs and their promises of chastity. I won't be going to the feast either."

"Did the messenger say anything about Egric?" Cate asked.

"No," Mary said, concern shining from her eyes. "But I wouldn't have expected him to."

"I am so sorry to have dragged you down," Cate said, using her sleeve to dry her eyes. "You could still be part of their lives if you weren't here with me."

"Dragged me down?" Mary scoffed. "This is the life I was meant to live. Before we left the ranch, I was trying to find a way to tell you I was planning to live at the abbey. Now we have a place with five other women and are respected as healers. I am happy! I wish you were."

"I'm content most days," Cate said. "Then other days I remember how I wanted Egric and his children and all my family around me. Those are the days I'm sad. Some days I think maybe I should find a way back to Brycgstow, marry someone—I'd guess Wulf is still looking—and be with family who love me. A silly dream, I know. At least here I feel useful."

Mary put her arm around Cate's shoulders. "Running away is no answer, and we are your family. Didn't you leave Brycgstow because you felt God called you here?" Cate nodded. "Then accept this is God's will too."

Cate shrugged. "Did God cause me to warn Tamu? To save a town of Moors from Christ's warriors?" Mary looked away and said nothing.

As they passed the Aljama neighborhood, a young boy with black hair and loose white clothing darted out in front of them, chasing a ball. For a moment Cate was sure he was Musa, although the growing dark made it hard to tell. The boy froze in fear when he saw them, then ran with his ball as quickly as he could to the sheltering walls he'd come from.

A sudden sadness washed over Cate that she shook away, reminding herself of the trouble she'd had because she let herself love Musa and Tamu. All it led to were questions and hesitations, she told herself. What good can come of that?

True to Sperleng's word, she hadn't seen him or Egric since the day Osbert and several soldiers took Cate and Mary to the Hospitaller's fortress in Amposta. The

Hospitallers welcomed the women, remembering their work in the year after the siege, how they'd helped in the infirmary and even dressed themselves as soldiers to give the illusion of strength as they awaited Berenguer's army when the Moors tried to retake Tortosa. And the Hospitallers knew Gilbert's gift of the village in the mountains came at Sperleng's request.

Cate could barely remember her novitiate, a year of routine and prayers that felt like a fog to her, then and now. But she remembered her loneliness and regret. All the people she had lost: her parents, her sisters, Sperleng, Willard, and Egric. Aedra, Cearl, and Oxa. Tamu and Musa.

Every day, Cate wondered *Is this what the rest of my life will be like? Loneliness and loss?* She consoled herself with the routine of the daily prayers and soothing chants during services. *Was saving the lives of a few villagers who'd never done them harm really so bad?* she asked God daily. She wished she had Willard's conviction of what right action was and prayed for it. *Where are you, Lord?*

Cate had waited for Sperleng and Egric to soften and take her back. Then she waited for a mystical experience that never came. Once she'd take her vows of poverty, chastity, and service, the Brothers asked Cate and Mary if they wished to help start an abbey in the village in the mountains, one where women could live in peace and contemplation, but both agreed they preferred living in the city near the cathedral, working with the poor and the sick in Tortosa. It was the right decision, she knew. Being busy was better than so much thinking.

Cate and Mary arrived home to laughter and the smell of vegetables roasting in olive oil, laughter that stilled when they entered. *Do they, too, know that Sperleng is getting married?* Cate wondered, *or am I just the kind of person that casts a gloom over everyone? I didn't use to be. I shouldn't be.*

"Put the trenchers on the table so we can eat," Sister Estafania commanded. "Where have you two been? Sunset was long ago."

"Walking off the kinks in my legs from standing too long," Mary answered with a smile. "I am getting old, you know."

"Ha!" Estafania replied. "You just aren't used to hard work, coming from that rich family. I'll bet you just sat around and commanded your servants to do everything. Well, those days are over, Sister."

Mary laughed. "Someday I'll tell you all about home. How cold it was, how hard we had to work to grow our medicines. Now where is my share of that melon?"

I am content, Cate assured herself.

~

Cate had trouble sleeping that night as she wondered about Sperleng and, inevitably, Egric. She tried to still her mind, but her dreams seemed worse than sleeplessness, dreams that seemed so real she could hardly tell if she were awake or dreaming. She saw a ladder, set precariously in sand and rocks against a high fortress wall, angels ascending and descending. Cate screamed but made no sound as she watched Sperleng and Egric climb that ladder. Egric looked at her from the top with accusation in his eyes before he fell into a muddy, rushing river. Cate ran along the river, never able to catch up, never able to see if he were alright. Suddenly she was being chased by men on dark horses. Who were they? Christians? Moors? They chased her up the mountains to an empty village. She checked every house; no one was there to help her. She was in Brycgstow, on streets that never led anywhere but back again. Then on Lisbon's streets that always ended at the fortress wall. Finally, she came to where she knew was home but couldn't recognize it as the empty rooms led to another and another. Thunder. A flood began to fill the house until she felt she was drowning and her whimpering sobs woke her again.

She got up and knelt beside her bed. Give me peace, Lord, she prayed.

In the dark, Cate walked to the cathedral for Lauds. She hoped sharing prayers with others would soothe her. As she listened to the chanting and mumblings surrounding her, she thought about forgiveness, hoping they all forgave her. She searched her soul, and realized she wanted their forgiveness, but wasn't as sorry as she knew she should be. She was sad for how things had worked out, and sorry she had hurt the people she loved.

I'm sorry, Lord, Cate prayed fervently; *sorry that I don't know what to confess. Forgive me.* But in her heart, she was thankful too. Thankful that Tamu and Musa and Al-Basir escaped. Thankful that Sperleng would be joining Gilbert's family. Thankful that Mary hadn't abandoned her. She bowed her head deeper so the sisters beside her wouldn't ask about her tears. She didn't need anyone else's judgment.

Cate hummed the *Gloria* as she kneaded bread to the peaceful sounds of birds waking and the occasional shifts of the sisters' bodies on their pallets. By the time Estafania arose, Cate already had fresh bread on the table. The sun brightened the room as the rest wandered in, brewed herbs for tea, and discussed the tasks for the day.

"Well, Cate, we see you can bake bread," Estafania said. "Maybe it's time you learned to make a decent meal of more than pottage and burned fish."

"Maybe it is," Cate admitted. "Show me how."

Historical Note

For those of you interested in the historical background to *The Way of Glory*, here's a list of important primary sources in translation that give a glimpse into the twelfth century world of the English Anarchy, pilgrimages to Santiago de Compostela and Jerusalem, the sieges of Lisbon and Tortosa, and medieval herbal medicine.

"The Anglo-Saxon Chronicle" (Everyman Press, London, 1912). Trans. Rev. James Ingram (London, 1823), with additional readings from the translation of Dr. J.A. Giles (London, 1847). Web. http://mcllibrary.org/Anglo/. [Also available online in translation at: http://www.britannia.com/history/docs/asintro2.html, and from the British Library in the original: http://blogs.bl.uk/digitisedmanuscripts/2016/02/anglo-saxon-chronicles-now-online.html

Bernard of Clairvaux. "Letter." Trans. J. H. Robinson. *The Crusades: A Reader.* Eds. S. J. Allen and Emilie Amt. Toronto: Toronto University Press, 2010. 134-38. Print

Caffaro Di Rustico. *The Capture of Almeria and Tortosa.* Trans. G. A. Loud, from *Annali* Genovesi di Caffaro e de'suoi continuatori, ed. L.T. Belgrano (Fonti per la storia d'Italia, Rome 1890), 79-89.

Faculty of Arts. University of Leeds, n.d. Web. 4 July 2013.
<http://www.leeds.ac.uk/arts/downloads/file/10 89/the_capture_of_almeria_and_tortosa_by_caff aro>.

Eugene III. "Summons to A Crusade." from Doeberl, *Monumenta Germania Selecta*, Trans. F. Henderson. *Select Historical Documents of the Middle Ages*. Vol. 4. London: George Bell and Sons, (1910): 333-36. *Internet History Sourcebooks Project*. Fordham University, 1996. Web. 22 July 2018. <https://sourcebooks.fordham.edu/source/euge ne3-2cde.asp>.

Medieval Herbal Remedies: The Old English Herbarium and Anglo-Saxon Medicine. Trans. & Ed. Anne Van Arsdall. London: Routledge, 2010. Print.

The Pilgrim's Guide to Santiago De Compostela. Trans. William Melczer. New York: Italica Press, 1993. Print.

Osbernus. *De Expugnatione Lyxbonensi: The Conquest of Lisbon*. Trans. & Ed. Charles W. David. New York: Columbia University Press, 2001. Print.

Winand. "The Lisbon Letter." Trans. Susan B. Edgington. *The Second Crusade: Scope and Consequences*. Ed. Jonathan Phillips and Martin Hoch. Manchester: Manchester University Press, 2001. 61-67. Print.

Acknowledgments

I am grateful for the support of my mentors and readers while I was working on this book at Queens University in Charlotte, especially Fred Leebron, Naeem Murr, Dana Spiotta, Pinckney Benedict, and Ashley Warlick. Thank you also to my editor, Teresa Bruce, whose generous comments and guidance made this a better book.

Thank you to all my friends, family, and workshop colleagues who have read and commented on the many drafts, including Jen McAlonan, Stacy Smith, Joyce Boomsma, John Wagner, Mara Kelly, David denBoer, Ian King, Fredda Bisman, Margaret Wilson, Gene Hetrick, Liisa Atva, and the many others who have listened patiently to me worry about one thing or another.

ABOUT THE AUTHOR

Patricia Boomsma is an Arizona lawyer. Her publications include poems in *Haiku Journal* and *Indolent Press* and short stories in *The Vignette Review, Persimmon Tree,* and *Scarlet Leaf Review.* She has a Master's in English from Purdue University, a J.D. from Indiana University in Indianapolis, and an M.F.A. in Creative Writing from Queens University of Charlotte. This is her first novel.

Find out more at patboomsma.com.

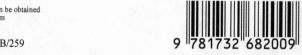